Pride Publishing books by Gin Vane

Southern Awakenings
From Bad to Worse

I0646173

Southern Awakenings

FROM BAD TO WORSE

GIN VANE

From Bad to Worse
ISBN # 978-1-80250-979-3
©Copyright Gin Vane 2022
Cover Art by Kelly Martin ©Copyright August 2022
Interior text design by Claire Siemaszkiewicz
Pride Publishing

Published in 2022 by Pride Publishing, United Kingdom.

Pride Publishing is an imprint of Totally Entwined Group Limited.

FROM BAD TO WORSE

Dedication

For Em, my partner in crime. Without you this series would not exist, and neither would I. Love you to the moon and back.

This book is dedicated to anyone exploring their identity "later in life". It's never too late to welcome all of you to the table. The people who get it will get it. And those who don't? They're missing out on the gift of you. Let it be their loss.

And also this book is for romance readers like me who fall in love with characters first (and *then* we care about the spice). I hope to do you proud with Everett and Colt.

Part One

REMEMBERING

Chapter One

Everett
Louisiana, 2018

"You know who you have to call, Everett."

Lead Detective Everett Kane sat at his desk with a single thought in his head, surrounded by files that looked like scrapbook memories. Because this Meyers case? Staging aside, it was Patrick Combs all over again.

Major Stapes leaned against the open office door, face unreadable in the light of dimmed fluorescents. "I'll be the first to admit I've no love for the bastard. And with how you all left things...well, there's a bigger picture now."

A hard laugh escaped Everett's throat. "He's the one who saw that in the first place. Back then."

The major nodded, but didn't look happy to agree. For all anyone ever said about *"that nutcase outsider,"* not to mention the legitimate grief he gave the bosses back in the day, it'd be easy to turn a blind eye and avoid an uncomfortable sight. But Major Stapes had a reputation for giving credit where it was due. He was the one who'd hired the bastard back when. He knew what he was asking Everett to do — again.

The older man picked at peeling black letters that read *E. Kane, Lead Detective.* "Maybe so," Stapes hedged. "But it doesn't change the facts. Now that there's another body...do it now or do it tomorrow, but you're out of time. We need him."

Everett eyed the locked drawer of his desk. They both knew exactly who he meant, but Everett wasn't stupid enough to go saying the man's name aloud, even to the only boss who could halfway stand him. This case had conjured up enough old ghosts without adding *him* to the mix.

Everett shook his head. "I'm not workin' with him."

The major snorted, a paternal sound that made Everett feel like a kid complaining over chores. With his silver hair and well-lined face, Stapes often reminded Everett of his grandfather, though he wrangled small-town cops instead of stallions. He rapped his knuckles against the door. "Believe that's the second time you've tried to convince me of that, Detective."

Shit. Stapes was right about that too.

The fight fell out of Everett with a heavy sigh, leaving him hunched over the desk. He fixed weary eyes on the photo in front of him — a young woman in a State Rodeo T-shirt and a puddle of her own blood — cut up and dead in a way no person ought to be. One look at those photos and the petty wilted in his gut.

Yeah. There's that bigger picture to think on.

He tried to rub the tiredness from his eyes. "I'm not gettin' out of this, am I?"

Stapes' attention darted around the room—at the photos stapled over the walls, the files that littered every surface, the theories and timelines connected by string and too many cards to count. It made his point too well.

"Not this time."

The major turned on his heel, leaving Everett to stew in his half-lit office. The station lights had long ago been dimmed, which made sense. Everett's colleagues all had homes to be getting to. There'd been a time he had the same—a couple different homes, if he were honest.

He clicked his pen twice, then chucked it at the desk. Broken pieces of plastic scattered to corners unknown.

Fuckin' Harkan. Why'd Colt always have to be right?

Alone and accustomed to being so, he cracked the small window in his smaller office and blazed up a Camel filter. On a normal day, Everett was a strict only-with-coffee smoker. He was down to a pack a week when things stayed the right kind of average. But this one was peeling fast, half-gone from yesterday—a soft pack because *fuck it,* they weren't gonna last long enough to matter. Not when the State Rodeo was once again the scene of a murder. And *certainly* not now the name Colt Harkan was playing on a loop in his mind...

* * * *

Louisiana, 2009, nine years earlier

"I'm not workin' with him, Stapes. Guys who come off undercover...they ain't *right.*"

"That's what I like about you, Kane. Got such heart."

Everett took the correction in stride. He slid into a chair with an easy smile, looking wry across the major's desk. A person would be hard-pressed not to give him the whole world when he turned on the charm like that—and Everett knew it. Just so damn likeable. People couldn't help but say yes. Sometimes before they even realized what he'd asked.

Everett had always been a force-of-personality type, though he wouldn't say the overall package was terrible to look at. The title of Lead Detective kept him clean-shaven and clean-cut, his thick sheaf of wheat-colored hair cropped short and threaded with sun. When he looked in the mirror, his cornflower eyes saw how family life and the nine-to-five grind had dulled the edges of his expression, creased careworn lines he was still getting used to in the corners of his honest face. Everett wasn't as fit as he had been in his rodeo days, but he'd been known to joke in a western bar or three how time made grown-ups of them all. Eventually.

Everett kicked his leg up, bracing his shoe against the major's desk. He propped an arm on his knee, looked down his nose and tilted his head—every trick in the book to get Stapes to go his way. "You know what I mean, Major. Can't hardly tell what he was up to, there's so much black in his file. Looks more like sheet music than Times New Roman. Reads like arty poetry with three words to a page."

Stapes kept typing. "He's had more career in months than most do in decades, I'll give him that."

Everett grunted as he thumbed through the file in his hands. "How can you tell? Even his start date is redacted. And don't tell me it's some clerical error." He closed the rust-colored folder. "What's he doin' in Mason? Ain't we a little back-country for someone with this kind of weight in his file?"

When Everett looked up, the major had that look that meant *stop askin' and I won't have to lie to you.*

Stapes returned attention to his computer monitor. "He's owed some favors. He'll be comin' in rough, but we're the lucky ones here. I've done my calling around and even with those complaints from the brass, he's got the clearances. Might be the real deal."

It wasn't what Everett wanted to hear, but he knew that tone in the major's voice by now.

He grumbled, "Don't see why I gotta hold his hand any."

"Choose your training strategy as you see fit, Kane." Stapes chuckled from behind his big desk. "But he's your partner until he learns the ropes."

Everett stared at the patchwork file labeled *C. Harkan* and decided it was too thick to contain so little fact. But he let it thunk on the major's desk and leaned back in his chair, lacing hands behind his head like he couldn't be bothered. Seemed he was getting a partner after all. He asked, "When's Mr. Sunshine reporting for duty?"

A new voice at the door replied, "Ten minutes ago."

That low, even tone turned Everett's head quick, and he got his first look at Detective Colton Harkan.

Somehow, he looked exactly like his file—a few broad strokes to make the outline of a man. A body by default, formed out of assumption and habit. Like he'd shrugged into life one day and hadn't figured out why. At first glance, Everett was struck with the thought that a man with his background, running thick as thieves with all manner of rough, shouldn't look so quiet, so worn. So tired. Colt's dark eyes and darker hair gave him the look of a shadow, like a piece of thread left to twist in the wind and well, maybe Everett could see it now, on that second look.

Everett knew much about different kinds of dangerous. There was the obvious threat, clocked and taken out on approach.

And there's the one you never see comin'...

Everett's curiosity got the better of him as he held Colt's gaze, a worn-wood ochre that spoke of knowledge learned through pain. Wisdom, some might call it. Colt seemed the type to call it *necessary means*. He had an angular face that might've looked kinder with a smile, but it didn't seem to Everett those were muscles Colt flexed often — though the rest of him was in decent shape. Golden skin shone like he was hardly without a tan. The purple under his eyes matched a bad night's sleep or two days' drunk. Having had his share of both, Everett figured he wasn't in much position to judge and decided to extract the foot from his mouth as fast as possible.

He walked to the door, hand extended. "Everett Kane, Lead Detective. I'll be your—"

"I know who you are."

Colt's assessing eyes swept up and down Everett's frame, radiating how unimpressed he was with anything he was seeing. From Everett's khaki work slacks, blue button-up and cheap tie, even the pleasant smile plastered across his face, Everett knew himself to be the very picture of politeness.

None of it seemed to matter to the man in the doorway. He stepped to the side, angled around Everett and inclined his head to the man behind the desk. "Major."

With that, he left the office.

Everett's outstretched arm felt cold in the empty air, like the handshake he'd expected and had decidedly *not* received was some missed opportunity. His fingers itched as he pulled up short, anxious to get a read on the mystery he'd be working with. Could tell a lot about a man from a handshake. Maybe more from one passed by.

Everett's hands braced on his hips, thumbs digging into the leather of his belt. He watched through the major's window as Colt ambled to the only empty desk, set down a yellow legal pad like he'd been there for years, then left for whereabouts unknown.

Everett swiveled his head to the major, not caring the door was open or that the squad could probably hear him. "You've gotta be fuckin' *kidding* me, Stapes."

"Just a couple of months till he gets his feet."

"And if he don't?"

"Then I'll fire him — and you, if you don't start doin' what it is I pay you for."

Everett mumbled something about "Seniority my ass," that he was careful not to finish too loudly. Before the major could ask him to repeat it, he cut Stapes a sarcastic salute and stuffed his fists in his pockets, resigning himself to follow a man whose training would *clearly* include *Workplace Etiquette for Dummies*. If they made it through training at all.

* * * *

"So what's wrong with you, Harkan? Some kind of fuckin' asshole?"

The words were harsh, but Everett kept his tone light and it all landed softer than it might've otherwise.

A little self-aware levity to fix whatever offended his new partner.

As far as Everett could tell, it had zero effect.

Colt hadn't looked his way since he stopped beside him at the coffee machine. The man stared straight ahead as he waited for the pot to fill, eyes fixed on the trickling stream of what he'd soon learn was underwhelming shop coffee. The silence stretched long enough that when Colt finally spoke, Everett almost didn't hear his baritone over the percolating machine.

"You're not my partner. You're my babysitter."

Colt snagged the coffee by the handle, flinching at the hiss of unlucky drops sizzling on the hotplate. He replaced the pot, then stared at Everett over his steaming white cup, a drawl like velvet over the steel of his words. "And I don't need one. Never have."

It wasn't a boast. It wasn't meant to start a fight—though it was clear if things got physical, Harkan wasn't worried over doing what needed done. Colt just...*said* it. Like it was obvious. Like a fact.

Ain't got no personality to him at all, Everett thought.

Unsure how to follow the major's orders with this man as his charge, Everett shrugged. "All right, Harkan. But I gotta give you the nickel tour anyhow, show you the ropes. So I can keep *my* job."

Colt blinked once in response.

To their right, a door opened and a redheaded woman breezed in, wearing a top too low for business casual and a skirt too tight for sitting. She looked up from the stack of files in her arms. Blue eyes landed on Everett and she smiled. "Detective Kane? Those files you were wantin'?"

She had the sweet affectation of a fine Southern lady, though she was doing her best with makeup, attire and attitude to disabuse the notion. Everett met her forward gaze and tilted his head at the door. Kelly would know what he meant.

"Leave 'em in my office, Kel. Take a look after lunch."

Kelly arched her auburn brow, but her curiosity was gone as soon as it came. She gave Colt an appreciative glance, and yeah, Everett supposed he should've guessed women would flock to this enigma he'd been saddled with. He had the exact kind of look that was honey to the fly—brooding, arrogant, unimpressed with life in general. But Everett had never been in so bad a mood he couldn't appreciate a beautiful woman, so as Kelly turned to leave, he let his gaze linger on a few points of those...*files* he planned to examine later.

When he faced Colt again, he hadn't expected what he found. The expression sat strangely on his placid face, but if Everett had to guess, it was something like a smile—full of implications he didn't much appreciate.

"What, Harkan?"

Colt's eyes fell to Everett's left hand. The ring on his fourth finger fairly burned with guilt. But when he leveled his anger on the man in front of him, ready to challenge the impending question, none followed. Colt only stared at the scratched golden band, then blinked back to Everett like it wasn't worth his trouble. He was just noticing. And telling without *telling* that yeah, he'd noticed.

Everett's jaw ticked as he inhaled sharp. His stance shifted to something ready for a fight. "Fuck you, man. Ain't a thing you need to be thinkin' over there."

Colt nodded over his coffee, obviously unconvinced. But when he flicked his eyes up to hold Everett's stare, those warm-wooded orbs seemed less empty, less sunk-in. More like a tracker on the trail. A predator in wait, contemplating the hunt. Everett was two seconds from decking him for something to do when Colt ignored all manner of space and checked into his shoulder, brushing past like Everett wasn't standing right there to follow Kelly out of the door.

"Let's wrap this tour up. Wanna get to something worth my time."

Not waiting for Everett to follow, Colt sipped his coffee and let the door slam. Everett massaged his shoulder, still tingling from the contact.

Fuckin'. Asshole.

* * * *

In the weeks following that nickel tour, the station weathered the storm of adapting a work environment to the likes of Colt Harkan. Mason was the sort of place where cops on the beat went to high school together, and the ones who had some college on them made rank, given time. Thanks to the nearby state schools and fairgrounds, Mason was big enough to get lost in, but outside of peak seasons it was easy to notice who was sticking out. Weren't many strangers that hung around for long — and Colt was stranger than most.

Some guys at the station were threatened by a file they didn't understand. Everett didn't blame them for that. The few pieces that made any sense kicked around his head as he tried to contextualize Colt, the man who'd sat a silent shotgun for nigh on a month, like he'd never heard of small talk before.

Two tours in the war, Middle East and Philippines. Medical discharge in '03...

Three years undercover working vice in Texas. Extracted once for six weeks before going back in. Contacts in various gangs, hate groups...

Married once, divorced. Still his emergency contact though...

Psych evals. Therapy recs. A couple months in hospital for traumatic brain injury...

Performance review anecdotes of – unmanageable, some vigilante fuck-up, a good mind for cases if you can stand an ungodly, pessimistic-type asshole...

Well. The file got that right, at least.

At first, Everett took the car silence personally. But after weeks of watching Colt miss every opportunity with anyone who mattered, he stopped being offended by the behavior. There was still some of the fine Southern graces crowd at Mason PD. They mostly made the mistake of thinking Colt needed a helping hand and got a different side of the man – depending on if he thought the offer genuine.

Colt ignored Kelly's attempt to sneak into a dinner date by way of *showin' him around some.* He told Detective Maynard the only way he'd come by for a beer is if he *"stopped droppin' the n-word some kind of regular"* when he thought no one else could hear. About started a full-on fight with that one, but Colt didn't so much as raise his guard in defense, just sipped shop coffee as Maynard barreled toward him, like he'd seen far worse to recognize Ralph as a threat.

Martha, the older woman who oversaw the filing room staff, got a kind *"S'all right, ma'am, I'll figure it out"* when Colt couldn't work the copier. She showed him anyways, and Colt tipped his head in quiet thanks, a move that made Everett wonder if this strange partner of his had spent time on horseback. It was somehow too easy to picture him in a cowboy hat.

So clearly, Colt Harkan left much to be desired in a conversationalist, a coworker and a human being to boot. But the case on that man...god*damn.* Taking a page from the major's book, Everett had to give credit where it was due. It was like working with a fucking machine.

They hadn't caught anything major in the month since Colt's arrival, but "major" didn't come to call too often in Mason. And yet it didn't seem to matter what sort of case they caught—robbery, missing persons, the occasional domestic. The second they'd step on a scene, Colt's eyes would go soft and somehow, he just *saw* what everyone else missed. Like a pessimistic sponge, he'd stand there and absorb, squeezing relevant details into lines of looping scrawl, fine black ink filling page after yellow page.

By the time they were back in the car, Colt would have it figured—a map to the next logical step, which alibis were full of holes, the perfect question, the missing answer.

Cuffs. Lunch.

Like the man was born with an extra sense, Colt spat out solves with lightning quickness. And never once had Everett heard him say a detective's least favorite words—*I don't know.*

So sure, Colt Harkan was a miserable son-of-a-bitch, but that didn't stop Everett from sticking up for him when the guys got to ragging on his Strangeness of the Day. If Colt even noticed, he didn't seem appreciative, and maybe that was why it came out of the clear blue for Everett when the man started voicing certain *opinions*.

A bad Tuesday night rolled into a worse-off Wednesday, another night of claiming case to Rachael and cruising bars for easy company. Not like a man his age could risk the circuit anymore, even on some casual thing. Not with a wife and two kids at home. Rodeo was a young man's game.

Nowadays, Everett's thrills came in the form of western bars, whiskey shots and a handful of wayward women. He'd stumbled into the locker room that morning expecting it to be empty. Instead, he'd found the *last* person he wanted to see in his uncaffeinated state. For all their weeks on the job together, they never seemed to hit the showers at the same time. For that matter, since their tour the first day, Everett hadn't seen Colt darken the door. Until now.

With the early hour and evidence of his own rough night on his face, Everett wondered what could make Colt want to wash up so early. Was it really just avoiding people? Around then, Everett had to admit that, sure, he was probably still drunk, or he might've answered his own question with one look.

Colt must've just gotten out of the shower. Beads of water spiked his dark hair and slid down the lines of his back, disappearing into the towel tied low around his waist. His arms tensed and flexed as he ran a broken comb through short waves of brown. As he tossed it inside his open locker, Colt caught Everett's eye in the mirrored door.

Another man might've asked what he was doing there or comment on how Everett was staring. But Colt didn't mumble a word, just held his gaze in the peeling mirror, and waited for Everett to have his say.

The shower-humid heat made him sway when he asked, "What's all the birds for?"

Everett coupled the question with a two-finger shove against Colt's right shoulder, which was covered in the diving arcs of tattooed wings.

Colt closed his locker and turned to face him. He tightened the towel at his waist. "Which one?"

Everett ran a whiskey-brave finger to the smallest bird on his chest, up by his left shoulder. "This?"

"It's a swallow," Colt said. "First tour. Tradition."

Everett nodded, but didn't look up, skimming his fingers over Colt's collarbone as he moved to another bird. This one spanned Colt's right shoulder with dusty checkerboard feathers. "This?"

"Northern harrier. My pop's favorite."

The start of a smile curled his lip, and Everett couldn't help the curiosity, couldn't help but trace the harrier's wings with the tip of his index finger. He was drawn to the succinct stories, etched into a man he'd thought cared for nothing at all. But of course he did. Everyone cared about something. Years as Lead Detective had taught Everett that much—and Colt cared enough to carve it in his body. Weren't his fault no one had asked, that no one had cared to understand.

Everett trailed his fingers down Colt's right arm, skimming the curve of his elbow to rest on the sensitive skin above the bend. With the slightest pressure, he could take Colt's pulse if he had a mind. Not wanting to examine the part that did, Everett asked in a voice gone quiet, "This?"

Colt stared hard at the stormy blackbird on his forearm, black wings tipped with splashes of red and rust. Something dark flickered in his eyes. "That...ain't a story to be telling."

Everett wasn't so drunk he didn't know he should be pulling back. He blinked up and met Colt's gaze, realizing all manner of things too fast. One, sometime during his questions, Everett had taken two steps forward and was now standing closer to Colt than he ever had before. Two, he was rubbing his thumb in circles over the red-winged blackbird Colt wouldn't discuss.

And three, his partner's eyes had the dark shine of fuel, ready to burn.

Everett could've pulled away. Probably should've. But he didn't. He felt himself swaying, still worse for whiskey, but the sight of the tattoo on Colt's left arm pulled him up short.

"What about that?"

Everett's eyes tracked the pattern of the interlocking Celtic cross. At the center were four thicker lines that, on second glance, were sharper — angled and spun like a fucked-up windmill that would only ever mean hate in these parts. It was a decent cover job if someone didn't look close, but that ship had sailed long ago.

"Looks like you know," was all Colt said.

Pieces of that patchwork file tumbled through Everett's mind...

Three years undercover working vice...

Contacts in various gangs, hate groups...

But, still, the emblem didn't fit with the man he'd worked beside for weeks, not even for some undercover op. By now, Everett knew he could ask part of a question and Colt would hear the whole thing — might even answer now they'd managed to talk at all. So though it weren't a bit his business, Everett took his best guess.

"What happened to the piece of shit who landed you *that*?"

Clear and even, Colt said, "I killed him."

Something electric shivered down Everett's spine. "And your man? The case?"

"I got him."

The answers weren't a shock. To hear otherwise would've surprised Everett more. The cold way Colt confirmed it settled something in Everett's opinion of him, though what, he couldn't say. "So, it was worth it?"

Colt's eyes flashed a mournful brown. "No. But it was necessary."

With that, Everett nodded and removed his hand from the half-naked man in front of him. Wouldn't be long before day shift showed up and caught some kind of wrong idea. Everett pushed at Colt's chest, ignoring the coolness of shower-damp skin, and let his arm fall to the side. "That's why you come in early? So people won't see your ink? We ain't *that* small-minded around here."

"It's one reason," Colt replied, then added, "What's yours?"

Everett wasn't touching him anymore, but neither had he added any distance. So when Colt leaned closer, took advantage of his height to nose the air near Everett's neck with an incriminating sniff, he froze — desperate not to make contact of another kind, if Colt was thinking what he thought he was...

Colt pulled back, eyes bright with amusement. "Where you been, Ev?"

"Excuse me —"

"Don't smell like you been home any."

"The fuck is that supposed to mean?"

Colt's half-smile was back and gone again, crammed in the corner of his mouth. "Nothin'. Not a goddamn thing, Ev."

Everett twitched in response to the nickname. Felt like something cold creeping down his back. "Don't call me that."

"What?"

"*Ev.* I'm not...I don't do nicknames. You call me Everett, Kane or Detective like everybody else, but don't get to thinkin' we're friends."

"Sure," Colt replied, crossing arms over his chest. "Why'd I want a thing like that?"

"Fuck you, man."

"Better than you have tried."

A switch flipped in Everett's mind, too fast to circle back to what the actual hell Colt might be suggesting. Everett shoved him in the chest and slammed Colt against the lockers — and suddenly, their distance really *was* that different kind of dangerous. The clanging crash of metal shocked some sense into him, but Everett didn't move and kept Colt pinned. His eyes went hard as ice, not a trace of kindness or placation to them.

"Shut your mouth, Colt."

"Watch your hands, Ev."

A quick downward glance showed exactly what Colt meant. Caught in this position with his hands around Colt's wrists, arms pulled close to the body, it wouldn't take but one wrap-around move for *Colt* to be in control, setting him free as those birds on his arm. The energy shifted as Everett nodded, his only acknowledgment of who really had the upper hand. Even with his eyes shut, he could feel Colt leaning closer.

"Need you to do some thinkin' for me, Rhett..."

There's another nickname to train out of him, Everett seethed, breathing heavy through Colt's even keel, unwilling to listen through the haze in his head.

"I ain't saying a word that's not mine to say," Colt drawled. "But you might want to wash up 'fore you get to your desk."

Bastard almost sounded like he was enjoying this. Everett huffed his response in short bursts of anger. "Got somethin' you wanna say, Harkan? Got opinions on where I been?"

"I'm saying, there's a certain scent you might want to eliminate. Since Rachael's waiting for you."

Colt had yet to meet Everett's wife, but the pictures around his office were plenty to recognize her by. He watched Colt catch the glint of shame in his eyes, but neither was Everett keen on admitting to nothing either. He doubled down with a challenging stare, barely able to form words around the rage. "How d'you know it's not her?"

Standing as they were, on the cusp of an out-and-out altercation, Colt found the audacity to smile. "I don't. But I reckon *she* will. Detective."

At the pressure on his fists, Everett's gaze dropped to their hands. He watched as Colt slowly turned the hold against him, and the way his arms strained as he forced Everett to yield —

Before the man could finish, Everett shoved him again. Harder this time.

It didn't help like he'd hoped.

Everett said nothing as he faced his own locker and kept his back to Colt. He struggled to control his breathing as he freed the buttons of yesterday's shirt, still stained with the scent of unfamiliar...perfume.

Fuck. This was not what Everett needed right now.

The guilt of the morning after was always worse when Rachael came by. Seemed these days, more often than not, he was too busy fucking up to put on his husband's best. A shower probably was in order. A cold one.

Everett kept his eyes forward as he undressed, ignoring the urge to turn his head at the light *pat-pat-pat* Colt tapped on his toweled thigh. In time, Everett recognized the sounds of clothes being pulled on, a locker closing and the hall door swinging shut.

Ten minutes later, Everett found exactly what Colt described at his desk. Rachael was there, all-knowing eyes and a fragile smile, breakfast in hand with a duplicate order on his desk. Everett leaned close and kissed the top of her head, avoiding the bun that pulled her thick brunette hair from her face. At the smell of decent coffee, he spent a moment thankful for the hospital's proximity. Breakfasts were easier to count on than dinners with Rachael's surgery schedule.

"Thanks, honey," he said. "Really appreciate it. Long night."

"Hope it was worth it."

There was a question in Rachael's hazel eyes that darkened every day, but today wouldn't be the one she dared ask after it. Instead, Rachael confirmed his schedule, that Everett was still good to pick up Gracie and Marcus from school, and reminded him her parents were still waiting to hear about dinner next month.

Everett confirmed the details of his family life as fast as possible, finishing his food by the end of the short discussion. He'd learned that filling his mouth with caffeine and egg sandwich was easier than lying outright. Gave him something to work on after swallowing his tongue.

Everett's office was one of the few with full walls, even if one was all glass and blinds. Down the hall, a door swung open and shut, and Everett clocked his partner's gait among the early-morning noise of the station. He turned from Rachael to watch through the blinds as Colt slid into his chair, thick slats of plastic cutting the man in pieces.

Everett looked away before he could be accused of something as ridiculous as staring. He darted his attention to the wall lined with bookshelves, department awards and a dusty trophy or two. The wall boasted one window that, if the weight of words unsaid between him and Rachael got any worse, he might be tempted to crawl through. When she finally broke the silence, it was with a sigh. She walked to the doorway and called to the only unknown face at the desks, "Colt Harkan?"

She said the name like a question. While he'd been working with Colt a while now, Everett had managed the interference well. With the little he knew about his partner's personal life—and the plenty he knew about his social graces—Everett figured he was saving Colt from the invitation he knew was coming, but there wasn't much he could do now Rachael was here, calling his name. Colt wasn't that kind of asshole.

The man ambled to the doorway, unwilling to step inside, like he didn't want to be getting close to any piece of this situation. Colt managed an expression that made him look more tired than miserable. "Rachael. Nice to meet you."

Didn't sound like it to Everett.

Rachael crossed the space between them and extended her hand to shake, which Colt did before returning his hands to his pockets. Everett tried to tamp down the part of him still waiting for his damn handshake, and the thought brought back the memory of those inky birds that hid beneath Colt's rolled shirtsleeves...fuck, but maybe it was good they hadn't done much touching at all.

Everett lost the thread of conversation, but when he tuned back in Rachael was smiling, making offers like *dinner* and *have you over* and *meet the kids*.

At the word *kids*, Colt stopped breathing for a long moment. He exhaled slowly, and the conversation stuttered on with brief, one-word responses to Rachael's friendly questions. Colt nodded a hasty agreement about coming by that weekend and it all wrapped fast and awkward. With a tip of his head, Colt made his exit.

Rachael turned to Everett in confusion, like she didn't know where to start. Everett breathed a laugh with hands on his hips, eyes tracking someone who—for a morning at least—had seemed more man than mystery.

"It ain't you, Rach. Colt's just...like that."

* * * *

Louisiana, 2018

Sitting alone in his office, Everett laughed bitterly, caught up in memories of the dinner that had never happened—and the many after that did.

He remembered how Colt had arrived that weekend at Rachael's request, swaying drunk and shaking on his doorstep like he was knocking on the gates of Hell itself. He'd seen the man green around the gills before, had assumed Colt wasn't a stranger to some hair of the dog, but Everett had known at once that this was something else.

At the sound of the doorbell, Gracie and Marcus came running from the backyard, dashing around the kitchen counter and giggling with squirt guns in their hands. Everett only turned his back for a second, throwing out a guiding arm to keep the kids from rushing him.

When he turned again to the door, Colt was in his truck, driving away.

Everett didn't need Rachael to tell him to forget dinner and follow Colt, but he appreciated that even she could see that something was a new kind of wrong. Everett didn't yet know the full story of the horrors plaguing him that night, but he followed Colt's tottering pieces all over town anyway. The trail ended at a too-seedy bar that was already working on throwing him out, so Everett flashed his badge and got the bouncer to put Colt in his passenger-side.

"Where d'you live?" Everett asked when the man came around.

Colt blinked out of the window and slurred, "Doesn't matter."

"Sure it does. Where's home? I'll take you."

"You can't."

Not having much else to work with, Everett called the major and got him to look up Colt's address. Wasn't a great spot, but it was only a few minutes from the man's questionable choice of watering hole.

When they arrived, he managed to wake Colt and stumble him to his feet, left arm slung over Everett's shoulder as they staggered through the lot. Colt was in no place for fine-motor skills, so he'd propped him against what he hoped was the right door and fished in the man's pockets for keys. Something like a laugh fell out of Colt's mouth, but the sound had no humor to it. "Sorry, Ev..."

"Whatever, man. Bad nights happen."

"M'sorry...shit, I'm sorry. This wasn't..." He knocked his head against the door. "Fuck."

That was all he got out before Everett turned the handle on somewhere closer to a flophouse than a thirty-year-old's apartment. But the key fit and Colt shoved in like it looked familiar, dissolving into a dingy brown couch without turning on the light. That left Everett to find and flip the single switch by the door. Just some entryway bulb, but enough to see by without shocking Colt's red-rimmed eyes with light.

"You uh...you wanna talk, man?"

"No point."

Everett couldn't say why he didn't leave it there. Would've been a fine thing to make sure Colt was okay and see him Monday. Weren't like they were friends. He'd been pretty damn clear in the locker room.

But instead, Everett found himself stepping outside, calling Rachael to say he wasn't sure Colt should be alone tonight and he'd be back for church with the kids in the morning. It had been nice to hear Rachael happy on the other end of the phone for once, like she was proud of him for sticking it out with his stick-in-the-mud partner. Everett went back inside, found a clean-enough glass to fill with water and brought it to Colt on the couch.

"Here. Drink this."

Colt sat up and took the water automatically, gulping half of it down in one go. Like the faster he did, maybe the faster Everett would leave. "You ain't gotta be here."

"I know."

Colt downed the rest and handed the glass over. Everett sat at the other end of the couch, leaning forward and rolling *the cup in his hands. They stayed like that for a few silent minutes. Everett's gaze fell to the floor between his feet. And when the sound of stuttered breathing gave way to what could only be a flood of tears, Everett didn't stare. He didn't say a word at all. He let Colt have it out, bearing side-eye witness to his misery and near-frantic tapping of hand to thigh – thumb then third finger in a clear, repeating pattern, a puzzle Everett wouldn't solve for years.*

In time, Colt's breathing evened out. He sniffed hard and stood, filled another glass with water and knocked it back like it was something stronger. He leaned against the living room wall.

"I had a daughter. Once."

Everett still remembered the way his stomach dropped at the confession. There was nothing to be said when someone shared their deepest grief. No placation that would fix it. No words to make it better.

"Colt, I'm sorry. That's terrible."

"Would've...would've been four years old, come Christmas."

Shit goddamn and fuck, but life wasn't any kind of fair. Everett rubbed his forehead. "Colt, I...damn, man. You ain't never had to come by the house, that wasn't – I mean, Rachael didn't know. Hell, I didn't know – "

Colt didn't say anything, but the shake of his head stopped Everett's litany in its tracks, empty words that could never fix a father's grief. Instead, Everett tried to pivot to something more tangible. He blew a long sigh from his mouth and asked, "You got a bed in this dump somewhere?"

Colt scrubbed his eyes. "Yeah."

"Good. I got the couch. You go on."

"You ain't gotta – "

But at that point, it wasn't even a question. "Look, I've got kids. I've got a..." Everett trailed off, unable to even frame the words. He raised his eyes to Colt's, saw the pain behind the wisdom and wished there was any damn thing that anyone could've done.

"All I know is, if it were me...someone would need to be here. To make sure I woke up in the morning."

"Ain't your job."

"Kind of is. Lead Detective and all."

It was barely a joke, but it got Colt to stop arguing. "Suit yourself."

Colt finished his second glass of water as Everett scouted for sleeping gear. And once he'd made up the couch, before he could talk himself out of it, he walked to where Colt lingered in the kitchen and took a risk he still couldn't explain.

"C'mere."

Maybe it was knowing he'd been a father. Maybe it was just instinct, an intrinsic need to care for a person who'd seen too much. If it were anyone else, Everett would've been too scared to show this sort of kindness, especially to another man. But Jesus, if Colt Harkan weren't the person in the world most in need of a hug, then Everett didn't know who was.

From the way his whole body froze, Colt didn't expect it at all.

But Everett was committed by then, so he stayed put and held Colt close, bestowing two friendly pats on the back like anything could make this better. Everett leaned away from the contact awkwardly, not entirely sure why his mouth felt so dry, and maybe a bit ashamed at the surprise in Colt's mahogany eyes. Like he'd never expected compassion could be in Everett at all.

Colt broke their staring match first and sniffed, looking away. He cleared his throat and pointed to a door down the hall. "Bathroom's there if you need. Ain't got a spare towel or nothin'."

"Not a problem. I'll be gone by breakfast."

Colt nodded and stepped back, leaving them both in their own space. Everett turned to the sofa as Colt walked down the hall. But before the bedroom door closed, a low voice called, "Ev?"

"Yeah?"

"Thanks."

And damn near a decade later, surrounded by the sprawl of a case he *could not solve*, Everett unlocked a drawer with a bottle of whiskey and two files he hadn't read in years. As he flipped through the pages, his mind lingered on that hug, that moment of honest decency that was possibly the start of it all.

Why hadn't it felt strange to reach for Colt that way? It was the least he could've done, yet Everett knew if anyone else had been there, he'd have stayed planted on that couch like he meant to grow and die there. But he'd had the second thought. He'd seen a human being in need of care and allowed himself to provide it. And it wasn't the kind of terrifying he'd thought.

Really, what was wrong with giving a friend some physical comfort?

"Yeah," Everett scoffed as he poured a healthy drink, swallowing hard against a throat gone rough. "What *was* wrong with it? Just a little compromise. Helpin' a friend in need."

The compromises continued in his head.

Just a roadside. A kiss. A gravel road. A case we solved but left undone.

A backseat. Some alleys. A fractured home. One month of mornings that burned bright in-between.

The going back. The good years and the bad break. The bottle of wine that changed it all.

And after, four years that've yawned wide as the Grand Canyon with the drudgery of a life on autopilot. A life like death.

But none of that changed the major's orders or the young woman bleeding on his wall.

No way around it, then.

Everett picked up his office phone, dialed a number he couldn't ever forget and prayed the man on the other end wouldn't answer. Like usual.

Chapter Two

Colt
Louisiana, 2018

In a rundown office near the state line, a man more booze than bloodstream listened to the phone ring out. He knew why the blocked number was calling. He recognized this pattern from too many trial runs and one *"if this is who I fuckin' think"* that left the line silent as the dead. He'd be the first to admit there was a bit of lost time he'd had to swim back from, but it beat the alternative for now. He still had work to do.

So Colton Harkan filled a coffee mug by emptying another bottle, tossed it to a pile of clattering green glass and waited. The machine picked up after five blaring bell tones, but there was no message — never any message these days.

Three sips later, the phone rang again.

Got some nerve, asking for my help now.

Because this wasn't the only time his line had lit up this way, a semi-regular occurrence in the years of lack and wandering. The first time the blocked number had called, Colt wasn't sure it was real. He was blacked out on more than booze, too shocked when he picked up to that familiar, staggered breathing...

"Hello?" he'd asked, expecting nothing.

It wasn't nothing.

An inhale, deep and slow. Then a held-breath quiet, tense as a budding thunderstorm. A stuttered, low exhale, too like a mountain mist and no, it couldn't —

"...Ev? Is that — "

Click.

Nope. Had to be a dream. Because if it were real, and Colt had asked after him like *that*, not caring if his voice were breaking? The line never would've gone dead. Couldn't be Everett. He'd have answered, once.

But damn if Colt hadn't broken that too.

The next time the phone rang late at night, Colt happened to be of clearer mind. He'd picked up to nothing but that breathing on the line and decided to let it ride, just to see what would happen. The call lasted a whole seven seconds. Colt gave no hint he suspected who it was.

When it kept happening, Colt wondered after his sanity — not for the first, or likely last time. It was one thing to know the man was calling, to let it ring out in annoyance, even pick up if he happened to be there. But Colt had started *waiting* for the calls, proof that somewhere, Everett was...well, he was somewhere.

Maybe he just wanted to see how long it would take for Everett to give up the game, to admit that *yes*, it was him, or *yes*, Colt was right about the Combs case all along. On particularly bad nights, he'd open his throat to the welcome burn of whiskey and wonder if Everett called when Rachael was home. Or maybe she did up and leave for good, even after that hospital scene on his last night in Mason.

Colt wasn't sure either way — not because he couldn't find out, but because he didn't want to know. Nothing Everett ever said about his wife seemed to matter. Couldn't imagine that changing after Rachael...had her say.

Either way, the calls kept coming, the space between them dwindling until finally, that shit was happening damn near every night. What could he even be calling for in the first place? Colt pondered that question for weeks, choosing to ignore that his fixation made him buy a better phone, a model closer to this century with an actual functioning machine. For the business and all. Told himself it was for clients. So he could pay the bills and track the bastards who mattered.

But it was all for four messages he would never delete.

The messages totaled not even thirty seconds, but they proved Colt's theory on the caller behind the blocked ID. The breathing...it sounded like him. Not Everett Kane, Lead Detective. Not the man at the head of an investigation. The messages Colt saved sounded like Ev, like a half-furnished apartment they'd almost called home.

The phone rang again and jolted Colt from his thoughts. He grunted and shot the last of his whiskey, lit up a cig and ripped the cord from the fucking wall. If he kept letting it ring, he'd answer in a rage fit to match one of Everett's — exactly how he'd scared him off last time.

Until now. When he needed something.
And that's just way too damn familiar.

He raked a hand through his overgrown hair and wandered to find today's bottle, purchased fresh from the corner store. He knew he was too tired to fight the memories tonight, but that wouldn't stop him from trying to numb them anyhow.

It always started with thinking back on that month they spent in his old one-bedroom, dubbed "serial killer chic" by an Everett in better spirits than the first time he'd seen it. But at the close of the State Rodeo investigation—their biggest case and even bigger mistake—Everett was busy worrying over a different kind of error.

Around the time they caught Combs, Rachael finally got her answers about Kelly, and Everett's new forwarding address had become Colt's rundown sofa. Colt was still unclear how much she knew about the others, but it'd been enough to kick him out for a time. Everett had gone by the house only once for some things, but every day after, he'd move bits from the house-pile into Colt's space.

A lamp for the living room. A pan for eggs in the morning. Everett himself in Colt's full-size bed.

But if Colt was honest, it started earlier than that.

Somewhere in their four years apart, he'd stopped trying to convince himself otherwise, stopped pretending there was a version of him that wouldn't always be gone on Everett Kane. It became more ritual than memory, edges worn soft as oft-folded paper, thinking back on that roadside that started it all.

So close to life undercover—to Rosa and Jared and all the forgetting that took—it was no wonder he'd picked a thrill with such a narrow margin for success. At that point, Colt was begging for a wreck, not so particular on the how.

But he got another miss with another bullet instead, because Colt wasn't ready for Everett's question that day, or the way his eyes bugged when Colt answered with nothing but silence. How at the same moment, Ev's lips parted for a short, stuttered breath...

Fuck. If he'd known then how it would all go now?

Well. He still probably would've done it anyway.

* * * *

Louisiana, 2009, nine years earlier

Colt flinched at the click of the seatbelt, and this time Everett asked, "Why you do that? Jump at the buckle? Wouldn't expect a guy like you to bother so easy."

Colt didn't feel like explaining, though he did wonder how long Everett had noticed and said nothing, how much of Colt's file he might've actually understood. His next stab at the problem revealed a piece of it.

"This about your brain and stuff?"

Thanks to an uncomfortable episode a week ago, Everett was now aware of the portion of Colt's damage that had undercover work to thank. Ever since he'd shared those few stories of his time in vice, and the hospital stay that followed, his partner had been hyper-focused on him — asking after every fogged-eye gaze, every break in conversation, like he expected Colt to slip into an episode at any moment.

Rhett hadn't tried to get him to talk this much since those first days in the car. Six months into their partnership, Colt figured it might be easiest to start with a different piece of his mind, though he hadn't done so in years. "Ain't always about what's wrong."

Everett flipped the turn signal as they drove, more habit than necessity on the empty road. "Then what is it?"

"Just somethin' I've always had. My pop is the same."

Everett stayed quiet, probably since Colt didn't talk about personal things. He found himself explaining. "It's called synesthesia. Got worse after my injury. Physiologically speaking, I've got some wires crossed when it comes to perceiving the world around me."

"Could've told you that."

Colt's eyes flashed to his partner, but the jibe was good-natured and delivered with a smile. He nodded out of the window to a bank of trees. "What's that look like to you?"

Everett turned his head, expecting a trick question, but gave the obvious answer eventually. "Just an old willow. Leaves dancing in the wind."

Colt ashed his cigarette out the passenger-side. He licked his bottom lip at the sensations brought up by the sight. "Willows taste like peppermint. Smell like an autumn breeze." He could tell Everett didn't understand, so he added, "It mostly affects sight and taste. Some scents. Lots of colors. I just…get more than I'm supposed to."

"And it's always there?"

"Pretty much, these days."

"So, the seatbelt?"

"Broken glass and asphalt."

Everett made a face, like he imagined that wasn't pleasant for how often it must happen. "Ain't nothin' that helps it?"

Colt shrugged. "Not somethin' to be fixed. Just is."

He could've left it there. The silence was almost comfortable and, for once, they'd managed to talk without it turning into a fight. As they drove, Colt found himself lulled into something like a conversation, his mouth telling truths he wasn't sure he wanted Everett to know.

"Used to draw, when I was a kid. Helped make some sense of it. No one ever knew what I was talkin' about."

"I imagine that hasn't changed much over the years."

Colt swallowed a laugh deep in his throat and pulled hard at the cigarette between his lips. He didn't have to hide his amusement now — something he still had to remember even this far from life undercover — but that saying about old habits never told a lie.

For lots of reasons, a blank face was still safest in Mason.

They hit a pothole, and the crucifix Everett kept around the rearview jumped and jangled, causing more sense-memories to spill out. "Sunday school teachers said I scared the other children," Colt mused. "Didn't like when I told 'em their angels tasted like dust or felt like a peeling sunburn. Pop stopped makin' me go after that."

Everett darted eyes between Colt's face and the tattoo on his left arm. "You ain't Christian then?"

"No."

"But you got a cross tattoo. Why, it taste like rock candy or somethin'?"

"It ain't — never mind."

"C'mon, don't be an asshole. Tell me. I wanna know."

Colt sighed smoke and braced for Everett's inevitable rebuttal. He stared at the too-familiar pattern as he explained, "The Celtic cross is a symbol of multiple and disputed origins. Far as folks can tell, it had more to do with the seasons. An acknowledgment of the power of the four elements in harmony. It's linked to Judeo-Christian imagery now, but that ain't all there is." His tone shifted to something more practical. "And there's only so much you can do to cover a fuckin' brand."

Everett nodded and didn't speak for a time, like he was chewing his words before spitting them out. "Hope you didn't pay any large sum for that one. Don't mean to be telling you your business, but it's not as nice as your others."

"Imagine not. Did the cover work myself."

"You some tattoo artist on the side?"

"No."

Everett was clearly waiting for more, but that was all the explanation Colt planned to give. He'd already let the conversation run long, got Everett thinking he was an open book, rifling through pages without the context to understand. Far as Colt could tell, Rhett had been raised to depend on a savior too well to consider a reality without one.

"So really," Everett tried again. "You don't believe in nothin' greater than yourself?"

The fastest way out of this was to turn the tables on him, so Colt aimed to wound and let the truth fly. "Seems to be doing you all manner of good. Bringin' health and happiness to your marriage."

It was a step over the line. Colt expected a fight. But for once, Everett didn't lash out. He stayed uncharacteristically quiet, then said, "Rachael's family is Jewish, you know."

"Assumed. Name like that."

"Yeah, well that was still some kind of deal around here when we got together. Like to start some holy war with the parents. But Gracie was on the way already and...well, both sides felt a *religiously complex* ceremony was better than the wrong side of the blanket."

Colt tried not to crack a smile at the thought of *Everett Kane* being responsible for someone's moral education, and was only partially successful. "What, you take 'em to church and all?"

"I do. On the Sundays I can swing it. Rachael does Passover with 'em — not really a temple around that's not a half-day's drive. The kids are young now, so it ain't all that hard but...I do wonder what they'll decide when they get minds of their own. Worries me."

The quiet held for longer as Everett worked up to the question he was *not* going to answer.

"So you don't believe in Heaven? Not the idea of...seein' folks again?"

Colt tried not to flinch at the itch that crept up his forearm, did his best to ignore the taste of pennies and chipped paint. He forced the dark memory away.

"Dead is dead, far as I can tell. Nobody comes back from that."

He could see Everett didn't expect him to be so blunt with it, yet he sat there waiting on more anyhow. So Colt gestured to the swaying crucifix and doubled down on his worldview. "Even your man came back to this shithole for three days and left for whereabouts unknown. Makes you wonder if we'd have been better off never existing at all."

"You can't mean that."

"Fine."

Everett mumbled his way through a few holy curses, but none caught the air fully formed. In time, he said, "Look...think what you like. But you need to button this shit up when you're at the station. You know those rednecks can't — "

"I'm not a fuckin' moron."

"Well, you do a great impression of one. Real convincing." Everett shook his head. "Jesus, like the guys need another reason to razz you any."

"Doesn't bother me."

"You ain't heard their latest theory."

The way Everett set it up, Colt found he might actually be curious. He said with mild lightness, "Any of their *theories* won't deserve the word."

Because the way Everett was ramping up to this had captured Colt's full attention.

Ev delivered it as a joke, like he expected Colt to brush it aside, clear and easy as cobwebs. "Maynard's tellin' the guys you're some high-falutin' city-queer. Said you must've took it up the ass for those boys undercover. Only way you could've hung with such a crew."

Well, Colt thought, *that didn't take long at all.*

Everett's face turned to shock — and something else — the longer Colt remained silent. He cleared his throat, toeing the truth in his even-measured drawl. "This, uh...this might be one of those times you'd want to be correctin' me."

Instead, Colt kept his gaze on the road and focused on his breathing, not the buzz in his ears or the leaves that swirled into dust in the rearview mirror. Colt knew what was real most days now — what was lingering trauma, what was crossed-wire sensation — but it was still a heady cocktail to bear. To Colt, the silence in the car sounded like a revolver, five of six chambers full.

Terrible odds.

Something dark whispered, *Pull the trigger.*

"I will," Colt told his partner. "When somethin' needs correcting."

Wide blue eyes shot to the road. Everett passed a semi-truck and merged back again, but Colt wasn't surprised at his reaction. These were early days on a new job for this kind of honesty. They were just settling into a semblance of routines, of knowing which fast-food joints the other could deal with, remembering preferred brands of smokes and sweet tea.

And into that uncomfortable newness, Colt had confessed to sleeping with men. In his experience, there were only a few ways this could go, none of them good. Was always the ones who talked loudest about their women that went runnin' for him first. Seemed Everett was no exception.

He held to skate-around-it humor to start. "Well…you must be one dedicated bastard. Don't think I could do it. Not even for a case."

Such a liar, Colt thought. But he said, "Leave it alone, Ev."

"And I'm not some bigot neither, just mean for me, it don't seem natural —"

That holier-than-thou tone from a man he'd caught breaking many a Commandment pulled an honest chuckle free. "You can tell yourself whatever you want, Rhett, but don't waste your energy lyin' to me."

Everett's temper came fast this time. "And what could you *possibly* mean by that?"

"Pull on over and I'll show you."

And it was good that Everett wasn't looking at him, that the closest their eyes came to meeting was one shared glance in the rearview. Everett's thumbs weren't tapping their usual beat on the steering wheel. He did seem to be flexing his fingers, though.

Eventually, Everett bounced the heel of his hand off the wheel. "Fuck you, man. Go ahead and sit all quiet 'n slick over there, but there ain't nothin' I can do but makes me look like half a faggot—"

"Keep driving and you're a coward. Pull over, you're what you say you are." Colt slid another Camel from the pack, flipped his silver Zippo and puffed the cherry to life. He took a long drag. "Seems simple enough to me."

Colt watched his partner from the side of his eye as Everett checked the mirrors, ensuring they were on a stretch of abandoned road and not *"out in fuckin' public for whatever antics you're pullin', Colt."* The wet, heavy air felt oppressive the moment the car shut off, even with windows down and the heat of the day a few hours off yet. When Everett turned to face him, Colt stared out of the windshield and smoked, wondering how long it would be till Rhett shook his head and put this off as some joke, a dare they'd look back and laugh on with distance.

The moment Everett found some words he might want to use, Colt cut off his impending *so what the fuck* by opening the passenger-side door. The light repeating ding of the alarm played in the space between them, and as Ev shouldered out of the car, he had the look of one who *knew* he wasn't some nancy who backed down from any dare.

Yeah, Colt thought as he followed. *This ends well.*

Colt leaned against the tail light and pulled the last drag deep into his lungs. He kicked a leg up, sole against the tire, thumb hooked in his pocket as he watched Everett circle the car. He stopped three steps away, an obvious roll in his sky-blue eyes. The hot wind tossed his tie and sunny hair as he brought hands to his hips. He was trying to seem the good-natured sport, but the man looked downright nervous.

"All right. Got me out here, Colt. What's it gonna take to get us back on the road? What're we doing here?"

Ev should've known better than to be asking questions like that. Colt looked his partner up and down and wondered if the lesson in broken wrists they'd skipped in the locker room had come for a second turn. The bright taste of watermelon burst on his tongue. Colt flicked his cigarette to the ground.

"I'm gonna show you, kindly as I can, just how much you don't know."

Everett's shock was something to behold.

"The fuck does that even — "

"Ain't gotta talk now, Ev."

Colt pushed off the car to close the space between them, invading all boundaries of professional working relationship. Ev swallowed hard as Colt dared him back with his body. He knew how to throw his height around without making a bit of contact, turning a sharp corner until it was *Everett* with his back up, leaning away — and into the car for support.

"Here's the truth, Rhett," Colt told him, voice low. "People collide. Bodies adapt. One constant about the human race? We're gonna find a way to hold onto what feels good when we find it. Even and especially if it kills us." His eyes snagged on Everett's mouth. "Everyone's an addict of some kind."

For as close as they stood, Colt still didn't touch him. But he might have let his head lean closer, let his dark hair fall over an appraising brown eye, let Everett wonder for a moment just what exactly he'd gotten himself into—and how it might already be having an effect, if the bulge in his slacks was any proof.

"Only few things worth it in the end," Colt said. "This is one of them."

Everett sounded surprised by the quality of his own voice. "You seem a bleak motherfucker for sex to be *that* high up your list—"

"Not sex. Connection's the real drug." Colt's eyes danced over Everett's face. "It's a primal directive, encoded in our DNA. We're all of us doomed to involve."

Colt knew that Ev hated his philosophizing, that academic pessimist shit that so often rained on his parade. But there was a different look in his partner's eyes now, like maybe he'd got to thinking about something Colt had said.

Connection...

In reality, he only caught a glimpse of Everett's face. It would be hours after, when he got to analyzing, that Colt would contemplate how the man's eyes had fallen to his own mouth, how Ev wet his lips as they parted with a heavy sigh, equally likely to start a fight as a fire in his chest.

Because in the moment, it wasn't more than a second before Colt went ahead and kissed him.

Colt wasn't about to change who he was for some rodeo-burnout's pride. If it mattered, his opinion was that Everett's masculinity wasn't yet so fragile he couldn't stand there and take it while a man hooked him around the neck. Wasn't really expecting to get lost in nothing. Damn sure didn't think it would be the start of something.

Colt kissed Everett Kane with the conviction born of proving a point—and a little bit because he could. There was no gentle give and take, nor was it anything resembling a tease.

Until it was.

Sharp as the ozone spark of a storm, something shifted as he cupped Everett's face, intending to hold him still, but it felt an awful lot like holding him close, and before he could stop himself, Colt was taking advantage of Everett's surprised sigh. He licked into his mouth and worked his jaw open, pressed his hip against Ev's hardening cock and was rewarded with a grumbling "*Oh fuck.*"

Colt's kiss made bold, unshakable claims even Everett couldn't seem to deny. Panic-idle hands twitched at his shoulders—afraid to touch him, like it would all stop if Everett so much as blinked. Certain he had to be pushing his luck, Colt started to pull back. But there was a light pressure on his neck as Everett followed after, blunt nails combing the short hairs at his nape. Before he could think too hard about it, Colt kissed him again, daring to linger as they woke from the spell of it. Like just maybe, Ev was getting accustomed to kissing another man back.

Breathing heavy into Everett's space, brushing their lips together light and easy, Colt opened the door to the backseat—and didn't hardly have to lay his partner down at all before kneeling in the gravel seemed the most natural thing in the world.

* * * *

Louisiana, 2018

Colt plugged the phone back in just to see what would happen.

In five minutes flat it went back to ringing, like it wasn't damn-near midnight at a business address. Like Ev couldn't be bothered to leave a fucking message. Because Colt wasn't about to be answering anything tonight. Now, he was thinking about other firsts too.

That first time Ev had bent him over in their backseat, Everett had pretended like he didn't know what he was doing. Got all shy and shit, like they hadn't spent weeks knocking into each other, all brushing shoulders and trailing hands. Like they weren't doing everything in their power to rile each other up. Like Everett hadn't just blown him in two minutes flat and come up smiling, something like pride in his joking *"Got you, didn't I?"*

Back then, there was a competitive side to their Russian roulette. It soothed something Everett seemed to crave and wouldn't name. Yet there he was, arms wrapped tight around Colt's waist, holding him close from behind, one hand fumbling to open his belt. Ev sucked hard at the pulse at his neck, biding his time, like they both didn't know what he wanted.

What Colt wanted to say was *don't lie to me like Rachael.* Didn't take a genius to see that Everett was grappling with something — couldn't handle, perhaps, that he had a separate set of rules for his women and his wife, like some acts were too crass to be spoken in the halls of a home. Instead of wondering what sort of rules Ev might make for him, Colt reached behind himself and damn the awkward angle, he held Everett close and ground against the hardened heat at his hip.

"Can't tell me you never fucked any of those pretty young things in the ass," Colt teased. "Don't need me holdin' your hand none."

Everett tossed him to the seat with a smile. "So hand-holding is where you draw the line?"

Doesn't have to be, he thought, but Colt said nothing of the kind.

Everett had eyed the bottle Colt pressed to his hand with surprise, but not ignorance. Colt had fished it from descending pockets before their pants tangled legs in the footwell. Ev arched an eyebrow, a clear tell of impending smartass commentary, but Colt cut him off at the jump.

"You wanna make fun for having it? Or be glad you've got it?"

Everett snorted, fished a condom from his own pocket and flipped the cap.

By that point, they could joke about it with moderate ease. There'd been enough over-the-console reach-overs and bobbed-head jack-offs that casual ribbing over *all that queer shit* only reminded Everett that, all evidence to the contrary, that was not what they were in the process of doing. So Colt never mentioned how when Ev's hands smoothed down his arms, lacing their fingers as they sank together that first time, it was the closest Colt had come to a hand worth holding in a long while. Wasn't really anyone but Rosa, and later Mira, who ever showed him a physical bit of kindness, was ever something more than an anonymous fuck.

And now, Everett. For all the good it was like to do.

Wasn't nothing wrong with what he and Mira would have later—it was just different. Felt compatible in a way that made keeping her and Rhett both seem pretty normal for those couple good years. Like they didn't have nothing to do with each other, just partnered different parts of him until again, he had to let a good woman down, unable to be all she wanted him to be.

Not a father. Not again.

Some lines were drawn in sand. Some in concrete. Ev understood about crumbling edges, when he could be bothered to think about it at all. So by then, Colt had figured if someone was settling for scraps, it'd be all right if it was him.

* * * *

The phone stopped ringing around two a.m. Message finally received.

But it also didn't change the facts. Even if the cops were playing catch-up on the Edwards family secrets and the State Rodeo too, Colt was willing to admit the jurisdiction he needed was getting more important than his pride. He needed someone else on this the way he was. Someone who, once they knew the stakes, would commit. Ready to root out the darkness at the source.

Someone with skin in the game.

Colt flipped through a collection of SIM cards he stored in a different coffee mug. He fit one into a battered flip phone. As it powered on, he paged through a wind-whipped, car-worn legal pad to find the notes he was after.

"Mason County Tip Line."

Colt doubted anyone who would've known him would be answering phones on the graveyard shift.

Hell, he hardly recognized himself with a mirror and eyes to aid him. Those jokers, by voice alone? Clock *him*? No way.

Colt kept it short, an anonymous breadcrumb to set Everett on the path — and to give himself a chance to get a read on his old partner. Then he opened a file he wasn't supposed to have and resolved to run it through, one last time. He'd start from the top with Combs and prepare. He was only going to get one shot at explaining things, if they even got that far.

Because the way it all broke four years ago, Colt wasn't sure he could trust a soul in Mason. Not even Ev.

Chapter Three

Everett
Louisiana, 2018

Everett stopped dialing around two a.m., having left no message because *what would I even say*. He'd have to make the drive tomorrow if the phone wasn't getting him anywhere. Stapes wouldn't let anything slide worse than it already had.

If Colt wasn't there—or more likely, wasn't answering out of spite—there was only one thing to do with his time before morning. Not like he'd be able to sleep anyway. He dropped the Meyers file atop the two cold cases, slid the stack off his desk and dragged ass to the breakroom. He nuked the dregs of cold coffee for the third time since morning and didn't wince as it passed his gullet. If this Meyers case really was connected to Patrick and Mary...there was plenty of brushing up to be done. Maybe new surroundings would help.

He opened the file labeled *P. Combs, 2011* and reread the officer's initial report. One male vic by the name of Patrick Combs, twenty-three years of age. Family said they hadn't seen him in months, but that wasn't strange for a kid fresh from college picking up seasonal work. Witness statements and initial canvas had confirmed Patrick had only worked at the State Rodeo half a year. Folks who knew him said he seemed down on his luck and kept to himself.

The man who owned the rodeo, Mason's own Richard Edwards, said security heard someone breaking into the office and found Patrick stealing cash from ticket sales. The guard claimed to have seen a gun in his hand and fired in self-defense. The officers on the scene weren't inclined to disagree — not with a man with the last name of Edwards.

Officially, Combs was an "attempted robbery" and nothing like a murder, but Colt had noticed more on that scene than any of them. From behind the official police reports, Everett pulled a stack of pages and read the rest from Colt's loopy scrawl.

Addict in recovery, probable religious affiliation. Raised middle class, likely gay. New in town. Look into whereabouts after Katrina...

Everett shook his head as he read over Colt's notes. He'd spun all kinds of theories in the days after Patrick's scene, theories that convinced Everett into actions they *never* should've taken. In the end, they'd worked Combs on the low for a month before the trail went cold — and Everett decided to let it. For all Colt's theorizing, too much seemed circumstantial then.

Everett rubbed his forehead and closed Patrick's file, then opened the other cold case labeled *M. Sawyer,*

2014. On the surface, Mary's scene had nothing to do with Combs, but the threads of connection Colt had uncovered tied Mary to Patrick with too neat a bow.

It took Colt a whole year before he'd come to him about Mary, admitting he'd never stopped working Combs despite Everett's clear instructions to the contrary. Colt was full of reasons why he barely understood, but he did his best to listen — even if Colt sounded like he should be wearing a tin foil hat. Apparently, if someone working the State Rodeo also attended religious rehab or Katrina support groups, was under twenty-five and hired as a seasonal temp, then to Colt, they were a person of interest. Someone to be watched.

Because people in this Venn Diagram had a habit of disappearing — or turning up dead.

That was the first time Colt ever showed him his list. Six people fit the pattern, and Patrick Combs was one. Mary Ann Sawyer was another, and thanks to Colt tearing up missing persons in his free time, he'd actually managed to find her. Alive.

Seeing it all laid out now, Everett wished they'd found her sooner, wished they could've talked to her, even just once. If they hadn't spooked her on that stakeout in 2012, maybe. But they had, and she'd gone, and that was that. Even Colt had finally let his theories go with Mary. He'd seemed pretty sure they'd never see her again.

So when she popped back up out of the blue in 2014, there was no talking Colt out of trying to make contact. Everett wondered if it was the first time he'd ever been wrong, the way he kicked up trouble with the bosses about the whole thing — and for what? All following Mary had led to was pain and death and more unanswered questions.

Everett tried not to let his thoughts derail to guilt, to get lost in anger or be torn away by grief. His hand flexed at his side. Nothing about the night of Mary's call had gone well. If they'd gotten there sooner, maybe. Everett rubbed his eyes.

Fuck, he hated this. Because he couldn't help but think...maybe if he and Colt hadn't had that dinner, if he hadn't run like he did and Rachael hadn't been so quick...maybe poor Mary would still be alive. He and Colt might still be working together. And this newest file of Andrea Meyers, open three long days, dead from knife work and bound torture that *nobody* should have to endure — maybe it never would've happened in the first place.

He leaned his palms against the breakroom table and ran through it all again.

Combs and the not-quite robbery, 2011.

That first sighting of Mary, 2012.

Secret doors and gunshots and Mary mumbling *"Run..."* in 2014.

Everett blew a long sigh from his lips. Three fucking weeks before the State Rodeo finals, the biggest event of Mason's economic calendar, and this Meyers case had broken with all the marks of a full-blown psycho-killer. And where was he? Stuck staring without a clue, wondering what exactly had been going on in his town. On his watch.

Everett was down to grounds in his mug when he admitted he'd had the right idea before. He re-stacked the files and returned to his office, foregoing a glass to take a pull straight from the bottle. If he was gonna figure this out, he needed to start at the very beginning, that first bit of common ground.

Patrick, Mary and Andrea had all worked the rodeo seasonally. They had overlapping traumas and similar ages—but more than that? There had to be more tying them together than Everett was seeing. Or was it all just coincidence, suggesting connections where none existed?

Even in his own head, that sounded like wishful thinking. No, Everett had that feeling. They had missed something—on that first scene with Combs or when they did their digging after. And if he had to go rifling through all those memories? He needed something stronger than coffee.

* * * *

Louisiana, 2011, seven years earlier

Everett was known to say a person could learn a lot about a man from his car. There was a reason the old timers called it the mobile office. Sure, they had desks at the station, but being out and about was where Everett had his ideas. Driving around the backwoods, looking out on the natural sprawl...something about it settled his thoughts, let him see the case for what it was.

Or it used to.

Used to be there was a time when the car was the best lunch spot in town, a quiet place to think, a respite for a smoke and a catchy tune all in one. All that ended when Colt Harkan took shotgun. And not much had changed in the two years since.

First of all, the man was staunchly opposed to driving on the job. Clearly *could*, as evidenced by that beat-up "silver" truck he drove around, though time and disrepair had faded the color to weathered-blue. But apparently, being on the job with Detective Harkan meant being a glorified cab driver. The second they entered their car, that damn legal pad was on Colt's lap, and he'd scratch away for pages that, admittedly, contained more than Everett had seen.

But still. It was the principle of it. And when their thing picked up by that roadside in '09, the car became a new kind of distracting.

Wasn't like it was an everyday situation, but it wasn't exactly infrequent either. A week or two would often pass before one of them would get the itch, make the reach, nod at properly abandoned parking lots. Everett spent a fair bit of time in-between reminding himself of all sorts of things—how it wasn't that big a deal, how they didn't mean anything by it. How it was just some fucking game.

Some people did crosswords. He did...this.

Because damn, did it liven up his workday some to watch Colt on a scene now, knowing on the way back, those long-fingered hands of his wouldn't be flipping pages for long. Colt could give the work a break for five minutes. Do something a bit more fun.

And in that way, even with the scene around them, today was a special kind of treat. Because everyone else was ready to phone this one in, but Colt wasn't having a piece of it.

Everett was surprised the actual owner of the rodeo was there to meet them at the gate. No one grew up in Mason without knowing Richard Edwards. Their family had the kind of money that polite folks didn't mention—that *old* Southern money, too stained with blood to go anywhere visible, so they buried it in assets and properties, in the unseen lavishness of indoor lives.

To be frank, Richard Edwards was wealthy enough not to care if a man was dead on his property. To him, the State Rodeo was one of many in a portfolio that'd likely scramble Everett's head. But the fact he'd come by to ensure assistance spoke of a genteel upbringing that didn't exist these days. To Everett, at least.

Not to Colt.

Colt spent his time grilling Richard in that quiet way of his, slowly turning up the heat not with threats or sarcasm, but with silence. There was a way Colt worked where something flipped in his storm-dark eyes. For a moment, it would seem like he could look straight through a person, like if he said a word in anything other than his muted drawl, they'd confess every sin they committed.

It was the tension of tipping his hand that put them over. Poor bastards were never ready for it.

Colt stood near the body and kept his eyes on his legal pad. "What's on your schedule today, Edwards?"

It always started benign, like a way to follow up.

"Busy, I'm afraid. But if you need anything" — Richard extended a crisp white business card — "Call here. My staff knows to send all calls from police straight to me, no matter the hour."

All Colt had to say was, "Kind of you to make the time."

Because *that* was the silence to let them fill.

Richard Edwards was a tall, silvered Southern gentleman, whose custom boots put him on par with Colt's six-foot-even. But Everett could hardly tell with how those proud shoulders fell — before swelling with outrage.

"If you mean to say — "

"That'll be all. Stay in town, Edwards."

Colt turned back to the body without another word. Edwards stormed off, unaccustomed to being so dismissed, but Colt couldn't hear him if he tried. He tossed his cell phone to a nearby uniformed officer, and Everett noticed it was the guy who'd done least all day, yet complained loudest about the heat. The officer fumbled the phone but caught it, unsure what he should do.

"Walk away," Colt told him. "Far as you can."

The officer's gaze swung to Everett, like he was supposed to make sense of this. Everett waved him off because honestly, it got Colt to shut up and do his job, and the uniform flapping his gums was wearing on his nerves anyway. Colt needed no distractions to think like this, and his phone was full of plenty. Even the possibility of interruption was enough to pull Colt from the important things, which apparently included going hard on a case it was clear the bosses didn't want.

But it wasn't just at crime scenes. Colt hardly answered his phone anywhere. Barely kept the damn thing charged. It was unacceptable to be pulled away from real work with reminders about petty tasks, like his ever-pending performance review with Stapes. Colt probably wasn't planning on going to that anyhow.

So as Everett watched him work the scene, he mentally added to the list of grievances that came with being Detective Harkan's partner — first on-demand cab driver, now a goddamn answering service. Because if anyone actually needed to get a hold of Colt, they didn't call his phone anymore. They called Everett's.

"Detective Kane? If it's all right with you?"

Everett turned at the sound of his name and remembered that at some point, he might've been interviewing someone. Colt's careful interrogation had caught his eye, and Everett had trailed off to watch without noticing. He'd have expected the man to say something sooner, but the richly attired fellow before him — one of those business-hotshot cowboy-wannabes — was already blowing past to follow Richard and other staff inside.

The hotshot's eyes landed on Colt in an appreciative fashion, and Everett didn't much care for the feeling that inspired. Something too close to jealousy, acidic like a bad whiskey, clawed up his throat and made it hard to breathe. Colt didn't so much as blink, his whole world narrowed to the body in front of him, taking in every detail.

The man finally left and Everett breathed a little easier. He looked around for other rodeo staff and, seeing none, asked Colt, "You plannin' on spending the whole night here?"

"I'm working."

Colt patted down the side of Patrick's jean jacket and pocketed a set of house keys. He kept searching the body, turning it over and untrapping the arm beneath. Colt pried the hand open and his eyes widened. Everett couldn't see what it was, but Colt quickly bagged the small item, slipping the plastic in his own back pocket.

"We've got the story, Colt. Can't imagine what you're looking for. This case is open and shut."

For all the response he got, Everett might've saved himself the trouble and stayed quiet. Colt remained in a low crouch, staring at Patrick's body for five silent minutes. Then ten. Then twenty. Eventually, they were the only ones left on the scene and he had to knock into Colt's shoulder with his knee to break the man's trance. Everett convinced him back to the car and drove around while Colt scratched pages of notes. They were good and lost in the back country when Everett pulled over out of spite. Just an experiment to see how long it'd take for Colt to notice.

Seven minutes later, focused brown eyes were looking up, adjusting to new surroundings and turning to Everett in the driver's seat. "So what's your take?"

"My *take* is you're writing an awful lot for a Friday night. I work day shift for a reason. I want my weekend."

Colt flipped a page to reread his notes with one hand, automatically slipping a Camel from the pack with the other. He puffed it alight and clinged his Zippo shut, but didn't stop reading.

"Lookin' forward to some quality time with the family?"

"Fuck you," Everett shot back with no real fire. He shifted in his seat. "C'mon over here."

"Why?"

"You know why."

Or maybe he didn't. Because when Colt looked up again, he seemed genuinely surprised, like he hadn't hardly noticed the state Everett was in at all. He reached across the console to flip yellow pages over his partner's hands, slid the cardboard from between Colt's fingers, then tossed the pad to the backseat.

Observant brown eyes read Everett like a book, now he was looking. "What happened?"

"Nothin'."

Colt glared in a way that said even Everett was smarter than that, so he tried to say a part of what he meant. "Just didn't like how that suit was lookin' at you, is all."

That got Colt's attention, but it wasn't the kind he wanted. Colt reached for his notes in the backseat again. "Who? What kinda look?"

"I dunno. Just a look."

Colt's interest faded as fast as it came. "Need to be more specific if you want my opinion, Ev."

Specific was the last thing Everett wanted to get on how that look had felt in real time, how relieved he'd been when Colt hadn't noticed. Everett did his best to deflect, but he'd wanted the man's attention, hadn't he? Just no clue what to do now that he had it.

"How specific can you get about a look?" Everett asked.

"From a seasoned lead detective, I'd hoped for more than its existence—"

"Oh, for Christ's sake. It was…y'know. *That* kind of look."

It was almost worth the heat in his cheeks for the way Colt's eyes brightened. Before, the man had been ready to howl in frustration at how little Everett noticed on the daily. Now, he was trying not to laugh.

"You think you know what *that* kind of look is?" Colt teased. "Got some vast experience I don't know about?"

"All right, asshole. Go on and have your laugh, but I might know a little 'bout *that* kind of look by now."

Colt hummed low in his chest and dropped the legal pad again. He flicked his cig out of the window, though plenty was left. His tone warmed with promise as he leaned across the console.

"Didn't like how he was lookin' at me, huh?"

And nope, Everett decided. Moment over. Because his face was burning hotter the closer Colt got, eyes near-sparkling with implications he didn't care to examine, daring him to say otherwise.

Looking too smug for comfort, Colt was.

So he flipped the turn signal and swerved them back to the road. Everett muttered darkly as they returned to civilized streets, hopeful it would distract from how his flush was blazing straight up to his ears.

"Swear to God, I ain't never tellin' you shit again, Harkan. Just gonna say you fuckin' missed something and watch you suffer. See how you like *that*."

* * * *

Shift change was long over when they made it back to the station. A few stragglers were still on their way out and everyone at the desks dropped their eyes when they walked in. There was something strange about it, though. For once, people weren't avoiding Colt's gaze.

They were avoiding Everett's.

The reason wasn't clear until he flipped his office lights. Two over-packed bags stood in front of his desk. Everett couldn't remember the last time he needed suitcases, but they looked like the ones he got Rachael a few Christmases ago, when she was going to some conference or other.

A folded note sat atop the retracted handle of the largest bag. There wasn't a name, but not like it could be from anyone else. Everett's mouth dried up as he opened the note.

I'm in the parking lot.

No signature, but it was definitely Rachael's hand.

Everett heard the shuffling of anxious feet in his doorway, but didn't turn to notice which coworkers were the brave ones, who was stepping up to fill the others in, whispering *Rachael* and *about time* and *showed up an hour ago*. Everett brushed past and made his way to the detective's lot and wondered how he'd missed Rachael's SUV, parked beside his personal vehicle as it was. She leaned against it, hazel eyes hard with a truth long ignored.

Everett could tell. The question was gone. Rachael *knew*.

He sent a prayer to anyone who might be listening that she didn't know about it all. He stopped beside their car and asked, "What's goin' on, babe? We got some trip I forgot?"

Rachael didn't acknowledge his feigned ignorance. She closed their distance and shoved hard against his chest, but her heart wasn't in it. He rocked back on his heel and looked at her, brow furrowed. "Rachael, what are you—"

"This is what you want, right? You want me to make a scene."

"Rach, you need to fill me in here if—"

"Don't pretend I don't know. I've known for *years*. All that's changed is now I have a name."

Everett's heart felt like it might explode out his ribcage. It was possible that, in this, Rachael knew more about some woman than he did. Too many nights fogged from shots and broken promises flashed in his mind as Rachael said, "She came by last weekend. When you said you were working. Kelly, is it? Guess I'm not the only woman you're standing up these days."

And God forgive him if his first thought was selfish, but to hear words like *her* and *Kelly* steadied the ground beneath Everett's feet. These were apologies he'd been meaning to make, lines he'd memorized—though he'd never really expected to need them.

"Rachael. Listen…"

"No, *you* listen, Everett. You wanted a show, right? That's why we couldn't do this like adults, why you couldn't be honest and opt out? Because you'd rather be screwing your secretary like it's 1985? God, but if you weren't so predictable…"

Rachael was well and into her temper now, not caring that her voice was pitching higher, that a small crowd had gathered under the station overhang, glass door ajar so everyone inside could hear.

"You've got some nerve to try to do this to me. Trying to make *me* into some small-town housewife pining for your attention." Rachael stifled an exasperated laugh, borne of the kind of hurt that wouldn't ever make sense. "I'm a doctor, Everett. I make *twice* what you do—and save the lies, because you've never been as okay with that as you pretend. Is that what this is? Some way to be the man? Spread some wild oats and relive your rodeo-glory days?"

"That's not—Rach, you're making a mistake."

"No. I'm fixing yours."

Rachael reached into the pocket of her scrubs and retrieved a shiny set of keys he didn't recognize, attached to a keyring he did. He swallowed hard as Rachael clenched the keys tight in her fist, like she needed something sharp to bleed the words out.

"This is the most I'll play this role you've made for me, Everett. This is the one and only time I will lower myself to what these assholes here must think of me, the *only* fit I'm gonna throw about you runnin' around as obvious as you do while I bring you breakfast and coffee after—"

"Rachael, I'm—"

"No. You try to come by the house? You'll find new locks on the door. You need something from there? You call first. The kids and I will be with my parents while you decide if home's someplace you want to be."

"Rachael, *please*—"

"Just take what you need and leave. At least I know you're good at that."

What Everett saw in Rachael's face was the only thing that cut worse than embarrassment, than betrayal, though that was there too. He recognized the worst of it from the countless claims of choosing their battles they'd scattered over their marriage, because

Rachael wasn't sad or even vengeful at the moment. Her hazel eyes glinted with the armor of indifference, because now, she'd done what she came to do. Everett's reasons never factored into it.

They might talk on it later. But for now, he'd been dismissed.

Everett wasn't sure how long he stared at his family sedan, the four-door they'd chosen for ease of children's car seats, the one he'd parked in too many bars on a mission to forget what he had at home, if he could be bothered to want it some. When he'd imagined this in the hypothetical, he always thought he'd get a chance to explain. Now the unspoken excuses clogged up his throat and left him short of breath.

He heard the grind of small wheels over pavement grow louder, then stop. At his side, Colt set the largest suitcase down. He had papers tucked under an arm and Everett's duffel slung over his shoulder. He let the Combs file fall open on the hood of the car.

"C'mon. The case ain't done because you want it to be."

Everett knew he could mouth off in anger or feign ignorance at the implication. He was halfway to making a decision between the two when Colt pointed at the open file. And it was only when Everett read his partner's notes — and eyed the growing crowd at the door — that he decided he'd rather leave without a fight.

Especially if Colt thought Patrick Combs was a murder.

Everett tossed his bags in the back with a grumbling "Fuck this, man," and followed Colt's truck from the lot.

* * * *

Wasn't like Everett didn't know what Colt was doing, trying to distract him with the case. It took most of a twelve pack and the better half of a bad pizza before Everett admitted fine, maybe Colt had an interesting theory about the key he found in Patrick's hand, or even how it related to Colt's redacted time undercover.

But after an hour of sitting on Colt's lumpy-ass sofa, listening to the same list of connections on repeat, Everett was starting to feel like he had after those college cram-sessions that set his head spinning. And he didn't have the effort to spend on what might be a murder. Not when the world as Everett knew it was crumbling beneath his feet.

For all he'd never expected to get caught, Everett was plenty accustomed to the burn of shame. Grew up in it, really. Across the years, he'd played the role of repentant sinner with mixed levels of conviction, but tonight, he was in rare form. He lashed himself over the coals, using any excuse to turn the conversation to his idiocy — what he was gonna do without Rachael, what life without her and the kids would be. And a part of him knew it was performance, but shit, trying to pull commiseration from Colt Harkan was worse than blood from a stone. Every time Everett let loose a self-deprecating line — waiting for confirmation, negation, or any reaction at all — Colt simply countered with facts about the case.

Damn him. How else were they supposed to talk about this?

Beer-hazy though he was, Everett could tell Colt had the bit between his teeth on Combs. The man was worse than any dog with a bone when he knew Everett was putting him off, giving noncommittal answers that really meant *drop it.* Colt took a long swallow of beer where he sat on a stack of still-packed boxes and shook his head, like he was holding Everett personally responsible for this mess since he'd told Colt that the State Rodeo case was closed.

"That weren't no attempted robbery, Rhett, and you know it."

"What good does that do us?" Everett asked from the couch. "The bosses said to give it a quick shake, and we did. To prove anything you've got would take weeks of surveillance. At the *end* of rodeo season. There just isn't time."

"Not if we had the right source."

Everett barked a laugh before he pulled it together. "And your Rolodex is just crawlin' with CIs for this, huh? Got someone ready to flip and tell you some big story? Because the kind of rocks you're trying to turn, you're gonna need one. Prolly a few."

Colt didn't elaborate at first, but Everett found he was curious as hell what that head tilt really meant, like he was peeking through the blacked-out lines of a file labeled *C. Harkan*.

"Might know some names. Depends what type of rough this rodeo draws." Colt blinked slowly at a point on the wall and added, "Only some parts of that scene where I'd be useful. Couldn't do it alone."

But even Everett wasn't drunk enough for that. "Get the thought out of your head. We ain't running some black-ops bullshit over what is absolutely *not* a big fuckin' deal."

"Those bull-riding trophies in your office all for show, then?"

Everett cut a look at Colt, whose mouth was attempting a sneer, and they sipped quiet at each other for a time, unspoken barbs lighting up their eyes. Because sure, there was a part of him that would love to show Colt how wrong he was—in more than a couple ways with how he looked just then, sitting there in his cotton tank, slacks pulled tight across his thighs, face mad as hell and just as bent on getting Everett to go his way.

Everett turned his chin side-to-side. "Stop badgering me, Colt. There's other work to be done. It can't just be this one case."

"Better late than never isn't true for all things. Sometimes, late's too late to matter."

Colt's tone said exactly two things, weighed with scientific precision. He was absolutely, without a doubt, talking about the case. And he was also careful to keep two women's names entirely out of his mouth.

Everett scratched his nose. "Thought you were tryin' to distract me from that. With the case and all."

Colt pulled a hand through his dark hair and looked away. Everett reached for his partner's pack of Camels on the dinged-up coffee table, having burned through his own cowboy-killers hours ago. Colt knocked the box from his hand without looking, like he'd expected the motion, and pocketed what was left.

"Two birds, one stone," Colt admitted. "Ev, we should at least—"

But Everett had already moved onto that other bird he wanted to examine, the one that spanned Colt's shoulder with a predator's wings. Got him thinking about the place where those feathers ended in the curve of Colt's neck. Such a tender spot, and Colt moaned downright pretty when he got his tongue over it—

Yeah. There were *far* better ways Colt could be distracting him right now.

"For fuck's sake, give it a rest. Tomorrow for that." Everett let a bit of what he wanted swirl into his eyes. He parted his lips as he ran his gaze over Colt's shoulders, the lines of his chest, the angular cut of his hip —

Everett smoothed his hands down the legs of his pants, but it was a move too familiar to car etiquette to be convincing. "C'mon over here."

Colt didn't say a word, but it was the absence of movement Everett found more impressive. Every bit of him froze, like he couldn't hardly breathe. But by the next blink it was gone and Colt was walking to the fridge, hand tapping fast at his thigh.

In the couple years they'd been doing whatever this was, this was only the third time Everett had been to Colt's place. And maybe, upon reflection, that was strange. It might've seemed that, with all they got up to on those long drives and stakeouts, sleepovers at Colt's would be some natural next step, unoccupied as it was by prying eyes. Yet it was a step they'd never seemed to take. Everett didn't call or text outside of work, didn't reach for him anywhere but their car, didn't acknowledge in any way that Detective Harkan was anything but his assigned partner and all-around pain in his neck.

But now they were here? Alone? The possibilities of time with Colt outside the confines of a car were intriguing. To say the least.

Everett rose from the sofa and downed the last of what was warm in his bottle. "Grab me one?"

Colt closed the fridge and leaned against it, popping the cap of the single beer in his hands. He took a long sip and wiped his mouth with the side of his fist, looking Everett up and down before shaking his head at the sink.

Colt walked over to flip the tap and pull a glass from the cabinet. "Think you might've had a few too many to be making plans."

Everett set his empty on the counter and maneuvered behind his partner, fitting his chin along the groove of one shoulder. Colt inhaled sharp as Everett shut off the water, though the cup was only half-full. Everett took the glass from him and set it down slowly, turned Colt by the hips and walked him to the wall, noses brushing. "Boy, you got no idea. Ain't got no other plans now but wearin' you out."

"Aren't you full of promises?"

They hit the wall hard as Everett caught Colt's mouth with his, and for a moment...*God,* but it was everything he wanted. Colt answered his kiss and Everett traced his side with a hand, reaching low for the prong of his belt. But it stayed a brief sort of thing once Colt caught hold of his wrist, steering Everett's hand to rest on a hip instead.

Colt broke off with a frustrated groan, like he was just as annoyed as Everett by the interruption. He watched something familiar rise in Colt's mahogany eyes, a look more at home on a crime scene than a kitchen. He asked, "What's your play here, Rhett? Just gonna crash on the couch till Rachael caves and takes you back?"

"You think she will?"

Do you want her to?

Colt's face went blank, and Everett wasn't sure the man heard the question he'd meant to ask. He toyed with the tag on the inside edge of Colt's undershirt, unwilling to give up contact, but equally unable to look at him.

"I know y'all must've heard some of what she said. And I know you heard more than most." Everett cheated a glance up and wondered what in Colt's face was shadowed half-light, what was that fourth beer and what was maybe hiding behind both.

Instead of answering, Colt leaned closer, sliding his hand along the counter at their side. Before Everett could think to take advantage, could do more than breathe deep of something earthy and purely Colt, the cold weight of a glass was pressing into his palm. Water sloshed against the front of his shirt as Colt strode across the kitchen.

Having retrieved his beer, Colt considered the question, stuck to the fridge like some life-sized magnet. "Rachael's known a while. Imagine with time to cool down, and you clockin' some hours in that doghouse, you got a shot if you want it."

"That your honest take?"

And maybe it was or maybe it wasn't, but Colt wouldn't look at him either way. His face was unreadable. Impassive and cold. And maybe, Everett was surprised to find just how much he cared about this answer. About this specific detective's analysis.

Colt leaned away from the fridge and headed for the couch. "That's what my gut's sayin'."

He'd practically had to beg that answer from him, but Everett was relieved to hear it all the same. If Colt was right, then all wasn't lost, and Everett had worked with him long enough to know it was good odds to go with Harkan. Man had a sixth sense for these things.

Maybe it wouldn't be so bad.

Everett knew he'd needed to call things off with Kelly — and the same was true for his late-night running around. Just wasn't worth it anymore, if it had ever really been. He followed after Colt, took a seat at the other end of the couch and drank some damn water. When the thought hit, he couldn't help but chuckle at Colt's choice of words.

"Whole thing went sideways in the first place thanks to you and your *gut instinct*."

"What d'you mean?"

Everett turned to face Colt's end of the couch, kicking the man's shoe with his. "Last weekend, when I told you I had plans? Went on and on how I didn't have time to sit on that motel with you, waiting for one sporty car to pull in...and what'd I do? Spent a whole day I could've been gettin' laid in a hot metal box with your sorry ass."

Everett swiped a handful of bottle caps from the coffee table. He ran his thumb around the bent edging of one, then flicked it at the box of bottles near the kitchen. "Kelly...well, sounds like she went by the house when she got tired of waiting. That was that."

He flipped another few caps and missed more than he made. All the while, the burn of rejection competed with the burn of shame, and neither was a train of thought Everett wanted to board at present. He cut a look to Colt, who was tracing the label of his beer.

"So what? Don't like me unless I'm some cheatin' asshole?"

"Just don't know what you are anymore."

Everett sensed this would be one of those moments to have the right thing to say, which was a shame, since he was drawing a total blank on what that might be. Colt wasn't the only one without a clue who Everett Kane was at present. All he knew was it was someone different than who he'd woke up as that morning, when he had a home and a wife and a life. Now, nothing was for sure.

If Everett hadn't dropped thinking from the night's agenda hours ago, he might've realized he could've said any of that. But it was so much easier to eye the slope of Colt's shoulders, run a hand down his partner's tension-tight back and hope like hell Colt would let him get away with this. Just one night of not having to think so hard.

Everett pitched his voice to make light of the moment. "What I *am* is tryin' to get laid here, Colt. Didn't think it'd be such an imposition to you."

He'd been trying to get some sort of rise out of him, but Colt kept his eyes level on his beer, his voice stubbornly even.

"Fucking me isn't gonna unfuck all those women. Not gonna erase what Rachael knows."

Jesus, but he did *not* want to talk about this part of it. "Colt, c'mon…"

And sure, his partner's voice was low, but it was almost worse that way. He sounded…disappointed.

"For fuck's sake, Ev. You keep acting like this just *happened* to you. Like someone's supposed to be feeling sorry for you, patting you on the back for realizing what you should've already known. Can't believe I've got to tell you this shit."

Colt swung his head to Everett at the end of the couch, nothing but fire in his coal-dark eyes. "You think I wanna give you advice about them? *Me?*" He looked away and worked his jaw, staring hard at a spot on the floor. He tapped his bottle with a thumbnail and mumbled, "You don't know what this is at all. Got no clue what you're doing."

Everett wondered who Colt was really talking to and watched him kick the leg of the coffee table. Maybe it wasn't too far off for both of them. Just because Colt and him were doing whatever this was didn't mean he had to make Colt his part-time therapist. These weren't his problems. Colt shouldn't have to deal with this.

It was just…maybe Everett wanted him to. Maybe there was some different option to examine here, if Colt was looking for one. And suddenly, it was far more distressing to not be holding eyes with the man standing from the couch, to not know what was turning in his mind as he pulled another Camel free.

"Colt, c'mon, wait—"

He stood in profile in the empty hall, turning enough to see Everett on the sofa. "She's right about one thing, though. A shame you're so fuckin' predictable."

Everett's ears were hot and his throat was dry. He didn't care how he sounded as he snapped, "The hell you mean by that?"

But Colt wasn't looking for a fight. He was just telling truth in that quiet way of his—though it blindsided Everett to hear it twice in one day.

"You don't give a person a chance to catch their breath, Ev. You just take."

Colt's bedroom door closed soundly behind him, leaving Everett alone in the living room. In time, the thought occurred that he'd spent too much of today staring down *no's* of his own creation, at family cars and slammed-shut doors. Now, he was on his own with no answers in sight—no distractions, no help and no way out.

Everett eyed the fifth of whiskey on the counter but shook his head, thinking better of it. And shit, weren't it almost funny how no one was there to witness his feat of better judgment. Far too little, too late.

Everett still passed the bottle by and picked up a nearby legal pad. He flipped through the pages for something to do and waited for fatigue to take over decision-making. Would probably do a better job than him anyhow.

Chapter Four

Everett
Louisiana, 2011, seven years earlier

Everett wouldn't categorize what he got as a good night's sleep, but thanks to his choice of bedtime reading, he awoke full of ideas. He braved the suitcases and found Rachael again making a point. The bags were full of everything he could need for a stay away from the house. Better than he would've packed for a trip he knew he was taking. Everett changed into a fresh T-shirt and jeans and made a mental note to ask Colt where that river was where he must beat his clothes. Everett hadn't seen hide nor hair of a laundry room.

Two hours later, the bedroom door swung open. Colt's eyes fixed immediately on the new additions to the case-wall.

"Coffee's on the table," Everett explained. "Need to get an early start if we're gonna be ready in time."

"In time for what?"

Everett tossed his phone over, open to a series of messages with the major. Colt thumbed through the conversation as he took the gas station coffee, leaving the breakfast sandwich untouched. "Hmm. Could be enough, if we work fast."

"As always, you're fuckin' *welcome* for runnin' them around for you. With me 'out for training', if you go in and make some excuse, we should have a few days to work with. Won't have no manner of backup if things go sideways, but far as I can tell, the main thing you need is data, right? Company servers, security footage and shit?"

"For starters," Colt agreed. "But I won't have that kind of access. My cover's not the office type."

"You ain't exactly the office type *now*. Can't imagine you gettin' much worse."

Colt actually smiled at that, and it was only then Everett realized how little he ever did. But maybe some of Everett's social skills were finally rubbing off. Only took two fucking years.

Everett gestured for his phone back and continued to explain the plan. "Lucky for you, the State Rodeo's amateur competitions are next weekend so I could get on the roster last minute. Once I'm in and registered, I should have time to sneak off and quick copy a few files.

"Meanwhile, you do...whatever it is you do and work out the criminal connections. You think that key you found is connected to your time in vice? Fine. Reach out to your contacts and find us a trail we can follow later — preferably one that leads to proof we could come about legally. Y'know, somethin' we could actually use in a court of law someday?"

Colt scratched his nose and made no comment. Everett rubbed his forehead. This was exactly why the man would never move up the ladder. No self-preservation to him at all. "We'll meet back here and you can do your 'stare until it makes sense' routine, and then we finish this case from behind a damn computer. And *you* can get off my back about this being bigger than some robbery. Agreed?"

Anyone else would be grateful for the risk Everett was taking, but Colt looked like he'd been offered scraps — and was considering turning them down. Everett watched him read over the bits of case file, yellow paper and gas station napkins turned temporary notepads they'd stapled across the walls last night.

Colt chewed the inside of his cheek. "You're asking for a lot, Ev."

"*I'm* asking? This was your idea. I'm just fillin' in the gaps."

Everett wasn't sure of much, but he knew for a fact he was the one risking more. If Stapes even caught a whiff of this, his desk would be packed by morning, no question. But Everett had done a lot of thinking last night, and the idea of letting this slide didn't sit so easy anymore. If Combs' death really was connected to something bigger, then the kid deserved better than he got. Someone ought to be looking for the truth.

"If we're doing this," Everett hedged, "I need to run by the house. Those suitcases don't have the right things for riding, and I could stand to grab a few things."

"You want help?"

The offer surprised him. With how they'd left it last night, Everett had planned on being grateful for the platonic couch he'd been offered. He looked up to find Colt's eyes heavy on him. "No, I, uh…I think I got it."

Colt nodded and hooked a cigarette from his pack, surprising Everett again as he tossed the box his way. Then he walked to the kitchen and pulled a small black kit from under the sink. He laid it on the counter and produced needles and ink.

"If we're really doin' this, there's things you should know," Colt said. "Before someone expects you to."

Everett sensed this was one of those times it'd be good if he shut up and listened, so he lit the smoke and leaned against the kitchen wall. Colt sat on a bar stool at the counter's edge, focused on the task of preparing needles and skin.

"There's only two rules the bosses care about with undercover work. Don't get involved, and don't kill anybody they don't want you to. You know from Day One if you do either, you're gone, buried in a desk somewhere or left to hang on the line. Unofficially of course, but you're just as fucked — official or otherwise. Guess they thought my time in the service would make me right for that sorta thing."

"That how you wound up in Mason?"

Colt shrugged. "They took their time in burying me, but yeah. Had their reasons to want me out of Texas."

"Why? Which rule did you break?"

"Both."

Colt assembled the tattoo gun and squeezed out a blob of black ink. He snapped on a pair of gloves and started to work on his own left arm. "I met my wife the first year I was undercover. I was working a ring of human traffickers with connections to the cartel. Got in with some bikers — small-time, cornfed supremacists the lot of them, but they had dealings with my stated targets. Wound up as second tier with them. Called themselves the Cobras.

"Taking up with Rosa changed things for my alias. Before her, I did whatever got me the best intel. After...well, it was the same with some, but not as many. It's all just currency out there—drugs, sex, women. Take or be taken. Eat or be eaten." Colt's eyes were darker than usual, but then they brightened, like he was remembering something better. "Having someone around to protect made them see me different, and Rosa needed something to cling to as badly as I did. When she told me she was pregnant...weren't really a surprise. But it was a wakeup call.

"Had to tell her truths I wasn't ready to trust her with, but even with the kind of life she'd had, Rosa was a genuine person. Didn't say words like *I love you* unless she meant them all the way. Plenty wouldn't have tried to preserve life. Still don't know why she did, and I never thought I would be...but I was glad of her choice.

"I had to tell my handlers. You can imagine how happy that made the brass. I agreed to stay under for as long as they wanted, work the case all the way to the top if they got Rosa out. Went to the courthouse the next day and set her up with whatever protection my name could give. She started seeing all kinds of doctors without me, but the job wasn't in a place that I could leave. Too much depended on making the bosses happy. So I stayed under.

"They got me out once for...for the birth. Spent six weeks in a WITSEC house in Kansas while my alias 'recovered' from getting shot in the leg. Got a Christmas and a New Year with them before I had to go back."

Colt stayed quiet for long enough that Everett risked a question. "How much longer were you on the job?"

Colt wiped a mix of blood and ink from his arm, then tossed the paper towel in the trash. "Eighteen months. Spent three years all told, making up for my mistakes. Gave me time to make some more."

"But then, what happened?" Everett asked, unable to help himself. "I mean, if Rosa and your...if they were *out* then—"

"Life happened. Sometimes, no matter where you go...there you are."

Everett felt like he was looking at the edges of a puzzle, glimpsing the shape of a much larger picture. "So, you weren't there? When it happened?"

"No." Colt cleared his throat. "I wasn't."

And *Jesus*, but Everett wished he could hug the kids about now. He blinked up at the ceiling, hating himself as he swiped the dampness from his eye, hardly able to focus. For a while the only sound in the room was the buzzing of Colt's tattoo gun, the pull and drag of rubber over skin. Everett tripped over his words, wanting the right thing to say and certain he'd never find it. "Can't, uh...can't really believe they let you keep workin' after..." He waved a hand and hoped the gesture summed up what he meant.

Colt's focus stayed heavy on his arm. The tattoo gun buzzed. "Didn't give them a choice. I dropped off the radar till I had what they wanted. Made a deal to deliver the marks if they kept me legally dead and let me go my own way. Except things didn't go as planned."

Everett watched as Colt pried the lid off his coffee to add a glug of whiskey. He gulped some down and snapped on fresh gloves. "You need to know, Rhett. If we run into any of these guys I knew, they're gonna talk some shit. Gonna say things you won't want to hear."

"Is it true?"

"Probably, but that ain't the point. The Cobras ain't much, but doesn't *take* much to shoot a man in the back of the head. If they make me, we're screwed." He pointed the tattoo gun straight at him. "So if you wind up talkin' to anybody who matters, Rosa's gone, crazy, and I got no idea where the kid is."

"Okay, Colt."

Everett stared as Colt chugged more "coffee". In time he asked, "How'd you get free at all?"

The answer must've been important, because Colt kept talking. "After my...I worked the job hard. Without usual precautions. Escalated some timelines to arrange a meet with the marks they wanted. Told my handlers where it was goin' down." Colt took another swig and set the cardboard cup aside. "Don't know how, but someone tipped them off. Walked right into a trap.

"The marks knew I was police, and were kind enough to demonstrate the finer points of interrogation. Lost consciousness somewhere in the fourth hour. When my handlers finally showed up to cuff anyone who mattered, everyone assumed I was dead. But some crime tech looking for a bullet wound found a pulse instead.

"Rushed me to the hospital. Lots of surgery. Worse recovery. Taking that beating kicked the stuff in my head into high gear. Used to be a background sort of thing. Nowadays, I turn a corner and walk straight into a memory." Colt trailed off, staring at nothing in particular. Everett could only wonder what he saw.

Colt shook his head and returned to the work on his arm. "Anyway. Spent some months rehabilitating before they called my debt paid and shipped me out to Mason. Never thought I'd see somethin' from those days again, but. Here we are."

"Jesus," Everett cursed under his breath. He rubbed his palms together. "Look, it's sad what happened to this Combs kid. It is. But it ain't worth —"

"Ev."

And there was something about the nickname that sounded different, too like the broken father who'd sobbed beside him on a rundown couch. Colt took a slow, steady breath and said, "If that key is what I think...this could get me a second run at settling some old debts. The ones that got away on the case that cost me my little girl. So if there's a chance of takin' *any* of them down with this?" Colt met his eye. "It's worth it. To me."

Everett thought it must be, because later, when Colt was finished sticking his arm with ink, the symbol at the center of that knotted-up cross was clear as a fucking picture. Colt wrapped the arm in plastic cling, covered the whole affair with a long-sleeved flannel, then buttoned up the cuff to keep things in place. That done, Colt turned to him, and he wasn't sure what he expected the man to look like, but completely blank-faced wasn't it.

"I need to get seen by the right people if this is gonna work. Not even sure where they hole up this far east. Gonna have to put the word out a few places." Colt pulled open one of the unpacked boxes in the corner, retrieved a gun that was definitely not his service weapon and started to break it apart. "I won't be around for some time. I'll check in every twenty-four hours unless I can't."

"And if you don't?"

"Wait some more. Two days pass and I'm still not back? You either finish this without me or call it off."

"Without you?" Everett choked on the question. "Like I'm gonna—"

"Save the hero shit." Colt held the barrel up to the light, then rummaged in the box for the tool to clean it. "If I'm gone for two days before we even get started, it's 'cause I'm dead. So I need to know. You really wanna do this?"

His gut impulse was *hell fucking no,* but Everett knew he'd never be able to hold to it. That redness in Colt's eyes was the only evidence of their talk at all, but the story sat heavy in Everett's heart just the same. He had to do something, or the anxious energy caught in his chest was gonna explode right out of him.

Everett nodded once and watched his partner clean the unfamiliar gun. When he held the barrel up again, this time Colt looked satisfied with the results.

* * * *

Getting things from the house wasn't anything he'd call comfortable, but Everett's first week living at Colt's was removing that word from his vocabulary. The place had no manner of anything he'd expect from an adult's place of habitation. Sure, Everett had his bachelor pads before him and Rachael shacked up, but even he'd had a dresser. A shower curtain that wasn't a see-through liner. A spare mirror outside the bathroom.

Right now, the lack of those last two wasn't an issue, as Colt was barely home except for random intervals of sleep. One day it was noon to four after staring at their wall of notes all night. Then Everett didn't see him for thirty-six hours, and was fit to be fucking tied when Colt rolled in — covered in gravel, mud and what Everett hoped wasn't his own blood.

Never got a chance to confirm that, though. The second he slammed the door, Colt told him to "*shut your mouth for once*" before collapsing in a heap on the couch. For fourteen hours.

Whoever this alias-persona was, Colt was going full method-actor with his bullshit. Either that, or there were more than the obvious reasons why Colt's file was so redacted. Considering all he'd told him, Everett was starting to think the brass had skipped a few things on behalf of his partner's image, blacking out words like *alcoholic* and *twitchy motherfucker* along with the horrors that wrought them.

So when Rachael agreed to meet him at the house, Everett gathered a list of items that served a two-fold purpose. One, it might drag Colt kicking and screaming out of the junkie-redneck aesthetic he'd acquired, not to mention improve both men's comfort in sharing a bathroom. And two, Everett hoped it would cover why he was really there — to get his rodeo leathers.

They talked some, too. It was stilted, but civil. Rachael even let him make plans to take the kids to dinner, and Everett wondered if he'd done a better job than he'd thought making himself look different for the case. His decision not to shave coupled with his food-stained T-shirt made him look pretty miserable. It wasn't far off the mark.

He tried to keep busy the rest of the week, but it was hard not to feel like Suzy fucking Homemaker, waiting on Colt to get back from who knew where, never sure what side of the man he was going to get. So when Friday night rolled around and Colt barreled through the door—fully strung out and barely holding it together—Everett was glad that, either way, tonight would be the end of this. Living with Colt was strange enough. His alias was a goddamn nightmare.

The man glared at Everett's pile of house-things, like they hadn't been taking up floorspace for half a week already. "The fuck do we need with floor lamps and kitchen shit?"

Everett sighed. "Yeah, well, leave your breakfast order on the counter and we'll see what we can do, sunshine. Believe the response you were lookin' for is *thank you*. Even you got to get tired of pizza and canned shit."

"What fuckin' for? What'd you ever do for me that didn't help yourself out more?"

"Wow," Everett deadpanned. "So, you're fun today."

Colt's answering grunt made Everett turn from the mirror he'd propped in the corner, another useful item from the pile, *thank you very much*. He paused in buttoning his shirt as he watched Colt stalk closer, and Everett decided to pull up on what was fast turning into a *biggest dick* competition—because hands down, Colt's alias would win.

They hadn't been this close since their first night here a week ago. But at the moment, Colt looked less like a threat and more like he was waiting to get hit for something. While Everett would be the first to admit the thought frequently crossed his mind, he wasn't sure of the reason Colt thought he'd given lately. Maybe he just...expected it?

Or maybe, this wasn't all Colt anymore.

Everett decided to let it lie and tried to ease the tension. "Should've figured your alias would be an even bigger asshole than you. Though I'm not sure how it's possible."

The word *alias* brought a familiar light into Colt's leathered eyes. He turned away and sat on the sofa, pulled off his ratty flannel and kept the sweat-stained, dirt-scuffed undershirt beneath. Palming something small from the shirt's front pocket, he stood and walked toward the bedroom.

Everett called, "You about ready, Colt?"

"Two minutes."

Thank God for small favors that he still answered to his name, because Colt's voice didn't sound familiar at all. His usually steady baritone was all scratched and faded. This version of Colt wouldn't be doing any finessing in the box, couldn't talk to anyone except a certain kind of rough.

Who does he think will be at this rodeo that he needs to be this person?

"We shouldn't show up together," Colt called from his room. "Never know who might be watching the entrance, and my kind of company won't be comin' in with the family crowd."

Everett scanned for his hat and spotted it on the counter. "Thought we were taking your truck."

"You're taking the truck. Fits better for you...dressed as you are."

He'd tried not to consider Colt's inevitable opinion when he picked up his least-ornate shirt at the house, but rodeo wear wasn't about blending in. Still, Everett thought his black button-up with embroidered roses cut a fairly muted picture with his Wranglers and riding boots. Colt could stand in the doorway with that *you kiddin' me* stare all he wanted.

Fuck him and his judging eyes. Everett liked this shirt.

"I thought you said you used to be in this scene some," he called back. "You should know this ain't nothin' compared to what most guys will be wearing."

"Guess I wasn't focused on the fancy clothes."

Everett flipped him the bird and put his cowboy hat on for good measure. Colt closed the bedroom door as Everett polished his belt buckle, only a bit oversized, and checked himself over again. "So if I'm taking the truck, how're you getting there?"

He watched in the mirror as Colt walked to the kitchen, wearing thick jeans and steel-toed boots. He slung a black leather jacket across his shoulders and over his dirty undershirt, tugging the sleeves over his refreshed ink. The jacket was road-rough and shaking out gravel. A coiled-up snake was stitched across the back. Then, like it was some natural habit of his, Colt dropped a line of powder on the counter and rolled up a dollar bill.

"Jesus, you can't be—"

Colt snorted the coke fast and shook his head once, then gathered up the spare bits and finished that for good measure. He tucked the rest away and removed a key from a nail on the kitchen wall. Blindsided, Everett followed his partner out through the side door, watching as he approached the nearest rolltop garage. Colt fit the key in the lock and yanked the garage open.

Standing beside the boxes and tools was a fucking motorcycle.

Everett took one look at the picture in front of him — a leather-clad Colt with eyes red as sunset, unstable from the powder in his nose and the memories on his mind, straddling some death machine of crimson and chrome, and he knew — knew in his soul that this was a bad, bad idea.

And, maybe, a darker part of Everett liked it that way.

But inconvenient truths aside, this still wasn't any kind of smart, and Everett found himself sputtering out worries like "Where's your fuckin' helmet?" and "How will I find you?" while Colt slid a phone into his jacket pocket. The bike roared to life, forcing Everett quiet long enough for Colt to answer.

"I'll find you."

"*How*?"

"Don't worry about it."

Well, that was easier said than done, because the man astride that bike wasn't anyone he'd ever met. Colt looked like a stranger — the kind that radiated violence and danger — and what he said next wasn't a threat. It was a fact.

"You fuck this up before I get there and I'll kill you myself."

Colt tore out of the neighborhood with skill that shouldn't be so sharp, considering all that was working against him. Everett stared at the empty road long after the exhaust had dissipated, certain that not a part of that had gone the way he'd wanted it to.

* * * *

Wearing the name *A. J. Cooper* along with his rodeo best, Everett blew past check-in with easy smiles, possessed of a boyish glee at the thought of riding again. 'Course, if all went as planned, Everett would be breaking his back on Colt's couch without having to sit the bull. But in lieu of other distractions the past week, the old itch was begging to be scratched. And Everett couldn't shake the feeling that, whatever they found at this rodeo, he was going to have a hard time saying no to the lesser stakes of some amateur ride.

It was the excuse of excitement he'd cling to later when Colt asked him how some intern had caught him copying files.

Colt had given him a long list of data he wanted — employee records, financial statements, company webs and corporate affiliations. Anything that had to do with shipping, company properties, assets...truth be told, it seemed to Everett like he was gathering quite the haystack to get lost in, but Detective Harkan had that knack for finding the needle, eyes too sharp to miss the glint of their own in the straw.

Everett managed to play it off with the intern like he was looking for a place to check his messages. He flipped the computer monitor off while the guy's back was turned and hoped the jump drive would keep downloading. That done, he graciously followed the intern and found himself corralled where the rest of the riders waited. The feeling in the tent was tense and focused, but familiar.

Of course, Everett's nerves had more to do with not knowing where Colt was — *or whoever he is right now* — than thinking about the bull that waited for him. He tried texting, but received no response. Come to think of it, Everett didn't recognize the phone Colt had pocketed before tearing out on that deathtrap, enough drugs in his system to blow any test if someone got to looking too hard. If he didn't even have a good number for Colt, how was he going to tell him that they had to go back for the drive, that they had to keep up appearances until he could find a way back to —

"The fuck are you doin', Ev?"

The rough voice startled him, but it was a welcome thing.

Colt. Thank God.

Everett stood at the back of the tent near a seam where two linen panels met, providing a window for talk. "That you?"

"Stupid question. Answer mine."

"I'm holding down my cover like you said. On threat of painful death, if I recall."

A pause. No laughter. The metallic clang of a Zippo. "What went wrong?"

"Office jockey found me," Everett said. "The drive is still downloading your shit. Gonna need a distraction to slip back in and grab it."

"Distractions are loud, and loud ain't the point right now."

"Why?"

"Haven't found who I'm lookin' for yet."

Caught in his worries as he was, Everett wasn't watching the rest of the riders, nor had he noticed how the tent was getting emptier, how the crowd cheered and yelled at each successive fall from grace. When the screen flashed *A. J. Cooper*, a thrill a decade gone rose in his blood, firing him up in ways he hadn't felt since that lifetime past. And maybe that's why it was so easy to tell even this version of Colt what he was going to do.

"Sit back on this. Got an idea."

"I told you, now ain't the right —"

"Just shut up and trust me a second. I'll get you the time you need."

Everett pulled his hat down firmly on his head, then adjusted the ties around the cuffs of his jeans, the pads and leathers and protective wear that felt so like a second skin. "The whole office is a graveyard," Everett told him. "You can slip right in. Third door on the right, second building from the entry. Don't get seen."

"Fuckin' *wait*, Rhett—"

He left the tent and steered toward the bull, raring to go in the cage, and there wasn't a single thing that felt like fear when the cool metal of the gate met Everett's hands. He swung up and over with practiced ease, hiked a leg over the animal and the crowd started to cheer. The sound felt heavy in his chest, but he just smiled and waved.

Sure, it'd been some years since he'd done this. That might matter more if he were like the rest of the cowboy-wannabes, these athletes with their trainers and money. The sort of balance Everett had was trained in years of summers at his grandfather's farm, from countless hours atop actual horses and bulls. None of that mechanical shit.

Colt could keep his motorcycle secrets. Everett astride a bull was the surest he ever felt, the quietest eight seconds his mind ever got. He shot a final look to the tent and found Colt staring back—spitting mad with hands on his hips, eyes like burning coals trained on Everett's every move.

And damn, if that didn't feel as good as the beast bucking beneath him…

The buzzer rang, the gate clanked free, and the clock and the bull began to run.

One…he needed to breathe. Gameplans were one thing and there was the game itself. To go in with a plan for something that was wild would get someone hurt every time. Riding was about reacting.

Everett let his body hang the right kind of loose, then tipped his mind to the spinning place where the jukes of the bull rippled through his limbs like water.

Two… that first buck set the tone, adrenaline surging and blood rushing in his veins. He held tight to the reins, hooked his foot hard in the stirrup and braced for the second kick up.

Three… Everett knew what he was in for now. Having survived the first two seconds, the game was on. Everett's arm flew up in ricochet reaction, but the other held fast to the saddle as they flew around the ring.

Four… it was something like serenity at the height of the ride, a dust-blown whirlwind of man and beast. Too many would see this and think of domination, the rider as tamer, the one in control. But Everett knew otherwise — felt it every time he sat the saddle.

Five…riding ain't a battle. It's a dance. And Everett knew how to follow.

Six… unable to help himself, he lifted his eyes to the whirl of the crowd, the cheers and surprise, and a set of black-brown eyes that were glued to Everett's thighs, too obvious to be doing anything but appreciating the sight. An easy grin split his face as he fought to keep track of the rough-haired bull he was riding, tried not to picture the many times he'd never appreciated having Colt beneath him much the same —

Seven… the bull bucked hard as that first again, catching a second wind and he had to focus, had to pull it together, had to hold on to get Colt the time he needed...

Eight...and the swell of the crowd meant he'd done it, meant he'd had the best ride of the night, and coming from a complete unknown, it was the kind of upset an audience adored. Everett rode the final throw to his feet and got clear to the side. The clowns corralled the bull by the fence, and Everett waved as the loudspeaker echoed, "*A. J. Cooper!*"

It was a familiar feeling, all eyes on him in the ring. Damn pleasant, even. But nothing could compete with the peak of the ride because now, with the cover of the cheering crowd, the only brown eyes that mattered were darting furtive in shadowed halls, picking through intel that Everett sure hoped was worth their careers...

Because that silvered head in the very front row belonged to Richard Edwards.

* * * *

Everett dodged over the fence as quickly as possible, but after a ride like that on the amateur circuit, there was a crowd of well-wishers out to block his path. He caught sight of Colt slipping around the office building. Richard Edwards was still in the seats, talking with important-looking people, so Everett pulled his hat down low and stayed on high alert. He answered questions and returned thankful replies while he watched, hoped and waited.

Edwards didn't look his way, nor did the man come by to say anything. A couple minutes later, Everett caught sight of Colt, ducking around the crowd — blessedly undetected. He breathed a grateful sigh, sure that relief was creeping onto his face. Everett watched his partner drop into an empty stable, and when he could make "A. J. Cooper's" excuses, he followed Colt inside.

Everett's was the last ride of the night, and there wasn't a soul in sight as he poked around looking for Colt. He'd managed not to go calling out just yet, realizing he should've gotten the man's alias before now, the moment he needed it. He wound his way deeper into the stable, ears sharp for any sign.

Turning into another empty room, Everett exhaled in frustration. "Come *on*, where are you?"

Then a dark figure was on him, pushing him fast and hard to the slatted-wood wall. He barely recognized the familiar scent amidst the gasoline and sweat. His head knocked back as a leather-clad arm pressed against his throat.

"Hey—hey! It's me."

Pupils blown wide, Colt's eyes were more black hole than earthy-brown. His breathing came harsh like he'd been running, and Everett felt his ramping up to match the longer he studied his partner's face. Because there was no mistaking it—not at this distance.

Desperation. Desire. And maybe, something like fear.

"You *fucker*," Colt growled in his face. It was all the warning he got before Colt's mouth crashed into his.

Everett hadn't known what to expect when he found Colt again, but hope as he might've, it surely wasn't this. Not that he was complaining. Far fucking from it. Colt's kiss was possessive—had him pinned and pining in quick, successive fashion—and he eagerly returned the embrace, pulling Colt bodily against him. The thrill of the ride and the recovered drive in Colt's pocket painted a smile on his face despite the man's every attempt to kiss it off. Or swallow his damn tongue from the feel of it.

Colt fit a hand fit around Everett's chin, angling his head away as he buried his face in Everett's neck. And he knew they were alone, but Everett still tried not to groan too loud as Colt scraped teeth over his pulse, as he tongued and sucked at sensitive skin, frantically working the black button-up from the back of his jeans with his hands. After a week of stilted distance, all Everett could do was hold on. He pressed hard against the wall and Colt to keep himself upright, ignoring the burn in his thighs, the weakness in his legs he could only partly blame on the bull. Which reminded him...

"How'd you find me before?" Everett asked.

"Please. You're easy to track." Colt worked his hands around to the front of Everett's belt, and he sounded more like himself when he asked, "How'd you do that?"

Everett grinned wider this time, knowing Colt would see those trophies in his office different come Monday. "Plenty of practice. Show you sometime."

Colt pulled back with a dangerous look, teeth flashing white in the dim light. "That a fact?"

"Absolutely."

To make his meaning clear, Everett snuck a hand under Colt's rucked-up jacket, smoothed fingers up his spine and thrust his hips against him. Colt swallowed a needy sound and returned to kiss him again. They rocked together and Everett relished the feel of Colt's arousal pressed against his.

Without a word, Colt dropped to his knees on a mission, pulled the rest of Everett's belt away and freed his cock. Everett's head thumped against the wall, sending his hat tumbling to the hay-littered ground. But despite their surroundings, Colt was hellbent on taking his time. He ran his tongue along the underside of his shaft, mouthed at the tip, pulled away as a rivulet of spit stretched from his kiss-bitten mouth. Everett watched it drip down to coat the head before Colt wrapped his lips around him and sucked—

"Jesus, *fuck*—"

Colt smirked obscenely around his dick, bobbing his dark head and pressing palms into hips, keeping Everett pinned. Colt worked his throat, hollowing his cheeks as he slid closer, till he had Everett so far down that Colt's nose brushed the hair near his navel. The feel of humid breath against the thin skin of his hip was too much to take, and the wet heat of Colt's mouth surrounding him...*God,* how did this always feel *so good?*

Everett fisted his hands in white-knuckled resolution, determined to make this last as long as possible. He didn't care what would happen when they got back to Colt's apartment, didn't let himself wonder if this intensity could stay on the job for long. Because the way Colt's tongue kept teasing down his shaft was too damn perfect to consider stopping.

One of Colt's hands left his hip to circle Everett's wrist. Colt unfolded his fist, then brought their hands to the back of his own head. Fresh sweat dampened the dark waves at Colt's neck, tempting Everett to more force than usual. He laced fingers through his hair and fit the heel of his hand by Colt's ear.

Unable to hold still any longer, Everett's hips stuttered forward on instinct. Colt moaned around him as his brown eyes danced in the dark, encouraging Everett to rock into his throat. So he moved again, experimentally pushing forward, deeper, not wanting to choke him unless *good goddamn*, that was exactly what Colt wanted, exactly what he was begging for.

Jesus H. Christ…

Everett could feel the moment Colt gave up control, how he stopped pushing and pulling of his own accord and started riding the force of Everett's arm. The motion became a guided rhythm as Everett bucked faster, fucking into his flushed mouth until he'd swallowed him all the way down. And Everett was close, *so close*, he should give Colt some kind of warning, but—

"Back off, cowboy. You're messin' with my ride."

The unknown voice sluiced down his spine like ice water. Everett's hands flew from Colt's neck, but he kept his eyes on the man kneeling in front of him. Colt slid off him with a wet sound, not hiding in the slightest what they were doing. Everett's blood rushed north to paint his face red as anything, but Colt sat unbothered on his heels, dragged his mouth across his arm and winked—fuckin' *winked*—before calling over his shoulder, "Jared."

"Switch."

Switch? Who the fuck is —

But Everett knew. He watched as the closed, quiet detective dissolved before his eyes. Gone was the man who sat back at a scene, analyzing every detail. No, it was Switch's head that ticked as a hand tapped his thigh, Switch who tried to stand and only stumbled closer, like he was too high to stand on his own. Everett caught him before he could think to do anything else. Something small pressed into his hand before the weight was gone, *Colt* was gone, and Switch only had eyes for Jared.

Whoever Jared was.

Everett did up his belt, discreetly slipping the jump drive in his pocket. He recovered his hat as an excuse to give the intruder a once-over, cementing every detail to memory. No hair in sight on this skinhead. Of a height with Colt, maybe two inches shorter. Not overly large, but not weak either. The kind of man that kept compact muscle beneath his leather jacket and black shirt. A familiar brand spiraled across his freckled neck.

Everett met Jared's dark eyes across the stable and saw the same kind of shakes that Colt had all evening. He put some pieces together and decided this Jared might be Colt's contact after all, that this whole thing in the barn was some plan to get them here...but why?

He didn't get long to think. Jared reached into the band of his jeans in a clear threat, and Everett recognized the flick of a gun's safety well enough to back away, hands raised, and edge out of the door. Switch's gaze stayed fixed on Jared like he was the only man in the room. Everett walked what he prayed was far enough away and turned a corner, hopeful to hear something to make sense of the last few minutes.

"Ho-ly shit. Switch. Back from the dead."

The shuffling sounds of boots on dirt. The scrape of leather against leather.

A handshake? A brushed shoulder? An embrace?

"Heard a rumor you were back on the road. Where you been?"

"Around."

"So far from home?"

Everett heard the shake of a plastic bag, the crinkle of what Switch was all-too-happy to pull from his pocket, then, "What was I ever doin' someplace like this?"

Two hard sniffs confirmed one of Everett's theories. He smelled the smoke of a wafting Camel as a voice he recognized set the trap. "Truth is, I'm in town on business. Got somethin' for ya, if there's somewhere we can talk."

"Follow me back and we could see about that."

Another flick of a lighter and more smoke joined the air. "Ain't so big a job. More somethin' you and I could see to—"

"No chance. I'm on business too. And a man with your skillset falling from the sky, needin' something from me?" Everett recognized the catch of leather on denim and something too like a swallowed groan for comfort. "Just when I'm needin' something too? Sure seems like old times, Switch."

Everett seethed in the darkness, hands fisted at his sides. Colt's reminder kicked unkindly in his head.

"Gonna say things you won't wanna hear."

"Is it true?"

"Probably…"

But Everett couldn't do what his jealousy wanted just yet—because yeah, that was what this was. Plain and simple. But he had exactly zero time to worry about that, because this venture here was *not* part of the plan. They had no backup, no way to communicate and from the looks of things, he'd be tailing his partner on a wing and a prayer to who knew where before this wrapped. Everett silently pleaded with any god that would listen that Colt was in there somewhere, would maybe realize how badly they needed to step back. They could come at this from another angle, try again later…

Do not agree to this, you dumb motherfucker—

"When?"

"Now," Jared said. "You in?"

Fuck. Even Everett knew the answer to that. "You're drivin'."

* * * *

Everett almost lost them in the crowds leaving the rodeo, but a persistent buzzing in his pocket eventually caught his attention. He didn't recognize the number, but he answered anyway, glad Colt had the presence of mind to dial his number at all. He picked up and muted the call, keeping the phone close to his ear. Sounded like it was in the pocket of Colt's jacket.

Everett could make out every third word at best as he searched for them in the lot. He recognized the click and slam of a truck door and turned his eyes from loiterers to higher ground. He spotted them in a black pickup splattered with mud and rocky dirt. Colt could probably tell where they were headed from that mess alone, but it was all just mud to Everett. He did a quick scout and found Colt's silvered-blue vehicle not far off. He slid across the hood of a neighboring car, then climbed into the cab. He propped the phone in the cupholder and put the call on speaker.

The noise of the engine made it hard to hear, but things got easier once they hit flatter road. Everett kept a couple cars between them and, when the traffic thinned, he tailed as close as he could without being seen.

"Where's the bitch?"

Jared's tinny leer bounced around the cab.

"Shit, Rosa's been gone," came Switch's scratchy reply. "Went crazy fast when she finally turned."

"Weren't she knocked up?"

"Maybe. Never heard for sure."

"Damn, Switch. Still a cold son-of-a-bitch, ain't you?"

"You'd know."

For a while, there was nothing but staticky country radio.

"So you ain't see her never?" Jared asked.

"No need. Was never much of one to be a father."

Oh, for God's sake...

Everett had managed to keep his panic to a minimum so far, but listening to Colt like this was a new kind of fucked up. Besides, what was he *thinking* — volunteering to get in a truck with this asshole? Should've taken his bike, should've followed him or something. Didn't Colt know what was coming?

"You're asking for a lot, Ev..."

Everett groaned in the empty cab, double-checked that the line was muted and fished in his pocket for the flask he'd hoped not to need so soon. There would never be a whiskey strong enough for this.

Jared's truck was the only car on the road as they wound through the fading twilight. Everett pulled hard at his flask as he watched the inevitable in silhouette, watched the driver pull his passenger close, two bodies blending into one solid form. Then only one man's head was visible, and the sounds coming over the line, echoing in the cab, turned Everett's stomach until he tasted bile.

But he only had to listen. Colt had to live it. And if that meant rolling down the window and letting some liquor go, he was gonna do it.

His mouth tasted sour as he cranked the window up. He slammed a fist on the steering wheel, his gaze trained on that single shadowed head—

Then all of a sudden, silence.

His eyes darted to the phone in the cupholder. Maybe the call had dropped. But no, they were still connected...just no sound coming through. Like someone muted it. Like someone took the risk of being discovered, just to quiet the line.

Everett bit through his lip and tasted blood. He took a moment to remind himself that he'd only brought his service weapon. Meant he had to care where the bullets ended up. Because otherwise, there'd be nothing stopping him from taking the shot once Jared cleared that truck — and *fuck* the case anyway.

Chapter Five

Switch
Louisiana, 2011, seven years earlier

He tucked a hand in his jacket pocket and swiped a thumb across the burner's screen. He kept the window rolled up as he lit a cigarette. Better not to have the wind fucking up the line. Ev would have a hard enough time hearing as it was.

Jared steered with one knee, using both hands to fasten his belt. Switch asked, "So what'd you need me for?"

"Besides that?"

Jared always was an obvious sort of man.

"Said you were in town on business," he tried again. "Don't be lyin' to me now."

The not-quite request landed with mixed success — as intended. Jared never liked him to pretend to be something he wasn't. He preferred to beat the lip out of him than to never hear it at all. Switch watched as Jared shifted in a way he recognized well. He was on the right track with his questions. "What were you and the boys doin' at the rodeo?"

"What were we ever doin' in a place like that?"

Switch nodded at the sound of his own words returned to him, but it was also the confirmation he needed. Jared was still the middle man for the Cobras — the organizer, who made sure the club had all the drugs and *recreation* their tastes required. It had burned to leave Jared and the rest of the Cobras standing, but for all the awful Switch had seen them do, it was a drop in the bucket compared to his "stated targets". The suppliers he was really after were a few rungs up the ladder, something his handlers had preached on repeat till he'd agreed to leave Jared and the rest alone. Another compromise that hadn't fucking mattered in the end.

Switch's heart kicked faster and he tried to steady his breathing. All on its own, his hand started tapping his thigh, rustling his jacket with every touch of finger to denim.

Thumb once, then the third finger. Thumb thrice, third again. Thumb short, third long.

He lit another cigarette and tried to focus. No doubt they were on their way to the warehouse. Only place they could be going. Switch had never been back when, but he'd heard plenty about it from Jared. Saw the key in his possession too many times to count. The question now was, how'd some seasonal rodeo hire score something the gang never let out of their sight?

How'd a kid like Patrick Combs get a key to the Cobras' warehouse?

Switch kept a close eye on the man beside him as they rolled through the wilderness, mentally retracing memories a lifetime gone for any connection to Combs or the State Rodeo. Then Jared checked the rearview twice in quick succession. Switch coughed and rolled down the window to spit. The sound snagged Jared's attention and he smirked, pulling onto a gravel road that explained the state of his pickup.

Switch watched in the side mirrors as another truck rolled past. A dark cowboy hat turned over a familiar shoulder. Wasn't anything out here for miles so Everett would have to hide the truck, then double back on foot. He'd need to stall until then or find his own way out.

Same as it ever was.

They rolled up to a row of muddy vans and the odd bike or two. Most guys wouldn't be risking their wheels on terrain like this, but he spotted Jared's ride — along with a few others he was hoping to avoid. A bonfire blazed some fifty feet from the warehouse. A half-dozen men sat in a circle around the flames.

Even with Jared's arm hooked around his neck, the grumbling caused by their entrance made it clear he wasn't welcome. A well-muscled man with a long mane and graying beard stood up. Green eyes glinted in the firelight.

"Switch. Ain't you some prodigal son."

"Leroy. Too long."

They traded nods, but Switch didn't move otherwise — not with Jared's hand on his shoulder like it was.

Without warning, some scratch in a jacket that barely fit stepped up, popped off and busted his lip with a sucker punch. The guys seemed split on if it was funny or a cheap shot, and before Switch could get to asking, the kid coughed up his reasons.

"You're lucky Leady's dead, or he'd have shot you himself."

Switch took a quick look at the young man and sure, he might've been some sort of kin. Could make sense to carry that grudge past a grave. He touched his bloodied face.

Leadfoot. Now there's a name I haven't heard in a while...

The campfire smelled the same as it did under Texas skies. Wafting scents of all kinds of smoke – some chemical, some machine – mixed with earthy tobacco. Would've been a time at a fire like this, he'd be sat up next to Jared, masquerading at pride of place, waiting for the hand on his neck to turn firm.

But that night he sat on a busted bench in the parking lot they'd taken over, too far out and too late at night for any locals to bother them. He was staring across the fire at Jared, whose jealous eyes hadn't left him all night. Leroy was going on about something – the trail, the business end, who knew – so he wrapped an arm around the waist at his side and pressed close to a body that felt like hope. His rope in the darkness. Rosa.

Couldn't have been more than twenty, but life had aged her early. In some ways just a girl, and in so many more the woman he'd been afraid of needing. He hadn't been looking for a partner to get him through this job, but Rosa wasn't the type to scare. She wanted someone to take care of, and he'd stopped trying so hard to tell her no.

But to these guys he was Twitch, and things were easy enough when he was second tier, not fighting for that alpha spot. At least until him and Rosa took up together. Then the old ways of gathering intel stopped working like they used to.

Some of the guys who'd grown accustomed to certain access made comments. Mostly harmless razzing. And the more Twitch turned their words around, the more they laughed it off. Besides, what was a man supposed to do but settle down with his Old Lady anyhow?

That was enough for most of them. Not Jared, though. And not Old Smokey either.

He moved Rosa's raven hair to rest his chin along the curve of her neck. Twitch let his other hand slide inside her shirt — one of his flannels, actually. Hidden from view, he gently brushed her stomach and sighed. Hadn't heard from his handler in over a week, but he had to keep trying. No child of his would know a thing about a place like this. He may not have planned to be a father, but getting Rosa and the baby out? It was his responsibility. It was all he cared about anymore.

So maybe he was more focused than he ought to be about Smokey runnin' his mouth, how what might've been jokes that fifth of whiskey ago were now obvious, sour barbs. He waited for Leroy to weigh in, but more guys wanted to know what he'd do. They wanted a show, and Twitch wasn't in the mood to care about an audience.

"I know you can hear me, Twitch," Smokey hissed across the fire. "Fucking some wet-backed cunt screw with your hearin' too? Got some magical fuckin' pussy or somethin'? Shit, maybe we all better try a round — "

The only round Smokey got was one clear through his foot, a quickdraw shot that Twitch didn't care if he made. Anyone in his crosshairs deserved that bullet, but he spared a moment of gladness that he'd found his mark. He kept the gun drawn as he looked into Rosa's eyes. She held his face softly between her palms and kissed him.

Across the fire, Smokey howled into the night. Cries of laughter and breaking bottles joined the racket, but Leroy was on it now. He stood and fired two shots in the air. Everyone turned and quieted — well, except Smokey, cursing a blue streak and bitchin' to Jared, who still only had eyes for Twitch.

The silence stretched on longer than it should. Rosa was tense at his side, but held her ground. She pinned Smokey with a glare of her own and Leroy started to chuckle. Laughter caught like tinder around the fire, and before long, conversation resumed.

"Nice shot. Switch."

That was all Jared said for the rest of the night. The new name stuck like tar and tacky gum.

Another name changed the next morning. Ain't no one called him Smokey after Leroy hit upon it. Ol' Smoke had his foot wrapped and was lagging something fierce from the start, and at the first gas station, Leroy rounded up the rear with a grin.

"C'mon, Leadfoot. Can't ride any faster than that?"

Switch moved his hand from his bloodied face and pulled himself from the memory, inspecting the way his fingers shone in the orange light. He ran his tongue across his teeth and tasted the iron that coated them. Then he looked the kid dead in the eye.

"Your old man should've thanked me. Any name's better than Smokey."

The kid looked ready to make an issue of it, but Switch's comment had turned the tide. With the support of the crowd behind him, it was easy to feel into that other part of his stance, the part that would keep anyone else from doing more reminiscing — the same part that caught up with Leadfoot years later to settle the balance for the only ink he'd never wanted.

But sure. Let the kid think a random raid did Leady in.

Remembering *that* nearly put a smile on his face, and he felt Jared's interest narrow on him, slick as gasoline and just as chemical in scent.

"We here on business or a social call?" Switch asked. "I'm feelin' less like company by the minute."

The way Jared looked him over didn't sit all the way friendly, but worrying over subtext wasn't going to change the facts. He was still past extraction with no damn clue where Everett was, or even a way out beside the keys he'd palmed in the truck. He'd rather not clue Jared in on that theft just yet, so Switch watched the bald man clap the kid on his lanky shoulder.

"Should be careful 'round this one, Smallfry. You'll think he's one way...but all of a sudden, it's the *other* way. And you don't really wanna be around for either one."

The crowd at the fire laughed and conversation returned to what it was. With a guiding hand on his shoulder, Jared led him toward the warehouse in the distance. Not really a place he wanted to be, knowing what was probably inside, but away from the crowd was the first step. If he could stall even ten minutes more, odds were good he'd have help getting out.

Jared's hand slid to his neck and squeezed tight. Switch wondered if he'd even get three.

* * * *

It took five minutes to blow all the way bad.

Switch stayed close as Jared flipped a breaker, lighting up the cavernous room. The whole place looked like a cross between a junkyard and an artillery. Boxes, crates and machine parts littered the floor. Jared steered them to the nearest table and Switch followed along, keeping his head on a swivel.

Now they were alone, he could tell Jared was itching to kill him. It was more a matter of when, of how many questions he wanted answered first. Because this was the real-deal warehouse with enough proof to put every one of these guys away for good. By sight alone, he could make shipments of smuggled bike parts, drugs, and even guns. Shit, but they'd seriously upped their game. If the Cobras'd had this kind of inventory years ago, even his old handlers would've had him changing targets.

So why was Jared showing him all this weight? Either he wanted Switch to think he was still his friend — or he knew for certain he wasn't. It was time to force the issue.

He ran the back of two fingers down Jared's spine. "So what's this job already?"

"Protection for a meet. You still remember how it's done?"

Switch leaned closer. "Remember a lot of things."

"So do I."

Jared spun fast and cracked a fist into his jaw, and after having his bell rung good for the second time that night, Switch stumbled. He managed to fall into Jared and sent them both reeling for the wall, but the other man got the upper hand and forced him flat against the metal.

"I fuckin' *told* Leroy we lost too many the day you died. Which is a shame, with the kind of hookup we got now. You see, Switch?" Jared gripped his chin tight and forced him to look around the warehouse. "You picked the wrong side."

Jared pulled his hair hard and forced his head back, exposing his throat. "Knew the second I saw you tonight," Jared told him. "If you're still alive, means you were a snitch from the start. Don't know why you came crawlin' back here. Should've stayed gone with your bitch and your daughter."

He felt his eyes close.

Not kid. *Daughter.*

Now how in the actual *fuck* did he know about Ava?

Jared still had him pinned, so he didn't waste energy struggling. Instead, he opened his eyes and stared straight at him, memorizing every bit of Jared's angry face.

"You stay away from Rosa or you're dead."

Darkly pleased with his reaction, Jared whistled over his shoulder, and that security Switch had been waiting for stepped forward. He drew a gun from the band of his jeans and let it hang at his side. "Always were protective of her," Jared mocked. "Hope you said goodbye…because you ain't never leavin' this place alive."

The percussive clicks of loading firearms ricocheted around the warehouse. The stench of the man's want filled Switch's mouth with the tang of rust. "'Course…" Jared looked him up and down. "We got some things to talk on first. Just you and me."

Jared pulled back and swung with the butt of his gun, but Switch was faster on the react than that. He'd been waiting for a window. This was it.

He dodged low and rounded on Jared, staying close so they made one target instead of two. He wrapped his hand around Jared's and the gun at once, forced the muzzle to the other man's thigh and squeezed, blowing away a chunk of muscle in a flash of blood. Felt like he might've snapped his trigger finger.

Good.

Jared yelled and his fist jolted open, giving Switch full control of the weapon. He got him in a chokehold with one arm secured around his neck, forcing the man's back flat to his chest. With his other hand, he pressed the hot barrel against Jared's freckled temple.

The three men holding semi-autos froze, unsure how to proceed.

"New offer for you boys," Switch said, addressing Jared first. "If you like livin' any, you and me are gonna take a walk." He pitched his voice to the others while Jared struggled against his hold. "And since y'all would rather ride home than take the fall for whatever's in this warehouse, you're gonna let us." He leaned close to Jared's ear and tightened the arm around his neck. "That sound right to you?"

"*Fuck* you, Switch—"

"Yeah, I know. C'mon."

He edged them out another exit—on the side *not* facing the bonfire. He closed the door as quietly as he could, then forced Jared to the warehouse's outer wall. He placed the gun's muzzle against the small of Jared's back, forcing him to walk in front. If anyone did see them as they made their way to the bikes, it'd look like they were walking close, at least till they noticed his stuttered gait.

Jared breathed heavily through the pain in his mangled leg, but Switch forced him on, ignoring the man's threats.

"Think me and the boys won't find you? Now we know what you are?"

He dragged the gun up Jared's back and ground the muzzle into his cheek. The sight scraped and cut, painting his face with a shallow swath of blood. "I'm leaving you with your life 'cause it's more convenient than shootin' you dead." Switch shoved him to the ground near the corner of the warehouse. "A smarter man would keep quiet before he changed that."

Jared, no doubt, had something to say to that, but he didn't give him the chance. Switch cracked the butt of his gun against Jared's skull and watched the bald man slump to the ground. He pushed Jared's unconscious form against the wall and took everything from his pockets, hoping somewhere there might be a clue for later. If he was around for later at all.

That done, he stepped from the warehouse's shadow — head down, pace steady. Seemed there'd been enough distance and other noise to keep anyone at the fire from hearing anything, but he was on borrowed time. Even if Jared stayed unconscious, there were at least three guys in the warehouse with guns they were ready to use. The threat of one limping hostage wouldn't stall them for long.

He made it to Jared's bike before the warehouse door banged open, and he only just got it started when the commotion broke loud. If any of these drunks got one good shot off, he was gone —

Two bullets whizzed by his head, but Switch didn't feel anything hit. He looked over his shoulder to where, a moment ago, a guard was lining up his shot — but the man was holding his knee now, cursing and crumpled in the mud. Unsure what happened, Switch turned toward the road.

Everett stared down the sight of his service weapon — feet squared, pistol level.

"Nice shot," he said.

"*Terrible* plan, Colt."

He waved Rhett over. "Get on the bike."

"You've got to be —"

Another shot in the distance kept Switch from having to repeat himself. Everett swung up and over, grabbed at his waist for balance and kept the gun on the campfire crowd.

"Hold on, Ev."

Gravel crunched beneath sliding wheels, but they missed the lead sailing by their heads and hit the pavement fast. Switch shifted gears and tore down the road like he was chasing the rising moon. Who knew? With Everett showing up with luck like that, they just might catch it.

He dared a look over his shoulder. No one after them. Yet.

"What about your truck?" Ev yelled in his ear.

"Later. Got to get clear."

He could tell it wasn't the answer Everett wanted. The man clung closer, forehead pressed between his shoulder blades as he held fast to their go-bag. They blazed at full speed till the buzz of adrenaline faded to static, and Switch's thoughts turned to all he'd learned.

He needed to get somewhere he could sit and record it fresh, but even with all the night had been — and the work still left ahead of him — he couldn't help but smile when he pictured Jared, hobbled up on the ground. Or how Everett must be looking now, muttering curses into the leather at his back.

Maybe it was the shock, and it wasn't saying much, but...he'd had worse nights.

So since Rhett would never be able to tell, he took the long way back and enjoyed the ride.

Chapter Six

Colt
Louisiana, 2011, seven years earlier

He slowed to acceptable speeds once they reached familiar streets. Before long, they were parked in the rolltop garage. He pulled the chain on the only bulb in the place and double-checked the doors. Everett leaned against the cement wall while Colt dug out a tool box from the shelves in the corner. At the bottom was an old flip phone.

He pulled open a drawer of ratchets, wrenches and the battery he was looking for, then popped it into place. He turned the phone on and tapped his thigh.

"Colt?"

"Not now."

He pressed call on the only contact and turned away from Everett.

"Hey, you there?" He held the phone close, but this would be quick anyway. For both their sakes. "Ran into some old friends. One mentioned seeing you. Wanted to…yeah. Okay."

It was never easy when they had to talk. At least she answered this time. She told him what he wanted to know, but it was obvious she wanted off the call as fast as possible. She didn't sound like a woman with any interest in catching up.

Her answers didn't bring much relief, but he felt less frantic than before. "Call if you need," he said. "I still check the messages."

But the line was already dead.

Everett must've heard enough, because he asked like he knew the answer, "Rosa?"

He nodded and disassembled the phone.

"She all right?"

If *that* weren't a loaded question. "She's in nursing school and well rid of me. That's as close to fine as she's like to get, but it's hers." He took a deep breath and shook his head. It did nothing for the ache in his chest. "She deserved better."

"I think that's true for both of you, Colt. No parent deserves—"

"Don't you say a fuckin' *word* about what a parent deserves. Not *you*. Not to me."

The fierceness of his reaction clearly surprised Everett, and he knew how out of control it'd make him seem. But Ev let it lie, like maybe he could see how hard Colt was fighting for control.

He'd barely felt the bag between his fingers till Everett asked, "Who's Ava?"

Goddamn…

Hadn't heard the name spoke aloud in years, yet it broke through his mind like sun on a cloudy day, tasted sharp as the sound of wings in winter air—

Too shocked to do more than stare, he watched Everett wave at his jacket pocket, then tap his own thigh in a too-familiar manner. "Didn't catch it until I heard it through the phone," Ev said. "One short, one long. Three short, one long. First again. A-V-A. Your daughter, right?"

All he could do was nod. Then words found a way. He cleared his throat. "Rosa picked it. Because of the birds on my arm."

"It's a good name."

"Yeah." He found he couldn't swallow the way he'd like and wished he had some water. Or something *much* stronger. "Can...can we not talk about this right now?"

He wasn't sure what Everett saw when he looked at him, but the man kept his mouth shut even as he set a line on the table. Colt sniffed hard and blinked at the expected rush, not wanting to meet his partner's judgmental eye. But Rhett was ready with another surprise and waved for him to toss the bag over.

He hesitated.

"What? You gonna share with your boyfriend and not with me?"

If Everett was looking for it, this was another clue that something still wasn't right, that maybe he couldn't shake off his alias quick as his leather coat. Because Colt never would've given him the bag.

But Switch would.

Everett laid out his own line and sniffed, pocketing the rest before he could ask for it back. And when the next question fell from his partner's mouth, Switch wondered just how much they could blame on the drugs.

"So before..." Everett hedged. "That was for the case, right? Establishing your cover?"

The sights, scents and colors of the stable burned down his cross-wired senses...

Fresh hay, horses, leather, Everett, the sandpaper grit of braided rope and something all anise and spice —

"Weren't a strange thing for me to do. Then."

Rhett looked like he had a few feelings about him dropping to his knees that kind of regular. He scratched his nose. "What'd Switch get up to? Back in the day?"

Colt knew he should be specific, but too much of tonight had pushed too hard. His whole body ached like the time he'd gone those rounds with a car battery — and Switch was too much in the saddle to say a word but the hard-up truth.

"Anything. So long as it killed me first."

Everett reached a hand toward his shoulder, but pulled up short. The halted motion didn't keep either of them from swaying closer. The air between them sparked with unfinished business. Colt didn't move his feet, and Everett didn't get close enough to touch, still trying to hold back. Still trying to be sure.

"When I was following you...looked for a moment like —"

Fuck it.

Switch closed the distance and grabbed Everett by the waist. He pulled their hips together, unwilling to let him retreat. Ev's hitching sigh was warm on his neck.

"Doesn't matter," he told him. "Familiar territory yields easy."

And that was too simple to be anywhere close to good, but the look on Everett's face said he feared it might be true. In the back rooms of his mind, Colt did a rough calculation. He knew Everett's flaws well. He was selfish, clueless — and determined to stick his head in the sand on *far* too much — but Rhett would never force him. He wouldn't assume in the wake of Jared. Everett had given him space all week, even after he'd brought him halfway home and left him in the stable, all to wind up with Jared, hunched over in that truck—

No. Don't remember.

So sure, Everett wanted him. But the way he was feeling right now...some quick trade of favors wouldn't cut it. He needed to be somewhere else, *needed* to be out of his head before the whole night crashed around him. Only one thing that might do the trick. And he was willing to do some convincing to get it.

So he breathed hot and heavy against Rhett's cheek, sliding a hand between their bodies and over the bulge in his partner's jeans. Everett bit off a whine and lasted all of two seconds before he was pressing into the contact, resting an eager hand over his backside to keep them close.

Everett's voice was honey-warm as he bargained. "Colt...if there was somethin' you were wantin', I figure...tonight doesn't count in no way that matters." Warm lips brushed his cheek. "What reports we gonna write off this shit?"

So since it didn't matter, he took Everett's hand in his, slid joined fingers up his chest and placed the man's palm on his neck. He held Everett's gaze and encouraged him to press at the sides, and even as Ev pulled back in surprise, his sapphire eyes sparked with longing.

Yeah, Switch could tell that Everett had it in him, that he was no stranger to these sorts of games. But if he was really offering to help with this, the man deserved the truth. "You don't wanna see me like this, Rhett."

Everett's breath stuttered as he scanned his face, but Switch could tell he'd won—familiar territory being what it was.

Ev leaned close to answer. "No, I don't. But someone needs to."

Fingers tightened around his throat and Everett pulled their mouths together.

A tandem moan escaped as they both held close, but it didn't stay soft for long. Lips parted and teeth clashed in a kiss more battle than caress before Ev shoved him hard to the ground. Knees thudded against concrete as Everett sank with him, crouching low, till the only things in his line of sight were eyes burning bright with blue fire.

He relished the heat of Everett's palm on his neck, how his Adam's apple pushed against the hold when he swallowed. A rough thumb strummed his bottom lip as Rhett pulled at his jacket. His mouth twisted as he tore the leather off one shoulder, then released him all at once.

"Take that off. All of it."

Colt did as instructed and shucked the jacket, then lost the shirt. Hands fell to his belt, loosening the buckle before Everett caught his wrists and twisted his arms back. The heaviness of eyelids was harder to ignore as something new started rolling off his partner, an emerald sheen coating his every word.

Everett exhaled slowly. "Where'd he touch you?"

He felt a pinch at his wrists and realized that the gentle clink of metal wasn't imagined. Everett snapped the other cuff on tight—a familiar sound on familiar ground—and pinned his arms to his back. Not like a pair of standard handcuffs presented much of a challenge, but it fit right for the moment, put him in the space he needed.

Finally restrained, Colt rocked on his knees, lost in the cerulean calm that meant it wasn't up to him anymore, that he was on the job, on the rock, on his way to that unconscious void after all…

A hand touched his face. "You can tell me, Col."

Far away, Colt heard himself answer, "My hair. My face. Mouth."

The air in the silent garage felt heavy with Everett's rage. He listened as Ev swallowed a yell and huffed, those hurt animal sounds that meant the fury was on him proper. He lived a lifetime in that stuttered inhale, the harsh exhalation that tossed his hair. Something in his chest knit back together when strong fingers gripped his scalp, intent on leaving different prints behind. The hold moved to the short hairs on his neck. Ev hiked his chin up as he stood to full height, forcing Colt to strain to hold his gaze.

Ev fished a hand inside their open go-bag and retrieved a bottle of water. He opened it with his mouth, twisting hard at the wrist to crack the plastic into spinning. He spit the cap aside and took a pull himself. Then Ev tipped his chin up and placed the bottle on the edge of his lip.

"Drink."

The sharp plastic edges cut into abraded skin. Colt hissed as the water flowed down his throat, his zipper-rough chin, across his naked chest. Everett adjusted the bottle but didn't let him stop, forcing him to take down as much as he could, and Colt wondered if water had ever tasted so sweet. Clear and clean, like it was drawn up a well.

When the bottle was empty Everett tossed it aside. The cheap plastic crinkled against the cement. And the way Ev was staring at his damp and battered face...*fuck him*, but it was like looking at an eclipse. Too bright to stare directly, but the man shone like a sun, like he saw something worthwhile, and for all the night had been, Colt knew he'd never been so hard in his life.

Swaying on his knees, he shivered when Everett told him, "Inside. On the bed."

They got him there in a blur of shuffling feet, guiding arms and a not-so-delicate toss to the mattress. Everett shut the bedroom door, loose pages of notes dancing across the floor, then pulled at his bootlaces to strip his feet bare. Ev trailed a hand lightly along the skin of his ankle, running a shiver up his legs, his spine, to where he wrapped his fingers tight around Colt's tattooed shoulder.

Colt wasn't sure what to expect next—and thank fuck for that. It wasn't till Everett had him lie on his back, cuffed hands be damned, that he started to see where they were headed. Ev positioned his neck to lie along the curve of the mattress, brushing his thumb lightly down the side of his throat.

Yes. He wet his lips. Everett's hands had told him exactly what they were about to do.

The metallic sounds of Ev's unbuckling belt rang in his ears like a bell, and Everett barely got those jeans down in time before he was reaching his neck, angling his head, unable to wait for Ev to press the tip past his swollen lips.

Please...

Colt felt the words bubble up, but forced them down. Even like this, he couldn't—*wouldn't* beg. Not with all those layers of what asking Rhett for anything would look like. Especially now his living room had become the man's temp housing.

So he took it for a kindness that Everett didn't make him. Because if he asked…Colt knew he would do it. And that balance might never be righted.

Instead, they held eyes as Everett positioned his jaw just so, smoothing fingers hot as brands over his collarbone. Then Everett slid himself across his tongue, slowly down his throat until he'd swallowed him whole. The man honest-to-God whimpered the first time he rocked forward, thrusting into the slippery sounds of Colt getting exactly what he'd asked for, what was promised hours ago, and between the coke and the unexpected thrill of survival, none of this was gonna take very long.

And all the while, Colt's only thoughts were of the weight of the man in his mouth, the salty-slick taste of Everett on his tongue, the way his throat spasmed and the need to hold on longer, to make Ev make that sound again that shook the room with the force of a hurricane. Everett pulled away so Colt could swipe his tongue down the shaft, over and around the head of his cock before taking him down again and *yes*, that was it. At Everett's broken moan, they spun in the eye of the storm, Ev panting hard as he outright fucked his throat, doing his best to keep some manner of pace.

But Colt wasn't worried over soreness in the morning, or saving a shred of dignity either. He wanted it all—needed it all—and when Everett tried to pull back, Colt slithered after, pushing against his nearly numb hands to follow him all the way down. He barely noticed how his own hips thrust in the air, desperate for the friction his part-buckled jeans could provide—

Everett slapped his hand hard against Colt's chest, the only thing that kept him from sliding clear off the bed. Five strong fingers anchored him against the mattress as Everett bucked into his mouth, erratic and necessary.

"*Fuck* — "

That was all the warning Colt got. It was more than Switch needed.

He hollowed his cheeks and sucked Everett down, desperate to forget everything from the night but this. Because here, in this moment, none of the rest could touch him — not ghosts in black trucks or the sting of red-winged memories. It all faded as Everett's cries echoed like thunder, shaking his foundations like a howling wind.

He barely felt himself being turned over or the quick release of the cuffs. Everett's mouth latched to the side of his neck as he pulled Colt to hands and knees, pushing aside jeans and boxers as he went. Rhett fit behind him easily, held him close with an arm across his chest, then brought his other hand to his own mouth.

Ev whispered, "It's all right," and licked his palm, because who fucking knew where that bottle might be. Ev's strong grip felt familiar around his cock, fisting him tight as he mouthed down his spine, and at the symphony of sensation, Colt nearly writhed apart. He tasted the smile he couldn't see — summer and sweet watermelon — as Everett kissed behind his ear, voice light with laughter as he said, "God*damn* it, man. What else you hidin' from me?"

And at the satisfaction Colt could sense in the man behind him, the way he clung close and encouraged

Colt to fuck into his hand — it wasn't long before he was seizing into the mattress, shaking in Ev's quaking arms.

Release washed over him, then all that mattered was the dark.

* * * *

Later, Colt heard the crack of another water bottle. A damp T-shirt passed over his skin. A cool sheet landed on his shoulders.

Fingers skimmed over his hair. A door swung open and closed.

The light went out, and consciousness took its cue.

* * * *

Colt usually wasn't up at dawn unless he caught it from the other side, but this time awareness stuck around with the daylight.

Memories faded in with the soreness of limbs and the prick of scabs, tight with healing. He supposed a part of him would be something like nervous if he hadn't felt what last night was doing to Everett too. Colt sighed and reasoned they could ride this off. Living like they were, they were bound to crash into each other. He blinked his eyes awake and decided not to worry. They could blame a lot on a bad night. Steer into the skid.

Except that didn't leave much explanation for the morning, because Everett was still there.

Colt had expected him to be gone — not for long, just to run out for coffee and breakfast. All they needed was intentional distance and that physical shit could keep being their fucked-up secret, hardly discussed between them at all. But when Colt rolled to his side, he met a pair of too-blue eyes, wide and real and staring. Everett was looking at him like he might be afraid to lose something, like it wouldn't be so awful to brush his sleep-tossed hair aside and ensure Colt was really there.

He closed his eyes at the soft touch of Everett's hand, not wanting to give anything away in the gray light of morning, this lull before the heat of day took hold. Then Everett's hand strayed from the safer terrain of hair. His thumb brushed easily over Colt's cheek, hollow from his time in another man's jacket.

He was still getting Switch's blow out of his nose, out of his system. Everett couldn't have picked a worse time for something so addictive.

Colt forced himself to ask, "What're you doin', Rhett?"

His voice was rough with the excuse of sleep, but Ev was already pulling him close.

"Hush a second."

Everett didn't often pull Colt to anything. It was more his way to make the right comment and wait, to be pulled himself toward their foregone conclusion. Without warning, Everett's words from last night played in his mind...

"What else you hidin' from me?"

And no way in hell was he answering that question with words. Whatever Everett's reasons, Colt met his kiss with a sigh.

They twined together easy, like they'd had more practice being horizontal in a bed than they did. Everett's mouth was on him and his kiss was almost tender, something meant to comfort and catalyze in equal measure. Colt usually kept his hands up by

Everett's shoulders, but he risked a tentative trek down the lines of biceps, curved soft around an elbow to fold Everett closer, to secure him more completely around his back.

And goddamn, but Rhett let him do it.

With each touch of the other, they passed permission, mapping planes of chests usually covered, hips and legs no longer hidden by unbuckled pants. And for a while, it was just the kissing, steady like thunder.

In time, mouths followed hands.

Everett kissed down his neck, caught the curve of Colt's shoulder in his mouth to tongue and suck and fuck, but that wasn't supposed to feel so good. His own breath was heavy in the hollow of the other man's neck, then Ev ventured lower, brought warm lips to Colt's reddened wrists and all across his chest. Everett traced his tongue down and around his hip, almost leisurely before taking Colt in his mouth, choking off a moan as he swallowed him down.

"Evvv..."

The nickname was out before he could stop it.

It wasn't the kind of thing he'd say when they were fucking around in their car. None of their fractured hideaways had heard a part of either of their names, not tinged with the desperation of a lover's sigh. Colt had been a special kind of vigilant about that. And to have it ripped from him now in his own damn bed was nothing short of humiliating. Because of course, this would be the line, the thing that'd make Everett rise up and realize what he'd been doing for two damn years —

Or maybe, Colt had finally reached a moment where the worst he'd braced for wasn't coming. Because all Everett did was slide off and kiss the tender skin of his thigh, eyes shut with something like rapture when he whispered, "Say it again."

God, Ev…

Everything Colt had been holding back spilled from his mouth in a flood, Everett's name falling from his lips at the slightest provocation. Everett hummed like he was pleased with his response and kissed lower, letting his tongue discover parts of Colt he'd only fumbled in the dark. He spread him wide, dove inside and the room was split apart by the purpling hues of heat lightning. A crunch and crackle like breaking glass snapped behind his eyes as Everett worked him open, kissed around his rim, went back again to reach for that sweet spot over and over, two fingers deep with nothing but spit to ease the way. Didn't need nothing else the way he ate him like a fucking prom date, and Colt's hips jerked with inevitable release, only just held at bay by a soft plea of, "Don't yet, Col. Not yet."

The words anchored him, pulled Colt back to reality, to the sun falling light across Everett's golden head, radiating warmth and a bit of wonder where he looked up from the foot of the bed. Colt blinked something sharp and hot out of his eyes, unwilling to acknowledge what they were. At the sight of the falling drops, Rhett levered over him to kiss the salt away. He reached between their bodies and took them both in hand, stroking them together, and wasn't nothing Colt could do but hold on and moan — didn't feel capable of nothing else.

In unhurried time, Everett had him on his back, holding his gaze as he entered him inch by rocking inch, head falling to Colt's shoulder when he was fully seated inside. And Colt was too wound up to give a shit about something like pride. Shot that to hell ages ago when he let this shit carry on. He shifted his hips, scared to even ask now their eyes were held together, but...

"God*damn* it, Ev. C'mon, I...I need it from you."

Everett answered with a steady thrust and shoved a pillow under his hips. He folded Colt's knees around his waist. "I got you, Col."

Colt knew then he'd never forget the cut of these jagged moments—how the vulnerability in Everett's eyes stung like a razor, how Ev kissed him full on the mouth as he stroked deep inside, sending shivers and sparks and something too much like nicotine rocketing down his hips, clenching in his gut, pulsing in time with his cock while Everett fisted his hand around him. As their rhythmic tempo rose hard and fast against the mattress, Colt took the risk and reached a hand to Everett's lips, nearly writhed out of his skin when the man sucked two fingers deep into his mouth, swirling his tongue and giving all kinds of permission in the process.

It was too much, *too much* –

It would never be enough.

Colt reached his peak with a fierceness he didn't expect, rioting against Everett's strength as it shattered and crested. His broken cries triggered something in Everett that made his hips ride faster, push harder, angle Colt just so. And the second he regained that smallest bit of sanity, he reached around to where Everett rocked above him, caressing in the way he'd never ask for, that Colt knew he'd wanted since the start.

"*Colll...*"

Colt smiled. He'd never seen his name in better colors.

"The fuck are you *doin'*," Ev moaned, weak with want, but it wasn't really a question. He'd managed to bite off the *to me* his tone implied—but only just, and Ev gripped him tight as he followed over the ledge. They tangled together, slick with sweat, each holding close to a man as broken as the one they shaved in the mirror, and Colt wondered if this was what people meant by words like inescapable. Fated.

Starstruck.

They stayed close in a pile of softly held limbs and one light kiss to the neck. And as sleep threatened to claim them again, Ev confessed a truth learned in a week of nights on the couch.

"I know what this is, Col. Just don't know how to keep it any."

Neither of them had much to say to that.

* * * *

When Colt woke again, Everett was on that coffee run.

An hour later, he was shuffling through scraps from the warehouse when Ev walked through his front door. He sat beside him on the couch, normal as anything, cracking jokes about the mountain of paperwork that was his alibi. Everett handed him the rodeo drive, which he plugged into his laptop, and both men pretended at breakfast.

Rhett didn't look at him when he asked, "Where you wanna start on this?"

Colt wished he knew how to answer that.

But he took Everett through what he'd found about the Edwards Corporation, and by the time they'd finished eating, the rough of last night and the balm of the morning had both faded to muddled gray. By unspoken agreement, they kept their attention on the case. When evening rolled around, Ev took the couch without complaint. Wasn't any other place Rhett was gonna go, really. Not the way things stood with Rachael.

And they didn't know it yet, but that was the start of a whole month Ev would spend crashing at Colt's, staring at dead ends until they looked like wallpaper, half the time winding up in Colt's bed before morning. It'd take two weeks for Ev to stop pretending to sleep on the sofa first.

And when Rachael did eventually take him back for those couple good years, Colt decided he wouldn't think about empty beds. Instead, he adjusted to the status quo, knowing it wouldn't be long before Rhett would say what had become their password, that joking *"c'mon over here"* that sounded so much like *"I need you."*

Shit. Maybe he did too.

* * * *

Louisiana, 2018

The clock read four a.m., if Colt's bleary eyes could be trusted. Going back through Combs again hadn't done a thing but pick at old wounds. Made him feel much like he did after Everett had left in 2011, gone from his bed and the case in quick succession.

Ev didn't have the patience for the deep dive on Combs then, nor maybe enough reason to try. Rachael taking him back meant life was returning to normal.

And if that meant listening to the bosses to let that rodeo mess slide, well, that was chain of command.

When he was feeling particularly morose, Colt wondered what he must've done in past lives to deserve this one. He pushed the thought away and closed his copy of the Combs file, looking around his office and reading odd bits off the case-wall. This one was at least three times the size of its predecessor. There was a whole section dedicated to Combs, and a list far longer than six names.

It wasn't time he needed to bring this in anymore. He needed the right leverage.

Colt stood slowly on unsteady legs. This detour to Mason wouldn't change the rest of his plans, but he'd put enough on hold to get this case done right, and like hell was he going to let *Everett Kane* stand in the way of his peace of mind again. He'd had enough of that for a lifetime.

Colt propped himself in the corner of the room and stared at the wall of photos. His eyes snagged on a familiar puddle of blood, the same one he'd been looking at for four long years, the last night of his life in Mason...

The last days of easy quiet in 2014 before two weeks that split his life wide open...

Missed calls and solo drives, dinners and driveways and that goddamn bottle of wine...

Mira's sharp eye, and Rachael's even keener one. Rhett's fear getting the better of him. Colt's frailty coming to bear...

That last stop by the Kanes' house that wouldn't ever be a home again – not after Ev smashed hell into his truck, glass stuck in his knuckles as they walked up to Mary's scene...

And a final look down a hospital hall they'd never once discussed...

Colt braced a hand against the wall, tripped over his feet and slumped to the ground. He pulled and crawled his way to the camping cot he called a bed, then set an alarm for a few hours closer to daylight, when sunrise would hold at least one bit of interest.

Tomorrow, he'd likely see Everett again. Would be best to get some sleep.

Too bad there weren't a chance of that happening.

Part Two

RECKONING

Chapter Seven

Colt
Louisiana, 2018

Conveniently tucked behind a billboard-for-rent, Colt sat in his truck and waited for Everett to post across the street. Calling a one-room shack like this a "bar" was a kindness, but it was as isolated as he could hope for this conversation. And since it was mostly empty, Everett would have time to wait once he arrived.

Plenty, if Colt had anything to say on it.

Everett rolled in at ten a.m. in a car Colt recognized well. His old partner entered the bar and left just as quick, a cheap suit jacket folded over his arm, blond hair dull in the bone-bright sun. He watched as Everett rolled his shoulder and slowly walked back to the car, obviously resigning himself to a long sit.

Colt decided the years had taken a piece of their toll, but only the dead got to skip on that. Everett was still there where it counted — and to be honest, the slump of his shoulders read a bit more solid and sure. His bogus tip had said to wait for a bar regular who'd known Andrea Meyers, so Colt wiped the sweat from his brow and cranked the working window down. Wasn't even the heat of the day yet, but he remembered how shoddy that sedan's A/C was and watching Rhett sweat it out held a certain pleasure, even if Colt suffered with him.

At twelve-thirty, Everett had loosed his tie and smoked through his pack, crumbling it up to toss out of the window. His head leaned against the seat like he was ready to call it. Forty minutes after that, he sighed and started his car. Colt did the same and edged his truck from behind the billboard. When Everett turned out of the lot, he'd be driving straight for him.

And as Colt looked around the corner, it seemed almost funny that what surprised him most was Everett's eyes. Never thought he'd forget that spark. So blue they burned with it, burned with everything Everett was feeling. Blue fire when he laughed. Blue fire when he yelled. Blue fire when he refused to look at him.

But Everett was looking now.

Colt blinked hard and stepped on the brakes. The air in the cab was pressing in on him. Everything felt hazy and, he'd admit, for a moment he thought it was just seeing Everett again, but this was different. This wasn't just nerves. Nerves didn't make sunlight leak across his windshield, yellow rays dripping with a patter like rain. The taste of watermelon burst on his tongue and fuck, but he knew what was happening now.

Just focus, Colt told himself. *You still know what's real.*

He breathed deeply and waited for the wires in his head to uncross. Should be able to get through a single day without the world crumbling at the edges. Reality had gotten harder to hold ever since the beating that ended Switch, and the decade of life that followed hadn't done much to help. But even Colt had to admit it was getting worse these days. If there was a chance Everett had something that could tie loose ends sooner, help him finally take action on what he knew was happening at the State Rodeo, then Colt had to do this.

Meant he'd finally get to be done with Mason. With everything he owed.

Then, he could get on with some other things that needed doing.

* * * *

Everett
Louisiana, 2018

He didn't really make the decision to pull over. That implied forethought. Something like a plan.

No, the second he saw that beat-up truck edge from behind the billboard on his right, Everett's hands veered left and sent his car off the side of the road. Took him a second to remember to let go of the steering wheel, to set the parking brake and breathe. He threw a look over his right shoulder, half-expecting there to be nothing, but a shadow the shape of Colton Harkan was strolling up to his car, pulled over on a roadside too much like their many others.

Fuck. Everett fell back in his seat and pushed hard against the headrest. Maybe he should've been, but he was not prepared to deal with the man ambling up to his passenger-side. Thought he'd have the long drive to the man's office to get his head right—but here Colt was. Like he'd never been anywhere else.

It's for the case, Everett reminded himself. *Don't hope.*

He lowered the window and Colt leaned in. His face was carefully blank.

"Everett."

He tried not to flinch at the sound of his full name. Instead, he watched Colt cup a hand around the cigarette on his lip. "Thought maybe we should talk," he said, sparking his lighter. "Since you seem to keep callin'."

Everett shook his head at the floormat. Straight to the point. Guess it was good to know some things didn't change, however rough the man looked. The day Colt Harkan made something like small talk, Everett just might die from shock. He turned his head and, for the first time, really processed what he was seeing, the changes that marked their four years apart. There were so many things he'd waited so long to ask —

"The fuck's with your hair? You undercover as some coked-out trucker?"

"No."

Well, that wasn't what Everett had planned to say, but wasn't like any of this was going the way he'd thought.

Colt scratched his week-old stubble and tied up the hair on his neck. "Why'd you call, Everett?"

He raised an eyebrow. "What, you don't know?"

"Didn't say that," Colt drawled.

"'Course not. You wouldn't."

Everett knew better than to bait him, but it seemed safer, at present, than the other thoughts in his head. He wasn't sure if it was the car he was driving, the clothes he was wearing or his general attitude of put together that had Colt in a mood, but the way Everett remembered things, there was wrong on both sides when they'd left it shattered in that driveway.

Not for nothing, but Colt was lucky that window was all he broke.

The old rage welled up in his gut, and he knew it was wrong, but right now, the case was the last thing on his mind. All Everett could do was close his eyes and breathe, mind racing with the reasons it'd been four years since they'd spoken at all…

"Gonna show you, kindly as I can, just how much you don't know…"

"Connection's the real drug…"

"Evvv…"

"Stay put, Everett."

"Fuck all that. Where is he?"

Swing and a fuckin' miss…

Everett pinched the bridge of his nose. He needed a moment to *think*, damn it.

"So you're my lead?" He narrowed eyes at Colt as he realized what that meant. "How long were you just sittin' out there, watching me wait?"

"A few hours."

"Jesus H. Christ…"

Everett was careful to mumble the rest. Every time, Col just had to be the asshole. And those intense brown eyes of his hadn't left Everett's yet.

He asked, "So, you do know why I called, right?"

Colt shrugged and smoked. "Only one reason you would."

"Well that reason's got a name. Andrea Meyers. Ever heard of her?"

Colt tipped his head and stayed quiet. Everett tried again. "She one of those on your list?"

His gaze strayed to the empty road, but Colt nodded. A breath later, he added, "Yeah."

"Shit." Everett drummed his hand against the steering wheel. "So…what's next, then?"

"Next is you stop askin' so many questions. You need to follow me somewhere. And we got a drive ahead of us."

Fuckin' Harkan. Like he could roll back into town and just…

"Just like that? You think I'm gonna follow you God-knows-where without so much — "

"Quit your bitchin'." Colt flicked his filter at the road and headed for his truck. "We both know you're gonna do it."

Everett found he had all manner of things to say once Colt was out of earshot. He mumbled a few of the better ones as Colt flipped his truck around. His old partner pulled up beside his sedan and, at this distance, Everett confirmed something that maybe he'd always known deep down, but the sight of that busted window stole the breath from his lungs all the same. He met Colt's eyes over the jagged edge of the glass, stubbornly sticking skyward even four years later.

Felt like he should say something. Anything, really.

Before he could open his mouth, Colt shifted gears and drove away. And just like the man said he would, Everett followed after.

* * * *

He'd only been following Colt for half an hour, but every minute stuck in their car with thoughts of before felt like an eternity. Even having lived it, Everett wasn't sure he could put words to how things ended up like they did. Or where they might go now.

In those couple good years after letting Combs slide, he and Colt didn't have much reason to be in each other's pockets. He was back home with Rachael, and while the occasional work call brought them side-by-side, gone were the days of endless cruising, or any of the other times they usually fell together.

Colt had seemed all right without it as much. Everett wanted to be the same.

And sure, things had picked up again later — after a year spent working up the nerve to ask for anything now that he was back at the house. But after those long months, things shifted more comfortable long term. They learned what questions not to ask. What fights not to have. Whatever it was, it worked. And the longer it worked, the less it felt like something to hide, or like something they'd been getting away with at all.

Everett wondered now, taking another turn after Colt's tore-up truck, if the settling was an extension of the ways they were easing into other dynamics back then — at work, with Rachael and Mira, even rare occasions with the family. By then, the kids weren't so little that it felt like an imposition, and he remembered thinking at one Fourth of July, watching Colt offer his Zippo so Gracie could light her sparklers that maybe, some years of stable quiet might've done his partner some good.

No telling what the years of distance might've done since.

They only felt like the good ol' days once they were gone, but Everett would swear he'd felt their fall coming, like the change in the air that signaled the shift of seasons. To his mind, the beginning of the end was borne of one bad habit in particular, a product of their years successfully avoiding detection. With so little in his world that he'd call interesting, Everett stopped worrying over precautions — and began taking bigger risks.

It'd started small enough. A hand tracing patterns up Colt's thigh in line for drive-thru, removed at the last moment before they reached the window. Colt would retaliate when they were getting drinks from the gas station, cop a feel on his way to reach for sweet tea. But when Everett took advantage of an empty locker room, sliding his arm around Colt's toweled waist, he hardly got to enjoy the man's startled sigh at all before Colt was trying to pull away. He pressed him against the metal shelves, and unless Colt was willing to make some noise about it, wasn't much he could do but let Everett nip at his tattooed shoulder and wait to make his escape.

He brushed Colt's hand away from tapping his thigh and tangled their fingers together, pressing their palms flush against Colt's hip. Even knowing how out of line it was, that a totally insane notion had possessed him, he couldn't help it. He ground himself against Colt's hip, thumb brushing over the back of their still-held hands, and breathed deep of a scent he wouldn't yet admit to missing.

"Still using that soap of yours, hmm?" Everett had whispered into his back, raining open-mouthed kisses through the thin cloth of his undershirt, and at that moment, he'd wished Colt could be as lost in the memory as he was...

In that month they'd lived together, waiting on Rachael to call her shot, Everett would eventually stop trying to convince Colt to buy some necessities. But that first week after the warehouse, the top item on his list was a real damn shower curtain. That cheap plastic liner might've been fine when Colt lived alone, but it left nothing to the imagination of his temporary roommate.

Honest to God, he'd just been trying to take a leak, unable to wait till Colt finished his long-ass shower. He was washing his hands when he looked up at the mirror, expecting to see his own reflection and a fogged plastic screen. What he saw was a fuckin' tease.

Colt was facing away from him, scrubbing down his shoulders with a sudsy cloth. Everett's eyes followed the streams of water down the slide of his spine, over the flesh of his backside, across his tattooed patches and too many scars to count.

Everett remembered wanting to try anyway.

But a choked-dry throat and a watering mouth were soon the least of his problems. When Colt turned to rinse in the shower's spray, their eyes locked in the mirror, and if the bathroom counter hadn't been the exact height it was, Colt would've known immediately how Everett felt after seeing all that.

He turned attention to drying his hands and cleared his throat. "What kind of soap is that? Smells funny."

Colt stayed watching him in the mirror. He passed the soapy towel over his chest, eyes warm and chocolate brown. "Rosemary. Makes the shower look like a mountain mist."

"What's it taste like?"

"You."

Everett decided pretty quick he didn't care if that was true or just something to rile him up, 'cause it was fuckin' working. He far preferred discussions of crossed-wire brain trauma when the lecture came from a wet and naked Colt, who by that point was lathering up too slow for it to be anything but a show. And the way the water slicked his hair over one eye...Jesus, but Colt needed an exhibitionist streak like a goddamn hole in the head.

Really, what was Colt Harkan but a man made of contradictions, determined to torment his peace?

"You better stop that," Everett warned.

A smirk curled Colt's lips, asking the question for him – or what?

"Or you might have to finish what you started here."

Everett thought it would be funny, more than a little hot and definitely a great way to get laid. He flipped the lid on the john and sat back like he was at some titty-bar, lacing hands through the back of his sunny hair to drive the joke home. He hadn't expected it to feel like that first morning together, to not be able to look away if the whole world burned around them.

Colt leveled his eyes on him and from that moment, Everett was hypnotized. He watched as Colt ran roughed-up knuckles across his chest, one hand sliding low to meet his rising erection, the other teasing a nipple, squeezing between thumb and forefinger. Brown eyes closed as he breathed deep through the sensation, turning up half-lidded as he swallowed a groan.

In time, Colt fully opened his eyes and watched where Everett sat staring. He grabbed the shower gel and squeezed another ribbon on the towel before closing it around his cock. He stroked himself with precise intention, arm pumping faster until he abandoned the cloth for the touch of his own hand. It didn't take long for Colt to reach the peak he was after, head and body both leaned against the tile wall. But when he took a bit of that convenient wetness spread across his stomach, reached slickened fingers back to tease himself open, holding Everett's gaze all the while – there were no ifs about it.

It was the hottest thing Everett had ever seen.

When Colt decided he was done torturing him – for there didn't seem to be no other reason – he shut the water off and walked to Everett by the towel rack. He reached for the white cotton and slung it casual around his waist, and it was the closest Everett ever got to catching the man's full-on grin.

Colt reached for the door, like he planned to open it wide to the hall with nothing said about the matter. And maybe he would've if Everett hadn't got to him first, something primal growling in his chest.

"Just where d'you think you're goin'?"

He ripped the towel away, almost certainly leaving a red-rough burn, and spun Colt to brace against the door. He slid a hand up the coolness of Colt's shower-damp back, then worked himself wet to slide into him from behind. And the way Colt pushed against him, the way he kept moaning Everett's name into the doorframe, he knew this would be a race to the finish line...

But their game of chicken in the locker room wasn't like that time in that shower. Colt struggled to catch his breath as Everett kissed and licked his neck from behind, pressing them both against the lockers. They were *at the station*, for Christ's sake, but for the life of him, Everett couldn't seem to care. It was a terrifying thrill to think someone might happen upon their secret, might force this shit into the open –

Which only made it better when Colt shoved his back against him, spun quick as a cat to press a hand to Everett's shoulder, forcing him to walk backward. Relief soared in his chest when Everett realized what he was about. He stepped into the shower of his own accord, head knocking against tile hard enough to dizzy him because finally, Colt's mouth was *finally* on his, possessing him body and soul with a kiss that felt like a cool, gray morning. Colt's hand cupped his face as he worked Everett's mouth open wider, coaxing with his tongue...

Goddamn it. Col...

But much too soon it was gone, and Colt was breathing in his face.

"Careful, Ev."

Something in his coffee-dark eyes said *please.*

But before Everett could ask what he meant, Colt spun away and pushed the tap on cold, full blast—entirely unbothered by the fact that he was still fully clothed.

* * * *

That day in the locker room wasn't the last shower Everett would take in his clothes. Had some dark nights himself in those lonely four years over no particular grief, borne of the weight of reconciling who'd he'd been with who he'd been trying to be. And sure, some nights he eased into the maudlin with too much cheap whiskey. But fuck it, weren't nobody there to complain. He wanted to sit in the shower in clothes he didn't like, a bad shirt picked for a date that didn't show? It was his goddamn right and no one's business anyhow.

When Everett did manage to keep a date, he always picked a table near the door. Saved time to get a read on her before she saw him. And when the women who matched their profiles walked in and out again, too fast to be anything but a dismissal? He figured it wasn't their fault for seeing what everyone did eventually. Made it easier, being by the door. It was where he shoved everyone he cared for sooner or later. Not such a bad place to be.

Those four years alone weren't all bad, but little was good. He called the kids regular as he could stomach, though the conversations were forced. The few times they talked, Rachael sounded something like glad, if a little sad too. She sounded like life, and Everett could empathize. Tried to, when he could. And more than anything, he tried not to think about Colt. Did pretty well most days.

But he couldn't always help it.

If ever a man deserved a break, it was Colton Harkan, but Everett couldn't seem to give him one, even in the courtroom of his own mind. Never felt like an option to track him down, to talk things through. That would mean thinking of some kind of anything to say, and they'd left it too raw — he'd left them too raw.

Not even worth some kind of goodbye…

When Everett remembered the night that broke it all, it wasn't the concussion or the glass in his fist that hurt worst, or even his throat, raw from screaming lies like *"We ain't done here."* The worst was the memory of that long hospital hallway, the last time he'd seen Colt before today.

He was drugged but lucid, and the hospital gown itched where Gracie and Marcus tugged, old enough to understand how close it had really been. Rachael was doing her best to keep them calm and explain what the doctor said. She'd checked his chart herself, but the worst damage was done before that drag-racer smashed into his ambulance. The crash killed that poor EMT, though. Driver got away clean — probably texting or some shit. To Everett, that burned worse than some glass in his hand, though the bulk of his stitches were from Colt's truck, Colt's precision blows and not the accident at all.

He honestly thought he was dreaming when he recognized his partner's voice, more worried than he'd ever heard before, because what would Colt be doing here after...after what he'd seen at the house —

Stapes called out to him, "Harkan. Surprised you'd show."

Colt's voice answered, rough and strained. "Fuck all that. Where is he?"

At this disturbance in the hall, a passing nurse closed Everett's door. His whole family was there, after all. Who else would be visiting at this hour?

He could only imagine what it looked like to Colt through the inset window of the door: him in bed, surrounded by his kids. Rachael's hand to the back of his head, taking his temp the old-fashioned way. If Everett didn't know Rach like he did, that she was in emergency mode where nothing else got to matter, he would've understood the expression on Colt's face.

But even so...it hurt to look at him too close. Rachael had been thorough. All he'd ever see when he looked at Colt now was him and Rach, clinging fast, pressing close against his kitchen wall in his own house, and God, had it been in his own bed —

Try as he might, Everett couldn't look at him any longer. He just needed a minute to figure why he was so angry at Colt for...exactly what he'd been doing for years. Screwing some woman and pretending it was his partner.

Almost didn't matter it was Rachael. Except for in the ways it did.

Everett's gaze stayed heavy on the foot of his hospital bed. He tried to focus on his breathing and not letting a bit of anything fall out his eyes, unsure how long it took to get himself under control. When he looked up again, Colt was gone.

In the morning, a resignation all of two words long sat on the major's desk — I quit.

Another copy was stapled to his office door with a postscript he'd never understood – Swing and a fuckin' miss.

Stapes tried to get him to talk about it. Everett found he didn't have much to say. When the guys around the station asked, the major said it was a "personal matter", but not a one was brave enough to ask what that meant. When he and Rachael split, most figured it out for themselves. Didn't take a detective for that one, really.

Occasionally, Everett would remind himself he didn't technically owe Colt a thing. Because technically, Colt was nothing but his crazy ex-work partner, the man who'd fucked his wife, and that meant he didn't have to care what his years after Everett had turned to. Wasn't his business if Colt was caught in a limbo as hellish as his past four years, an imprint of a former self fading into TV and frozen dinners.

Life without Colt developed into a pattern. Solve a case. Pretend it mattered. Home, bed, dread. Lather, rinse, repeat. And when he watched it, Everett's porn was full of all sorts of women. But the men looked a lot like Colt.

* * * *

An hour later, Colt parked at a gas station that felt uncannily familiar. Everett pulled in a few spaces down, though there was only one other car in the lot. He put his phone to his ear – *like anyone would be calling me* – and waved at Colt through the windshield.

Colt turned away to smoke and Everett looked at his phone. He dropped it in the cupholder and thought back to when he'd been too afraid to do so. With two different people, considering the secrets his messages used to keep.

He remembered that conversation with Rachael like it was yesterday. Two weeks out of the hospital and back in the usual swing — or as close as he was like to get once Colt had gone and quit — saw Rachael and him sitting at the table, kids at her folks' so they could talk. And God, the guilt. The rage. The jealousy he felt at the mention of his ex-partner's name, how all that name had meant had been replaced by the image of that night in the kitchen.

She tried explaining why she'd done it. Told him she knew he was cheating again, that she knew about the woman on his phone, how he'd picked up his bad habits when the case got hot again. How she'd warned him last time. How she'd thought she made herself clear. How maybe now, he knew a bit of how she used to feel.

When Everett stayed silent in response to her reasons, Rachael went for the jugular. "Don't know why you're so surprised I picked Colt. Only seemed fair that I got to fuck him too."

She set her purse on the table and produced a manilla envelope, then slid a single photo across the polished wood. In it, Colt was leaving their car, arms at an angle that could've meant rummaging in his pockets — but he was fixing up his belt. On the other side of the vehicle, Everett was staring at his cell phone, a look as guilty as anything clear on his photographed face. Where he sat in the kitchen, throat dry and breathing fast, he was certain of what was on that screen, of exactly what he'd been looking at and the woman it was from. Probably what sent Rachael after his phone in the first place.

Looking at *this* photo, it made a sick sort of sense that she'd picked Colt to blow their marriage apart for good. Two birds, one stone. Rachael was nothing if not practical.

"Is Colt just your work partner? Or something else?"

Everett still wasn't sure what to tell her.

* * * *

A blue van parked beside him, and the slam of a passenger door snapped Everett back to the present. This wasn't no average gas station they'd driven an hour to park at. He knew exactly where they were now. If he trekked into the overgrown woods beside the station, he'd find the trailer they used to stake this spot six years ago.

Damn it, Col. What are we doing here again?

Everett got out of the car and walked to where Colt was smoking. He leaned against the store wall an arm's length away and kept his gaze forward, but the view he got wasn't much better, lined up as he was with Colt's truck.

"See you've made a habit of bustin' that window," was all the mention Everett planned to make of it.

"Don't reckon that's it."

Everett swiveled his head. Now they were standing closer, he had a better view of just how ragged Colt was looking, how his clothes hung loose from a sickly thin frame. As if sensing his scrutiny, Colt walked to his truck, gathered a stack of legal pads in a backpack, then jerked his neck in that *c'mon then* fashion.

He followed Colt toward the woods and watched him pull a flask from his flannel pocket. Colt took a long drink before he asked, "So where you been?"

Dark eyes demanded *for so goddamn long.*

Everett swallowed hard. He knew better than to shrug and hitched his chin up. "Around. I'm not the one who fell off the map."

"Like you were lookin'."

"Could've been."

He watched Colt pick up the pace and finished the thought in his head. *Could've been a lot.*

Everett wondered at the Colt Harkan before him, all ash-faced and turning gray. He had the kind of strength now that reminded him of a willow, but Colt was never one for getting to keep his roots, and weathering decay was creeping red around his watery eyes. That ponytail of his made him look like a fucking pirate. The flask wasn't helping any of it.

Christ. He looks terrible.

Everett wondered how many threads Colt was clinging to, but didn't dare to ask himself the same. Staring in the face of what Colt had done to himself, at the proof of the sin he couldn't hardly name, all Everett felt was the old anger again.

Not like I asked for this. You come out of nowhere and kiss me like you got a right to it – like you know something about me I ain't never *thought to ask – and turn mad when I don't know what to do with you? Wouldn't let me into any manner of what you were thinking. All I could do was ask, then take or leave what comes.*

How'd you let her do it, Col? How'd Rachael fool you so easy? Why couldn't you, of all people, see she had our number sooner?

Why'd we only get one month that felt like home?

But Everett didn't ask any of that. He turned from Colt's gaze but got no kind of relief when his eyes found that trailer in the distance.

"Jesus, man..." He cleared his throat and tried again. "Of all places, why bring me here?"

Colt's eyes narrowed, cold and resolute. "We're here because we have to be. Now, you gonna stow your shit and let me solve this for you?"

And that about took the goddamn cake, busted any tolerance he'd built for Colt's high-and-mighty bullshit. Everett rounded on him, marched two steps into his space and demanded, "What'd you *ever* solve for me, Colt? What'd you do but bring big fuckin' problems down on my life?"

"Then maybe you should've stayed gone."

"You know why I called," Everett spat. "There's been action on this case, Colt—"

"Not the case. Us. Back then."

And with a nod to the trailer they'd both failed to ignore, Colt emptied his flask and turned tail to the store—apparently not willing to take this walk without provisions. Everett swallowed a yell as Colt stormed into the station, but weren't no stopping the memories now. And he couldn't help but wonder if Colt was thinking the same thing.

Chapter Eight

Everett
Louisiana, 2012, six years earlier

Everett's partner never cared much what was going on when he entered his office, though over time, even Colt learned to knock first. So when he blew into Everett's meeting with Major Stapes and assorted higher-ups — men that Everett would rather his least-personable detective *not* piss off — he stood immediately and met Colt's eye, bright with a lead.

"Rhett. We gotta go."

Colt was out of the door before he could ask a question further. It told Everett all he needed to know.

This is about that State Rodeo case. The one that got away.

He turned on the Lead Detective charm and made apologies to the brass. In five minutes flat, they were in the car, tearing down Louisiana roadways. After a long, silent drive to that address of Colt's, he eventually closed his notes and let Everett in on the lead.

"You remember that net I told you about? From the rodeo drive last year?"

"The drive you told me you destroyed? And wouldn't *ever* be looking at again?"

"That'd be the one."

"Shit," Everett cursed, but he couldn't help the smile that followed. Not when Colt started it, having the grace to look regretful, yet somehow, not a bit sorry.

"Well, we drove all this way." Everett sighed. "What'd I put my career on the line for this time?"

"I've been working six names that fit the same pattern as Combs," Colt told him. "Young people, mostly men. All members of different recovery groups and hired to work the rodeo as seasonal help. All reported missing, never found. I assumed they were dead, but I got a hit on a Mary Ann Sawyer a month back. Last known address had her living around here.

"I took her photo to a couple stores. A clerk at a gas station called and said she'd been gone a while, but started coming back not long ago. Looked real different too. Wouldn't talk to anyone."

"So what?" Everett asked. "Some missing broad shows up and we tear ass across the county to get here because..."

Colt's shoulders fell, like he was having to spell out more than he should. "Because I think Mary and the rest of my list wound up workin' the rodeo the same way as Combs. I think they were recruited. On purpose."

"For what?"

Colt clicked his pen. "Not sure yet."

"Got any theories?"

"None worth sharing."

Everett couldn't help but laugh. "So you wanna wait out here for some sob story to come through and answer your questions, just in case she's got a background like Combs? On a hope and a prayer she comes past today?"

"If you'd rather I do this alone, just leave. I can get back on my own." Colt thumbed through his legal pad, disappointment clear in his tone as he added, "Thought you'd care more about wrapping up Combs, though."

"And why's that?"

"Because if I'm right, then Richard Edwards knows a *lot* more about these people on my list. And with all that man is around here? The way you all just—" Colt cut himself off and buried his head in his notes. "Forget it. Drop me off and go."

Everett weighed his partner's words and let out a sigh. "All right, Colt. Where we settin' up?"

Colt spotted an old silver bullet trailer at the edge of the woods. Looked like it had been a fruit stand once upon a time, but it had a good view of the road and station both.

"Over there."

* * * *

A particular sort of douchebag moseyed into the station store, and after an hour's stilted silence, Everett let go a low chuckle. "You remember that time with—"

"The sunglasses?"

He grinned. "Exactly. Those fuckin' sunglasses. Who'd that guy think he was?"

Colt said only one word, but his tone conveyed all manner of disdain. "Aviators."

"His girlfriend seemed to like 'em, with the way they got to rockin' in that car of his. Couldn't hardly see the mark till they rolled out."

Colt stared out of the trailer window and took a pull from the Camel in the corner of his mouth. "Women always like things they've been told to. At least until they realize it some. Not their fault—we do the same. We're all following some programming or other."

Choosing to leave that observation alone, Everett nodded, but offered nothing else on the topic at hand. He kept his eyes pinned on the station when he finally asked, "How's Mira?"

His partner's back stiffened as the name landed between them.

Everett knew he'd have to be the one to bring it up. That was his to do, considering how their time together had ended last year. He'd known leaving Colt's place would be stopping certain parts of their…friendship. And he'd done it anyway. That made it his job to skirt the pleasantries friends were supposed to ask. To give the expected answers an ex never would.

Good thing they weren't *that*, then. Whatever they'd had wasn't official anything—except maybe evidence they were both officially insane.

"Mira's good," said Colt.

"What's she do again?"

"Prosecutor."

Everett snorted, unable to help himself. "Well shit, that'll do for you."

"She's lookin' to teach eventually. She'd be good at it."

And if it weren't like pulling teeth, Everett might find it in his heart to feel happy for them. He knew he didn't have to explain to Colt why dinners were often canceled, why work would come up last minute. Didn't help that Rachael was so proud of her little fix, to have a matchmaking venture with Colt go well after many failed attempts.

It shouldn't be so hard to just be happy.

But Everett had decided to be a man who kept his promises, and he knew it weren't much to put on some pedestal, but it'd been a God's-honest year since he'd so much as looked at another woman. He knew it wasn't a mistake he could afford to make again. Only reason Rachael had taken him back was for Gracie and Marcus. However terrible a husband he was, when Everett showed up, he was a pretty good dad. The kids were happy to have him home, and he was genuinely happy to be with them. Things with Rachael were stilted still, but getting easier every day. It took time for new habits to wear out the old ruts, but Rachael deserved that. He could do that. Everett knew he could.

None of that made it easier to see Colt and Mira together. Or to be sitting this close to the man now.

"Hold up," Colt said, raising his binoculars. "Ten o'clock."

Everett turned and saw a thin rail of a woman, stringy blonde hair half-pulled off her neck. She looked much older than her supposed years. "Is that your girl? Mary?"

Colt nodded. A faded-blue sundress trailed behind her as she walked. "According to the clerk, she comes past this time every couple days. Gets the same stuff and leaves. Always pays cash."

"You wanna follow her?"

"Not yet. She's in a routine here. We'll learn more by watching first."

Everett stretched his legs, already restless. "You wanna stake this place for how long then?"

"Weekend to start. Might need longer."

He snorted. "You'll be lucky to get half of that before Stapes is on our ass."

"Then stall him."

Everett shot a look at the trailer wall in frustration, then bit off his impulse response. "Why? You still ain't gone into anything resembling convincing detail."

Colt always sounded tired these days, but especially so as the man sighed his name. "Ev, at this point, you either trust me or you don't. What's it gonna be?"

Years of working with Detective Harkan shut Everett's mouth on the matter. Momentarily placated, Colt explained, "This might be a delicate psychological situation. Needs to be treated carefully."

That caught Everett's attention. "You think she's been...what? Kidnapped?"

"Maybe. I can only rule it out with time." Colt flipped his legal pad open as Mary left the way she came, plastic bag swinging from her hand. "So get it for me."

* * * *

Colt
Louisiana, 2012, six years earlier

It didn't take long once Mary left to set his plan with the clerk, just like it didn't take long for Ev to call Stapes and negotiate. Those isolated tasks took ten minutes of their first hour of surveillance, and thanks to Everett, they had forty-seven more to turn this lead around.

That meant a whole lot of the thing they'd been avoiding at all costs—extended time alone.

Colt might still be The New Guy in a town that never changed, but after three years on the job, he didn't need much supervision. Made it easier to keep the time they spent together on the comfortable side of friendship. These days, they worked more cases at their desks. Everett's office door and wall of windows were always wide open. Leads were run down alone. The car was difficult.

But eventually, even those tense silences eased into case talk—or once Rachael got a taste for them, confirming reservations for those double dates of theirs. Colt hadn't planned to fall for Mira on principle, but it seemed to help Rachael to know Colt was okay. Over the years, they'd found a polite-distance friendship that could stand to trade an evening of stories across a dinner table. Still, Colt didn't like to think what it might mean that Rachael found a woman to partner him so well.

Not to mention if Ev bailed on one more dinner, leaving him to make excuses to both women, then Colt would not be liable for his actions. He was starting to wonder why he bothered to ignore the heat between them at all, because it had never gone away, despite that long year of trying. At least before there was a benefit to the lying. Now it was just lying and going back to Mira's, pretending one kind of comfortable meant he didn't miss another.

"I know what this is, Col. Just don't know how to keep it any..."

Colt shook the memory away. Hadn't seemed to matter in the end—how he felt, how Everett felt. People could care for each other as deeply as they liked, but it wouldn't keep them safe. Often the opposite.

He breathed deep and slow to settle his senses. He could do this. Everett still had enough shame on him not to try anything, and Colt was doing his best not to let Ev endear himself with his stupid jokes, the way he'd stop and stare when he thought Colt couldn't see.

Yeah. He'd hold tight to his dignity — or failing that, spite. It weren't always good, but sometimes, petty had a point. Could serve as quite the reminder about making the same mistake twice.

And as Colt left the station store, he almost believed he could do it. Believed it till the moment he swung the trailer door open and a blond head swiveled his way, until Colt noticed the way seeing him warmed the blue of Everett's eyes, just for a second before he turned to the trailer window...*yeah, right.*

Maybe for a second Colt believed he could do this. But more of him knew he didn't want to.

* * * *

Everett
Louisiana, 2012, six years earlier

Everett cleared his throat as he turned to the trailer window, pointedly not watching as Colt sat on the floor beside him. The trailer's only bit of blank wall was only a few feet across, tucked between two rounded rectangles of glass. To Everett, it was like being stuck between two magnets. The way Colt was sitting with legs sprawled loose and one knee bent up, *inches* separated their feet, not the arm's-length chasm that held their shoulders apart.

"How're the kids?"

Damn, but Col must be doing worse than him if he was willing to talk about the family.

"They're, uh...they're good. They're both at the middle school now. Got play practice in the evenings. *Midsummer*, I think. Guess it's Shakespeare or whatever."

Colt lowered his binoculars and smirked, gone as fast as it came, but Everett knew what he was thinking. He asked anyway, "What?"

"Just tryin' to picture you following along to somethin' more than NASCAR."

"I'll have you know I'm running lines with them these days." Everett smiled. "Don't understand a word I'm saying, but I think Gracie likes correcting me as much as gettin' to hear herself talk. She's Helena."

"What about Mark?"

Everett laughed, only a little embarrassed. "Swear to God, he's playing some guy who turns into a jackass. Asked me to teach him how to imitate a donkey."

"Like father, like son."

He knocked his boot into Colt's, still smiling. "Shut the fuck up. Jesus, I hope not."

That was when he noticed...Colt wasn't looking out of the window anymore.

Everett really meant to move his leg. Didn't think it'd be so hard to make himself shift, to turn his ankle the other way and remove that bit of contact. They weren't even really touching, but knowing they could...the worn toe of Everett's boot held both men's attention. Suddenly, the trailer seemed exactly as small as it was.

Everett flexed his fingers as his eyes ran the length of Colt's leg, because maybe, he just wanted to see if Colt was gonna move first or...

He wasn't.

And Everett couldn't stop his arm from reaching all on its own. Before he knew it, he felt the rough seam of Colt's jeans on the outside of his finger, just the barest brush of denim and damn, but how was he gonna handle *two days* of this?

He closed his eyes. Two whole days with Colt. Maybe...maybe it couldn't be like it was. But once? They were owed a slide back, right? How different was it really from a three a.m. text from an ex — just looking to make things easy, since nothing was going to change the facts on the ground?

Everett took a shaky breath and blinked his eyes open, right hand skating the edge of Colt's calf, following the raised line over knee and thigh. And he was going to leave it there, had every intention of apologizing and pulling back, but Colt's legs slid open on a fractured sigh and it would take a man stronger than Everett to resist that kind of temptation.

Fuck it, then.

Everett slid a hand around his neck and pulled him close, claiming Colt's mouth with a kiss too right to refuse. And maybe he was a little drunk on permission, on the gift of Colt kissing him back so completely, his hands combing rough through dark wavy hair, the feel of Colt's tongue stroking his...or maybe it'd just been too damn long, because Everett couldn't stop the sounds escaping his throat, something closer to a whine than he'd ever admit to making.

God, it'd been a year. How'd he go without this for a *year?*

Because yes, Colt was kissing him back like he wasn't the only one to miss this. Like maybe Everett wasn't the only one who took too long in the shower, how the only thing that got him there anymore was picturing Colt on his back, not bent over in the backseat...

But before coherent thought was lost to the bliss of relief, there was a question Everett had to ask. The part of him too scared to stop, too afraid of living without again, fought his better judgment, but Everett remembered that night of too rough and now, he had to know —

"Colt. Why aren't you stoppin' me?"

It wasn't perfectly phrased, but he knew Colt would understand. Slowly, he regained awareness of where they were against the trailer wall. He was kneeling astride Colt's lap, leaning close to control their kiss. Colt sounded almost ashamed to admit what he was holding onto, but eventually, he answered the question.

Why aren't you stoppin' me?

He said low in his throat, "I don't know."

It was the first and only time he'd heard those words pass Detective Harkan's lips.

Need flooded down his spine and Everett shivered. He pressed a kiss to Colt's temple, unable to keep his voice steady. "I still...I still want this. Why can't we have this?"

Colt rested a hand on his ribcage, thumb tracing over the lines of his shirt. "Ev. It won't change things."

"I know," Everett told him. "But just...just for this job, huh? Once can't be so wrong."

Brown eyes slipped closed as Colt hummed, considering. Everett hid his face in the man's neck and braced for rejection, but he hoped that maybe, Colt was just as tired of worrying about right, that he'd let them just have this. Besides, things were different now. Colt had Mira. He had Rachael. Weren't nothing either of them would do to change that. This time.

He pulled back to look at Colt, lost in that faraway stare of his, like he could see it all rolled out, clear as a fucking picture. And Everett had to remind himself that crossed-wire projections were not prophecy, were not visions, had no ability to predict the future. Because something about how Colt looked just then...he couldn't help but think. However bad this was bound to end? It might still be worth it.

He leaned his forehead against Colt's and forced his hands still on the man's shoulders. "Col, just...just tell me, either way. Because I can't keep pretending this isn't killin' me. Not seein' each other as regular as we do. I just *can't*."

A warm sigh broke across his face, and Everett could tell he'd won. Colt groaned in defeat, slid his hands to the front of Everett's shirt and pulled hard on either side to heave him in to kiss.

God, yes. Colt...

There was a strength in this Everett had missed. Colt didn't ask—he *took*. The moment he decided to end their misery, Everett knew there was a list that could fill a few legal pads working in the man's mind, every action designed to drive him insane. Colt started with a kiss that hit like a freight train, working his jaw open to bring them closer still, tongue tasting deeply as he sighed. He caught Everett's bottom lip between his teeth, nipped and teased while Everett tugged at his shirt, desperate for the heat of skin beneath his fingers.

Because Colt wasn't the only one with a list he was trying to work through. This whole last year, Everett had kept track of too many things he'd missed, things he'd do if only given the chance. He kept finding more to add through too many sit-downs at his desk, always furniture between them, careful to keep apart. Like they knew at one touch, they would fall together.

Turned out, they were right.

So Everett wasn't shy about getting Colt undressed as fast as possible. And when he pushed Colt firmly against the trailer wall, kissing down his chest as Colt gasped for breath, he let his tongue sweep out to tease a nipple, tight with need...and *God,* but every hitch of Colt's breath, every swallowed groan was music to his waiting ears. He made quick work of Colt's belt and got him in hand, stroked the beaded wetness from the tip and down his shaft and yes — that sound, that thunk of Colt's head snapping back, the way he hummed and thrust into his fist...Everett couldn't help but smile.

Yeah. He'd missed this.

Colt was hard as he'd ever seen him, and Everett wondered if the car was as miserable for Colt as it was for him, for reasons other than seat belts that tasted like glass and asphalt. Everett knelt beside him, kissing down Colt's stomach, grazing his lips against the sensitive skin of his hip before he licked the head of his dick.

The way Colt moaned at that should be illegal.

Everett got his mouth around him and Colt rocked where he sat, hips rolling up and into the softness at the back of his throat. His eyes burned as he swallowed around him, but Everett didn't care about anything but the taste of him, how this one act of giving had him harder than he'd been all year — a fact that pushed to the forefront of his mind as Colt pulled open his belt.

Christ...just like that...

Colt stroked him in a move that spoke of history, someone who knew which buttons to push, how to brush thumb and knuckle around the sensitive head of his cock. He was almost glad they didn't have what they needed for something more drawn out. Impatience, desperation and a fair bit of downright giddiness had distilled into something too powerful to ignore, pushing them toward whatever release could be found the fastest.

Everett moaned around Colt's cock, deeper down his throat than was any kind of comfortable, but he didn't care. He'd had a whole year of comfortable and it was nothing, *nothing* compared to winning a hoarse "Fuck, that's good," from Colt's bitten-red lips. Colt refused to stop working Everett either, kept on though he had to reach to make it work, but nothing about this was for prying eyes. They didn't care how they looked, how ridiculous they probably sounded—like a couple of lust-drunk teenagers skipping off for a go in the woods. So Everett didn't stop his contented sigh when Colt's other hand fit around the back of his neck, guiding as he sucked, until Colt was pulling him up and away, visibly shaking.

"*Fuck*, Ev. Just...come here, already. C'mon—"

Colt caught his mouth in a kiss more brand than bruise, and Everett wondered if he'd have scars tomorrow from the searing heat of his lips. Colt barely let him get settled astride his lap before taking hold of both of them in the wide spread of one hand. Their mouths were engaged in a battle of wills, each daring the other to give it up first. And it seemed impossible to want Colt more, but as he broke their kiss, Colt licked across his open palm, holding Everett's gaze all the while.

His cheeks burned hot as Everett honed in on the only thing that mattered—Colt's mouth and just how exactly he made licking another man's hand look so goddamn natural. Everett watched, mesmerized, as Colt's tongue flicked over the lines of his palm, then his own. Desire pooled in his belly, his whole body tight like a coiled spring. Colt brought their readied hands to fist around them again and they slid together, fucking hard into joined fingers, racing toward completion.

As if only now realizing he'd never stripped off any layers, Colt's free hand fit under the back of Everett's shirt, pushing it up so their chests brushed together. And more than anything, it was the slide of that rough-heeled hand, steady up his spine, that sent Everett hurtling off the ledge, had him sucking hard on Colt's lower lip as he shuddered his release. He came hard across the other man's chest, spurring Colt into oblivion fast behind. They held close as hips jerked, arms falling around shoulders and backs of necks, lips brushing light over sweaty skin, unwilling to move despite the mess pressed between them. When Everett caught a bit of his breath, he couldn't help the laugh that bubbled up, though he couldn't really say what was funny.

He drew back to look at Colt and was glad not to have to explain. The same baffled contentment creased the corners of those brown eyes, like he was just as surprised as Everett that any of this could really feel this kind of good, that wrong didn't feel so wrong anymore. And maybe it was because they both knew what *once* meant, but Everett also thought that sometimes, a bone had to break worse before it set. Got to have the right parts beside each other for the body to heal what was wrong.

He'd never be able to tell her, but it helped to think that Rachael might understand, phrased that way. But if he was really being honest, Everett found he just couldn't care. If he could have Colt, even sometimes, then fuck the rest. It'd be enough. Rachael and Mira never had to know.

Colt wiped them off with his twisted-up undershirt, then pulled his button-down over his shoulders. He left it hanging open in deference to the heat — and the fact that Everett had yet to clamber off his lap. Everett did so and fastened up, deciding this silence wasn't as awkward as those first few, but also no kind of comfortable.

In time, Colt confirmed they hadn't missed the cashier's call. They settled in to watch for Mary, both sitting close to the same small window.

* * * *

Two hours past the forty-eight they'd negotiated, Colt's inability to let it go paid off. They watched from the trailer window as Mary stumbled past. She was in the store for the same amount of time and stumbled out minutes later. To Everett, she looked exactly the same.

But not to Colt.

The second Mary was out of sight, Colt was sprinting to the gas station, leaving the trailer door to swing in the humid air. Everett followed after, since apparently the need for quiet was gone, but even the chime of the store door didn't turn Colt's eyes from the checkout.

"What's that?" Everett asked.

Colt smoothed a hand over a torn bit of paper. "Contingency plan."

"And?"

But he could already tell it wasn't good. From the slump of Colt's shoulders to his fist on the counter, white-knuckled and furious...whatever this contingency was, it hadn't gone well. Colt told the cashier to call if Mary came back, but the way he said it, Everett wondered how likely that really was.

He followed a rage-silent Colt to their car, and it was a quarter pack of Camels before Colt managed to say, "Should've followed her. Shouldn't have tried to make contact."

Everett checked the rearview, then eyed his partner. "You wanna clue me in on what you're beating yourself up for?"

Colt flicked a smoldering filter out through the crack in the window, rubbed the heel of his hand over his forehead and pulled at the roots of his hair. He smoothed it back and looked to the road. "Told the clerk to give her a note. Just had her name on it. Wanted her to know that somewhere, someone knew who she was. I thought maybe she'd come out, look around for who'd wrote it."

"Makes sense. So what makes you think she's gone for good?"

Colt passed a scrap of yellow paper across the console. What was once Colt's looping print of *Mary Ann Sawyer* had been ripped in two. In the space below the tear was a short, shaky word, made of lines closer to the kid's younger years, when Everett's fridge was filled with stick-figure families.

Mary had written one word — *Run.*

He couldn't quite keep the awe from his voice as he asked, "How'd you know? She seemed the same kind of wandering crazy as that first time."

"She just...looked different. To me."

Colt hadn't said a thing to confirm it, but Everett wondered what it might be about Mary that kicked up old ghosts for his partner. Colt had been rubbing his arm since Mary left, fussing with the cuff of his right sleeve, trying to ease an ache centered on that red-winged blackbird of his. So Everett took a shot in the dark.

"It's okay that you wanted to help, you know. If she doesn't come back...weren't your fault."

"Maybe not," said Colt. "But it's someone's."

Everett sighed and settled in for a silent drive back. About twenty minutes from the station, he started thinking about home. Maybe he'd pick up something for dinner on the way, surprise the kids with burgers since he'd had to work all weekend. Rachael would probably appreciate not having to ask —

"Pull over a sec."

Everett noticed where they were, and the tension eased in his chest. Thanks to Mary turning up, they'd blown past any talk about those sweaty hours *once* had seemed to cover.

But this wasn't once. This would be again.

Thank God.

Before, a stop like this would've been a ten-minute detour. Now Everett knew that, this time at least, was about distraction, about ignoring something deeper that Colt might never want to talk about — and that was fine. Because he'd learned something else too.

Now, Everett knew he didn't have to know specifics to want to make it better, to give his partner the only escape he could. So if they spent just as long in back after the passion had passed, Colt tucked against his chest as his thumb traced checkerboard feathers...well.

Everyone deserved some comfort now and again.

Chapter Nine

Everett
Louisiana, 2018

"C'mon. There's things you need to see."

Everett turned and caught whatever it was Colt tossed his way, having assumed he was paying attention. Colt produced a flashlight from his bag then slung a strap over his shoulder, shining the cone of light down the darkening trail ahead.

The overcast sky had trapped the heat between the ground and the clouds all day. Everett was already sweating. He wiped his brow, then looked to his hand and found a pack of smokes. Cowboy-killers—his old brand. Not like a box of cancer sticks was some great olive branch, but it was something.

Colt stayed a few steps ahead as Everett pocketed the cigs. It was easier to ignore that trailer and all the rest the further they went down the trail. They walked for fifteen quiet minutes and Everett wondered how far these wilds went. He was about to ask when Colt broke the silence.

"I'm gonna guess on some things here."

"Yours are better than most. Have at it."

Colt pointed at a rundown structure a few hundred feet ahead. Everett nodded, keeping pace as best he could.

"I'm guessin' there's a list of things you're not supposed to tell me since I'm not police anymore," Colt said. "I'm guessin' Stapes made you call because he had to, and that no one of importance wants to so much as read my name again."

Everett snorted. "After the fit you threw when Mary popped back up, callin' every boss in the place a bunch of useless empty suits? Ignoring your suspension whenever it pleased you? And then *quitting* as soon as you got reinstated? When you was here on some favor in the first place?"

Colt pushed a branch out of his own way. "Like I said. I'm expecting you showed up with some red tape, but there ain't time for it, Everett. Never was, but 'specially not now."

"Why's that?"

"Because it's almost time for the hunt," Colt seethed, brown eyes hard as river stones. "And I'm not waitin' another year 'cause Mason's finest are playing catch-up."

Colt was far enough away that he'd have to yell, so Everett hoofed it to close the distance. "What're you talking about, *hunt*? Ain't the season yet."

"Your new vic Meyers, the body last week—"

"I didn't say nothin' about a body—"

"If you're just gonna lie, you can keep your mouth shut. Save us both some time." Colt paused his hike, pulled at his hair then tried again. "Late last week, you caught a body that had been skinned and marked, trussed up like a deer for slaughter and left on display at the rodeo. That right?"

Everett stayed quiet. Had to make sure nothing came pushing past his mouth in front of Colt. Hearing the scene laid out so plain brought the pictures up fresh in his mind —

"I know *why*, man. I know why she was recruited to work there, and I know why no one's seen her in weeks. Any of that sound important enough to break a rule or two? *Detective?*"

Colt wielded a look that might've once been intimidating, but there was a shake to him now that hadn't been there before. Everett was still sharp enough to catch the quiver in Colt's eyes, how a part of him might need this more than the booze and regret. At first, he was angry Colt thought he had the right, but that was just the shame. Nothing could've prepared him for how bad this hurt, having to face this version of Colt, the wreck Everett had made of the best detective he'd ever known.

So he swallowed it all down and followed Colt to a rundown building that, the closer they got, made less and less sense. That shack where Mary died was a mile off at least.

"It's not the same, but it's similar," Colt said, ever two steps ahead of him. "There's a few of 'em scattered around this patch of forest." He held the decomposing door open and handed Everett the flashlight. In a fit of self-restraint, he ignored the brush of Colt's fingers, grabbed the light and stepped inside.

This shack looked much the same as that dirt-floor number they'd tracked Mary to four years ago. She'd sat down in the center of the room and stared at the wall—for what then seemed like no good reason. Everett noticed there was a wooden chair in the middle of this room too. Seemed too specific to both scenes to be random. He sat down and aimed the light at the wall across from him. Without a word, Colt nodded and started tapping the wood, confirming the presence of a hollow panel they both knew to look for. Now.

He held the light steady and Colt slid the panel aside. A human skeleton rattled to the ground, a mess of dusty bones long past ID.

"*Jesus*, Colt—"

"I hadn't looked yet. Thought it'd be better to have a witness."

Everett put his head between his legs, bracing hands on either side of the chair's seat. The smell that escaped was evidence of the years it took to turn a human being to a pile of bones, and Everett tried to distract himself by thinking how they might find a name off dental records. They'd need to narrow the scope to have a prayer of—

"That's Eric Robins." Colt pulled a stick from the ground outside and hooked it through something Everett couldn't see. He tugged on a deteriorating strap and pulled a cloth messenger bag free. The time-brittle material snapped and it thudded to the ground.

The dust made Colt cough. "Bag was a present from his mother. Mentioned it in the description for missing persons."

"He one of those you worked off-the-record? The same list that gave you Mary?"

"And her brother."

"Brother?" Everett asked. "Her file said nothin' about siblings. No living family or next of kin."

Colt slid his fingers around the edges of the now-revealed panel, feeling for anything else that might trip. "Mary was in the system. They fostered together when they were young. Found each other again once they hit eighteen. If you look at rental history, she shared an apartment with one Elliott Caster for two years before she moved to a one-bedroom on her own.

"I'm not sure what separated them back then. That solo spot is her last known address. But if I had to guess...if Mary found her brother again, she wouldn't let him go anywhere on his own. Might've both wound up trapped."

"Trapped? By who? Colt, you're not making any sense." Everett rubbed his forehead. "What's any of this got to do with some rodeo?"

"There's something you never put together that you ought've about Combs. But you start lookin' close? It gets obvious." Colt pulled a plastic glove from his bag to paw through the broken satchel. There was nothing inside but a low-budget cell phone, probably long out of minutes, but Colt slipped it in plastic anyway.

"Start at the beginning," he said as he zipped the bag. "Patrick Combs, twenty-three years of age. New to town, addict in recovery and dealin' with Katrina fallout to boot. Got hired at the rodeo through a group called Heartland Staffing Solutions. They specialize in community service jobs, getting work to folks in need. Edwards' family businesses have worked with them for years. It's a publicity stunt that provides practically free labor for outdoor events, fairgrounds — "

"And the State Rodeo."

"Exactly. That's also how Mary's brother started working there. And if you'd let me see the file on Meyers, I'll bet she's the same. Most of the names on my list had a tie to Heartland that was *proactive*," Colt emphasized. "In all the stories I could trace, it was someone goin' out of their way to recruit them — telling them about a job fair, taking them out to lunch. For a temp agency gig. That sound right to you?"

"And you think that's Richard Edwards? That he's responsible for this?"

Colt leaned his back against the wall, having finished his inspection of the hidden panel. "For a time I did, but no. More likely it's someone in his business, maybe someone at the rodeo itself. Someone powerful, or someone close."

"That could be any number of people, most of whom are influential-type assholes who'd love to silence you for good."

"Why d'you think we're talkin' way out here? Out where they keep the bodies?"

Everett's head was spinning. The stench of death was heavy in the room. Was like to turn his stomach if he didn't get out soon. Yeah, he just needed some air —

Everett got around back before the breakfast he barely ate made a repeat appearance. He spat into the underbrush and leaned against the dirty shack. Staring into the foggy canopy, he thought about all Colt had said. Before long, the man himself appeared at his side, having followed the skeleton's hidden hall to exit out through the back. Another similarity to Mary's scene.

Colt offered a bottle of water and Everett rinsed his mouth. He drained the rest, took a few deep breaths and, for lack of other occupation, started packing those smokes against the heel of his hand. "Lay this out for me, Colt. One time, plain language. What d'you think is happening to the people on your list?"

Colt flipped his Zippo and Everett leaned into the fire, too shaken to begrudge himself the vice. Because for once, Colt answered his question in spades.

"I think someone in Edwards' business has been scouting people to work this rodeo for years. I think he's a predator who's been gettin' away with too much for most of his life, and he found a way to level up when he met more dangerous company. I think Patrick Combs stole a key he didn't recognize from a desk he did and wound up shot for his trouble. And I think the only reason any women are involved at all is 'cause this predator's gone from hunter to supplier, since 2013 at least."

Jesus fuckin'…

"How can you *possibly* think all that from anything you've found?"

Colt dug in his backpack and produced a file he wasn't supposed to have, the spitting image of the one labeled *P. Combs* in Everett's backseat. He handed his copy to Everett and lit up a cig of his own. At first glance it looked the same, but Colt's had an extra report at page two, a second autopsy with a different examiner's opinion circled in fine black ink.

"Combs wasn't a robbery," Colt said definitively. "And it weren't just a murder, either. He was assaulted."

* * * *

"You've got to have more proof than this to be makin' these sorts of claims, Colt. About anyone connected to the Edwards family? I mean…" Everett blew a hard sigh from his lips. Colt kept walking, but didn't refute the point.

Everett continued, "And I know, I *know* it shouldn't matter, but the fact it was mostly *men* that this guy...I mean, no one's gonna want to believe this. Even if it's true."

"You don't know the half of it."

After they'd tucked Eric's skeleton back in his closet for the time being, they'd returned to the trail and were now almost back to the parking lot. Colt was doing a better job keeping pace with him this time, though he looked more annoyed the longer Everett kept talking.

"I grew up in Mason, Colt. I think I know what I'm talkin' about."

"This is so much bigger than Mason. Or any small-town, small-minded shit. The Edwards family money's got legs. I tracked it through political campaigns in seven different states. Development projects in three. And that's just what was showin' up legally."

"How do you know?"

"Got plenty of proof at my office. On more than just the bodies and what's happening to these people," Colt said. "Didn't want to risk bringing it here."

"Why? You think I was gonna turn you in or something?"

Colt didn't answer right away, and Everett worried the man might think he was serious. He kept his eyes fixed on the approaching clearing as Colt slowed their pace to a crawl.

"Sorts of things I said to the bosses before droppin' off the map..." Colt mused. "Then this Meyers thing kickin' up, same spot as the case I wouldn't shut up about? Small-town logic's done worse deeds."

Everett stopped at the edge of the trees, that old trailer and both their vehicles just visible. He reached for Colt's arm and thought better of it too late. The briefness of the contact stung worse than if he'd never tried at all.

"Colt. It's me. You really think I'd do that?"

"Might've felt you had a right."

A hot breeze rustled through the trees, and the birdsong above them seemed awful loud. Everett wasn't sure who looked away first, but it was a close call. Neither of them seemed to be able to stand the weight of it — being here, looking at that trailer and Colt's busted truck, back working the case that had ended it all.

Colt sniffed hard and looked at the stars poking through the twilight. He didn't seem to notice how the wind caught his long hair, blowing loose strands about his face. "One last guess?"

Everett nodded.

"There's an open-and-shut option for your new vic, Meyers. A way it could all go easy. And you could let it, like Combs. Like who knows how many others." Colt cleared his throat, and the longer he talked, the more he sounded like his old self. "But if you're serious about putting this down for good, following this wherever — and I mean *wherever* it goes — then we've got three weeks before we miss this window. Three weeks or we have to wait another year till next season, and any bodies we find after will be on our heads.

"So don't say you're in unless you've made peace with a one-way trip. I'm not stopping at the bosses' say-so this time. Got enough fuckin' murders on my conscience."

Colt tossed an empty pack in the parking lot trash, then wound the plastic from another. He'd just reached his truck when Everett called out, "And what about you? If I let this solve easy?"

Colt's shoulders fell, but he squared up and pulled into the cab of his truck. "Me? I'll be workin' three weeks straight whether you show up or not. After that…sort of depends."

"On what?"

Colt didn't answer. He took a searching look down Everett's entire body, committing the sight to memory like it was his last chance to do so. And for once, Colt wasn't hiding behind a mask of indifference. He looked…*God*, but Everett didn't know if he'd ever seen Colt look this sad.

"Say hey to the family for me, Ev."

Phrased another way, he might've been too mad to catch it. But Colt's eyes were too flat for Everett not to see what was happening. If there was one thing he knew the look of, it was shame.

He watched Colt start up his truck, navigating the lot with mirrors so he wouldn't have to face him. And yet…

He called me Ev.

Colt drove away without a backward glance. Everett sat in their old car for too long before taking the same idea.

Chapter Ten

Colt
Louisiana, 2014, four years earlier

In the middle of some state-wide ceremony, the clerk he'd never expected to hear from again had called Colt's cell directly. Heads had turned fast at the buzzing that was just as loud as some ringer, and half-whispered grumbles of *"fuckin' Harkan"* rumbled around the room. When Everett elbowed him to turn that shit off, gave a gesture that meant no way was Colt to leave the room in the middle of the commissioner's remarks, he let it go to voicemail. But a text followed after, and when he'd read those two words, he couldn't believe he'd let Rhett guilt him into staying put.

She's back.

Colt was out of his chair before he gave a thought to standing, pulling Everett by the arm all unwillingly out of his seat. Proceedings truly disturbed, the commissioner had turned his attention to the back row and asked what was so all-fired important it couldn't wait.

So, Colt told him. "Kidnapping. Murder. Probably worse, if I don't leave now."

It wasn't the right thing to say. The truth hardly ever was.

Everett groaned beside him, stood the rest of the way up with a grumbled "Here we go," and started ushering him out of the room. "Shut your mouth and c'mon. There's fuckin' *press* here, man."

And that was about all of Everett picking which truths mattered that Colt was willing to take. He rounded on his partner, threw the guiding hand off his shoulder and stormed the stage, addressing the commissioner himself. "It'd be a goddamn travesty if someone outside this room knew somethin', hmm? Might mean we had to *solve* a case or two, ask questions that you all just want to ignore — "

"Harkan! My office. Now."

But even his grudging respect for the major wasn't going to quell this fire. He halted his march to the podium, thought better of where he wanted to spend his time, and strode up the aisle toward the exit. "Fuck this."

The crowd buzzed with different levels of shock, amusement and outrage. Stapes yelled above it all, "He's suspended, Kane. Starting immediately. Two weeks minimum."

Colt called over his shoulder, though no one had been talking to him. "You useless, empty suits. Two weeks without you all interfering? I'm like to have this solved for good."

Three days into his *at least two-week suspension*, he and Everett sat at a table across from Mira and Rachael, having had no good excuse to move their usual double date. Truth be told, once he and Ev picked things up again, the dinners were better. Whole thing felt like a script he'd memorized, but Colt knew his part and played it well. And over the course of those couple good years, something strange started happening. Colt found himself talking, not just listening, telling the kind of tales that only shook loose on some social excuse.

One time, Mira asked Everett about his family, and Ev had gone on about how his parents had moved downstate, helping out on the family farm once his grandfather had passed. It was a year last June, and maybe that still felt fresher than it should. In the quiet that followed, Everett turned the question to Colt, and he shocked the whole table when he actually answered. Pop was still in Texas on the empty acreage where he'd grown up. No clue on his parents. They'd spend most of his life missing anything that mattered, more faithful to their drugs of choice than the son they'd never wanted. But Pop was never one for leaving a man behind, though maybe growing up saying *sir* and responding to things like *c'mon soldier* set Colt on his course to do those tours overseas.

Another time, a failed night of coaxing Colt into dancing, Rachael had asked, "And outside of work? You don't do anything for fun?"

Colt said he used to draw but didn't share why, and maybe Rhett looked glad to have known that already. Everett admitted over a terrible-looking steak that he'd once considered journalism school, maybe wanted to be a writer of some kind. But his English classes never held his attention — too much reading. Essays weren't his game. After a story like that, since they'd met in college, Ev and Rachael would get to looking at each other, and Colt would watch the shadows of their former selves in their eyes, the shades of people who'd loved each other and were clinging to what pieces remained.

So even though they were in the middle of a stressful case that, thanks to Colt, had all manner of media attention, the four of them were at their usual table at their usual weekend spot. Because apparently, they had one.

Colt hadn't liked being away from the case, but being suspended, there was only so much he could do. He'd made Ev confirm at least five times that night there was round-the-clock surveillance on the gas station, ready to call at the first sight of Mary. Colt knew, whether Rhett would admit it or not, that whenever that call did come, his suspension would be called off with it. And the nature of the dinner had been amicable enough that he didn't feel too bad for saying it.

"You know you're gonna need me eventually, Ev. Stapes does too. You'll have to call and he'll have to reinstate me, and then we can get to doin' what needed to be done in the first place."

"What didn't get done that needed to?"

Everett had groaned at Mira's question. Rachael chuckled, and Colt tried to hide a smile behind his beer. His partner said, "Oh Mira, you don't know what you started with that question."

Mira had laughed, brown eyes sparkling. "Is that so?"

But for all they'd become the entertainment of the moment, Colt believed every word he was saying. "If we'd looked for more connections on the Combs case three years ago…"

"We found all kinds of loopholes to investigate Combs, if you'll remember, Colt—"

"For all the good it did—"

"And whose fault was *that*?"

"They're like some married couple, aren't they?"

Mira probably didn't expect her aside to Rachael to affect the whole table. Everett stilled at once, a hot flush on his cheek, unable to do anything but stare at Mira. Like she might've just told him something he didn't really know. And at that, Colt was looking for any reason to keep his eyes away, running tongue over teeth to hide the tick in his jaw. Three minutes later, Everett was making noise about a work call Colt didn't hear. Ten minutes after that, Rachael had similar excuses, though she traded the phrase "case files" for "patient notes".

The departure of the Kanes left him alone across the table from Mira, that long-avoided conversation stretching out like plans in front of them.

"What do you want from this, Colt? Really?"

After that talk with Mira, Colt couldn't help but wonder...if either of them had looked at *Rachael* after Mira's comment, maybe the rest might've played out different.

* * * *

Colt
Louisiana, 2014, four years earlier

Colt wasn't sure where Everett went when he left the restaurant, but after Mira's comment, it wouldn't be home with Rachael. Ev just had a knack for being exactly where he shouldn't.

It was a rare change of pace to have Stapes call *him* for the whereabouts of his Lead Detective, which meant Ev hadn't stopped by work. And by the time he and Mira were done talking over the inevitable, Colt could also confirm he wasn't at their secondary office, also known as his living room. He considered calling Ev himself, but it felt too much like begging to be lied to. He was getting enough of that from the chafe of his work suspension.

That really only left one place Everett could be. Colt didn't let himself think about it.

There wasn't much sleep to be had that night, so Colt rearranged the photos on his living room walls and puzzled over the case until dawn. Dawn when, heedless of his suspension, Colt snuck into the station for some of his stuff — and to confirm another theory in the process.

Colt was at his locker when Everett wandered in, but he didn't pause to talk. Didn't even mention the suspension. Just nodded and walked briskly to the other side of the row, undressing in the stilted hurry of one trying not to look as harried as they were.

So, Colt ran the experiment. When Everett tossed his phone and keys to the bench, Colt looked over like he'd just thought of something. He reached for Everett's cell and said, "Mine's dead. What time is it?"

His hand didn't even get halfway there before Everett spun around and scooped up his phone. Everett's eyes stayed on the screen when he answered, "Quarter past."

Like they didn't both know Colt could smell it on him. Like he'd be washing up here for any other reason. One casual observation had scared Everett into a night of cheap thrills, and all the while, Colt had been sitting there with Mira, talking around the truth and thinking *they* mattered...what a joke.

That would've been enough insult to injury for most people. But when the major found Colt at the copier in the records room and walked him out before the clock hit seven-thirty, harping on about the definition of suspended, he knew he'd need Everett to keep up to speed. That meant they'd be seeing a lot of each other in the off-hours. And Everett was, for lack of a better term, cheating.

Colt wasn't sure how mad he really got to be about that, seeing as Everett had always worn that ring on his finger, no plans to take it off unless forced. But in the days that followed, the hours spent at his apartment were stretching longer, and Ev was getting too comfortable calling home with half-truths about crashing at Colt's. If he was honest, he'd admit it was worse the nights Rhett didn't come past, leaving him to wonder if Rachael's bed was just as empty, if some unknown woman's was full.

The next time Everett stopped by after work, things went the same kind of usual. They reviewed the case and waited for updates about Mary. When nothing came, slipping into habits from that month long gone was too easy. By ten p.m., they were both sitting in his bed, which thanks to Mira's time in his life was now on a proper frame, watching the TV Colt had deigned to purchase a year ago.

And Everett? In the middle of all this? Was watching some professional rodeo show.

Apparently all it took was staying at the case-wall too long for Rhett to decide he could watch whatever he pleased. And maybe, Colt was a bit amazed at the audacity of the man beside him — stretched out cozy in

Colt's bed like he wasn't some married father, like he wasn't fucking around with some easy excuse on the side, like it might be some kind of normal thing at all to make a comment to Colt about the television.

Everett gestured at the screen with his beer, where a bull had tossed its rider. "Useless, most of these young guys. Their game plan doesn't work? They got no idea where to go. Most of 'em panic and bail."

"You don't say."

Everett sipped and nodded once, ever unaware of his own patchwork wisdom. "Can't force an animal to be anything but what it is. Wild, unpredictable. You pick your plan right, and yeah, you might get away lookin' like the rider. But sometimes, that bull's ridin' you. All you can do is hold on and hope."

Colt grunted in response, and finally had to admit he was angrier about Ev's side-project than he'd realized. Because the only thought in his head was *now there's an idea.*

Everett didn't notice when he rose from bed to shower, didn't notice Colt leaving without grabbing clothes at all. This wasn't a *think deep thoughts* shower, or a *mull the case over* shower. This was about remembering who he was — someone who'd always had too much wild in him. And maybe, reminding Everett in the process.

Colt returned from a shower of mountain mist naked as the day he was born. He pulled a bottle from the nightstand and set it down brusquely, the gathering of necessary tools. He pulled a condom too, where maybe he wouldn't before.

Rhett turned at the slam of the drawer. He muted the TV. "What're you —"

"Shut up."

Ev's spine went stiff where he sat in bed, but Colt was pretty sure his partner knew what was happening. Everett's expressive face, while eager, was also conflicted. Like he knew he was being rewarded for bad behavior, but wasn't about to argue.

And that confirmed it for Colt. Because shit, he had to do something. It was too hard keeping on like life was the same when everything was falling to pieces around them. There was no work to cling to, no Mira to tease with, no way Colt could let himself get lost in Everett when…when he was so attached to old habits.

"They're like some married couple," Mira had said.

Well, not for long.

Colt slicked his hand and ran a fist over his rising erection, holding eyes with Everett all the while. He pumped the bottle again and reached around, doubling down on his work in the shower, then dropped his gaze to Everett's hand. He was still clutching the remote in his lap. Colt blinked slowly at him, making it clear exactly was needed. Everett shoved the blankets off and pushed his pajamas down, providing all the proof Colt needed about that bit of wild that thrived in Everett too.

Blue eyes darkened like a gathering storm as Everett shouldered off his shirt, but Colt was never one to change course for some thunder. Rhett wanted someone to follow him down the rabbit hole of bad decisions? Well, that suited Colt fine. For tonight.

Colt knelt on the bed and settled over his partner's lap, hit hands away to fit the condom over Everett himself then fisted them both together. Both men shuddered as they rocked against each other. Ev leaned close to kiss him but Colt pulled away, forcing his partner to chase after. Their lips skimmed light in the humid space between mouths. Ev breathed a laugh and got a hand around Colt's back, steadying them both as Colt raised up to take him inside — all at once.

Everett choked out, "Holy *fuck*. Easy now…"

But that weren't the point. Never was.

And Colt would never be the one to tell him, because some things a man had to figure for himself, but while it was his opinion that while Everett Kane might not be some full-time homosexual, neither was he cut from a husband's cloth. Rachael could stitch whatever pieces she liked to him, try to pretty him up, but Rhett was always going to be what he was. Impulsive. Driven.

A thorn in my goddamn side…

Colt settled in for a hard ride, meeting fiery blue eyes in a declaration of war, daring the man beneath him to do anything but sit there and take it. Everett tried to pull him close, to kiss the side of his neck, but Colt arched and rolled his head away. Ev tried again and reached for his cock, pressed to the wet expanse of his torso, but he swatted him fast with a definitive smack, and Ev pulled a hand away, stinging.

"Col…c'mon, I wanna —"

"You want to *what*?"

Colt rolled his hips with practiced precision, like he could pull this answer loose with the stuttered jerk at the end of each thrust, the way Ev was catching and sliding inside him. Instead of answering his question, Everett tried another tactic.

"Are you…I mean, I want you to —"

"Like you care."

He shoved Everett back to the mattress and pushed off his lap, ready and willing to leave Ev on the precipice until he caught some sense.

"Where you goin'?" Everett asked.

"Where I please. It's my apartment. *My* fuckin' bed."

Colt shoved to his side, but Everett caught his ankle quick, curled strong fingers around his calf and yanked him toward the headboard.

"That a fact?"

Colt tried to get back on top, but Ev was faster, up on his knees with a hand on Colt's back before he had much to say about it. Colt tried to ignore the heat burning down his spine, but Everett's touch had always felt too much like sunlight to keep from arching into it. So for a moment, he abandoned his plan and let Everett take control.

Ev's hands slid down his shoulders and arms to set his wrists. He ran calloused fingers down Colt's back, around the swell of his ass, the slickness at his rim. When Ev lined up to take him again, neither man could bite back a moan as Everett slid home. Rhett gripped his hips like he could mold flesh with his fingerprints, twisted his torso to fuck into him deeper, hitting that spot that made Colt go a bit boneless. And when he spoke, Everett sounded like he did after that case-frenzied bull ride, carrying on about what he might show him sometime.

"Don't act like it don't get lonely here without Mira keepin' you company."

The accusation stirred him from the summer-warm haze in his head and Colt pushed back—hard. "You really want me to answer that?"

"Maybe," Everett stuttered. "Maybe I do."

Everett slowed his thrusts, but he was grinding against him perfectly, pressing forward with his hips until Colt was choking off a whimper, biting his own forearm enough to bleed. But a hard fuck and *maybe* wasn't going to cut it tonight. Not after five years of wondering, of never calling this shit what it was...

"Not good enough," Colt told him.

"I'll show you good enough."

And fuck him, but for a moment, Everett did just that, and he let himself imagine that Ev meant this the way he seemed to think, that his conviction wouldn't fade with the rush of intoxicants produced by exertion like theirs. Everett had always been a dopamine fiend. It was the fall that fucked him after.

So he only let himself imagine for a moment, then locked the thought away in a memory chest full of all kinds of heartache. Ev kissed down his back, tried to hide how he was moaning Colt's name over and over, and at the dangerous jolt of hope that followed, he forced himself awake and took charge again. Everett might be on top, but the man claimed to know how to follow.

Let's see him try.

"Col...Col, you gotta...god*damn* it, man—"

It wasn't long before Everett couldn't be folded on top of him quite the same, not the way Colt rolled and bucked beneath him. Colt fisted his hands in the sheets, gripped the mattress edge between his fingers, desperate to make Everett feel every bit of what was here, if he'd bother to see it. Ev's breathing grew ragged, and something caught between a laugh and a groan escaped. Their pace grew faster and frantic as Ev pressed a hand low against Colt's body, low enough that he wondered if Ev was feeling himself on purpose, buried deep as he was on every stroke. And Colt had managed to stay nearly silent so far, but damn it, this might break him after all.

"Fuck *off*, Rhett...just take what you want already."

The room tinged blue and faded as Everett seized behind him, harsh fingers gripping his hips as he cried a frustrated sob. Like maybe Ev had gotten the message after all. He rolled onto his back in haste and blinked at the ceiling, chest heaving. Colt stroked himself to finish fast and stood shortly after, snagging one of Rhett's undershirts from the growing pile on his floor.

Colt schooled his face as he cleaned up and turned to face the bed. He tossed the dirtied shirt at Everett, then palmed his smokes from the nightstand. He was pulling into sweatpants when something *buzz-buzz-buzzed* on the floor.

Guilty blue eyes didn't dart to the cell immediately, but the crease of his crow's feet and the blush on Ev's cheek told Colt all he needed to know. He worked his jaw, damn-near awestruck at how careful Rhett was not to break their staring match, like doing so was admitting defeat.

Colt gestured in his direction and said, "You should take care of that."

Before he could reply, Colt went to smoke outside, leaving Everett to decide if he was talking about that rubber at all or the phone buzzing sharp through the silence.

* * * *

Colt didn't brave the bedroom until he heard Everett's light snoring, and in the morning, Ev was up before the alarm had the chance to ring. Being suspended and deciding to give a fuck, Colt spent the morning with the beers in the fridge and ran himself in case-circles all day.

Everett came past at lunch, but it was a ten-minute bit of work talk in the living room before he was alone again. For the rest of the afternoon, Colt wondered if Mary was ever coming back, or if they'd already missed their shot at solving Combs. Maybe something else too.

Early that evening, Rachael called about a dinner at the house he'd forgotten about. Colt broke the news that Mira wouldn't be around anymore, and Rachael shouldn't take it too hard, being the one who set them up. Sometimes, things just didn't work out.

She sounded sad to hear it and invited him to come past anyway, brushing aside his objections by insisting he and Everett needed a break from "*that case on the news*." He could almost picture the resolved tilt of her head as she chided him through the phone.

"I'm suspended, Rachael."

She snorted in amusement. "Like you're not still working it. Dinner's at eight."

Chapter Eleven

Colt
Louisiana, 2014, four years earlier

"Where's the children, Rachael?"

A yellow light clicked on as she peeked through the oven door, then added some minutes to the timer. "My parents' for the weekend. Things have been so crazy since that case reopened. Thought a little space might be good for everyone."

It was a plausible explanation, but not a comfortable one. With one word, Colt asked a larger question. "Everett?"

"At the station, working. So I'm told." Rachael raised her eyes to Colt's, and he could tell how little she believed it. "Not like you'd know. Being suspended and all."

It changed things, being alone with Rachael in an empty house. Only reason he'd agreed to come was for the hope of talking to Ev about Mary, since Stapes had officially cut him out of the loop on his own damn case.

The longer surveillance sat on that gas station, day after Mary-less day, the less inclined the major was to be lenient if this didn't turn into the big deal he'd promised.

Colt fished his pack from his pocket and gestured toward the door. "We can do this another time if — "

"It only needs another ten minutes. Might as well stay, or take a plate." Rachael shot him a playful look. "We both know you won't eat otherwise."

Even for Colt, that was a long time to stand outside ignoring what was going on here. He kept the width of the kitchen table between them and thought on what was best to do.

"It's not necessary," he tried.

"Have you eaten today at all?"

Colt shrugged and she smiled. "It's fine, Colt. Just stay."

From where Rachael stood at the counter came the distinctive *pop* of cork from a bottleneck, the stuttered glug and splash of liquid filling a glass. She turned with an empty in hand and set it down in front of him, eyes flashing as the heavy bottle *clunked* on the table.

He said, "I don't drink wine," and hoped she'd leave it there.

"Suit yourself." Rachael collected her glass from the counter and leaned on the wall across from him. She sipped her wine. "Did you know? That's he doing it again?"

"Doin' what?"

Rachael's look of *don't lie to me* was almost as good as his own.

"I went through his phone. Saw the pictures she sent."

Colt closed his eyes and tried to freeze his face. Rachael kept talking.

"You were married before, right?"

He blinked his eyes open. "Once. Short sort of thing."

Rachael took another sip — and two steps around the table. "You ever cheat on her?"

There was no good answer to that, but in the way Rachael meant? "No."

"You're a better man than Everett," she said, trailing closer, staring into his eyes as she moved into his space, planting her bare foot between his laced-up boots. Colt tried to look up and over her head — and not down her low-cut sundress. His pulse beat loudly in his ears. She smelled of cotton and clean soap. Good things. Hardy things. Nothing like the fire that was dancing in her eyes.

"I think you're settin' a low bar of comparison," he told her. "Rachael, what're you doin'?"

She set her wine on the table beside them, letting loose four words that held the grief of too many years. "What's *wrong* with me?"

At first, he was too pissed at Everett to remember what Rachael was after. Because it was Ev's avoidance making him have to explain this to her, and it weren't even the piece he was a part of. Damn, but did Rhett know how to hide from his fuckin' problems.

"Nothing's wrong with you. Don't blame yourself for his bull."

"Sounds like you know."

Wasn't like he was feeling all that fond of Everett himself at present, but Rachael's tone suspected too much to have chosen those words on accident. So Colt remained silent and hoped she'd steer them to safer territory — or at least to a different kind of dangerous.

Rachael didn't disappoint. She ran tentative hands up the front of Colt's flannel, then slowly down, testing how far he'd let her go as she said this to someone.

"They're all so much younger. Fresh faced, unbroken by the world. I used to be like that, Colt. Used to have hope, aspirations. But I'm not that person anymore."

"Ain't a thing wrong with you."

"Prove it."

Colt counted the bumps in the popcorn ceiling, leaned away as much as he dared when warm lips kissed up his neck...and wished it didn't feel so good. Wished it didn't feel like being understood. But it was too late to pretend he didn't know what this was at the absence of children's laughter. She kissed him first, had to hold him still to manage it, and it was stuttered and awkward and strange — not because Colt didn't want it, because a sad, lonely part of him did. To tell her no would only confirm the fears Everett had instilled. It would be better to stop her, but it wouldn't be a kindness.

So a part of Colt hoped she'd be done with a kiss, that she'd leave them both with a bit of dignity to be getting on with. That maybe all she needed was confirmation to get her courage up, maybe leave Everett on her own. There was enough about Rachael that Colt found attractive to not pretend on *that* score. So he kissed her back, and he could taste her soft *yes* against his lips, like it was all she really needed. At first.

When he tried to pull away, Rachael wasn't having it. "Please," she whispered. "I just want to forget. Forget I ever let him change me like this. Made me live out this made-for-TV movie of a marriage, just to leave me anyway."

That rang far too true to think on. Colt looked in her eyes with a detective's scrutiny and read her motive, plain as day. Rachael wasn't looking for rescue. No, Rachael wanted to drown. And after last night, Colt felt too much like the tide to keep from crashing his mouth into hers.

And sure. Maybe it appeased some other part of him to give a different Kane a taste of his own medicine.

It wasn't sweet. They were hasty and rushed. Hands grabbed too tightly, pushed clothes aside too messily. Teeth scraped in their clattering kiss as Rachael's soft chest pressed against his front. She tore a bit of nail scraping at his belt, but Colt was no better, peeling aside layers of floral and lace, pushing her hard to the table before he entered her, fast and fumbled from behind.

It wasn't about feeling good. It wasn't about making sure anything happened in the proper order. Because the way she directed him, Rachael just wanted to stand there and take it, to know she was being used on purpose for once — but not by Colt. By herself.

For a few fractured minutes, they clung fast against the table, hips rocking together as Rachael ground against him. And when the oven timer went off as Colt seized silent behind her, she let loose a moan that sounded like salvation. Like maybe, she was finally free.

He caught a glimpse of their tangled reflection in the opaque black of the oven, shining like polished obsidian.

Jesus fuckin' Christ...
What had he just *done?*

He couldn't look at himself without tasting bile, had to turn his gaze to keep from shouting or worse. Colt shoved away from her exposed backside, couldn't watch as Rachael rolled lace up her legs and under her falling skirt.

What were they *thinking?* How could he do this to Everett? To *them?*

How could he look in a mirror ever again?

"I'm sorry," she whispered, pulling at her dress. "I didn't…I tried to do this some other way, but…I didn't think I could with a stranger." Rachael's tone was different from the syrupy sad-and-blue from before. This sounded calculated. Edged with diamond and slate.

It didn't happen often, but Colt could tell when he'd been played. Unable to believe she had this depth of hurt in her, that she'd use either one of them like this, Colt dared her against the wall with eyes dark as pitch, violence in his body he wouldn't ever let loose, but he wasn't afraid to scare with it some. Not after this.

"The *fuck* are you sayin' to me, Rachael?"

Her tears fell freely, and Colt wondered if she knew the true cost of what she'd done. But she'd paid it anyway, cashed him in to do it. She'd planned every part of this, and now, Colt was an accomplice to her crimes. Accessory after the fact, but he doubted Ev would care much about that.

"He'll just keep doin' what's easiest. You know he will," Rachael pleaded. "I had to do something. Because *this?* He won't stand for it."

Colt wanted to shout in her face, force her retreat, thought maybe if he screamed loud enough, fast enough, the shame would leave when he did. This was next-level stupid for so many reasons, but he couldn't swallow down the hurt as he stared at her, trapped between his hands against sunny yellow walls — the ones he'd helped them paint last summer. The straps of her sundress were still falling off, and Colt found himself disgusted with what reflected in her hazel eyes.

She was terrified. Vindicated. A Valkyrie throwing herself on a pyre and *Jesus*, but Colt didn't sign up for this shit. He was many things, but he wasn't a sacrifice. And maybe if he'd kept to silence, refused to have the last word, he could've walked out of the world of the Kanes' marital drama and good fucking riddance anyhow.

But he never did learn to keep his mouth shut.

"Rachael, you just ruined your life. Blown it all to shit."

She shook her head, like it was Colt who was slow on the uptake. Like she pitied him in all this. "We'll see how you do, when you go looking for fidelity. And you can ask yourself...are you the only? Or the first?"

And Colt felt it in a way he couldn't ever explain — that was the moment Rachael knew. Which meant somehow, he'd been the one to give it up, that this proximity of a pity-fuck would be evidence someday in the court of Everett's indiscretions. He wracked his brain for any sort of response when he heard a sound that couldn't be real. There was no way. Not now.

He'd never been one for prayer, but Colt wished hard as he could that what he'd heard was the start of a crossed-wire episode.

Thunk.

Behind him, another bottle hit the table.

Then strong hands were on him, ripping him from Rachael at the wall. Before he could register the sight of blazing blue eyes, the world spun white, and a punishing blow knocked him into the dark.

* * * *

He was only out a few seconds. A brief respite in the void. As he came to, Colt's face was pressed against cold kitchen tile. He wished the floor would swallow him whole.

Ev...I'm so sorry...

"What did I just walk in on here, Rach? Gonna need you to be clear on that for me."

Colt heard the question Everett was really asking, but even through his ringing skull, he knew it was never a card she'd play. Rachael made every choice tonight to bring them to this conclusion, whether she thought her husband would be stopping by or not.

"You know what it was, Everett."

She sounded stronger than she had since that parking lot three years ago.

"How could...*how* could you—"

"How could *I*? How's your girlfriend tonight? Decide to drop by the wife's to unwind for once?"

Colt blinked in and out of consciousness, but he heard Rachael's bare feet padding over tile, a bottle lifted and set. "Guess I should be impressed you got the right brand. This time."

"Rach, stop...just, what's goin'—"

Buzz-buzz. Buzz-buzz.

The vibrating chime of Everett's phone echoed in the kitchen. The smell of lasagna hung thick in the air, and it should've been a homey scent, comforting and fond, but Colt tasted cinders and gasoline—smelled fumes just as oppressive.

He heard a rustle of fabric, coins in a pocket, then Ev's brittle voice demanded, *"What?"*

From where Colt laid on the floor, he could see the change in how Everett held himself, how the tension shifted from the rage of attack to the ticks and flexes of attempted control, some outside force being brought to bear on what would otherwise be a goddamn fistfight.

"Yeah. He's with me. On our way."

The call ended and the whole room waited, silent as a budding storm. Everett didn't look at him when he said, "Mary's on the move. Stapes will text you the address."

"Ev, listen—"

"Do not. Fucking. *Speak* to me."

Everett kept his eyes on Rachael as Colt got to his feet behind them both. The sound of him finally doing up his zip shook the house with each metallic stutter, but there wasn't any good alternative. Ev blew a sigh from his mouth too much like hyperventilation, wrapped a hand around the bottle he'd brought for nothing and walked out his own front door.

Rachael's look of shock was too complete to be fabricated, but that was a small consolation. Colt could hardly stand to look at her tear-stained, kiss-rough face, knowing all he'd done to help bring them to this conclusion. How'd he let this—

Smash.

The melodic clatter of breaking glass pulled both their eyes to the driveway. Rachael's instinct was the same as his and they both moved to the door—but Colt wasn't sure that was a good idea. The kind of anger, betrayal, and hurt rolling off Everett? Wasn't anything logical.

"Stay here," Colt told her. "And maybe...lock the door."

* * * *

His truck looked like a crime scene.

Greenish bottle glass mixed with the crunched white of the driver's window. Blood-dark wine pooled in the seat and footwell. He watched Ev smash the sideview for good measure, but the force was too much for the broken bottle in his fist and he tossed the shrapnel to the lawn.

Everett was picking glass from bleeding knuckles when he spotted Colt, expressive face contorted in pain. He shook his head quickly and turned for his own car, walking fast as his legs would carry him. Colt had to jog to catch up.

"Rhett, just *wait* a minute —"

Everett rounded on him and swung hard with his left hand, his dominant being full of bloody fragments, and that was likely the only reason Colt managed to take the blow standing up. He caught Everett's arm when he went for a second swing, trying to force his body to come down from the shock. If he could get to the part of the man who might listen for a fucking second —

Everett threw him off with a yell but bit off the rest. He swiped his eyes with the back of his good hand and looked for distant neighbors. Even with the sprawl of the subdivision, the commotion Rhett was making was the sort that, if he weren't police himself, might've sparked some calls from concerned citizens. His breath came fast and heavy, and when he seemed to catch enough of it, Everett murmured in a voice so low that Colt could barely hear.

"Keep your hands off me, Colt. Do not. Fuckin'. Touch me." Rhett's voice caught in his throat. "*Ever* again."

One tear caught the glint of porch lights as Everett turned away. "*Jesus*, I can't even look at you right now."

Colt followed anyway, slow and distant behind him. Something sharp as a hook pulled deep in his chest, and Colt trailed after like so much fishing line, a tether he'd never be able to cut and would always be pulled back toward. He watched Everett get in the car and slam the door shut, could almost feel the weight of his shuddered sigh as Colt stopped by the passenger-side.

Ev stared through the half-lowered window — what used to be *his* window — and Colt had to turn away. When he looked again, the man in the driver's seat was Lead Detective Kane, and he wasn't in the mood for insubordinate bullshit.

"Get to the scene and do your job, Harkan. You're reinstated. Major's orders."

He rolled the window up and backed out of the driveway alone.

* * * *

Louisiana, 2018

Back in his office parking lot, Colt slammed the door of his truck. His storefront wasn't much to look at, but the mini-mall landlord was happy to rent to anyone with cash in hand and he didn't pitch a fit about Colt shacking up in back. Most of the other units were empty, but the streetlights still clicked on at night. Only one worked at present.

Once inside, Colt found a bottle of whiskey that—thank fuck—had a bit left. It kept the taste of battery acid and juniper from overwhelming his senses, the taste of that solo drive to Mary's scene. He'd never been a gin man in any of his many lives, but he'd sworn off the stuff since that night four years ago spoiled all enjoyment of the flavor. Of so many things.

Colt stared hard at the case-wall, the one he'd moved from station to apartment to office and over again, but never seemed able to solve. He let his eyes unfocus, let them skip over the photos and settle on the worst of it, the one death in all of this he should've been able to stop.

Mary. This all hinged on Mary. There was something about her they missed, or else why would he—whoever *he* was—bother killing her? After keeping her alive so long? Colt shook his head. It didn't matter now. Mary would still be just as dead either way.

They were too late.

By the time he and Everett arrived separately to the scene, it was already over, though they didn't know it yet.

* * * *

Louisiana, 2014, four years earlier

Surveillance had tracked Mary to a shack much like Eric's today, and they huddled a hundred feet away, briefing Stapes and other late-comers on the situation. Mary sat in a chair in the center of the room—entirely silent, staring at the wall. According to the cops on duty, she'd walked from the gas station forest and deep into the wilds. They'd followed on foot and passed a couple similar structures, but hadn't seen anyone else.

Colt was about to go in when the shot went off. Him and Everett both had their heads on a swivel, scouting for where it must've come from, because it *couldn't* have been from some empty shack. Mary didn't have a gun, she was sitting there alone —

"Detectives? Where'd she go?"

Shit.

Colt whipped his head to the cop asking the question, then over to the shack. Mary was no longer visible in the window. But a growing puddle of blood was.

He ran in first, Everett fast behind him. Mary laid on the ground, slumped over from the chair, face down. The bullet had gone straight through her chest and she was bleeding out quick. Everett took one look and was back out of the door, yelling, "We need an ambulance here. Now!"

Colt eased his arms under her neck and back, gently turning Mary over to lie more comfortably. He heard the other cops circle them and secure the room, searching for her attacker and finding no one. Confusion flashed in her fading eyes. A tear rolled down her face.

"Run...run..."

"Run *where*, Mary? Who you runnin' from?"

Mary shook her head and coughed up blood, spattering Colt's shirt. He pressed his hand into the wound, tried to stymie the bleeding till the ambulance could get there — but where they were in the wilds, they'd have some ground to cover. Not like there was easy road access. A boat might actually be faster.

But Colt knew it wouldn't matter how they sent for help. Mary was dying. The least he could do was witness her final words.

"Run...they always...run, E..."

The life left Mary's eyes as she gave up her final sigh. Everett ushered the other cops out. Colt brought a hand to her face. He closed her eyelids, gently. He lay her body on the dirt-packed floor and watched her blood soak the earth, the only mark Mary was like to leave on this world.

Mary...I'm so sorry...

The other cops were smoking outside while Everett talked to the major. He was already running damage control, like wasting everyone's time was the worst thing to happen that night. Colt shook his head and left the shack, determined to pull every bit of intel from surveillance, whatever it took. No way he'd waited this long just to meet with another dead end.

He marched up to the nearest uniform and hit the cigarette out of his hand. "Y'all *missed something*. Who followed you?"

The cop squared up and stayed in Colt's face. "Screw you, Harkan. Nobody followed us. There's nothin' out here for miles."

"Then explain why there's a girl inside with a bullet stuck in her chest. You fuckin' stupid? I need to spell it out for you – "

"Harkan. Ain't their fault."

And yeah, it might've been Everett's job to cut in, but it wasn't a *bit* his business – like them showing up late wasn't on his head too. Colt turned to Everett in a mockery of manners, drawing all attention to them.

"I'm sorry, *Detective*. Whose fault would it be exactly?"

Everett worked his jaw and pushed his sleeves up, jacket and all. He tightened the scrap of cloth around his knuckles. "Need to step on back, Colt. Immediately."

"We should've been here, Ev. Should've got here faster—"

"You want to do this now? Really?"

"Why? Make it better that the neighbors won't see?"

"Watch it, Col—"

Stapes tried to intervene, hands extended. "C'mon now, Harkan. Kane. Get a hold of yourselves—"

But neither man was in the mood for the major's good advice. Colt could tell Everett was about to snap. That rage he'd tempered back at the house was breaking every chain he'd used to lash it down.

"You wanna blame me for this? After what you did to me? Fuck you."

The truth burned in his throat as he sized his partner up. Colt knew what a terrible idea it was to keep talking, but hell if that weren't the point. Maybe he wanted a reason to hurt this *bad* that came with a bit of bloodshed. So he pushed that one step further and said as much as he dared with such an audience.

"Finally found what it was you wouldn't stand for, hmm? Good to see you commit to something."

Lead Detective Kane turned on his heel and stormed away.

But Ev circled back, dropping phone, keys and gun from his belt, shucking his jacket as he hauled off in a sprint. There was time to move or stop him. The others were too shocked to see it coming, but Colt didn't move a muscle. He stared his partner down and spared a thought for that savior of Everett's. The morality of allowing one's own demise.

Never would've caught his breath again if he hadn't.

Rhett took him down hard, but it was a wild thing not meant to last.

You knew that when you let it start. When you let it go too long. Take the lumps you're owed —

After a few more blows, Colt managed to stand, self-defense kicking in without conscious thought. He caught Everett by the arm, fought the instinct telling him to break the limb in two —

But Colt didn't want to hurt him. So he hit him instead.

He hooked a fist into his partner's bloody cheek, stumbling Everett back to land hard against the ground. His head cracked loudly on an oak's veiny root, and the silence that followed was immediate for Colt — like cotton in his ears he couldn't pull out. The rest was a blur of dirty leaves and a stink like chlorine and regret.

Colt was the first to get to him, fearing a fractured spine. "Stay put, Everett."

Please.

But Ev was always made of stronger stuff than people gave him credit for. He rolled to his side, and before good sense could tell him otherwise, was on his feet tearing after Colt again. This time the major caught his lead detective around the waist. One of the beat cops held back Everett's swinging arm.

Restrained as he was with no outlet for the rage, he started yelling all sorts of things Colt didn't believe.

"Fuck you, Harkan. We ain't done here. You ain't blaming me for your bullshit —"

The men holding him back put more distance between them, only then letting Everett throw their grip. "Get off me, Stapes," he said, defeated. "I swear to God—leave me be."

After that kind of fall, Stapes didn't trust a word Everett had to say. When the ambulance arrived too late for Mary, he ordered him in back and sent Everett to the hospital. Stapes organized the scene and gave orders to the crime techs, then finally returned to deal with Colt where he sat on the bumper of his truck.

They both watched through the shack's open door as the techs got to work moving Mary.

He hadn't expected the major to say much, but the little he did made it worse.

"I don't know what that was, and I don't know what's going on…but that man is the only friend you had here. You know that."

Not keen on refuting an obvious truth, he'd let the major keep talking.

"Solve this, Harkan," Stapes said. He sounded tired. "I don't like you much, but I dislike being in the dark more. Just…steer clear of the station for a time. Let whatever this is blow over."

Like Colt was ever going to work there again. Like this would ever be water under the bridge. It was clear to him then if he was going to solve this thing, he'd be on his own—no partner, no help. Like it always had been.

The major left a small team on scene to watch his six. Colt tossed his phone to a scowling officer and followed Ev's final instruction.

He did his job. He got to work.

Not thirty minutes later, the cops peeled off without him, convinced Colt was insane to stare so long at nothing. He didn't worry over the lack of his cell. Who would be calling him anyhow?

Hour three of tapping and careful stepping revealed that passage in the wall. It explained how Mary's killer got in and out undetected, but the passage itself yielded no further clues. Resigned, Colt packed up and returned to his truck, sitting gingerly around broken glass and tacky pools of wine.

Checking himself in the rearview was the first look he got at his face. He'd had worse, but at that moment, Colt felt every inch the black hole his eye was blooming into. He found some loose napkins that looked clean enough and held them out of the remains of his driver's window, into the sprinkling rain. He wiped off the crusted blood as best he could while driving. It would have to do till he got to the station and the first aid still in his locker. It flew in the face of Stapes' advice, but the place would be a ghost town this time of night.

It was a long drive in the rain with a broken window. Colt hardly noticed the chill.

The station was strangely full when he got there — too full for some late-night call — and he wasn't sure what to make of the looks he was getting either. Sure, some were staring at his injuries. He'd expected more, and choice words as well, since he was no kind of popular with the rank and file. Five years meant nothing in Mason. Colt was still an outsider.

The whispers began in earnest as he walked to the coffee pot, and the station faded to grayscale the more Colt put together.

"Fuckin' Harkan...what's it been, two hours since..."

"Crashed into his ambulance —"

"One dead..."

"Some partner."

The Styrofoam cup slid from his hand and fell to the tile with a splash. He didn't stop to clean it, didn't ask any questions. He barely remembered keys on the way to his truck—had it in his head that running might be faster—and if Everett hadn't just kicked his ass, maybe so.

Please, no. Don't let that be the last time I—

But he couldn't even finish the thought. Colt's whole world narrowed to his feet, his windshield, frantic turns down empty streets, the parking lot, the intake desk, then he was demanding from an overnight nurse, "Everett Kane. Which room?"

The woman looked up from her screen, annoyed. "Excuse me? And you are?"

"Harkan. Surprised you'd show."

The major's voice pulled his attention from the desk, and in two long strides he stood next to Stapes, unable to hide the tremor roughing up his voice.

"Fuck all that. Where *is* he?"

"Down the hall," Stapes said. "We tried calling you—"

The major stopped there because Colt was already gone, already barreling down the hall to confirm with his own eyes what he'd feared since the station wasn't true. And yes, Everett was there in bed. *Alive.* Wearing a shiner to match his own...and something that looked like a smile. Some color bled back into Colt's world, but the scene framed in the glass of that door was too much to intrude upon.

The cold-water reality check sluiced down his spine, and Colt was left to wonder again why he'd thought anything would be different this time.

Couldn't save Rosa. Or Ava. Or Mary.
Couldn't keep Everett. Not for real.

Colt blinked hard and cleared his throat. Made it simple, then. He would leave—and fuck a two-week notice. Memorizing the familial scene before him, Colt thought back on those words he'd told Everett years ago, pissed at how much it sounded like prophecy.

"Connection's the real drug…"

Yeah. And he was hooked. Tried to wean off it, but there weren't no methadone for this. Cold turkey was all he had.

Everett turned his head and it was obvious he'd noticed him, frozen in the middle of the hall, arms hanging useless at his side. The room was too far away to tell what he might be thinking. All Colt could see for sure was Ev was looking, then he wasn't, and the fear of what would happen if he never looked back again was enough to turn Colt's head, then his heel, and start him down the hall.

He turned from where Rachael held her hand to Everett's forehead, where Grace and Marcus stood beside their father's bed, from the picture-perfect ending that swept the sins of the night aside in a rush of *thank God, you're alive*. He went home to his empty apartment and spent the night reconciling a familiar truth. Colt wouldn't ever be good for people, but maybe, he was still a good detective. He packed up his few belongings the next morning and was gone by the end of the day.

He made one stop by the station and delivered a letter more form than function, turned in with a final report of Mary's scene. According to his research, Edwards' hub of business was near the state line. Seemed like a good enough place to start. Anywhere would be better than Mason.

* * * *

Louisiana, 2018

And this office at the state line was where he'd stayed for four years, trading off between drinking himself to death and using the meantime best he could. This case was everything now — his charge, his burden. He *had* to solve it. These people deserved rest...and hell, maybe he did too.

Colt had always known he was one of those not long for this world. A morose sort of thing to know about himself, but it just made too much sense. At least this way, he'd have done some good first. He'd balance some scales on the way out. He nodded his head and rolled onto his cot, but in his mind he was back in that hospital — staring down a man he'd never thought to see again.

It made waking up to Everett's racket, tearing down his door at the end of a different hall, feel a bit like hope.

Chapter Twelve

Everett
Louisiana, 2018

It took ten minutes of knocking before the door swung open. Everett's watch said one p.m., but his old partner looked like he'd just gotten out of bed, the same sort of rough as the first day they met. Wary brown eyes fell to the box in his hands.

"Got more in the trunk," Everett explained. "Where am I going with this stuff?"

There was no verbal response, but Colt held the door and let him edge inside, a look of honest relief passing quickly over his face.

Everett followed him down the hall, and a quick survey of the office showed just how rough he'd been living. He decided right then he was definitely getting a motel. Colt didn't even have a room for himself, judging by that cot in the corner. No chance he'd have a spare anything that Everett could borrow.

He set the box of files on a folding table and retraced his steps outside. Colt already had the other in hand, so Everett snagged his computer bag and pocketed his keys. His family sedan and Colt's busted truck were the only two cars in the lot.

Everett paused by the truck's broken window, unable to keep from asking, "What happens when it rains?"

Colt hitched the box up in his arms. "It gets wet."

Everett laughed once, shook his head and followed him back inside.

Once there, Colt didn't have to explain his setup. Everett took one look at the over-full bulletin boards, swung a stapler open and started piecing his work into Colt's. The old quiet returned as they parsed through the paper — not the one filled with glances and wishful thinking, though they'd be a pair of liars to say that wasn't there too. The quiet that settled in the office that afternoon felt focused. Familiar. The turning of practiced parts in motion, of unused gears beginning again to spin.

It was good, but it wasn't the same.

For one thing, Colt was making God's-honest small talk while he sorted photos, asking careful questions like how Everett was besides work. And when that heart attack he'd predicted didn't come after all, Everett told him the truth because *hell*, Colt wasn't in any position to judge.

"I'm okay, mostly. Keep things quiet. Just go to work, punch the clock and come home. Not much of a social life." He swallowed down the lump in his throat and stapled a photo to the wall. "I see the kids when I can since…since Rachael and I split."

The world didn't end at the sound of his ex-wife's name, but Everett clocked the tension in Colt's shoulders all the same. "That's why I didn't get here sooner," he added. "Wanted to see the kids before..." Everett shrugged and lightened his tone. "But if I'd known the sorts of hours you keep, I wouldn't have rushed."

Colt looked up guiltily, but Everett waved him off and turned the question around. He did his best not to care about the answer—especially since he already knew. No woman in her right mind would let Colt run around as he clearly had, too broke down to be anything worth fixing.

Colt shrugged, like it weren't no surprise, and stapled another picture to the wall in front of them. "Keep it simple myself. No distractions. Just the work."

Everett nodded, chest warm with confirmation, but he let it lie. Too much to be doing.

Colt's next comment steered them toward less-neutral territory, but he didn't ask after the $100,000 question. Instead, he asked about *that girl on your phone*," commenting on a fact that could've gone snide, but stayed a casual observation.

"I'm sure *that* ended well. You always liked 'em wild." Colt's eyes flashed with amusement and he opened a folder, smirking.

Everett turned from the wall and really looked at what he thought he'd never see again, glad for many reasons that Colt's head was stuck in a file. Not just because it was so damn familiar, but also since it kept Colt from catching the way he grinned at that truth, at the irony of who it was coming from.

"S'pose I did."

They kept on like that for the first couple days, reviewing what they knew and circling each other like wounded deer, each doing their best not to force instinctive flight. They mostly seemed content to find there wasn't much fight in them now, at least not for each other. Everett imagined they were saving those skills for the man behind the murders, the specter they'd chased for damn near a decade.

Maybe they had different plans on what would happen after, if there *was* some kind of after to be worrying over. But until then, Everett knew they were on the same page. Until they found their man, nothing else in the world existed. And they'd do whatever it took to put the case down for good.

* * * *

After two days and nights of non-stop work, Colt finally agreed to share his whole theory. He pulled hard from his flask as he stood in front of the case-wall.

"What I'm about to tell you took almost a decade to put together. I know how it sounds, and I know how this is gonna look. I mean, when I started seeing the pieces..." Colt dragged a hand down his face and sighed, like there was no way around it. "But I can't keep looking at this and tryin' to convince myself otherwise. I need a second opinion. Someone to check my work."

The starkness of the request surprised him. "Can't remember you ever askin' for that before."

Colt let go a smoky exhalation. "'Course I did. Asked for your take all the time."

"You ever *use* it?"

The silence was answer enough. Colt blinked to where he sat hunched over his knees, chair backed against a long table. "Ev. Please."

Having heard that word maybe twice in the time he'd known him, Everett sighed and leaned back in his seat. "Look, I said I'd help, didn't I? Don't know what you thought I was doin' here otherwise, so get on with it." The words hit his own ears a bit harsh, so he added, "I'll hold my comments to the end. As I do, in fact, recall how you like stupid questions."

Colt actually laughed at that, and it might be an unpracticed thing, but there was a warmth to it he hadn't heard before. It was a pleasant sound, Colt's laughter. Even with him looking so sad.

"This time," Colt said, shaking his head, "ain't no such thing as stupid."

They were only a few steps into Colt's explanation before Everett was glad for the distinction. But the more he asked those follow-ups, looked for alternatives or ways this could go otherwise, he felt a weight sink low in his gut, something he'd learned to trust from his years on the job—in particular, those years with Detective Harkan.

"The people on my list," Colt explained. "They were all new to support groups in the area and made it known they were looking for work. Our man, whoever he is, would go to these meetings to look for marks. He'd get them seasonal jobs at the rodeo through Heartland. He'd make them feel indebted, and when he had their trust, he'd take advantage, like Combs. Not sure if he always killed his victims, but the earliest names have been missing since 2005. There were plenty of bodies to go around after Katrina. No one was gonna notice a few more."

"And since they were men," Everett added, "I doubt many examiners were doin' the proper tests to get 'em flagged."

"'Course not," Colt said, eyes on Patrick's file. "Men don't get raped."

It took everything Everett had to turn his attention from *that word* and the blank way Colt said it. Didn't do much for the rage burning in his belly, the kind that sparked anytime he caught sight of a muddy truck—

"I never got more than vague descriptions of our guy from the support groups," Colt continued. "Light hair, light eyes. Nice clothes. When the leads on Patrick dried up, I dug into the files we took from the rodeo. Found a whole web of trouble."

Colt stubbed out his cigarette and walked to the wall of financials, pointing out important documents as he went. "A few months after Katrina, early 2006, Richard Edwards reorganized his businesses. Drew up new wills and contracts that had him working more with his sister's boys than his own. The State Rodeo is run by a nephew, Phillip Edwards, and by reported incomes there's no way the business should've made it—not with how the recession hit in '08. There's off-the-books money coming in."

Everett nodded, following along for now. "Enter your kindly motorcycle friends."

"Exactly. Somewhere an introduction was made, and this nephew—or someone he trusts—made them movers for all kinds of illegal operations. Explains how the Cobras jumped up the food chain so fast. With the access a legitimate business gets with shipping and storage?" Colt hummed low in his chest, like he was almost giving credit where it was due. "Somethin' as small-time as the Cobras couldn't beat it. So now, our guy's in with Leroy's crowd, and with the Edwards' name to keep anyone from lookin' too close, he had everything he needed. Could up the stakes of his *hobby* without fear."

"Jesus..." Everett cursed under his breath.

Colt tipped his head in agreement. "Psychopathy on a serial rapist ain't so different from a certain kind of animal. There's a reason we call them predators. Predators hunt." Colt swallowed and squinted, like the whole thing put a sour taste in his mouth. "The more they get away with it...what they need changes. If it was ever about sex, it's not anymore."

Colt tapped a finger below the shack photos, the ones where Mary and Eric had died, though years apart. "He started bringing them here. Out in the wilds, where he could take his time. Started keeping people longer and disappearing more than one a season." He pointed to a photo of a larger cabin Everett had never seen. "If you keep walking past Eric and Mary's shacks, there's a structure about three times the size. Long abandoned, but enough space to hold people for a few days. Until our guy and his buddies were ready."

"*Buddies*? You mean he ain't workin' alone?"

Colt looked him right in the eye. "Did you know the Cobras' warehouse is a five-minute drive from Mary's gas station?"

Everett felt his eyebrows shoot to his hairline. He shook his head. "Can't say I paid much mind to road signs that night."

Colt continued on, not acknowledging the comment. "His pattern also shifted in strange ways over the years. For the longest time, the only woman on my list was Mary. But around 2013, more female names start croppin' up. So either our guy changed his tastes on a whim, or he wasn't workin' alone. Why else spend time building multiple shacks? Multiple shacks, multiple hunters."

"But..." Everett exhaled and rubbed his forehead. He was definitely getting a headache. "I mean, c'mon. Who in the blue-blazed fuck would *help* this kind of person?"

"You think he's walkin' around advertising what he's doing? 'Course not. Probably has even better people skills than you. He's gotta blend in to get people to open up to him. Had to learn who he could trust with his secrets." Colt pointed to the bit of wall that held details of the newest scene. "Besides, the time of death on Meyers proves he's keeping them longer — she'd only been dead twelve hours when they found the body, but she'd been missing for three weeks. To hold people that long, he'd need partners. Or a fuckin' fortress. But I'm getting ahead of myself."

He gestured to a different corner of wall covered in scene photos four years old. "After Patrick was Mary. Her leaving us cold in 2012 didn't make no sense till I found out about her foster brother. Had the name Elliott Caster on my list for years never knowing what they were to each other.

"Mary and Elliott disappeared from public record in 2009. We didn't find her until 2012, and she didn't get shot till two years after that. So why would our guy keep her around? Especially when she wasn't his type?"

"This is a fucked-up game of twenty questions, Colt..."

"Because she was *useful*," Colt finished for him. "I think when Mary found her brother again, *he* got her a job at the rodeo. And if our guy had already marked

Elliott, it might not have mattered if Mary tagged along. He could use them against each other to keep them both in line. Send one out while he kept the other under lock and key. Hell, they might've been his first partners once he knew he could trust them.

"Which brings us to our stakeout. If Mary had made it that long, he must've believed her loyal, though I think *traumatized* is a better word. When she got my note with only her name, she wasn't gonna go lookin' for who might've written it — especially since Elliott's was nowhere to be found." Colt shook his head, like he didn't want to guess at the horrors they'd seen, the psychological toll it had taken. "I don't doubt she went straight to our guy that night. Probably told him herself that someone was looking for her. Maybe thought if she was honest, it would keep her and Elliott safe."

Everett rubbed his hands and sighed. Jesus, this was all too much. "All right, Colt. Let's say you're right and Mary ran to our guy on some bona fide Stockholm shit. Still doesn't explain why she came back two years later."

A familiar spark lit Colt's mahogany eyes. "Now you're asking the right questions.

"Think about it from his point of view. He couldn't use the shacks anymore if Mary had made a friend, and he'd beat the cops last time with Patrick. So he got his ducks in a row to disappear, and when he was good and ready, he sent Mary to get our attention. Then all at once, he got rid of her *and* that way of doing business. The only person who might've known where he was going? He left bleeding in the dirt."

Disappointment and anger swelled in his old partner's voice and he wondered...all this dark shit...this fuckin' case. How many nights had Colt stared at these walls alone? It was too much for one man to handle.

"What'd he get up to after Mary?" Everett prompted. The question seemed to wake Colt from another line of thought.

"He was quiet for a time, but a person like that...he's not gonna stop being what he is." Colt walked to a clearer corner of the room, leaned against the wall and lit up another smoke. "There's been a few bodies, but more missing persons. It's not anyone from Mason proper gettin' took these days. My best guess? Him and his buddies are holed up someplace. Somewhere better hidden than those shacks. And he's been doin' this long enough now that not even the seclusion is enough."

"You're talkin' about the knife work. All the cuts and..."

"Andrea's just for starters." Colt huffed and stared down the mostly-empty wall. A hand tapped his thigh as he fought to keep himself focused. "Ev, I've got evidence of what he's doing to the people he takes, how he drugs them, even how they're killed. I just don't know *who* or *where*."

The room chilled as Colt admitted to things he didn't know. It was a new kind of uncomfortable. Everett didn't care much for it. He stood and walked to the photos of Andrea Meyers, that scene of torture and terror that still kept him up at night. "If," he started, "and I mean *if* all that's true — why'd he leave this scene for us to find a week ago?"

Colt flipped his Zippo open and shut. "Might be taunting us again, like he did with Mary. Could've evolved to be part of his pattern. But I'm not sure it was him. Andrea's not his type. We both know that scene was just the dump site. You put a body that tore up in a place that visible, it's a message. And our guy hasn't been workin' alone for years."

"So the real question is, who's sending the message? And why?"

Colt nodded. "We won't know anything until we find this new hideaway — and Ev, we gotta find it soon. Because come the end of rodeo season, I'm like to be adding to my list again. And I don't know how many more I can stand to find."

The way Colt's voice rasped at that was worrisome. "Last I saw," Everett said, "your list had six names."

Colt stared at the floor. "Yep."

"And now?"

"Seventeen."

Jesus...

"How many are you sure of?"

Colt took a long drag of his Camel. "Seventeen."

Angry brown eyes cast around the room. Colt cleared his throat and returned to his flask. Everett wished he had something to ease the weight of this reality too, but he wasn't about to ask Colt for the only thing holding him together. Silent minutes rolled between them like tumbleweeds as he searched for another explanation. His eyes followed the same trail as Colt's across the case-wall, and far more sentences ended before they'd begun.

Yeah. Everett was starting to see it.

"How d'you know all this? How *could* you, even?"

Colt took a seat in his vacated chair and leaned forearms on his knees. He pulled a hand through his overgrown hair. "Too much time staring at too long of lists to find the first names that fit the pattern. I interviewed people at support groups where recruitment might've happened, cross-referenced that with hiring documents on the rodeo drive. Some lucky receipts from Jared's pockets and files at the warehouse." Then Colt sighed, the only clue that he knew how insane his next confession was. "And a few late-night trips to Edwards' headquarters. For updated company information."

"Fuckin' *Christ*, Colt. Are you kidding—"

"Edwards' corporate offices are only twenty minutes away. Part of why I set up here in the first place. I took specific clients to get certain access. Stole the rest. Gonna be honest, I haven't worried about a court of law in years." He swallowed hard. "Not after what I found."

Colt pushed out of the chair and walked to a filing cabinet. He punched numbers into the small safe on top as he said, "I came upon some things in my travels. Predators like our guy…often keep trophies."

Colt retrieved four burner phones from the safe, all in separate plastic bags. Everett recognized one as the cell they found with Eric Robins.

"These burners…the story's all there. Filled in most of what I hadn't guessed." Colt slid a bag to him down the long tabletop. "Check the messages. All the phones are the same."

When Everett powered it up through the plastic, there was a single text, three letters long.

Run.

"He gives these to his victims before he turns them loose," said Colt. "No minutes on the phone, so they can't call or send for help. But the cameras work." He cleared his throat again. "Some…documented their last moments."

The thought turned Everett's stomach inside-out. He put the phone down. "Good Lord. Why would they keep these things?"

Colt turned Eric's phone over in his hands. "It's human nature to cling to any chance at rescue. You don't throw away the only lifeline you've got. Phones meant flashlights to see by, but it also made them easy targets in the dark. Ingenious kind of cruel, really."

Everett couldn't stop staring at the bags on the table. He swallowed against a dry throat and the question he had to ask. "You watch them all?"

Colt nodded. "Had to see if anyone caught our guy on camera. Or gave up his name."

"Did they?"

He shook his head. "Doubt he would've kept them otherwise, even locked up."

Damn. Everett chewed the inside of his cheek. "What'd you learn?"

"No city noise or cars at all. Different voices, multiple attackers. Thought I heard horses in one, but can't be sure. I think...I think it's some kind of event. Some fucked-up hunting party to wine and dine his criminal contacts. A way to indulge shared interests."

Thinking about *that* too hard would do him in for good. Everett covered his mouth with the back of his hand and dragged tired eyes to Colt's.

"How bad is it?" he asked.

Colt set his flask beside the phones. "Worse."

* * * *

"He seemed so friendly, like he understood..."
"Never would have thought..."
"Said we were going for a drive, to pick up supplies..."

"Don't remember how I got here. Woke up in some kind of stables..."

"Could see three or four other people. Recognized one from group..."

"A man gave us food. There's drugs in the water, but I swear, I stopped caring..."

"No idea what we're doing here or how long it's been..."

"Today, we got phones...a text that said 'Run'..."

"I have no clue where I am –"

"I can hear them laughing –"

"If anyone finds this, tell my mother..."

"Tell my partner –"

"My brother –"

"I love you. It's not your fault."

"Someone's coming..."

"I'm sorry. I'm so sorry –"

* * * *

Both detectives spent the night at the grindstone, working any lead to dull the edge of a guilty conscience.

Chapter Thirteen

Everett
Louisiana, 2018

It took most of the next day and a round of Chinese takeout before they caught a break. Colt was reading off a list of company vendors when Everett stopped him short. "Hold up. Read that last one back."

"K. Maynard of Serendipitous Events," Colt repeated. "Shows up in the ledgers for lots of Edwards' businesses. What of it?"

Everett opened a new tab on his laptop and typed the name. When the page loaded, he hit the edge of the table with his fingers. "I thought that was...*shit*, you're never gonna guess who just became relevant."

Colt narrowed his eyes and circled the table, leaning close to look over his shoulder. "I'll be damned."

"Ralph Maynard's wife runs this company. Maiden name of Catherine 'Kitty' Edwards."

Colt returned to the list of payees and other company documents. "And if she's done events for Edwards' businesses..."

"Good odds she's done family parties too." Everett scratched his chin. "With the family connection, Kitty might be the perfect person to ask about Edwards' properties. Might even have some pictures we could compare to the burner videos. Photos of past events and such."

Colt nodded and walked to the corner that held his few personal effects. He began filling a duffel bag on his cot. "It's a start. When we leavin'?"

"Hold on there, soldier. Things have changed at the station since you were there." Everett clicked over to the Mason PD homepage and swiveled the screen so Colt could see. The story was still front and center, complete with the photo from the paper, headline proclaiming, "*Congratulations to Lt. Colonel Ralph Maynard —* "

"So?"

He turned the screen from Colt. Apparently, it was his turn to spell some things out. "There's been a Maynard at Mason PD for as long as anyone can remember. Ralph's got pull in places you've never heard of."

"Doesn't mean anything — "

"It *means* we can't just roll up on him and ask these sorts of questions."

Colt broke his gun apart and began to clean the pieces, hands steady with the practiced motion. "Wasn't plannin' on asking."

Everett barked a laugh. "I'm gonna pretend I didn't hear that. For both our sakes."

"Best we play to our strengths."

His eyes snapped immediately to Colt's and both of them could say something. They each had ammunition a'plenty if they wanted to take the shot. But the relative peace of the last few days kept Everett from mouthing off, and after a tense moment, Colt returned attention to his gun.

"You wanna try it simple first? Fine," said Colt. "Do what you do, Ev. Call the bosses. Make nice."

* * * *

Colt
Louisiana, 2018

Everett's quiet working lunch with Ralph went about as expected. Colt tried his best not to think *I told you so* too loud.

They closed out their first week making plans Ev clearly never thought he'd make. But Colt convinced him to leave the right kind of message on Ralph's cell, just enough incentive to pop his head out one more time. Tomorrow, they'd drive to their new base for the rest of it—the dive where Everett had sweat it out on Colt's bogus tip.

The bar was owned by one Patrick Combs, Sr., who was more than willing to loan Colt his back room.

But their return to Mason was a night away yet, and riding this case as hard as they had, both men's vices were out in full-effect. They'd been emptying bottles and filling boxes all night and still had over half the case-wall to pack. Taking it all down was quite the task after years of adding to it. Colt refilled his glass again while he watched Everett work. He managed to keep quiet until Ev got to Mary's scene.

"Careful," he said. "Only copies I've got."

Everett raised an eyebrow but, for once, didn't tease.

Even dulled by whiskey, Everett would mark his overreaction. But he pried the staples on the next photo up with his thumbnail and placed Mary's shack in the folder. He followed it up with a long drink of his own, and Colt returned his gaze to the wall. For a moment, he let himself get lost in the pattern of it—how his scrawled-out notes circled Mary like a halo of unknowns, all rippling out from that static puddle of blood. The silence in the room felt thick in his chest, heavy with guilt...considering all that night had been.

Everett's question still surprised him.

"How'd Rachael get you? The night we got that call?"

It was the most they'd ever said about it. Colt heard the question beneath, clear as day.

How'd you do that to me?

At this turn in conversation they retreated to seated postures, each on their own side of the long folding table. Colt would say he was better than Everett at a lot of things, and after four years working at it, functional alcoholism was one. Rhett probably wouldn't want to talk about this if they weren't so far down the bottle.

"Ev...we ain't gotta talk particulars about—"

"I'm asking, man. Times have changed some. I want to know."

Looking at his old partner now, Colt could see there might be some truth to that. This comparatively gentle inquiry was nothing like the Everett he'd baited in that locker room years ago, ready to shove him through the metal itself for daring to comment on the beds he frequented at all. This Everett had lost enough to know the brittleness of false bravado. Might be that something more resilient had grown in its place.

"She started cryin' about the other women," he said. "Bottle of wine in her hand."

"Boy, you didn't stand a chance. Ran her game on you, didn't she?"

Colt's eyes flicked up. Everett cocked his head and smirked, taking a drag off the cig he'd fished from Colt's pack. He knew Ev had plenty of those cowboy-killers left, but the man was always stealing his Camels these days.

Colt said carefully, "She'd known what you were doing for a while. Imagine she'd thought about what revenge she'd take. When you got to tryin' it again."

Everett nodded along, still smiling despite that truth, because yeah, that was Rachael. They passed some time in long drags and healthy sips before Colt added, "I knew too. What you were up to. When the case picked up again."

Everett blew smoke at the floor. "Figured you did."

He chewed the inside of his cheek and tried to remind himself what he was doing here, that this wasn't about righting past wrongs or clearing any of their history up. Shit, if all it took was a lack of physical violence to get Colt thinking after how he'd changed, then those years on the bottle had done him worse than he'd thought.

"Y'know, that was Rachael's go-to move back in the day," Everett said, a sad fondness spread across his face. "Strollin' in with a smile for date night? Bottle of wine. Showin' up pissed as hell like she wanted a fight—bottle of wine." Everett ashed in the coffee mug between them on the table. "'Round the time I started leavin' a glass out for her was prolly when she made her first mistake. Thinking I was *husband material*. But I'd just gotten wise to her tricks."

Colt snorted into his whiskey. Couldn't help himself. Everett always was a natural with words, and it was times like these where he could see that creative spark, that in a different life, Everett could've been a writer, waiting on a story to tell. His smile broke like sun from behind the clouds as he leaned in to tell this next, like he was letting Colt in on the secret.

"If Rachael was drinking wine, it's because she was tryin' to get her courage up. Least that's how it started. Later on, I think she did it 'cause we both knew what it meant. She'd show up at home, kids asleep, and just — " Everett mimed along as if holding a bottle by the neck, treating the empty air with all the weight of the real thing.

"She'd just *set* that heavy bottle on the counter. And I kid you not, it was like I'd taken one of those pills or somethin'. Shit was *automatic*."

The room bloomed out in orange and rosemary at the smile on Everett's face. He chuckled twice, then once at himself and the mood turned blue and faded. "Been over it so many times now, and I still can't see how I let it go so wrong. Just too many left turns, I guess. By that time, you're long past Albuquerque, and the fuck you got to do then but keep driving?"

Everett was still staring at the floor, so Colt let himself linger. He traced the lines of hard years etched into Everett's face and decided they hadn't stolen any strength. Ev looked healthy in some ways and not in others, like for the past few years, convenience was his main concern. A life about making it easy. Not having to try so hard. Made him wonder...

"Why'd you finally call me in? What's the real reason?"

Everett shook his head, a little worse for whiskey. "You tell me why you're helping—me, of all people. For real."

Colt waved that away and stayed the course. "Mine first. Why'd you cave?"

Everett contemplated the ice in his glass that hadn't had time to melt. "Wasn't just for Stapes. That newest murder, Meyers…it *got* to me, man. Ain't right."

"He's been maturing," Colt told him, clinging to facts for minimal comfort. "Was only a matter of time."

"Yeah, well I don't know if skinning a woman like game is anything I'd call *mature*."

That would be the only thing that'd force Everett to bite the bullet—the thought that his previous inaction was responsible for this. That he wasn't the shiny Prince Charming he'd never admit to wanting to be, that no matter how many dragons he slew, there was never going to be a happy ending.

Everett let the silence stretch and crunched the ice in his glass. In time, he cashed in his marker, having been the one to go first. "Now you. Why'd you, uh…" Ev's voice caught in his throat, and he was looking too close for anything Colt would call comfortable. "Why'd you agree to help?"

He tipped his head and stared at the wall. "For this. For them. Mary most of all. If I hadn't left her that note, hadn't…" Colt dropped eyes to his drink. "That shit was on me."

Everett didn't look like he agreed with every piece of that, but neither did he press for more. And hell, Ev had been all kinds of honest tonight. He'd meet him like-for-like. "Besides. Never liked leaving things undone before movin' down the road. No need to change that for a permanent destination."

The shift in Everett's attention felt like static tuning in, but wasn't like anything he could say had the power to change Colt's plans. That wasn't why he said it. Call it a professional interest. He wanted to know what it'd be like to sit in the box across from him. He wanted to see if Everett had it figured, or if it would take these words to catch a clue.

"I'm tired of the ups and downs of this particular roller coaster. S'just the same mistakes in different places, never going anywhere but 'round the tracks another turn. Nothing ever changes." Colt finished his drink. "I'm ready to stop the ride. I want off."

He decided he wasn't going to look at Everett for the rest of the night. Telling truth to get him gone was one thing, but watching him listen wasn't on the table. Because if Everett reached for him now, Colt wasn't sure he could tell himself no. And the heartbreak bound to follow would put him in the ground for good.

It'd be a hell of a way to go.

But there was too much to do to get lost in *what ifs* and *maybes*. Colt pushed away from the table and stood, hoping it'd prompt him to leave. "I'll see you tomorrow."

There was a time Everett would've let him leave on a line like that.

"Times have changed some…"

"Motherfucker, hold a second. You don't get to drop that on me and leave. Not *me*."

Colt stopped in the light of that one good streetlamp filtering through the office window. He listened as Everett pushed his chair back and walked to stand behind him — and his voice, while firm, was softer than before.

It almost sounded like Everett understood.

"I'm sure that...when you made this plan of yours, it seemed like a good idea. Maybe the only idea. And I'm not gonna try to convince you otherwise. Learned a long time ago I can't change *your* mind about shit, but...you're gonna do me one favor, Col. Just one for...for old time's sake."

Colt closed his eyes against the memories pressing in. He couldn't afford to get lost in them now. He was too close to done, too close to rest —

He found himself asking, "What's that, Rhett?"

"If we get done with this case and we're both still standing? We're gonna talk about this first. It ain't...ain't just your decision to be makin' anymore. There's things we need to talk on, you and me. If we get out of this."

Colt blinked his eyes open and saw how his old partner was staring, arms folded across his chest where he stood between him and the door. Like he wasn't about to budge until Colt met that gaze of honest blue.

"All right?"

It was so little to ask. Too much to deny. Colt turned his head and said, "Fine."

The tension eased out of the room as Everett nodded, like that settled things. He edged them back to safer territory. "Okay. I'll see you tomorrow then."

"Yeah."

Everett eyed him again, and though he knew it was good-natured overkill, Colt doubled down. "I said, *yeah.*"

Everett clapped him on the shoulder, reaching his other arm for his keys on the table. He took a deep breath and a step toward his cot before he noticed, Rhett wasn't moving his hand —

"One more thing, Colt."

A strong arm pulled him close as Everett fit their mouths together.

Oh, fuck. Ev...

Colt was well acquainted with how it felt to go years without something, how a different kind of forgetting took place. Was like forgetting on a cellular level — like the things he'd touched, the things he'd held, didn't just stop being there. It was like they never existed at all. With all the time, distance and whiskey Colt had been drowning in, he'd been thankful for the blunted senses, how it felt as close to happiness as he was like to get. So when the thought crossed his mind of *I'd forgotten what this was like*, the remembering was a bolt of lightning, grounded through his body, to jolt Colton Harkan back to life.

Because yes, he *had* forgotten what this was like — the warmth of compassionate touch. What it was like to be held. To be heard and seen. To have some part of his body not feel like a burden, like some weight he was carrying around. There was nothing mocking, casual or cavalier about the way Everett's lips were claiming his, how his tongue swept and tasted like he could stay there forever if only Colt kept making that sound, that soft, surprised hum at the back of his throat, stuttered breath escaping on a sigh.

Everett cupped his face, thumb running the ridge of his cheek. Colt wrapped his arms around his back to pull him closer, but this wisdom-weathered Everett didn't push and smiled against his lips.

His kiss said *stick around*. Like maybe now, Colt might be inclined to agree.

They spent a moment swaying together as the kiss died a natural death. The soft parting of lips echoed in the quiet office, and he wasn't the only one breathing heavy after. There was still the hint of a smile in his spark-bright eyes when Ev whispered, "Good. Okay."

He stepped back to get himself right, returning Colt's words on his way out.

"See you tomorrow."

Chapter Fourteen

Everett
Louisiana, 2018

"Ralph, Kitty. Thanks for meeting me here. Really savin' my life on this."

Kitty Maynard — the former Catherine Edwards — looked exactly the kind of person who'd own a property like this. From Kitty's heels, skirt suit and diamond-encrusted cross to her perfectly styled, dyed-blonde hair, Everett was getting some clarity on where Maynard's attitude 'round the station might've come from.

Kitty's suit aside, it was clear who wore the pants in this relationship.

She waved at her husband with a ring that could put a dent in the national debt. Ralph, recognizing the gesture, handed off a tablet from the bag over his shoulder. Her manicured hands clacked across the screen.

"Usually, I don't work under such short notice. But of course, for a *friend*, we can bend the rules a bit."

Everett flashed a smile warm enough to be convincing, if no one was looking too hard. The faint crease of frozen laugh lines only hinted at her mood, but so far, Kitty seemed to be buying it. Ralph kept an eye on him as he scouted the grandness of the entryway.

The large house sprawled beside a small lake on acres of land. Everett told them as much as he led the Maynards down the hall, done-up with décor instead of knick-knacks. Kitty's approving tuts and hmms seemed to say maybe, this job wouldn't be so bad. Everett bit back a smile and walked on.

He knew there was no noise coming from the second floor, but the frantic beating of his pulse in his ears kept making him think he'd heard something. When they reached the kitchen of granite and steel, Kitty smiled at the space. "Lovely spot for hosting. What'd you say this was for again?"

"Parents' anniversary. Kind of fell to me last minute. Ralph here mentioned you had experience with these family events."

"I've done every event for my uncle's businesses for twenty years now," Kitty said with pride. "Family and business have always been a blended affair for us."

"You don't say."

Kitty took a seat on the leather sofa past the kitchen. Ralph's eyes landed on the bar and Everett gestured in welcome. "Please, help yourself. You'd be doing me a favor."

He returned his attention to Kitty on the couch. "You got examples of things you've done? We want to be outside mostly, on the grounds."

Kitty hummed in agreement and turned again to her husband. He set a fresh martini on the bar and pulled a laptop from her bag, placing it carefully on the glass coffee table. Everett nodded at the external drive and cords that followed.

"Bringin' out the big guns for this, huh?"

Kitty smiled. "This computer is my *life*. If there's not something on this drive that works perfectly for your party, I'll do the whole thing for free."

"Quite a claim, Miss Kitty."

She scrolled through photos of events she'd done, name dropping all the while. There was a collection of lakehouses, old Southern manors and the sorts of extravagance Everett had only seen on television. None of the properties included stables of any kind, but that didn't mean what they were looking for wasn't there.

This drive was an important puzzle piece. Time to press for more.

"I'll show you the patio out back," Everett said. "Can take whatever photos you need."

At Kitty's once-again outstretched hand, Maynard rummaged through the bag and produced a digital camera. She left the rest of her tech on the table and followed Everett outside, full of *oohs* and *ahhs* as she scouted the space. Kitty paused at the edge of the small dock, watching the waves ripple the ink-blue lake. Near the house, Everett pulled a cig from his pack and offered one to Maynard.

Ralph declined. "You know I don't smoke."

Everett lit up and inhaled deep into his lungs, appreciating the burn in a way he didn't usually. "Yeah, Ralph. I do. Just thought you might want one anyways. Something to take the edge off."

"Edge off what?"

Everett pitched his voice to where Kitty was turned away, but his eyes stayed fixed on Ralph. "How you do with surprise parties, Kitty?"

Ralph swiveled his slow head back to the house. He saw Colt, standing steady in the open door, looking all manner of comfortable with a silenced pistol between his hands.

Maynard was never quick on the uptake, but even he knew enough to grab for his holster. Everett caught his arm and relieved him of the weapon, ensuring the safety was on. He cleaned the barrel with a rag from his pocket, careful to avoid the grip, then pulled on his own pair of gloves. With every step he took to preserve Ralph's prints and remove his own, his old partner's eyes darkened like smoldering coal.

It was all Colt, but seemed like Switch approved the message too.

"Maynard," said Colt, calm as anything.

The colonel went red as a ripe tomato. "What the hell is this, Kane? What's this ignorant cocksucker doin' with a gun in my face?"

"Taking you hostage, by the looks of it."

Kitty finally turned and took in the scene with a scream. Her camera fell to the wooden deck, but he hardly noticed the glass shatter over her ruckus. On a property this far out, wasn't like anyone would hear her, but the kind of hysteria Kitty kicked up wasn't pleasant to listen to.

Colt gestured with his gun to keep Maynard where he was. Everett approached Kitty slowly. "Let's not be stupid, now. You ain't wanna run in those heels any more than I want to chase you. Just wanna talk."

Having her husband's weapon aimed her way shut Kitty up quick. Her hands shook beside her head, like she'd seen it in a movie. "Please, I…I don't know what's going on."

"You know more than you think," Everett told her. "Go stand by him. Over there."

Kitty walked on unsteady legs to where her husband glared at both men, but at Colt's tip of the muzzle, they stayed apart as two separate targets. Everett tossed Maynard's gun to Colt. He caught it with one hand and lowered his silenced pistol. Everett pulled out his own weapon as Colt examined the colonel's piece.

"Here's the thing, Maynard. You or your wife's been somewhere we need to go. Can't afford to wait or be told it doesn't exist. Because if we don't find it soon, people are gonna die in ways no one ever should. And that ought to mean something. Even to *you*."

Kitty's face blanched. Everett worried the woman might faint. Maynard looked to his wife and turned a darker red. "I'll get you for this, Harkan. Mark my words, you swaggerin' faggot mother*fucker* — "

"Always did have a taste for callin' me that," Colt commented, like they were discussing the weather. "But y'know what they say about guys like you, always callin' it out about others."

Ralph's usually dull eyes were bright with rage. "What do they say?"

Colt tipped his head. "Means you know what you're lookin' for."

Everett barked a laugh he tried to cover with a cough. Kitty broke free of the shock and launched into a list of accusations, all designed to pull focus from that telltale ring of truth. Her voice skipped across octaves in her rage.

"You're *disgusting*. My husband would *never* — my *family* would never — "

"That's right," Colt said, turning his gun to Kitty. "Got family secrets on that score you don't want us to know, hmm?"

Everett had to thumb back the safety of his weapon to keep Ralph still, but Kitty was another story. Insulted enough to risk some defiance, she took a step toward Colt.

"Watch it," he said, clear this would be her only reminder.

She took another step forward. "You gonna shoot me if I do? You just said you need us." Kitty hitched a proud chin upward and declared, "You wouldn't dare."

Crack.

Colt fired over Kitty's shoulder, aiming for the empty lake. Mostly.

She dropped to the ground with a scream like she was dying. Maynard thundered profanity at Colt, whose steady hand tracked to where she howled on the ground. He spoke evenly over the noise of the Maynards.

"Reckon we're past that point of things I wouldn't do." Colt sniffed once and stared down the gun's sight, like he was truly considering the notion. "What you think, Ralph? You think I care if I shoot your wife with *your gun* to get her to talk some sense?"

For cryin' out loud...

It took everything he had not to bust his gut laughing, but that wouldn't be helping matters. He really shouldn't be encouraging him. Whatever contingencies Colt had planned, every dig at Ralph was more dirt on the grave of Everett's career. Hell, they'd be lucky to escape a cell on this.

But Everett couldn't make himself care about that just now. Ever since he'd walked outside, it'd been one line after another with Colt, and it did him good to hear something like amusement in the man's tone. Been happening all day, really. Now that Colt was behind the business end of a gun again, he seemed steadier on his feet. There were times that afternoon he almost looked familiar, like two parts of himself finally blending into a whole.

Dangerous and driven. Focused and fatal.

Goddamn lethal combination, you ask me...

Colt flicked his wrist and pointed Ralph's gun at the house. Maynard walked inside, scowling. Everett had to haul Kitty up from the ground to get her started, but she followed in time.

Glowering, Maynard sat on the couch by the laptop. Colt tossed him a flash drive. "Plug that in. Open it up."

Everett knew what he'd see if he looked at the screen, but he'd never have to watch those videos again, the way the horrors had fixed in his mind. Couldn't ever forget seeing something like that. He hoped the same would hold true for Maynard. However much of a shitbag he was, Ralph was still human.

Maynard turned his gaze to where Everett ushered Kitty upstairs. "Jesus, you sick fucks. You didn't have to include my family in this horseshit — "

Everett kept his eyes on Kitty. "No hard feelings, Ralph. Just play nice and answer Harkan's questions."

"After *this*?" Ralph asked, incredulous. "What makes you think I'd help *you*?"

He and Colt traded a look. Everett nodded, and Colt slowly circled the couch. He reached a gloved finger over Maynard's shoulder and hit play, turning to stare through the patio doors.

"He seemed so friendly, like he understood..."

Everett hurried Kitty up the rest of the stairs. She made a noise of complaint he ignored.

"Believe it or not, ma'am, I'm doing you a favor. Up you go."

* * * *

Everett didn't expect to get much out of Kitty, but the real reason they were upstairs was insurance on their clean getaway. Whole thing was almost too easy — rolling out like clockwork, just as Colt had described.

Right now, Colt was downstairs with Ralph, showing what needed to be shown to get some honest answers. But even if Ralph was no help, they'd have Kitty's files to look through. If their guy *was* using an Edwards-affiliated property, then Kitty's drive was their best shot at pulling an address. They just had to figure out which one was the winner, and Kitty was bound to say something useful eventually.

There's a finite combination of words in the English language. The way Kitty was rambling in fear, she'd get there soon enough.

Everett asked if there was anyone in the family she hadn't seen in a while, someone who made a regular habit of being gone from the public eye. Kitty turned her nose to the ceiling and actually shut up for a second, but Colt must have scared her good, because she kept on, despite her distaste for the topic.

"You know, my side of the family has always been brighter," Kitty told him. "My mother was just as much a genius as her brother. Just as stubborn. She kept the family name when she married my daddy, and back then? *That* was a statement. Mama always said it meant something to be an Edwards. If Ralph weren't known around the force, I'd have never changed to Maynard.

"When my brothers started working more closely with Uncle Richard, it was good for everyone. They have the mind for it, like me. It's in our blood. But not all of them deserve it."

"Which one of your brothers you talkin' about, Kitty?"

She pressed her embellished cross close to her chest and shook her head. "Phil. My brother, Phillip. He was never one to turn away a business opportunity…cares more for money than connections."

"That's a problem?"

Kitty scoffed. "When they're *criminals*, certainly. I've never done a State Rodeo event for that very reason. Don't know where Phil's money comes from." She crossed her arms. "But as long as Phil keeps his personal life quiet, my uncle doesn't care. Or doesn't know."

"Personal life?"

Kitty twisted her mouth. "It's the only way Phil can be involved in the family business with the sort of…*company* he chooses to keep. Disgusting, really. The way people like him just out and flaunt it now."

The feeling that comment inspired was a new one for Everett. Felt like laughing at a joke no one else could hear. For a moment, he considered shaking this woman's worldview with a well-placed word, but when he opened his mouth, an angry yell bellowed from downstairs. Everett only nodded, having expected it sooner.

Kitty's eyes flew to the bedroom door. "What's happening?"

"Progress."

He took a painting off the wall and waved Kitty closer, pointing at the safe he'd revealed. Practically requisite for a house like this. "Do me a favor, Kitty. Then we'll go see."

* * * *

When they descended the stairs, he heard the sound of someone spitting and the unwell sighs of the sick. Colt's voice filtered up the stairs, cold as he'd ever heard him.

"That's five minutes of a hell at least a decade long. We need to know where it's happening. You or your wife might know the place without realizing. Could help us save the people that are trapped there even now. You wanna prove your people ain't at fault? Then help us, Ralph. For once in your useless life."

Everett waved his gun at Kitty. She sat beside Ralph on the couch. He was doubled over in front of a small wastebasket, face blanched and dripping with sweat. Kitty stared at her husband like he had two heads, but before she could get a word in, Ralph said, "Kit. Just answer their questions. Please."

Colt ran her through the same list as Everett had. She gave more specifics about the properties on her drive. Maynard hadn't recognized anything from the videos, and Kitty didn't either when Colt pulled out the printed stills. Ralph turned his eyes even at these snatches of scenery. Everett, at least, didn't blame him.

When Colt asked about suspicious family, Kitty doubled down on her brother's "abominable proclivities," adding this time that "perverts like him" got up to "all manner of things," and if it *was* Phil they were looking for, she hoped he got what was coming to him.

"Nothin' like family, is there?" Colt asked. Everett snorted in agreement.

Around then, the Maynards remembered their indignation. Ralph was still sour from being confronted with so much truth, and Kitty was going on about how they'd both be sorry, making promises of what would happen once her family got a hold of this.

Colt hummed, amused. "I wouldn't go mouthin' off once we leave. Especially you, Kitty. With your prints all over that safe."

Maynard faced his wife on the couch. "What safe?"

Kitty twisted her oversized ring. "Kane told me the combination and I opened a safe upstairs. So what? It was empty."

Colt's eyes shone bright as polished mahogany. "Sure. *Now.*"

With his gloved hand, he patted the duffel at his side. He slung it over his shoulder and Kitty's eyes went wide as saucers. Everett packed up the drive and followed Colt around the couch. They both kept their guns on the Maynards as they backed into the kitchen.

Kitty took her time piecing it together. "But...why do you care if I opened *your* safe?"

Colt furrowed his brow and cut a look his way, like the thought hadn't occurred to him. "This your house?"

Everett sniffed and shrugged. "Never been here in my life. You?"

"Can't say I have." Colt waved a gloved hand at Ralph.

The colonel's face purpled in fury. "You *fuckers.*" Maynard huffed. "Whose house is this?"

Everett eyed the crystal decanters on the bar, the richly wooded accents — and the many, *many* places that now bore the Maynards' fingerprints. "I believe this piece of property belongs to our illustrious senator. Busy man, doesn't get down here much."

"Security is for shit," Colt added. "I don't blame him."

Everett continued on, thoroughly pleased. "Seeing how he was busy with his visit to the station today — "

"According to your assistant, at least. Bad day to be out of office, Ralph."

"The way we figure, you not wantin' to explain why you broke in and drank the man's liquor while Kitty cleared out his safe..." Everett whistled through his teeth. Colt was damn-near grinning. "That just might buy us a bit of your silence — if doin' the right thing is too much for you to handle."

They'd wrapped it all in too tidy a bow for either of the Maynards to unravel. Everett watched Ralph do the math in his head and come up with the same proof.

"You're *done*, Kane. After this shit? You'll never work another day in the department."

Everett's steady chuckle told him just how fine that was. "Consider this my two weeks', asshole. I'll try to wrap this case before then. Call it my goin' away present."

Colt opened the ornate front door and Everett looked over his shoulder, adjusted the strap of Kitty's bag and winked at Ralph for good measure.

"Be seein' you, Maynard."

The door shut soundly behind them.

Colt kept his eyes on their exit until Everett cleared the house. Wouldn't be long before the fear kicked in, and Ralph would go running for his own vehicle in the drive. Good thing Colt had thought of that too.

They got into Everett's car and Colt dropped the duffel in the backseat. Everett nodded at the bag. "Thought we talked about you puttin' that back."

Colt looked like the cat who ate the fuckin' canary, smirking even as he buckled on his seat belt. "If we get out of this? Ain't no way I'm puttin' this back. Senator's a piece of shit too."

By the time he started the car, Everett was grinning like a kid on Christmas Day. Not so much at Maynard bursting through the door as Kitty marched behind, or even Ralph's stilted journey to the ground to check the tire that somehow came up slashed.

What really got his attention was the look in Colt's eyes as they left the lake house. Everett knew that look. Seen it plenty of times before—and returned it plenty more. As they drove from the scene of their various crimes, he wondered what *that* look at this moment might mean.

"Connection's the real drug..."

Maynard's grounded Hummer was a square speck in the rearview, but visible, when Colt dusted off a different line.

"Pull over a sec."

Everett's hands obeyed before he could question the notion, pulling them off the scenic drive that cut across the property's acreage. The car hadn't even made a full stop before Colt's seatbelt clanked against the door and rough, efficient hands were reaching for his zip. Before he could so much as slam on the brakes, Colt had him halfway down his throat.

Holy...

"*Fuck*, you ain't gotta...what're you—"

Colt slid off with a groan, and there was too much of Switch staring back for comfort—a man with zero thought of self-preservation, who only cared for the high.

He tipped his head and said, "Just collateral damage. Don't fret over it none," before returning to the task at hand.

Christ, Colt...

It wasn't that it didn't feel good, wasn't every damn thing he'd wanted all day and longer. It was just somehow, watching Colt like that, bent over the console to suck him hard and fast...that wasn't all he was after anymore. Everett wondered if it ever was.

But good goddamn, he was only human, and despite their time apart, Colt hadn't forgot a bit of what he knew. And it was so close to what he actually wanted, had so many of the same components—

Then Colt moaned at the taste of him, throat vibrating around him, and shit, but that was it for Everett's good sense. He couldn't help but let it ride.

Colt still knew exactly where to stroke to send his head slamming back against the seat. He knew when to press hips down as he bobbed his head, how to get the best angle Everett's seatbelt would allow because damn, Colt didn't give him no kind of warning, and he couldn't move at all how he'd like. But that was never their style anyhow.

"Col, I...fuckin' *hell*, just—"

The world flashed white behind his eyelids and he reached a rapid peak, sending it down Colt's throat as he sucked him dry, leaving no worries after cleanup. Like it was easiest or something. Most obvious course forward, so might as well.

When Everett calmed enough to think, he realized that didn't sit all-the-way comfortable.

For his part, Colt sat up looking pleased with himself and lit a smoke. He kept his eyes on the side mirror, watching Maynard, who was still fighting to pry off that slashed tire. Colt smothered a downright chuckle and took a drag. Everett watched the smoke curl from his lips and a few extra gears got to turning.

"Maynard's sayin' you're some high-falutin' city-queer. Must've taken it up the ass for those boys undercover..."

And, yeah. All right. Blowing him in no time flat, in partial view of that asshole and his churchy wife? It *was* funny. Goddamn hilarious, actually.

So Everett laughed along, did up his belt and steered the car back to the driveway. And also, he told himself, *next time*. Next time, he'd say something. Because as much as it still surprised him *this* time, he needed to know the physical mattered in the way it was supposed to.

He was still too worried Colt was out here trying to die to believe in easy lies like *"don't fret over it none."* And if by the end of this, all Colt was grabbing for was his belt across the console...well, he wasn't sure what would come next. Because then they wouldn't be on the same page at all.

Everett turned onto well-traveled roads before attempting conversation. "So, what's next?"

He let Colt decide if he was talking about the case.

The detective at his side flipped through pages in a yellow legal pad, punching buttons into the GPS on the car's display. He entered an address two hours away. With traffic, they'd get there by sundown.

"Got some questions for Phillip Edwards," Colt said. "How 'bout you?"

Everett flipped the turn signal and pulled onto the highway. "Could make time for a social call."

Colt shrugged. "Or somethin'."

* * * *

Colt
Louisiana, 2018

He levered back the safety and aimed at the man he assumed was Phillip Edwards. But he couldn't be sure, since there were two men in the bed, and either one could be Phil.

One way to tell.

Colt demanded, "Who shot Patrick Combs?"

The dark-haired man yanked the sheet up to his chin. He shut his eyes and muttered, "Jesus, Mary and Joseph." The other man didn't budge, eyes fixed on the gun.

Phil, then.

Everett kept his own weapon pointed down the hall. He was watching the door more from habit than anything, since Colt hadn't said a word about a plan for the hour they'd watched the house. He'd been waiting for a distraction, or failing that, the cover of dark. Both arrived as a black sedan parked in Phillip Edwards' drive. The sole male visitor was quickly ushered inside, and Colt had waited ten more minutes before following after.

And now, in Phil's very-occupied bedroom, Colt angled his head and asked the question again. "Who. Shot. Patrick. Combs?"

Phillip's eyes were too wide to be hiding anything but a guilty conscience. The man stuttered, "I didn't...I mean it wasn't—it wasn't me."

"I asked who it *was*," Colt clarified. He eyed Phil down the gun's sight. "Tell me. Or die knowing."

The man beside him gasped and hit Phillip's shoulder, terrified and clearly out of the loop. At the contact, Phillip threw his hands up and said, "Keith. My cousin. Keith shot that temp."

"Richard's youngest son?"

Phillip nodded nervously. "What did he...what do you think he did?"

"We're way past *think*, Phil." He walked to the side of the bed and pressed the muzzle to the pillow, right next to Phil's ear. "Talk."

"Keith works for me at the rodeo," Phillip said immediately. "Small stuff. He's in charge of the seasonals."

Ev inhaled sharply behind him. He looked at Phil more closely. "You were there. On the scene in 2011. I interviewed you."

Colt imagined the man in rhinestone-cowboy best and recalled a faint impression of Phillip, looking him over while he examined Patrick's body. Phillip nodded to Everett, and Colt waved with his other hand for him to continue. "Uncle Richard kicked him out of the family after...well, I never knew, exactly. Didn't *want* to. I'd seen Keith get away with enough to know if he finally got cut off...had to be bad."

"But you're still in business with him," Colt prompted. "You let your cousin work the rodeo even after your uncle cut ties."

"Keith has his uses. Handles a certain part of the business for me."

"You mean Jared and Leroy?"

Phillip nodded again, but didn't ask how he knew such names. Colt's attention slid to the frozen bedmate, then returned to the man in front of him. Real terror shone in Phillip's blue-green eyes, more and more as Colt kept talking.

"Your only hope of stayin' out of a cell is to give us something we can use. Where's Keith now? Where's he stay at?"

"I don't know," Phil clamored. "I *swear* I don't. If I knew, I'd tell you."

"Can you call him?" Everett asked from the door.

Phillip's face turned to one of genuine frustration, like this was a request he routinely had to field. "I can try, but he's got terrible reception. Even with the rodeo doin' so well, he uses these shitty phones. Says they're cheaper."

Cheap phones…

"Disposable burners?" Colt asked.

"Yeah," said Phillip. "Never know what number he's using. Which is a pain, since he disappears for days at a time. Can't trust him with anything but Leroy's crowd anymore."

"Where's he buy the phones?"

It wasn't the home run he was hoping for, but with a name, Colt could do a lot he couldn't before. Something dangerously like hope unfurled in his chest. He nodded to Everett at the door, then moved the cool muzzle to rest on Phil's sweat-slick forehead. The man whimpered as his lids slipped closed, and when he opened his eyes again, Colt was staring straight through him.

"Wouldn't mention this at the next family reunion."

Phillip gulped and nodded, perspiration dripping down his face.

Colt backed to the doorway and finally lowered his weapon, then took a moment to consider all he'd seen that night — the clothing on the floor, the car downstairs, the specific tenor of one man's expletives.

He tipped his head at the bed in farewell. "Gonna need you to write some things down in the morning, Phil. Be seein' you."

And to the man fairly hiding beneath the sheet, he said, "Father."

The holy man's eyes went wide in confirmation.

As they left the house, Colt could tell Ev wanted to ask how he knew, but he figured the Good Book in the back of that black sedan should've been clue enough for anyone. Once they were outside, Colt watched his old partner notice the gold-edged text, plant hands on his hips and mutter to himself. Ev's chuckle mixed with familiar words.

"Fuckin' Harkan…"

Colt allowed a small smile, remembering the many times he'd heard that line, the go-to phrase for any of Mason's finest when, once again, Colt the Outsider had been the one to break the case, to find the details no one seemed to see.

Colt just hoped he could do it one more time.

Chapter Fifteen

Colt
Louisiana, 2018

He only knew it was morning when Ev pulled the bar door open and let the light in. He hadn't slept a wink, but his old partner had come prepared and dropped two double-shot coffees on the bar top. When Colt reached for one, Rhett pushed a sandwich into his hand instead. He coupled it with a look that said he wasn't above shoving it down his throat, so Colt took a bite. Wasn't half bad.

They spent the day in the back at an old card table, remaking their case-wall and piecing through Kitty's drive. They dug deep on Keith Edwards, but all they found for an address was a house he'd lost in Katrina. As the hours stretched and the lists grew longer, Colt felt the storm-cloud worry set in.

They *still* might not have enough to put this down. Not in time.

They'd narrowed the new list of possibles to fourteen properties across the state — but that's if it *was* some family property. What if Keith had gone to ground with the Cobras after all? What if the family lead was a bust? For a moment, Colt worried they'd gone too hard with Maynard. If Kitty's drive didn't pan out, what then? Try to pick Keith up at the rodeo and wait for the lawyers to show, crying words like *circumstantial* over murders a decade cold?

It was realities like those that worried Colt most of all.

They spent a working dinner sorting files to avoid it, but Colt knew the dead end he'd dreaded was upon them. He tried not to let his mind run with how little time was left, with what it would mean to lose Keith again, but all he could feel was the weight of *another year*, the heaviness of what it'd take to finally put this down for good —

Gotta solve this. Gotta find a way.

"If all we've got is checking possible properties," Colt thought out loud, "each wrong one we pick gives Keith a chance to run. We're only gonna get one shot at this."

"I know," Everett agreed, his voice exhausted. "You've been sayin' that for hours."

Colt lit his last cigarette.

A silent minute later, Ev addressed the elephant in the room. "Well, if we're not gettin' anywhere with what we've got, what's next?"

He let his breath out slow and dragged a box of files closer. "The shot in the dark," Colt answered, raking a hand through his hair before tying it up in its band. "We go through the files again and hope something jumps. You want business records or old case files?"

Wasn't much of a choice, but Everett made one. "Business."

Colt handed the relevant folders across the square table. "Need to go through every piece of this with a fine-tooth comb. Every sight, smell, sound, every name we find—you think it through and look for connections." Colt opened a file of his own and licked the taste of ash from his lips. "We're close. It's there...waitin' to bubble up."

Then it happened.

He didn't know what it was that made it all click, but to Colt, Ev was the center of all light when the thought went off in his head.

"That night we found Mary...what'd it smell like to you?"

Colt paused in rifling through the box of files and thought back. "The woods. Different kinds of smoke. Chemical static. Decay. There was a lot to focus on that night."

But he couldn't help but watch as Ev stood there thinking, because Colt could tell that answer wasn't sitting right. Everett had his own look brewing that meant he was on it now, that he was following a thread only he could see and for once, Colt was left to watch from outside—to not know where he was going and be surprised by Everett's mind.

He hummed in anticipation. "What you got?"

Everett leafed through his stack of documents. "I'm lookin' for that shipping list you found on the rodeo drive. From our bit of undercover after Combs."

"Why?"

Warm hues of excitement bled into Everett's tone. "Well..."

Without warning, he dropped the rest of what was in his hand, letting the file fall with a definitive slap to the table. He pulled Colt's box toward him, rummaged through the photos and walked to the wall to pin one up.

"Colt. C'mon over here."

It wasn't a request, but Colt moved to his side. He knew the sound of a case cracked wide.

Everett pointed at a photo of Andrea Meyer's fingernails, broken and dirtied, with an unknown powder beneath. When the scene was first examined, initial testing returned a list of chemicals even Colt couldn't pronounce, and the lead had ended there. But the second pin on the board held a manifest for a shipping contract — with an order from a company that sold aquatic herbicides. And a lot of the chemical makeup looked the same as those tests.

Everett pointed between the two. "Edwards ain't connected to any chemical businesses. No company properties back up to water. So why buy aquatic herbicide in bulk if you're not making money from it?"

Through Everett's eyes, it clicked. He remembered what Kitty said yesterday.

"Family and business are a blended affair for us..."

"They bought those chemicals for personal use. For property upkeep."

"Exactly," Everett agreed. His eyes were bright. "I think *that's* what's under Andrea's nails. If the herbicide is from the actual scene, we might get an address from warehouse delivery records."

Colt moved to consult the relevant paperwork. Everett fished his phone from his pocket. "I don't remember much from that ambulance hit," he said, "but when the doors knocked open, there was this…tangy chemical smell. Was all over Mary's clothes too. Recognized it from when I was a kid."

Everett drummed fingers on his hip as he waited on hold. "My grandmother's people lived all over the bayous. Used to help her spread that shit to keep algae from growin' or it'd fuck up the motors on the boats. I thought it was just the concussion kicking old memories loose, but now…"

Colt followed his partner's conclusions and tried not to look as shocked as he felt. "You're sayin' it was our guy who hit you that night? It wasn't some random accident?"

"We knew Keith went somewhere after he shot Mary." Everett turned excited eyes to Colt, phone pressed to his ear. "Think about it. Where's the other people from those burner videos? Why d'you keep finding missing persons, but hardly any bodies? He's weighing them down in the water to make them disappear. *Got* to be. Easiest place to do that is waterfront property you own."

Colt walked to the list of properties at the other end of the room. He ticked off land-locked addresses with a marker. "Only three family properties from Kitty's drive back up to water."

Everett circled the table to stand beside him. He pointed at the map near the list of addresses. "I'll do you one better. They're in totally different parts of the state. Different quality of water at each, which means different plant life—"

"Which might mean different herbicides."

Everett took the marker from him, drew three circles and snapped the cap in place. "We find which herbicide that is under her nails? We find the right door to bash in."

Colt stared blankly at the three red circles.

Fuck. He actually did it.

"That's…god*damn* it, Ev."

Colt shook his head at the map, unable to believe how so much was *right there* and he couldn't see it. Not till now. The missing piece, courtesy of Everett Kane.

But Colt couldn't hold onto that truth for long — not without remembering, without wanting so badly he could burst. The thrill of the car yesterday was front and center in his mind, the close but not quite that only served to whet his appetite. And now, Everett had gone and solved it.

Solved *the whole damn thing*, just standing there.

Colt watched his old partner pace and stubbed out his cigarette. Finally off hold, Everett was talking to some buddy in the crime lab, asking for a second run of the chemical against the manifest's list. After a few traded favors and the promise of Stapes' support, it was agreed. They'd have results by morning.

But right now? Too much was falling into place for even Colt to ignore.

Everett ended the call and tossed his phone to the paper-strewn table. He knew he should look away, but there was nothing better than the sight of Everett's smile, full and hopeful and true. He tasted watermelon and sunshine despite himself. Laughing blue eyes met his. The muffled melody of jukebox country filtered through the wall, and their smiles were stuck on a feedback loop, a chuckle shared between.

When the smiles fell, neither detective looked away.

Rhett swallowed hard. Colt blinked once.

Then Colt was making the first move to him. Ev damn-near tossed his folding chair aside. In a matter of three urgent steps, they pulled each other into an inevitable kiss.

Since they'd been thrown back into each other's lives, there'd been none of Ev's shy shit from before. From his heartfelt request that Colt live a bit longer to the tenderness that followed, he'd been nothing but genuine. It was thoughts like those that had him holding the sides of Everett's face, and *yeah,* he should probably back off, shouldn't try to devour this moment whole, but as he walked them against the wall, the way Ev winced and still leaned into his touch…after all they'd done to each other, he still wanted this. Wanted him.

Goddamn…

It was only ever the shit that was really going to kill him that felt this kind of necessary, *this* kind of essential…and it kept getting worse the more Everett melted into him. Colt kept all his focus on kissing him, on rediscovering every place that made Everett sigh into his mouth. Tongues brushed and teased and he tasted the sweetness of relief, sharp desperation and something more terrifying he didn't think he could name.

Colt slowed their progress, pulling back to really look at him. He took in every bit of his partner—amped-up, kiss-flushed, completely hard in his jeans.

All of it was miraculously his fault. And Colt didn't much believe in those.

Everett grinned at him. "Not bad, huh?"

Then a new thought landed like a gut punch. Fear kicked hot in his throat. He touched Ev's cheek in wonder.

How'd I do anything without you?

But Colt knew the answer. He didn't.

* * * *

Everett
Louisiana, 2018

He might not've known what Colt was thinking, looking down at him like that, but he could see the intensity, could feel the depth of it even as Colt said nothing at all.

This would be that next time you told yourself about.

And Everett *knew* that. He did. But he needed to get his courage first.

He nudged their mouths together and kissed Colt again, stoking the growing fire as much as the man would let him. He twined a hand in the back of Colt's hair, the glide of the extra length silky between his fingers. He tugged lightly at the roots and Colt bit back a moan and fuck, but Everett had missed that sound. He pulled again and counted the minutes gone in teasing licks and soft nips at Colt's tragedy of a beard.

At least he'd trimmed it now.

But somehow, it still wasn't enough. He wasn't above begging—not for this man, the *only* person he'd let manacle his wrists against the wall with nothing but the strength of his hands. He couldn't tell if Colt even knew he was doing it, or if he was too far gone to notice. Colt angled their hips together and he writhed at the once-familiar feeling, too scared to ask for what he feared he'd already missed.

Because this? God help him, but it was everything he wanted.

Colt rocked against him, sucked on his bottom lip and *shit*, Everett couldn't take it anymore. He dug deep for bravery he hoped he had and didn't try to edit the thought, ignoring the soft press of lips down his neck and letting the words fall as they may.

"Col...don't tell me no. Not now — *please*, not now."

Colt fell against him with a sigh and released his arms. He held onto Colt's waist and slid hands up the sides of his ribcage. Their cheeks leaned hard against each other as they struggled to stay upright, and Everett slipped a newly freed hand between their bodies, let his fingers ride the ridge of him. He turned to nose Colt's cheek, to kiss tender down his jaw, around his ear to whisper, to beg for scraps if he had to —

"Come by tonight, Col. Just tonight. C'mon, now."

Colt would probably call it junkie talk and have all manner of things to blame it on, but for once, Everett didn't want to talk him off that ledge. Maybe it was pathetic, but Christ, he'd take what he could get.

Colt pressed a kiss to his temple. "All right, Ev."

They took his car with the GPS that could automatically store all sorts of addresses. They'd plan their next steps from his two-bedroom tomorrow, and there wouldn't be no lingering vehicle in the driveway to manage either.

As they left the bar, he caught Colt staring at his busted-up truck. He thought back on that camping cot the man had called a bed for years, the flophouse apartment that came before, and wondered when the last time was that Colt Harkan had somewhere like a home. Not that Everett's place was all that cozy, and he wasn't assuming home was a place Colt would be needing, if his plans for "*gettin' off the ride*" didn't change after the case.

But the thought of a home with Colt? It eased Everett's worries anyway.

Tomorrow was a world away. He could let himself dream tonight.

* * * *

Everett's small house wasn't much to look at, but the inside was clean and mostly furnished, filled with signs of the life he'd been trying to lead.

In the kitchen was a box of assorted teas and a stale can of coffee. Stacks of TV dinners lined the freezer. The fridge was all takeout and condiments. Only a six pack of beer, though there was space for more. Everett supposed it was still an empty life, but things were filling in at the edges. He watched Colt set his few belongings on the couch and amended the thought.

More and more all the time.

Colt put his phone to his ear to dial up some grub. He gestured to the freezer, but Colt cut that off quick. "Ain't eatin' that shit tonight. Could be a big day tomorrow."

And it was just pizza and beer and sitcom reruns, but it felt so free and easy that Everett was afraid to blink. They joked with each other. They ragged on the TV show, the commercials, all of it. While they ate, Colt only pulled two cigs from the pack, where before he might've gone for an uneven five. Everett stayed with water after his first beer, preferring to keep his wits about him the closer they got to sleep.

"You want the shower first?" he asked.

"Go ahead," said Colt.

"Ain't got the guest room set up, but the sofa's comfortable."

Everett dropped his eyes before they had to admit they wouldn't need it. Talking about the shower was hard enough. He walked to the bathroom and closed the door. Better to get clean fast as possible and be done with it...maybe in more ways than one.

Everett was out and done in a quick ten. He pulled on comfortable lounge pants and an old college T-shirt, then checked what Colt was up to on the couch. Looked like he was sketching in the corner of his legal pad, but Everett couldn't tell what of.

He cleared his throat and Colt looked up. "All yours, if you want it. I put a towel on the sink."

"All right."

He sat at the edge of his bed as Colt shut the bathroom door. He grabbed the book he'd normally read this time of night and listened to the unfamiliar sounds of someone else in his home. Running a thumb down the book's spine, he breathed through the splash of water against tile and wondered if he'd hear when Colt saw the biggest sign of just exactly what type of life he'd been living. Because there were two soaps in the shower, and he could've hidden one. But he didn't.

Everett had always been a bar soap man, but beside his suddy brick was a bottle labeled *travel size* that smelled like mountains in the mist. Or so he'd been told.

It all sounded like a normal shower to Everett. He hoped Colt spent the time in a cloud.

Twenty minutes later, the water stopped. Everett was reading, for lack of other occupation, and as part of his determined stance that he was *not* going to look at what Colt had been doodling. Not before he decided to show him.

At the creak of his bedroom door, Everett looked up to meet Colt's mahogany eyes. They were warm and scared and shining, but he didn't look away. Colt's wet hair was tied up at the back of his neck. Standing in a towel, he was more or less dry.

And the sharp scent of rosemary cut through the air.

Colt stood in the amber light of the bedside lamp. "Got me in here, Ev. What're we doin'? What do you want?"

Maybe it was because it reminded him so strongly of his own question years ago, when a dustbowl pessimist named Colton Harkan blew his nearly-stable life apart. Maybe it was all the years he'd spent wanting and trying and *failing* and hurting that made him more comfortable flailing some. Whatever it was, as he stood before Colt in the bedroom, all Everett said was the truth.

"You. Just want you."

Colt stepped into his space and smoothed hands up Everett's chest, then slowly along his shoulders, daring to pull him close. "Didn't use to."

Everett closed his eyes at the conviction in Colt's tone — like it was a fact. Like it was something he'd told himself, over and over in their years without, and goddamn but they had to get through this somehow. There was too much he had to make up for. Too much he'd never said.

He tried to say some of it now. Just in case.

"Yes, I did. You know I did."

Everett dropped his head to kiss Colt's neck, unwinding the towel from around his waist. It stuttered the man's speech, but Colt dared to tease anyway, "And how...how would I know a thing like that?"

"Because you were there that morning too. The only time I worked up the courage to make love to you like you deserved."

278

Colt didn't hide the heavy sigh that drew from him and angled his chin for a kiss. He walked them back to the bed, lips never leaving each other, and there was maybe a little levity in his tone when he asked, "So that's what that was? Makin' love?"

Everett nipped his ear and tightened arms around his back. "Asshole. Like I didn't have your number by then too."

"Maybe so."

He pulled a naked Colt to settle over him on the bed. Narrow hips rocked against his cotton pajamas. His breath hitched as Colt pressed close, finally where he wanted him most, but as Everett leaned in, Colt tilted his head away. There was a playful spark in his chocolate eyes.

"So that's how it is?" Everett asked. "Gonna make me prove this to you again?"

Colt brushed his nose with the tip of his own. "If you've a mind. If you're up for it."

"Watch yourself, now…"

And maybe there were some words he wished they'd already said — words they could say at all without complicating things further — but the time for talk was over when Colt angled his mouth over his, kissing him full and deep, and the relief was so raw they didn't tease each other for the sounds that escaped. Instead, they traced the planes of time-altered bodies and found so much still the same.

Everett tried to keep his shirt on. Colt wouldn't let him. So he spent an age at least kissing up Colt's new scars. It was the kind of soft and steady that built to something desperate, something urgent as the heat of sliding skin, bubbling under the surface since that very first roadside, when Colt promised to show him a bit of what he didn't know.

"Times have changed some..."

For the years he didn't take the time, Everett did now. He worked Colt open gently, relished every sigh and sharp inhale and "Get a fuckin' move on, Rhett," he could draw from the man beneath him. When he reached in the bedside table for a condom, Colt wrapped a hand around his wrist, sliding to twine their fingers together, a little breathless when he said, "Don't have to. Unless you're needin' one."

Colt wasn't talking about lasting. This wasn't some jibe about stamina or old age. Colt was asking if anyone had been where he planned to be, in any kind of recent to have mattered. And that answer had been the same for *years*.

Everett slammed the drawer shut.

He worked what he needed from the bottle he'd retrieved first, slicked a hand down the length of his cock and pressed slowly into Colt, skin-to-skin. With Colt on his back, it was just like that first morning — the one he'd imagined for years of mornings after.

They'd had this a few times in that month of playing house. But God, did it feel all manner of different now.

"Holy *fuck*, Col..."

"Ev...*goddamn* — "

"I don't wanna — "

"I know, just move."

"Are you — "

"*Move*, Ev. Now, right fuckin' now."

So he did, and Colt tipped his hips as they rolled together, catching his lips in a searing kiss. And Everett knew that this was the shit people meant when they said *"with my body, I thee worship,"* 'cause it was only through some manner of grace this man was in his life again. And he wasn't letting him go without a fight.

So for a night, Everett made love to Colt as completely as he knew how. He laced their hands together. He stroked Colt's face and the curve of his knee. He kissed down his chin and rolled his hips, grinding against that sweet spot deep inside. He thumbed Colt's nipples and nipped at his jaw as he brought their tempo faster, slower, whatever would make the tortured perfection last just a second longer, just a moment, just a minute —

As much time as Colt would give, Everett would take, and gladly. And when he wasn't sure he could last much longer, Colt let loose a confession Everett prayed wouldn't leave with the dawn.

"*Evvv*...I fuckin' *need* you, man..."

"I know, I'm here. I'm here, Col."

Like all he required was that final reminder, Colt's eyes dropped shut and his hips jerked up as he spilled across Everett's adoring fingers. He watched in a kind of wonder — thought there must be fireworks going off behind Colt's eyelids, the way he was looking now — and before long, Everett was coming hard and fast after him, an arm wrapped strong around Colt all the while.

Damp brown eyes blinked open to meet his, and there was no mistaking what he saw in those darkened depths.

"*So that's what that was? Makin' love?*"

As far as Everett could tell, yeah. Sure enough.

Chapter Sixteen

Colt
Louisiana, 2018

Colt woke first in the dark.

Mostly when he woke up, Colt wished he hadn't. This wasn't one of those times. But even as Everett rolled closer in his sleep, draped an arm over his hip and returned to contented unconsciousness, Colt knew that tomorrow could be complicated. Whatever else had happened that night, he still wasn't ready to trust Everett in the mornings.

Sincerity of a moment was never Rhett's problem. Sticking to it was.

Besides, he hadn't promised nothing beyond a night, and they still had work to do. So Colt didn't let himself feel too bad about sneaking to the couch and tried his best to focus on what tomorrow might bring.

* * * *

Everett
Louisiana, 2018

Everett woke in his bed alone. He'd halfway expected as much. He scrubbed a hand down his face and tried not to take it personally that one of them had some good sense to spare. Probably was best they kept focus on the case.

He got dressed before braving the kitchen, where he fixed a plate of the breakfast of champions—leftover pizza, antacids and a microwaved cup of black tea. Colt was dressed for the day and sat on the single bar stool at the island. He picked at a sad piece of toast, but looked amused when he spotted the box of tea in Everett's hand.

"They say it's better for you," he explained. "Less acidic or somethin'."

Colt's gaze dropped to the plate of cold pizza in his hand. He raised a wary eyebrow, but that was quite the double standard in Everett's view. "Fuck you, Mr. Takeout-and-SpaghettiOs-off-a-hotplate. I saw that office. You got no room to judge."

Colt set his coffee on the counter. His lack of verbal comment made his stare almost audible. He'd never known someone who could think as loudly as Colt Harkan.

Everett leaned against the cabinets and shifted gears. "So what's the plan then?"

Colt clicked his pen. "Thanks to your guy in the lab, we got results fast. Good odds it's goin' down here." He slid the notepad his way. Everett nodded at the circled address. "With the spread of dates from the burner videos, there's still a few days before it makes sense to go in. Better to wait till all the vipers are home before we torch the nest."

"And how were you thinking we'd do that, exactly?"

"You're the one working for government-funded forces. Might be time to let Stapes in on what we know."

Everett shook his head. "He ain't gonna like it. This kind of heat on the Edwards' name...they're gonna want more proof than we have before they take the right steps here. Legal proof, at least."

Colt scowled darkly. "We can't go to Keith with a kind request to talk. He'll lawyer up, clean up or go to ground again. Hide behind his daddy's money because the family can't stand the scandal—"

"I'm not sayin' I like it, Col. I'm sayin' that's how things are."

"Planning for *how things are* is the same as accepting it that way."

Colt said it like he thought Everett should've known that already, and for a moment, he wondered if Colt was talking about the case at all. His phone buzzed on the counter and saved him from having to respond. The ID lit up with *Major Stapes* and he figured, may as well bite the bullet now.

"Major. Was just about to—"

"Turn on the news, Kane."

He felt his brow crease, but Stapes sounded too pissed for it to be some joke. He walked to the sofa in the living room and grabbed the remote off the coffee table. When the TV clicked on, the banner text on the morning news read "*Lt. Colonel Maynard criticizes use of police resources to solve violent murder...*"

At Ralph's nasally voice, Colt's head swiveled to the living room. On the phone, Stapes cleared his throat. "You wanna tell me what that's about?"

"You really wanna know?"

Stapes didn't answer, so he tuned into the press conference, certain the major was doing the same on the other side of the line. It was quite the bit of speechifying, Everett would give him that. Maynard did a nice job stepping 'round the bits of truth that might incriminate his wife's people — and laid all the blame on Everett in the process.

No wonder they made Ralph a boss.

"The primary detective on this case has been working unmonitored for weeks. Why was he left to work this alone? If there's violent murder happening in our own backyard, we should be dedicating every resource, lending all possible assistance, sparing *no expense* to protect our citizens from — "

"You gotta be kidding me, Stapes."

"He didn't call you by name, but I'm gettin' pressure to have you bring this in fast. Can't keep them off your back for much longer." The major sighed. "You're gonna be getting help whether you like it or not. Probably a whole oversight team."

Colt moved to stand beside him in the living room, murderous eyes on Maynard. He sipped his coffee. "Should've shot him when I had the chance."

Stapes coughed in his ear. "I think you're breaking up there, Kane. Can't hear you on my end."

"I can hear you just fine — "

"I *said* there's some interference or something. Getting some other call mixed in on this line." Everett took the major's cue and moved away from Colt and his list of regrets. His mind spun with ways to get

Stapes on their side, but the major didn't let him start on any of them. He only said, "We need to talk, Everett. My office. One hour."

Not a single thing in the major's tone sounded comforting.

Everett tossed his cell to the coffee table and sat on the couch, head hanging between spread legs. His hands rested on the back of his neck, scratching at the short hairs before sliding off the top. He fell against the cushions with a huff.

"Well. Fuck."

Colt only shrugged. "Doesn't change anything."

"You watchin' some other newscast over there?"

The volume was low, but Colt's attention stayed on the television, like he was memorizing every bit of Maynard's face for the next time he saw him. "We're not the only ones feelin' the pressure now. Keith will move things up. It'll be tonight, tomorrow at the latest." Colt's eyes went darker than his coffee. "And we know where he is."

Colt took a seat at the other end of the couch. He ran a finger around the rim of his mug. "They're gonna want to rally some troops. Make a show of this." He stayed quiet a moment, then nodded his way. "Talk to Stapes. Get him to hold off until he gets our call tonight. Tell him as little as you can—I don't want anyone gettin' tipped off any further."

"What about you?"

Colt set his mug aside and opened Everett's laptop. "I've got the contingencies. The media wants to know what we're doin'? Wants the full story? Well, they're gonna get it. Even if we don't come back to tell 'em."

Everett nodded, and maybe it was agreeing to some suicide mission, but it felt better than the fear. He was about to head to the station when his phone buzzed again on the coffee table. The ID flashed *Rachael cell*.

And the way the man froze, there was no pretending Colt didn't see.

Rachael wouldn't have had to do much figuring to guess what Maynard's press conference really meant. Everett might not be her husband anymore, but he was still her children's father, still someone she cared about. Rach was good people. When she chose to be.

"Should've seen this comin'," he sighed and palmed his cell again. He walked to stand behind the couch. "Rachael, how's it — what d'you mean, news?"

Colt snorted and moved to the kitchen, but even with the printer working noisily on the countertop, he wondered how much Colt could hear. He paced behind the couch and watched the birds at the backyard feeder, letting Rachael ramble the worry out of her system. "It's fine, really. We're about to wrap this up if we have the kind of day I think. Just...you want to *what*?"

Colt raised his eyes from the printer with an unknowable look. Everett stammered into the phone. "I don't...I don't know if that's a good idea..."

Colt returned his gaze to the laptop, but extended his hand, palm up.

"Give it here."

* * * *

Colt
Louisiana, 2018

Everett handed his cell over but stayed too close for comfort. He'd expected this, just maybe not so soon. He mentally boxed the memories of yellow walls, lasagna, the taste of blood and cinders, then brought the phone to his ear.

"You know I won't talk about the case."

"I'm not asking you to," came Rachael's cool reply.

"Then what *are* you askin'?"

Everett winced in the key of *this is going well* and tried to recover the phone, but Colt's glare stopped him cold. He spotted his shoes by the door and decided on a walk around the block. The last thing this conversation needed was an audience.

Rachael, able to read a room by sound alone, waited until the front door closed to try again. "I appreciate you talking to me."

"Let's not start with lyin'. Though it feels familiar."

That kept her quiet until he turned the corner. Colt lit a necessary cigarette.

"When Everett came by, he said you were working together again, and…" She trailed off and tried again. "I just remember what the two of you were like back then. The kinds of risks you used to take when your backs were against the wall."

"What of it?"

"Look, I know it's not my business, but…" He heard a scratching noise and could almost picture Rachael, phone pressed to her ear as she nervously picked her nails. "Just tell me I'm overreacting. Tell me it's all fine, that he's not gonna wind up dead. I'm worried about him. You too, for what it's worth."

Colt flicked his smoke to the sidewalk.

What a load of shit…

Didn't sit right with him, Rachael coming through like she cared. There was no question in Colt's mind she thought she was checking on Everett, but it was clear that on another level, she was calling for something else too. Rachael wanted to know where things stood now Colt was back in town—like she had a right to it. Like she weren't the one who blew it all up.

Like he wasn't just as guilty as her.

Still couldn't hardly think her name without the cool slime of shame flooding down his back, all tied up in failing Mary and Ev in one terrible night. Dealt a bad hand, Rachael had chosen the nuclear option—and with four years of distance, Colt could understand that. Sometimes, things blew all to hell because different was all that mattered.

Well, different she got.

Rachael had made her choices, mended the fences she cared to mend and set herself up in a great big house a whole lot nicer than Everett's. If he was to be believed, she'd left that marriage on a mission to get everything she'd ever wanted, this time on her own. That was fine. Good, even. Didn't mean he had to hold her hand through the destruction left in her wake.

Whatever happened next—with the case, Everett or any of it—Colt meant to make one thing perfectly clear.

"If you called him just to ask me to lie to you, then I think you've got an awful short memory. Should know by now that's somethin' I won't do."

He couldn't talk about this—especially not with her. The last time he'd seen Rachael was in her kitchen four years ago, the last night of a life he was just getting used to living.

"I'm sorry about...about how that all happened. What it meant for you and the case, it wasn't..." She sighed. "I had to do something."

"That's not much of an apology."

"Not much of a reason to."

Well, at least we're back to truth.

Having completed a circuit around the block, he walked up Everett's drive and opened the door. He was exactly where Colt had left him in the kitchen, watching the printer spit pages of proof. Everett's head snapped up at the sound of the door, eyes full of questions he'd never ask aloud.

And if that weren't half the problem in the first place...

Rachael said in his ear, "Just look out for him, will you?"

Colt held Everett's gaze, but couldn't keep his stare as pointed as he'd like. Exhaustion fell like a curtain around his shoulders. All he wanted was to be off the phone and left alone. He was sick and tired of being pulled between Rachael and Everett, like some fucked-up tug-of-war.

He said into the phone, "I didn't need *you* to tell me that."

Colt ended the call and tossed the cell back to Everett. He caught it against his chest. "What'd she say?"

"Why d'you care?"

Colt was too thin on patience to talk this out now, too full of soured shame to make any of this ride easy. He couldn't help but feel last night should've solved more than it did, and he hadn't figured out why. Maybe because with every move he made, every embrace, Everett was saying *stay*—and a part of Colt was still stuck on *goodbye*. On that conversation they hadn't had yet.

He closed his eyes as the memory played in his mind—

"Ain't like it's goodbye or nothin'. We'll still see each other all the time...right, Colt?"

"Sure, Everett..."

So now, much as he didn't want to, Colt decided to answer honestly. He pinched the bridge of his nose. "She's worried about you. Thinks you're walkin' into trouble."

"Which I am."

"You gonna stop because she's scared?"

"No."

"Then what's it matter?"

Everett scratched his chin. His blond stubble rasped like sandpaper. He wasn't angry, but exasperated might fit. "With the amount we've all dealt with each other's bullshit? I think it's not outside the realm of courtesy to keep all parties informed."

Everett might be talking sense, but it didn't change the pain that bloomed fresh in Colt's gut, having to stand there and listen to him talk about Rachael, obviously pleased with her worrying after him at all. Fuck, not *this* again...

"What's your play here, Rhett? Just gonna crash on the couch till Rachael caves?"

"You think she will?"

He knew he'd been silent too long when Everett tried another tactic — deflection. "Look, you're the one gettin' all testy and judgmental. And you didn't have to talk to her."

He decided to only address that first part. "Everybody judges. I just don't keep quiet about it."

"You keep quiet about anything? News to me."

"This ain't a joke, Ev."

"I know it's...damn, Col." He laughed once, but there was no humor to it. "Excuse me for tryin' to ease off this tension some." He rapped the linoleum where he leaned at the kitchen counter. Everett watched the printer work and muttered, "Jesus, if I don't sound like I'm talkin' to my ex-wife…"

"Ain't so different."

He was never sure how Ev would react to a truth staring him in the face, but this time, it wasn't bad. Everett shrugged in that *well, there you have it* fashion and the silence returned. It wasn't comfortable.

Everett cleared his plate and drank the last of his tea. His lips were pressed together in a tight line as he rinsed his dish. When the printer was finally done, Colt ripped the pages from the tray and stuffed them in Kitty's bag. He could tell Everett wanted to find some right with him before they plunged back into reality, but it was just as clear he had no idea what to say.

Ev tossed the dish towel over his shoulder. "Just…don't forget we still got talkin' to do, you and me. When this is over."

Colt shouldered Kitty's bag and grabbed his duffel for good measure. He was in no sort of mood to keep pulling this particular punch. "Yeah, well you're right about that, Everett. Because in all the time we've known each other, we still ain't talked about the one thing that fuckin' matters."

"And what's that?"

"The real reason we only got a month before you went scamperin' back to Rachael."

"Ain't like it's goodbye or nothin'…"

The words landed like a slap, but Colt couldn't stand to be stuck in the house or memories of them any longer. He let that be the last word he'd regret and slammed the door on his way out. He'd walk to his truck if he had to.

Because Colt had too much to do that day to be worrying if Everett Kane was capable of change.

Chapter Seventeen

Everett
Louisiana, 2018

Never was a good sign when Col called him "*Everett*."

So he didn't bother going after him, didn't ask if Colt wanted a ride to the bar. Colt would get in touch when he was good and ready, about the case if nothing else, thanks to Maynard's press conference. Trying to push things now would only make it worse.

Everett stopped by the station and survived the meeting without giving too much up. With grace, charm and promises he secured Stapes' word that the cavalry would only be a phone call away. It probably helped that Everett said he'd be putting in papers to retire once they closed the case. The major could give him some leeway on this. Hell, he'd earned it.

Two hours later, Colt texted him coordinates and a message.

Get there before dark. Be ready to go.

Everett arrived at dusk in a dark shirt, darker jeans and hiking boots, his freshly cleaned gun safe in its holster. He pulled into a gravel lot to find Colt's weathered truck beside a backwoods dock, miles from anything one might call 'civilization'.

"You find us a ride?" he asked, hauling their go-bag over his shoulder.

Colt pointed at the motor boat tied to the dock, then pulled a muddy-brown shirt over his cotton tank. "Guy owed me a favor. He'll get us close and hang back in case, but we'd be better off if Stapes is ready. Maybe with those reinforcements Maynard's been promising."

He snorted and followed Colt to the boat. "Stapes will be there. He wants this down, just doesn't want to know about it."

"Same as it ever was."

"How 'bout you?" Everett asked, unsure how much time there really was for chatter. How personal Colt would let him get. "Combs, Sr. all set?"

Colt nodded. "He's got copies of everything to send to the press if he doesn't hear from me in twenty-four hours."

"Not leavin' us much wiggle room."

Weathered brown eyes considered the sky. "I disagree," said Colt. "Think we'll be lucky to be alive in two."

Everett wanted to convince him that wasn't so, but he didn't get the chance. Colt doubled his pace, stepped into the boat and called to the man at the motor, "All set, Carver?"

And a face he'd never expected to see again looked up from beneath a wide-brimmed hat.

Carver's barely familiar form sat hunched at the stern, a box of tools sprawled open at his feet. The arms of his flannel were rolled and the shirt hung open, framing his grease-stained undershirt. The sight sent Everett back to that night, smack in the middle of those four years of nothing when Carv had that same grease all down his arm, a kind face in a sea of strangers…

"Need a light?"

"Don't mind obvious, myself."

"Dance with me some."

"C'mon, Everett. What's it gonna be? Omelets or eggs?"

"Just about ready," Carver called to Colt. "Been a while since it ran."

Colt asked, "Think she'll hold?"

Everett decided to shut his mouth before anyone noticed it was hanging open.

"Yeah, well, I gave it my best. Business at the shop's been slow." Carver wiped his hands on a rag. "Maybe now you'll let me at that bike of yours again."

Colt lit a smoke and tossed Carver the pack. "Got two now, actually. Both could use a tune-up."

Everett wasn't entirely sure what was best to do here. On the one hand, he and Colt needed a ride — and if Stapes did fall through, Carver was all they had. To have a chance in hell at getting to Keith undetected, they couldn't risk driving. Stapes and crew could roll right through after they secured the area, but the road was the way out, not in.

On the other hand, after the morning they'd had? Everett wasn't keen on making nice with his one-night stand. Not in front of the man he planned to spend the rest of them with.

Just my fuckin' luck he knows Carver…

He was saved from having to play it cool when Carver returned Colt's smokes. He tossed them over and spotted Everett, still as a statue in the gravel lot. Recognition sparked in Carv's light brown eyes. He darted a look to Colt, then back at him, and Everett wasn't sure what in about that barely there nod righted things, but the unease settled in his gut.

He kicked the ground and shoved hands in his pockets. Carver swallowed a smile and kept working on the boat. He'd just have to add this to the list of problems for tomorrow, if Everett was around to worry about it at all.

He climbed on board and Carver gestured his way, asking Colt, "Who's your partner?"

He only stumbled the final step, and Everett thought that was damn well done, all things considered. The word sounded different in Carver's knowing tone and he wondered if Colt picked up on it. Probably so, the all-knowing bastard.

Whether he noticed or not, Colt motioned for him to get on the boat. "Detective Kane. He's the official side of this operation."

A smirk curled in the corner of Carver's mouth as he packed away his tools. "You a cop or something?"

"Yeah," Everett said, aware he was repeating himself, and prayed this was the most fun Carv would have at his expense. "Hope that's okay."

Carver shrugged and tested the engine. "A friend of Colt's is a friend of mine."

"Think you might be the only person I've heard say that. Least not sarcastically."

Carver motioned for them both to sit. "We better get going before it's too much darker. Black Ops over here doesn't wanna use the searchlight."

Colt entered coordinates in a GPS device Everett had never seen and handed it to Carver. The mechanic looked at his map as well, and after conferring between the two, he nodded to Colt.

"No problem. Half an hour, tops."

* * * *

Back on land, they rode the line between fast and silent as they trekked through the marshy fields. The darkness was all-encompassing, making the lights in the distance seem brighter. The main house was much further than it'd seemed from Carver's boat, and it was a twenty-minute hike before they finally arrived.

Kitty's files had named the place *Foxland Hall*, an abandoned manor house from the old days of the family. Hadn't been used for events since the early 2000s, and it had suffered damage in Katrina. Officially, the property was condemned.

Foxland wasn't large for the time it was built, but that was back when a family's plot of land was their own private kingdom. Besides the main house, there was a chapel, guesthouse and small stable where hostages might be held. Based on the burner videos, Colt wanted to start at the stables then track down Keith and his partners. He'd been less forthcoming on how he planned to manage that second part. Everett had kept quiet, but he noticed. He noticed all right.

They'd left Carver with the boat, but the bayous wound through much of Foxland's grounds. They'd passed two makeshift docks already, and a third was coming up on their right. The glassy shine of animal eyes flashed from the side of the water. Everett raised his gun, but Colt stayed his arm.

"What?" he whispered. "Jesus, can't see a thing out here."

Colt peered into the darkness and didn't flinch at what he found. "There's nothing there wants a problem."

But soon as he'd said it, Colt looked like he wanted to make amendments. His mouth twisted and he spat at the ground. Almost looked like he was going to be sick.

"You okay?"

"This is the place, Ev. Can fuckin' taste it, it's all chlorine and rust..."

He put his hand on Colt's shoulder. "Just breathe, man. I'll make the call." He held the screen to his chest, trying to block the light from any unseen eyes. "Signal is for shit out here. Might take a minute."

Colt nodded and pointed to the nearest building on their left, a small wooden stable beside a half-full trough. "Keep checkin' it."

He went to do just that when he heard the click of a safety release, the shush of fabric as Colt raised his arms.

"Hold on. Don't move."

A stick-thin man with ratty hair stood in the door of the stables. Behind him, a horse sniffed and whinnied. A State Rodeo T-shirt and jean overalls hung off his shoulders, looking like a stiff wind might bowl him over. This wasn't Keith Edwards.

"Elliott?" Colt asked.

A faint tilt of his head was all the answer they got, but it seemed a good guess to Everett. He kept his gun on Elliott as Colt pulled a scrap of paper from his pockets, scrawled a name across it, then held it out for Elliott to examine. The man's gaunt face went pale.

"Mary's dead, isn't she?"

Colt nodded.

Elliott dropped his eyes to the ground. "I *knew* it. Knew he was lyin'…"

"Where's he now, Elliott?"

"With the others. Not as many since…things got moved. But three men are with him in the house."

"The people he's got?"

Elliott pointed to the stables. Colt kept probing for information. "How long before they start?"

"I don't know. Not long."

Colt darted eyes over to Everett and flexed the hand on his gun. He kept his weapon low, pointed away but readied as he slowly approached. "We need to get these people clear. Get you and everyone else out."

Elliott's face broke with guilt. Tears slid down his cheeks. It made him look painfully young. "The things…the things I've *done*, there's no way—"

"You're sayin' you and Mary stayed of your own free will?"

Elliott was fast with the refusal, a litany borne of years of reminders. "He said he'd *kill* her, kill *both* of us. He'd find us, no matter where. And the kind of money he's got—"

A door slammed in the distant manor house, followed by the crash of breaking glass. The sounds made Elliott jump and he whimpered under his breath.

Colt kept talking, trying to keep him calm. "I know. I'm here because I know, Elliott. We got people ready to help, but we need a phone. Where's the landline?"

But Elliott's focus was slipping, his eyes unfocused. Everett wondered if he was on the same cocktail of drugs as Keith's other victims. "The people he's got," Elliott slurred, "may not want to see me. I was the one...lockin' them away and...and lookin' after the place..."

Colt closed the distance to stand in front of Elliott, but Everett shored up his stance, still not ready to trust the kid. He didn't *think* Elliott was dangerous, but trauma like his could have a light trigger. He wasn't about to risk tripping it.

Colt's voice was clear and deep. "Elliott. Where's the phone?"

The shaking man stuttered, but he nodded toward the house. "In his office."

"Keith give them the burners already?"

Elliott waved at the stable. "On the table. I was just leading them out."

Everett watched the whole exchange in stunned disbelief. He could hardly stand to hear this casual discussion of the hell Elliott had been through. But this was that other side of Colt, when he turned a part of himself off to meet a person in the darkness. Still, it was like some grisly car crash. He couldn't help but stare.

"What's his name, Elliott?" Colt asked, looking for confirmation. "The man doing all this?"

Elliott furrowed his brow. "*The* man? You mean—"

More glass shattered, accompanied by the raucous shouts of men. Another door slammed. Everett gestured with his gun and motioned Elliott into the stable. He went without a fuss, and Colt closed the door behind them.

Elliott sat on a stool beside a table with four burner phones. Colt extended his hand, palm up, and he gave over a ring of keys. Colt pocketed one of the phones and tossed another to Everett in an easy motion—like somehow, this was all in a day's fucking work.

"Take this as evidence," said Colt, voice low and urgent. "Go with Elliott and call Stapes. Tell him to bring everything he can. A fuckin' helicopter if they got it. Don't want a single one gettin' away in the dark."

"And you?"

Colt jerked his head to the locked stalls behind them. "Got people to see to. Wait until that text comes through and you'll be clear to enter the house."

Everett was well aware that Colt hadn't answered his question. Just because folks needed looking after didn't mean he wouldn't run off on his own. "Colt, I think—"

"*Now*, Ev. Please."

He shook his head at Colt's stubbornness, but the man was already trying keys in locked stable doors. He checked his own phone again. Elliott piped up from the stool. "Don't bother. He's always complaining how long it takes to send the texts…to get started…"

God *damn* it. He bit back his need to argue and told Colt, "Just…just wait, okay?" He pointed his gun back at Elliott and motioned toward the door. "C'mon. Show me the way."

The natural leavings of willow, oak and walnut crunched beneath their feet. It was a short walk through shadows and distant lantern lighting before they slid in back of the deteriorating manor — something closer to a construction site than anywhere Everett would've looked for an office. Inside, a gruff and distant voice touched a familiar memory, but this far away, there was no telling for sure. The voice disappeared down the hall and the *buzz* in Everett's pocket stole his focus.

He knew what three-letter message he'd find if he looked, so he didn't bother with the text and surveyed the room. The walls of the office were lined with furniture from mismatched eras, shelves filled floor-to-ceiling with decaying memorabilia. On the scratched wooden desk was a laptop and an old corded phone. Everett checked the immediate area to be sure and, seeing no one, called Stapes.

The major promised help in no more than ten minutes, but when Everett pulled the burner from his pocket, his heart dropped into his stomach. Stapes might as well be years away.

Because somehow, this message was more than three letters. It was five whole words that could only be for one man.

Catch me if you can.

Everett swore and sprinted for the door.

* * * *

He found what he expected back at the stable — the most lucid hostage set up with a knife, ready to drop him as he rounded the corner. Everett disarmed the man and demanded, "What happened to the other detective?"

The terrified hostage waved at the door. "I don't know. He just dropped the phone, gave me the knife and told me to wait. Then he was gone."

Motherfucker...

Everett turned to Elliott. "Where's Keith now?"

"If they start in the usual places, he'll be out by the old chapel, but —"

"Works for me."

Everett compared the time of Keith's text to the clock on his phone, and the math of minutes gone had him cursing an obvious fact. He could run all he liked, but Colt had too big a head start. No way was he gonna catch up, unless...

The thought went off in his head and Everett braced hands on his hips. He huffed at the dirt-packed ground, tried not to laugh or groan and landed somewhere in-between...and turned his head to the chestnut mare saddled in the stable.

The things I fuckin' do for Colt Harkan...

Deciding not to look his *actual* gift horse in the mouth, Everett swung up and over the saddle. He gathered the reins, dug the flashlight from his bag, then adjusted the gun on his belt.

"Look out for each other," he told Elliott. "Help's coming."

He steered them out of the stable door and coaxed the horse to trot, building to the gallop he'd need to reach that chapel in the distance. The crack of a faraway gunshot split the night in two. He cursed and urged the mare with his heel. Out in the pitch dark, he turned on the flashlight. The world shrank to a bright, dancing circle, illuminating snatches of scenery — and a bald-headed man with a familiar tattoo, confirming that voice he'd heard in the house.

Everett pulled his weapon before Jared could wonder at the light. He saw the whites of his eyes, a familiar silhouette, felt the squeeze of a trigger, easy as lying —

He told himself to think on what fell as summer rain, and rode through the ruddy cloud like so much dust.

Chapter Eighteen

Colt
Louisiana, 2018

One thing became clear as Colt entered the old chapel. Those burners he'd found? Were only pieces of Keith's collection.

The *missing* pieces.

Colt pushed open a peeling white door on a room that, long ago, might've held a hundred parishioners. The remaining pews and tables had been press-ganged into service as shrines. Bits of clothing, jewelry and burner phones lay scattered across worn tabletops. A long-fallen oak tree reached branches across the pulpit, and the tumbling growth that wound through the aisles spoke of years of undisturbed quiet.

The work lights at the door nearly blinded him. The rest of the room was poorly lit by sputtering altar candles. Colt put his back to the wall and closed his eyes while he could. He needed to readjust to the dark, and fast. Those holes in the ceiling weren't helping much, and a flashlight would give his position away. His own ragged breathing echoed in the vaulted rafters...and in time, he heard another pattern join his own.

Keith. He's here.

"Took you long enough."

The voice slithered toward him in the dark. The acrid taste of rust burned on his tongue. Colt pulled out his phone and placed it screen-down on the floor. At the last second, he turned on the light, sending it skidding to the center of the room. The shadowed outline of a man flickered behind the pulpit, then the harsh crack of a gunshot sent the room back into darkness. A second bullet sailed through the wall beside him, but Colt managed not to flinch. He anxiously tapped his thigh. Dark laughter bounced around the room.

"I'd expect nothing less from you."

Colt knew it was too much to hope for more light, but the shot made noise. Maybe that'd be enough for Ev to find him. He'd have to buy some time.

"Not sure we've been introduced," Colt said. He kept close to the wall as he circled toward the pulpit, but the altars and plant life left only one path. He wound through the serpentine trail and kept his head on a swivel.

"Can't *believe* you don't remember the day we met," Keith mocked, tutting his tongue, percussive and patronizing. "But I guess you only had eyes for Patrick that day. Not even Phil caught your attention. And Phil catches everyone's attention."

Colt didn't have time to consider how unsettling that really was. He'd *missed* him? How could he have—

no. He swallowed against a dry throat and gripped the gun in his hand.

"I suppose that shouldn't surprise me," Keith continued, condescension dripping from every word. "Wasn't just me and Phil you ignored that day. Tell me, does he always throw himself at you like that?"

The way Keith said *he* made it clear who he meant. Colt blinked the thought of blue eyes away. "Ain't nobody here but you and me."

"Not a chance. If he's alive, he's out there somewhere. My guys are too. Wonder who'll win if they find each other?" Keith sneered. "Too bad I missed him with that car crash. Should've finished it then."

So Ev was right. It *was* Keith who'd smashed up his ambulance. "Why'd you do it?"

"He was boring. A distraction. And you were taking too long."

The more Keith talked, the more nails he put in his own coffin. "That why you dumped the last body at the rodeo? To hurry me up to get here?"

"You know what's funny? She wasn't even one of mine."

"Not your type?"

"Clearly. No clue how she got there, either."

"So one of your psycho-killer pals isn't trustworthy? I'm shocked." Colt tasted bile as he made the offer, but he made it all the same. "You got an idea who's tryin' to frame you? Say some names and tonight might turn out different."

"You're disappointing me, Colt."

The wooden floor creaked as Keith's displeasure echoed through the chapel. "You don't want to catch me. Because without this case, what are you? You're not even real police anymore. Just a washed-up drunk with a few crazy theories. Kitty's husband had *lots* to say about you once he got that good scotch in him. Family dinners are so dull, you know. Got to pass the time somehow."

"If you're basing a damn thing on the say-so of Ralph Maynard, you're dumber than I thought."

Keith laughed, but it was a brittle thing. Hollow. "People have their uses. Like Ralph. Like Jared. Even *you* have your use. It's why I brought you here."

"Is that right?"

"You," Keith said grandly, "will be my greatest prize. Because you're just like me, Colt. We deserve each other. You don't know how long I've dreamed of bringing you here."

Colt could count on one hand the people who'd ever said his first name that kind of comfortable. Keith Edwards was nowhere on that list, yet the way he said his name…it was like he'd said it before.

It sounded *fond.*

A sickening thought slid down his back. A psychopathy like Keith's…he was fixated. On *him.* He'd killed people and worse. To get *Colt's* attention.

And now, Keith had him cornered. On his turf.

Colt's vision spun, but he had to keep it together, *had* to give these people some chance at vindication. For fuck's sake, it was the least he could do.

How many on his list were dead because of *him?*

He'd cleared half the room, but sounded like Keith was circling too and it was still too dark to see much. Waiting on Everett was all he had. So much as he disliked it, Colt tapped into the part of him that could play any role and soldiered on. "How you figure we're the same?"

Keith made a pleased sound, like they were trading stories on a smoke break, not circling a goddamn crypt. "You noticed more than anyone on that scene. Saw more about Patrick than any of them. So did I." He made a contemplative noise. "Guess I always have. It's so easy to make them dance for you, isn't it? When you can just see what they want? What they need? And they always fall for it. It's pathetic. The world doesn't wait for weak people."

Colt couldn't tell for sure, but he thought he saw a darker shadow stop at an altar. It sounded like Keith had picked something up. "Patrick was the only one who even got close to figuring me out. Had to shoot him before he ever got to this place." Keith set the small item down again. "But then Patrick brought me you. And *you*, Colt? You found Mary. One of the only two I ever kept. You were impressive.

"I'd never been on the other side of it before. Never had someone stalking after me, searching for *me*. Made it all so...exhilarating. Every one of them I hunted, I thought about you. Wondered if I'd ever get to tell you...if you'd ever know."

If Colt had to listen to another second of this, he might actually vomit. He might never stop. His mouth tasted sour as he forced out, "So I'm observant. Don't make me any different than—"

"Don't lie," Keith rasped, and he was angry. *Real* angry. Crimson waves of tension rippled toward him in the dark, and for lack of a better option, Colt pointed his gun that direction.

"You're nothing like them," Keith spat. "They barely look. But you, Colt? You *see*."

Clouds shifted in the sky and a shaft of moonlight fell through the broken rafters. It was enough to watch a ball of yellow paper bounce against the floor. Colt didn't have to open it to know he'd see his own torn penmanship staring back. It was the confirmation he needed.

"Mary...you used her as bait the night she died. Tried to get me to follow you then."

"You couldn't seem to find me once I moved out here. I'm not above giving a hint. Since you needed one."

"Because by then, you'd turned Phil's criminal contacts into a whole new revenue stream. Hosting those hunts must've brought in more than the guns and drugs together."

"Never leave money on the table," said Keith, almost sing-song. "I have to ask. How'd you know?"

"Your pattern changed. Pretty obvious by your choice of victims when you went from addict to supply."

Keith chuckled low in his throat. "*Very* good. You know, my father says I've got no instinct. Weak is what he is. All I did, all I built? I did it myself. No help from him."

"And how's that workin' out? You've got to know we've got backup coming."

Keith made a dismissive noise. "You still don't get it, Colt. You're here because *I* want you to be. The things I know, about the people I know...no one can touch me. Doesn't matter what you find. They'd never arrest me. And we'll be gone before they can try."

"Wasn't planning on lettin' you see some cell. Padded or otherwise."

He wasn't sure what response he'd expected, but the way Keith sighed...it was like he'd been asked to dance.

"Oh, Colt...now *that's* more like it. You know what they say about great minds."

The sharp pop of a gunshot cut Keith off, much closer than Colt had dared to hope. He turned toward the floodlights at the door —

Crack.

The butt of Keith's gun hit heavy against his head. His vision spun wildly as he staggered to the wall, barely keeping ahold of his weapon. Keith had him dead to rights, must've been circling alongside him after all, and the grim weight of failure threatened to consume Colt whole —

But the next thing he felt was the prick of a needle, then two arms pulled him close in a cloud of chlorine stink. Before long, he was being pushed forward, out the back of the chapel and into the night.

Whatever drugs were in that syringe, they were strong stuff. Had to be, or it wouldn't be affecting Colt at all. For a person without his history, it'd probably be enough for total sedation. His eyes were lethargic, but he could tell when they got outside. His feet felt loose and clumsy beneath him. His left stuck on a bit of stone, sending them tumbling to the ground. Colt groaned and rolled to his back, but Keith was on him fast — seaglass eyes staring vicious in his face.

A golden sound rang out from the chapel. "Colt? The fuck are you?"

"*Ev!*"

Or that's what he tried to say. Colt's tongue was lead in his mouth and he wasn't sure how much got out. Keith looked to the chapel, displeased with the interruption, and slid a long knife from a sheath on his belt. The sharpened edge dripped cool moonlight on his skin.

"Be back for you later," Keith promised, staking the blade in the marshy ground. It was only when cold slickness gave way to the burn of flesh that Colt realized what had happened. And in that, at least, it was over. A stab wound in the gut? More than enough to punch his clock for good.

Colt was dying. *Finally.* He just had to finish this first.

Keith was watching him bleed with greedy eyes, but the noise Everett made in the chapel pulled his attention. Keith ducked behind a headstone, and Colt realized with a bit of dark humor they were in a graveyard — he was gonna die in a *graveyard* — and shit, if that weren't saving people trouble in a way he'd never managed in life.

He couldn't do much staked to the ground like he was. He was forced to watch in slow motion as Keith drew his firearm and palmed a smaller knife from his belt. Everett appeared at the chapel's side door and ducked at Keith's first shot. They traded back and forth, sharp cracks and pops piercing the night as Everett used the doorway for cover. Wasn't long before they were both out of ammo and Everett crouched to reload. He finished first and stood, confident he'd be fastest on the draw, but Ev didn't know about Keith's plan for his lack of another clip.

And Colt realized that, knife in his gut or otherwise, there was only one way Ev was getting out alive. Knowing it was the end gave him the strength to do what was necessary, to twist and reach for his own discarded weapon, barely out of reach at his side...

Because Everett had caught sight of him now, wide blue eyes fixed on his injured stomach... but then he *stayed* frozen. An easy target, gaping at his growing puddle of blood —

Keith's blade sliced through the air and sank into Everett's shoulder.

He never saw it coming.

Wearing a look of genuine surprise, Everett fell against the chapel's outer wall. The gun tumbled from his hand and he slid down the chipped-white siding, a streak of blood and hopelessness behind him.

No. Please, no.

Ev…

On luck, instinct and a dying gasp, Colt's fingers reached his gun and slid it close. He lined up his final shot, aimed true, pulled the trigger —

Keith Edwards crumpled in a burst of red.

Colt's pounding heart and cicada song raged in his ears. He watched the body fall — now missing part of the forehead — watched as blood mixed to mud in the dirt…but the silence held. It was over. He could rest.

"Col…"

Fuck.

Not yet.

* * * *

Everett
Louisiana, 2018

Everett rolled away from the chapel wall with a yell. He pulled the knife free from his shoulder before he could think how much it hurt. Fumbling with his shirt, he pushed to his feet, tripping over himself to get to Colt as fast as he could.

"Col! Just wait, I'm —"

But words failed further as Colt's chest went entirely still, on some Zen-master bullshit as he slid an eight-inch knife from his gut. The blade was crimson-wet in the moonlight.

God, not like this. You got him. You got him, Colt...

The knife pulled free and some words came with it.

"It go all the way through?" Colt rasped. "You gotta...gotta tell me what it looks like..."

Dangerously dark blood pooled fast around the wound. He kneeled at Colt's side, tore his T-shirt open and used it to mop the blood now soaking his white tank. A high ringing sounded in Everett's ears, and he didn't know when he'd started talking, but his mouth was spouting all kinds of nonsense, like one of them might believe him anyway.

"Don't worry, Colt...it's not — it's not so bad."

It's worse.

"Won't be long now," Everett told him. "I called Stapes. They're comin' in with full force."

"That's good." Colt grimaced. "How's your arm?"

Everett eyed it, unsure when he'd torn his own sleeve off and tied it around his shoulder, but he'd take whatever help his muscle memory offered. A distant part of his mind noted he was probably still in shock, but none of that mattered as much as answering Colt's question.

"Still hurts, but I reckon that's a good thing."

It was barely even a joke, but Colt still laughed. It turned to a hacking cough real fast. "Fuck you, man. Need to...work on your timing some."

"If I stop talkin', you're like to stop answering, and help is *almost here*, Colt. Just hold on."

"I thought it weren't so bad."

He looked up from their bloody hands and met Colt's gaze. His voice broke on the single syllable. "Ev…"

Those knowing brown eyes said it all. Everett didn't want him to be right, but it was a good bet to go with Harkan. Man had a sixth sense for these things.

Colt knew it was over, but he wasn't angry. He just looked sad.

"That talk you were wantin' to have? Might need a rain check."

Everett couldn't listen to this. *Refused* to listen to this. "Shut your mouth, Col. We'll have plenty of time to talk —"

"No, listen. Wanna…wanna say it once."

He couldn't imagine what the man had to say that Everett didn't already know, but he'd listen, *anything* to prove he wasn't fading out red into the white of his cotton tank, dying for *no damn reason* because *help is coming, Col —*

"What we had? That month and the rest of it? It was enough…it was enough for me."

Just hold on, Colt…

"It was worth it…it was — we…"

He coughed wet and harsh, tried to ramble through it, but that was the last that made any sense and Everett couldn't stand to hear it anyway. Because Colton Harkan was using his last breath to lie to him, and he could've sworn that was something he'd said he'd never do.

Everett knew he wasn't listening. His eyes were fogged and his breathing was slow. But just in case Colt *could* hear a little something, could feel anything besides the pain, he pressed a kiss to his feverish forehead — and corrected the bastard one last time.

"No, it wasn't, Col. Not for me."

Then, a distant brightness caught Everett's eye.

Fireworks? A searchlight.

Stapes. A *chance.*

Colt was stone silent, but Everett yelled loud. "Major! Over here!"

* * * *

Everett woke in a wash of white hospital light. Threads of the last few hours tangled in his mind...

"That's all I remember. Promise, Sir..."

"Fired one shot on approach, didn't see where it went..."

"Bald, tattooed man? Can't say I did..."

All those sirens and searchlights...paintin' the church walls like jelly...

Just remember bein' in that graveyard, tryin' to get him to talk...

When he was conscious, the major told him what no one else would — Colt hadn't woken up yet.

And in some ways, thank God for Rachael and the kids. After spending so long in a place of such death, Everett needed to be reminded of some good, some honest. Something true. But *goddamn,* if Colt didn't wake up...it was too much for too little. Too high a cost.

"It was worth it..."

So if he let some of it out while he had familial arms to hold him, Everett hoped no one would blame him, and the tears fell like rain.

Just wake up, Col. C'mon, for me. Please.

* * * *

In a room two floors below him, a dark-haired man opened his eyes and thought, *This is not how this was supposed to go.*

Part Three

RECOVERY

Chapter Nineteen

Everett
Louisiana, 2018

"The fuck are you doin' here?"

He was sipping a cup of water when he realized Colt was awake, looking madder than hell. It was an improvement.

"Are you...watching me sleep?"

Everett rolled his eyes. Like he'd never done *that* before. "You're a barrel of monkeys today." Colt scowled, and it reminded him so strongly of the day they met, Everett tried the old joke again. "What's the matter with you, Harkan? Some kind of fuckin' asshole?"

Annoyed eyes raised to his. Colt shifted in his hospital bed.

"Why're you here?"

Like he has to ask...

Colt finally kicked that coma three days ago, but this was the first time Everett's nurses had let him visit. The stitches in his shoulder didn't allow for crutches yet, but he'd made the trip in Old Ironsides anyway. Rachael and the kids had been visiting every day, and maybe it felt strange to think of Colt's room in those moments, quiet and empty, while his own was so full.

The news played low on the TV in the corner, and at the sound of a too-familiar name, Colt's head snapped up. A picture of Keith Edwards filled the screen, the same one they'd been running all week—an old mugshot from '05, when Richard had kicked him out of the family business, an anecdote that every reporter on every channel included.

"He was there," Colt mumbled. "On the Combs scene. He was walking inside with Phillip once I was done talkin' to Richard. And after that, he did what he did...because of *me*."

Everett let his breath out slow. He'd read Colt's debrief with the major, the only interview allowed once he'd finally woke up. Couldn't believe some of the things they'd pulled out of that chapel, and to be honest, Everett didn't plan on reading the report once it was finished. All he cared about now was sitting in that hospital bed, determined to blame himself for far too much. Colt *would* think that Keith's fixation put himself at fault.

"So what? You should've known he was a murdering psychopath at first glance?"

Colt flopped his head to the thin pillow, angry eyes fixed on the ceiling. "Keith wasn't working alone. He bragged about it."

"Yeah. And odds are good we'll never catch them that got away. Maybe Stapes will find something, but I'm not holdin' my breath." Everett waited for Colt to look at him before saying the rest. He placed his hand on the edge of the bed. "But we got Keith. And the Combs case that started it all, Mary's case? Those and so many more…they're all down, Colt."

Another time, that might provide some comfort, but today, Colt looked more like a frightened deer than anyone Everett remembered knowing. He kept staring at the ceiling, too focused on his breathing, even for someone with his injuries.

"I'm not…" Colt stuttered, voice low. "I didn't plan for this…contingency."

He refused to acknowledge all that word meant and aimed for levity instead. "Can't imagine anyone plans for the kinds of surgery *you* needed—"

"It's not that. I shouldn't be here, Ev. At all."

And *that* was a conversation neither of them were ready for. Everett retracted his hand from the bed and picked at his peeling armrest. "Yeah, well, how about we take this one step at a time, huh? Not sure we need to talk on this five minutes after your third nap of the day."

Colt rolled to his side, away from the TV and Everett both. He pointed his chair toward the door. "I'll be back later."

"Why?"

The genuine confusion in his voice told Everett all he needed to know. It was going to take a gentle touch to get Colt through this. Gentler than he might be capable of.

But Colt was alive, and he'd passed some days of late when that didn't seem possible. Couple of nightmares, too. So Everett decided he could be patient, if patience looked like picking a fight as he wheeled out of the door.

"Dunno. Thought we might try somethin' new. Take things slow for a change."

Colt grunted at that, like the very idea was insulting. He told Colt he'd see him after lunch and got no response at all, but he leaned up from the mattress as Everett left. Like maybe, he was watching him go.

They carried on like that most days of Everett's hospital stay. In the mornings, he'd roll down and regale Colt with inane bits of news. He'd mostly sit there, performing what Everett called his "*cantankerous crabapple impression.*" With a bad wig. And an overgrown beard.

Lines like that got him a dark-eyed glare, on a good day.

On Everett's last night before discharge, he turned on the lead-detective charm and convinced his night nurse to let him see Colt at lights out. He was too quiet that day at lunch, didn't rise to any of Everett's bait, didn't even say what he wanted him to sneak in first, since Colt had to be tired of hospital food. And Everett had a feeling why.

"*Because in all the time we've known each other, we still ain't talked about the one thing that matters...*"

He leaned against the open door and waited for Colt to notice him. Colt pointedly did not.

Everett only crossed his arms, making it clear he wasn't leaving.

Colt said, "You're getting out tomorrow. Goin' home."

"I am."

"Glad for you."

Didn't sound like it, but he played along. "Thanks, Colt. So listen, let me know what would be a good time for ya. Visiting hours aren't the same for people comin' from outside, but I can be here at three tomorrow if—"

"Ain't gotta worry yourself. I'm not your problem, Ev."

"Yeah, you are."

"Didn't ask to be."

"Didn't *have* to."

And to be honest, the only similar things were the tone of Colt's voice and the way he wouldn't look at him. The room was completely different, Colt had a fuckin' ponytail and Everett wasn't holding a box of his things, heading to Rachael's on a second chance. But he could see how enough might seem the same to Colt.

A flat voice called from the couch, "You look like she took you back."

Everett shut the door and pocketed Colt's spare key, turning to face the man he'd hoped wouldn't be there. "What makes you say that?"

"Wore your good shirt on a Saturday. Instead of that ratty State number."

"Kind of you to notice."

"Weren't no kindness."

He wasn't sure how to read Colt just then. He'd hoped to get the last of his stuff while Colt was on the job, that they could have this talk without boxes in his hands. This felt too much like that quick move out of the house, Rachael staring daggers while he grabbed the essentials. Holding those boxes made it all too domestic, and entirely *unlike the temporary stop this was supposed to have been, before he'd crawled into a bed that felt too much like his—*

No. He had a family to get to. A life. And a good woman willing to give it a second try. Besides, Colt could be the part of that he'd always been, right? Nothing had to change.

Maybe he'd hoped a bit of Colt would be pleased.

Colt had been there for him this past month, but he shouldn't have had to lean on whatever this was so much. Wasn't fair. Maybe Colt wanted something like what he had with Rachael. Something that could stand in the light of day, that didn't have to hide in plain sight behind the word 'partner'.

Everett packed his belongings and waited for Colt to say a word, but he didn't ask for reasons, didn't tell him to stay, to fuck off — nothing. Didn't give a clue that any of it mattered enough to say a word. Colt just stared at the wall, unwilling to meet Everett's eyes. So he sighed with box in hand and tried his best with what he knew.

"Ain't like it's goodbye or nothin'. We'll still see each other all the time...right, Colt?"

His answer came in a cloud of smoke. "Sure, Everett."

Not Ev. Not even Rhett.

Might as well call him Lead Detective Kane...

"I'm gonna be here," Everett told him. "Tomorrow and every day I can till you're out."

Colt silently worked his jaw, but Everett wasn't trying to convince him. Just felt the need to state some facts before he left.

"Look, Colt...I've lost you a few times now. And I know you've got a lot goin' on, healing up and such. But you might wanna consider givin' some credit for time served. Could ask yourself what I might've learned between then and now."

Colt tipped his head toward the door. "Why'd I wanna do that?"

Everett smiled. "So you can tell me all about it. Tomorrow."

* * * *

Everett was damn busy settling his life after Foxland, but he kept his three o'clock appointment — and every one he made in the days after. Colt was staring down quite the schedule of rehab, and was maybe a bit embarrassed to be living at all. But every time Everett knocked on his door, road snacks in tow to bitch about his day, they shifted closer to familiar territory.

Everett's departure from the station processed easy, and he reminded Colt every day he was holding down the fort at Harkan Investigations "*till the boss is back on his feet.*" He told Colt he was working on his investigator's license, more as a passing comment than anything. Pretty much no matter what he said during their visits, Colt would listen quietly, only responding when forced. And every time Everett came past with some trinket or diversion, Colt still looked surprised, like he couldn't quite believe it. Like he didn't understand why Everett might've bothered.

Jesus, but they needed to get Colt out of that hospital. They might be looking after his body, but Everett wasn't sure they were doing enough for his mind. The mostly-female staff at the hospital was all manner of charmed by that Cowboy Jesus look of his, with Colt's wavy hair and beard so overgrown. Especially since he was a hero now, the way their names had been all over the news. It'd be too easy for Colt to put on a smile, make them think he was "*fine, just fine, ma'am*" and take what he needed from their pockets.

Everett wouldn't judge him if he had a stash. Probably a fucking reflex for Colt at this point. But he wanted to know where it was. And more than that, he wanted to convince him such a thing wasn't necessary.

That as long as Colt was still around, there were options.

He hadn't figured out how. But Everett kept showing up.

Colt's last week at the hospital brought an unexpected change in demeanor. He hadn't thought Colt would be jumping for joy or anything, but neither did this quiet stillness make sense. Any time he tried to bring up where Colt was going to stay, if he'd scheduled his out-patient therapy, he'd find a way to change the subject. His favorite excuse was he'd yet to find an apartment that'd let him smoke inside. That usually devolved into begging for a cigarette which, Everett was proud to say, had yet to work.

"Don't know why you're still asking," Everett told him his last day in the hospital. "You ain't gettin' one from me. You're on the mend — whether you like it or not."

"Fuck off, Ev. C'mon, I know you've got one."

"I do not. I quit."

Wasn't often that Everett got to surprise the man with anything. He tried not to look too smug as Colt repeated, "You *quit*?"

"I did."

"You, Everett Kane, quit smoking?"

"Surely did. Before all...this." He gestured between them, like any wave of the hand could summarize their past few months. "I'd cut things back to a pack a week. Figured I'd give quittin' it all another try."

"Why?"

"Maybe I've got some things to stick around for."

The look that crossed Colt's face was pained, but soft. He wanted to ask after it, but a gentle knock on the door turned both their heads. A nurse leaned her head in, looked at Everett and said, "Dr. Stern would like a word. When you can."

Colt shifted to his side, a clear signal he was done for the day. Everett decided not to push the matter and let him sleep. He'd need all the rest he could get before discharge tomorrow.

It was still a bit strange to hear that name and see Rachael's face when he turned the corner. Her mouth curved in a tight smile, but she kept her distance, arms crossed. They fell into step and headed toward the elevators. Rachael slipped her hands in the pockets of her long white coat.

"This is me not asking if you've got what you need. For tomorrow."

Everett slowed his gait and pushed the down arrow. "We'll manage. And you can ask." He caught Rachael's eye and amended, "If you have to."

They shared a short smile, but it was nice. Didn't feel forced.

"Apparently, I do," Rachael replied. She looked over her shoulder and, confirming there was no other staff nearby, added, "I didn't want to let him leave without knowing he had somewhere to go."

"Of course he's got somewhere to go."

"Does he know that?"

The elevator doors opened and Rachael got in alone, which was fine. He'd take the next one. Because maybe Everett needed to sit with that before heading back at all.

* * * *

The next morning, Everett arrived at Colt's room bright and early. He tossed a pack of Camel filters at his chest. Colt caught it against his hospital gown with his good arm.

"You fuckin' serious? The day they let me out and *now* you cave?"

"Absolutely not," Everett said. He started folding the few clothes Colt might want. "I'm just not above some bribery, now and again."

He watched from the corner of his eye as Colt inspected the pack. "It's a present, asshole. Open it."

"What, we got some anniversary I don't know about?"

Everett had learned to pay attention to the jokes.

"What's it taste like? You..."

"So that's what that was? Makin' love?"

"We got some anniversary?"

Everett shook his head at the half-packed duffel and laughed. "Just open it."

Colt finally did and found the box full of wads of shredded paper. When he pulled those out, a single cigarette remained. Beside it was a small silver loop he lifted into the air.

"It's your set," Everett explained.

"Of..."

"Keys."

Colt looked at him blankly and Everett laughed. "House keys, man. I know you won't be doin' much moving on your own yet, but..." He shrugged and tossed another T-shirt in the bag. "Wanted you to have 'em anyway."

Colt folded the jagged pieces of metal carefully into his palm, staring like those keys held the secrets of the universe. Hell, maybe from his perspective, they did. Never knew what Colt was seeing.

It didn't take long for everything to process. By nine-thirty that morning, Everett was wheeling Colt across the lot to his sedan. Had themselves a small adventure getting inside the house, but eventually Colt was safe on the couch, the walker he'd finally agreed to use open at his side. He managed a bath mostly by himself, and Everett knew it was due to convenience, but watching Colt amble around in *his* rolled-up sweats put a smile on his face all the same.

Colt sat on that single cigarette all day as daytime television played low in the living room. When he wasn't making plates of turkey sandwiches or changing bandages, Everett did a lot of pretending to read the paper. He suspected Colt was doing much the same, letting him pretend.

And Everett had never spent much time on the bit of concrete out back that passed for a porch, but that night, taking the evening air had a strange appeal to it. Like it might be the start of some new habit. Colt joined him, moving slow with the walker, and they sat beside each other in a pair of lawn chairs. Everett took the left naturally. Maybe it was all their time in the car, but something about that felt right.

He cracked open a beer. Colt finally lit his cigarette. Cicadas hummed in the warm night air, and the sounds of the neighbors' radio made the whole thing play like music. Despite their many years getting used to each other's silences, Everett felt the anxious need for small talk creep in. Never was very good at discussing things that mattered.

He waved at the dusting of stars overhead. "See? Ain't this better than the view from your room?"

"S'fine." Colt pulled the next inhale deep into his lungs. "I'll be out of your hair soon as I can. Get you your key back."

"Whatever, man. No rush." He took a sip of his beer. "Still gotta set up the guest room. Get you an actual bed for once in your life."

"Could've stayed at a hotel until —"

"Col, do us both a favor and shut up."

He did for a while, and they sipped and smoked. Everett had finished half his beer when he decided to float the idea he'd been working on. "You know, it's not like I put out an ad or anything, but with the press from this Foxland stuff, you could make a real go of your firm."

"I guess." Colt ashed over the arm of his lawn chair. "Was only any good at one thing. Spent most of my life gettin' shit for it."

He narrowed his eyes and Colt added, "I've been a soldier, a cop and a drunk. Which of those sounds like a good place for pointin' out truth?"

Everett laughed into his beer and tried not to choke. He wondered if somewhere there was a meeting for the poor souls who'd tried to manage Colt Harkan. Certainly put Everett in some interesting company.

"So," he tried again, clearing his throat, "you gonna start things at the office, then? You'll need one hell of a decorator."

"Doesn't seem to matter what I choose to do. Always wind up doing the same thing over."

"You wanna try that again? Preferably in English?"

Colt's tone was contemplative and his eyes stayed on the sky. "My time in the service made me right for undercover. Bein' Switch that long made me wrong for anything else. Even in my retirement, I still almost got you killed because I couldn't leave it alone. Because I had to know."

"Colt, that's not what happened — "

"I'm sayin', Rhett. I don't know how to do...this." He gestured with the butt of his cigarette, then dropped it to the cement.

"Do what?"

"Life. Normal life. Last time I tried..."

Colt didn't have to say it. Everett's throat felt tight as he waited for silence, but unlike the other times they'd broached this subject, Colt seemed determined to keep talking.

"I ever tell you what happened to my daughter?"

Everett exhaled and leaned forward on his knees. He toyed with the tab on his beer. "I think you know you didn't. And you don't have to...but you can."

He didn't say a word in protest when Colt stole his beer and finished it. He crushed the can in his hands and threw it deeper into the yard. "That WITSEC house in Kansas...I only got those six weeks with them at the start, and I knew it was temporary...but that was it. Closest I ever got to normal." Colt's voice grew harsher the longer he spoke. "Once I was back on the job, Rosa called whenever she could. Left messages for me. She'd hold the phone up and Ava would babble away. Her first ever words were on the phone.

"She liked to sing. Rosa said she was copyin' the birdsong. Only thing that kept her quiet was 'watching the pretties' at the feeder out front." Colt tried to keep his breathing steady and got mixed results. He watched Colt dig his thumb into the red-tipped wings on his arm, tracing the tattoo with pressure hard enough to bruise. "She was chasin' one of her favorites when...neighbor's kid. Driver's permit. Never saw her."

Jesus Christ.

"Colt...I mean, fuck, man—"

"I should've been there." Colt kept talking like he hadn't heard him. "Should've...I mean, when I got that call, when I heard what..." Colt cut himself off and scrubbed at his eyes. Everett did the same.

"Spent weeks in a fuckin' daze. Went no contact with my handlers. I only kept up with the job in the hopes it'd kill me. Thought I could finish that mess up before I went...considering all it'd cost."

Colt's hand twitched with the need for a cigarette, and Everett was glad he'd dumped the rest of the pack. Right now, he'd give Colt any damn thing he asked for. Anything he could.

"She'd have been thirteen this Christmas." Colt swallowed audibly, letting his head drop forward. "A teenager. Can't hardly picture it."

Colt stayed hunched in his chair. Everett didn't know why this felt like the biggest risk considering all they'd been through, but he reached for Colt's hand anyway and linked their fingers together. He squeezed lightly and looked at the ground.

"I'm sorry, Colt. I'm just..." If there were words for a time like this, he didn't know them. "Fuck. Just so sorry."

Colt stayed quiet, and Everett listened to the sounds of the night. He tried to pick out the song on the distant radio with no success. He rubbed Colt's knuckles with his thumb, back and forth. And as long as they were talking this honest...well, it seemed a shame not to ask.

"Col, before we left for all this, you said...well, you know what you said." Everett cleared his throat and didn't let go of Colt's hand. "You still feel that way? You still wanna die?"

"That's the whole damn problem," Colt said, shaking his head. "I thought there'd be peace. That it would finally be the end, but...look, I don't believe in God. Yours or any others. But I swear, Ev. She was with me in that graveyard. I felt it, like a presence...a warmth, right here. Like I only ever felt holdin' her." Colt placed his empty hand on his own chest and said through gritted teeth, "She came to find me in the dark. Even when I wasn't...when I didn't – " Colt cut himself off and gripped Everett's hand tight.

"Not once after she died did I let myself think about Heaven. Not the idea of seeing her again, angels, none of it." Colt turned to face him, wild-eyed with grief. "But Ev, it felt so real. Like she was right there, like I could reach out and...what am I supposed to do with that? How do I go on, now I know she's out there, waitin' for me?"

And that was it for Everett. He couldn't listen to a single second more without trying to make this better. He knelt in front of Colt and threw his arms around the man's shoulders. He didn't move to accept it, but he didn't shove him off either.

"First off," Everett mumbled, "not a thing about what happened to your girl was...I mean, and the shit you've..." There were too many thoughts in his head. Couldn't pin one down long enough to make any sense. He pushed back Colt's overgrown hair. "Col, I'm not sure what I'm supposed to say."

Colt didn't raise his head from where it laid on his arms. A shuddered breath later, he said, "Never stopped you before."

Everett couldn't hold back the laugh that broke through his own tears. He cursed under his breath. "Got no clue what you're gonna think about this, but if you're askin'? I think you've got some things backwards."

Colt remained quiet, but he could tell the man was listening. "You don't gotta believe in God to believe in miracles. Are you, of all people, gonna ignore what you saw with your own eyes? What you felt in that moment?" He shook his head at the ground and bounced a hand off Colt's knee. "You wanna know how you're supposed to live now that you know she's out there...and all I can think, sittin' here listening, is how could you wanna die knowing all she did to save you? Now that you know she's lookin' out for you? Sounds to me like she answered a prayer."

Everett didn't feel the need to state whose prayer specifically. They both knew it was his.

Colt was silent a long while. Everett didn't mind. Eventually, he whispered low, "You think?"

"Yeah, Col. I do." He chewed the corner of his lip and shot a look at the stars for luck. "And I also think...I think you should stay. At the house, here with me." He chanced a look at Colt. "Until you find somewhere, at least."

Colt kept staring at the ground, but he let his breath out slow. "All right."

"All right, then." Everett rubbed the back of his neck. "You hungry?"

"No."

"Me neither. Can of soup it is." Everett braced against the arms of Colt's lawn chair and pushed to standing. He walked to the sliding glass door, then looked behind him. "You uh…you want help gettin' inside?"

Colt stood on shaky legs, but he made it to the house easier than before. The track at the bottom of the door caught the wheel on his walker, but Everett was close enough to get an arm 'round his waist.

"S'all right, I got you." He set Colt back on his feet.

And maybe it was wishful thinking, but he swore he heard Colt mumble, "I know."

Chapter Twenty

Colt
Louisiana, 2018

Back inside, he watched Everett soothe himself with the rituals of caring for the sick and healing and thought, *That's the second time you've saved me from myself now.*

Wasn't really a plan to it, just got lucky one morning. The wrong nurse dropped the right bottle too close to a kindly hero in his chair, someone too good at giving something back while palming something else. He'd had the means for a week now. Probably lucky it hadn't happened sooner, that he hadn't been in a state of mind to seek things out on purpose. He'd been working up the nerve to toss them ever since. If Everett hadn't showed up so early...no telling how the rest might've played out.

But after getting used to a new set of keys and leeching some poison from that red-and-black wound, Colt was getting a certain feeling again, something he'd only felt twice in his life. The moment Everett caught him, just to set him back on his feet, he was decided.

Life, then.

Time to try again.

So he sat on the couch and sipped the water Ev handed off. He took all his pills but one. And minutes later, when a bowl of chicken noodle followed the water, he watched Everett pick up the remaining tablet and return it to the bottle of pain meds.

Colt reached for the soup and said, "You should get rid of those. Don't need 'em."

"You can't tell me you're not in pain."

"Not what I meant." He forced down a spoonful. Wasn't bad. "Better not to have them in the house."

He heard the shake of the bottle and imagined Everett standing behind him, staring back and forth between the pills and the top of his head. With how long he took to answer, Colt knew he understood what he was really being said.

"You sure?"

"Yeah." He turned from the television and caught Everett's eye. He let a small smile stay on his face. "Might've heard somewhere I'm on the mend."

"Okay. Well...good, then."

They ate in mostly comfortable silence. After, Everett cleared their bowls, and Colt tried not to wince as he lay down on the sofa.

"Hold on. You don't really think you're sleeping on this couch?"

"You said the guest room —"

"I know what I said. But my back's not so bad I can't do a night out here while we get some house-things. Now c'mon, let's get you settled."

"I'm not kickin' you out of your own bed, Rhett —"

"Listen, you. If it was *my* ass who'd been knifed to shit, had major goddamn surgery, spent time in a coma and barely come back alive and *you* were puttin' *me* on some couch, you wouldn't ever hear the end of it." In three even strides, Everett was in front of him, bundling the blanket off his lap. "And *I'm* the one of us with somethin' resembling a sunny disposition."

Everett walked to the kitchen, blanket stuffed under his arm, and returned to his own nightly meds. "So shut your mouth, and get on up so you can sleep in the only bed in the house, because we ain't having this conversation again."

He drained his water and set the glass down, like that settled things, so Colt didn't fight any further. Because in the scenario Everett just pitched, Colt would be around to bicker with him.

It was a thought.

* * * *

Everett
Louisiana, 2018

They passed a few days getting Colt acclimated to the house. This included buying him some clothes of his own, but, more often, Everett's closet still waved hello from Colt's slowly building frame. Everett found he didn't mind and stopped sorting when he did the laundry. All wound up in the same place.

At the start of the second week, he won their ongoing argument about Colt's need for facial hair. After a day of meeting clients out at coffee shops, Everett found him in front of the television, clean-shaven and scowling at an excuse for news.

"Jesus Lord and the Saints be praised," he exclaimed, tossing his coat over the back of the living room armchair. "Careful, Col, or I might actually recognize you."

Colt ran a hand over his chin. "Yeah, fine."

"Surprised you ain't cut the rest off too."

He rolled his shoulder and pain flared in his face—too much for such a motion. "Tried. Couldn't reach."

Everett popped the buttons on his cuffs and rolled the sleeves of his shirt. "Idiot. You know you're not supposed to be stretchin' like that yet."

Colt shrugged, but even that was enough to crease his eyes in pain. Everett knew what he'd say, but he couldn't help but offer. "You sure you don't want—"

"No. And I thought you got rid of them."

"I did."

"Then don't offer." Colt turned back to the television.

Unsure what else to do, he settled on something he could control. He flicked the tail of Colt's hair off his neck. "Well, c'mon then. I'll help you."

By the time Colt made it to the bathroom with the walker, he was finished digging the clippers from under the sink. Everett got out of his way and nabbed a chair from the kitchen. That done, he turned to Colt at the wall, pulling at his cotton tee, wincing too much to get away with it. Without a word, Everett stepped in to help.

He pulled Colt's shirt—*his* shirt, actually—up and over, and tried not to let his hands linger. The stitches across his stomach had come out yesterday. The raised ridge of his scar was still an angry red, glossy in the light thanks to the ointment that kept it from itching. If

Colt could go some time without re-injuring himself, he just might make a full recovery.

Everett tossed the shirt to the floor as Colt sat down. He picked up the scissors and gathered the ponytail in his other hand. An obvious chunk was missing. "What'd you try to use?"

Colt waved at the kitchen knife on the bathroom counter, and Everett asked the ceiling how this man survived a single day without someone looking after him, let alone four years in that live-work hole of an office. Everett snipped the tail and set it aside, but his eyes snagged on that knife by the sink.

"Is that, uh...something we need to be worried about?"

Colt sniffed. "Not really. When my head gets like that...pain's not the point."

Everett adjusted the head in question. The clippers buzzed along Colt's neck. "Well, try to keep it on as straight as possible. Don't wanna fuck up the back here."

"That's not how I remember it."

The shine in Colt's eye confirmed exactly what he meant.

Laughter bubbled up in his throat and the feeling caught Everett off-guard. It was the first time conversation had veered to something like them since Foxland. He knocked into Colt's shoulder, then angled his head to trim by the ear. "Oh, come on. Too easy."

"Might be owed some easy."

Everett moved to the other side and continued. "I'll second that."

He did his best to replicate Colt's old cut from back in the day—a bit shaggy on top, shorter at the sides, though not as much as it once was. He'd noticed Colt didn't seem to mind the extra length now. And if he were honest, it might've done something for him, the way Colt tied up that bit at the back of his neck, combing it out of his face so those dark eyes could concentrate, how when he raised his arms, his shirt rucked up over his hip—

But thoughts like those would only lead to embarrassing scenarios they were both doing their best to avoid. He flexed a hand at his side and mentally reviewed his schedule, anything to distract from the *other* lines of thought that were starting to crop up. He set the clippers down and checked Colt's hair, threading fingers through the top to make sure he didn't miss anything.

He was about to call it when he dared a look at the mirror. Colt's eyelids dripped closed as he inhaled slowly. The corners creased as Colt held his breath, then let it out even as he could. Everett swallowed as his mouth went dry, again carding his hand through Colt's thick waves, slower this time, and was rewarded with a low hum of pleasure. The sound vibrated in Everett's chest, and maybe Colt was leaning into the touch, *his* touch—

Like the thought was enough to wake them both, Colt blinked his eyes open and they both looked away. Everett cleared his throat and swept a hand across his dewy forehead.

"M'kay. Done."

Colt leaned forward, turning his chin to examine the work in the mirror. Everett dropped his gaze to the fine hairs that sprinkled Colt's shoulders—and cut that train of thought off *quick*. The *last* thing he needed to think about was Colt in the shower.

Keep it together, man...

He raised his eyes to Colt's reflection and forced a smile. "You almost look somethin' like a professional again." Colt narrowed his eyes. Everett repeated, "Almost."

Colt stroked his hairless chin. He tossed the front of his hair, getting used to the shorter length. "Y'know...was thinking about what you said. About the firm."

His heart beat faster, but Everett knew a thing or two about time, place and Colt by now. Best way to get him to keep talking was to stay quiet. He focused on cleaning the mess of his barbering.

"Was thinkin' of looking for office space in town. Maybe an apartment nicer than my old spot. Since I've got the time to look." Colt met his eye in the mirror. "You think you know someone who could help me with that?"

He grinned at the floor as he swept. "Might know a guy."

* * * *

They spent most of the afternoon on the couch looking at Everett's laptop, and once Colt was done razzing him for having a list of options ready to show, a silent middle finger and the utility of the thing shut Colt's mouth on the matter. What Everett refused to compromise on was keeping the office separate from Colt's living space. Quitting the force had renewed his interest in this life-work balance he'd heard so much about, and he was pulling Colt into the experiment whether he liked it or not.

Colt was noncommittal about the office listings, but agreed he'd look at places if Everett found someone to take them around. As far as apartments, they had more luck. He pointed to the fourth on his list and said, "This one's not available for a month, but it's checkin' most of your boxes."

Colt leaned over his right shoulder to read, a comfortable habit from their many years on the job. "Second floor, not too many stairs. Got a nice balcony."

"Sit out in the mornings. You can sketch me somethin'."

It was a newer joke to add to their repertoire, borne of their new routines of breakfast — Everett reading the paper, Colt with his head in his legal-pad replacement. Everett had gotten it as one of those small distractions for *"when he was feelin' up to it,"* a spiral-bound sketchbook of thick, crisp pages with a few pens and pencils to start. Some kid at the shop had to help him find it all, and damn if the proper inks weren't double the office supply, but Everett hadn't wanted to risk getting it wrong.

Colt got his name on the apartment's list — practically hung up blushing when the lady recognized him as *"that detective from the news."* Everett could only hear snatches through the phone, but she found all sorts of reasons to talk to Colt — how nice it'd be to have a *"good man"* around, someone to *"keep the neighborhood safe."* Everett laughed quietly, but he couldn't blame her. He'd told plenty of lies to get close to Colt in his time. Not surprising others might do the same.

When he finally weaseled his way off the phone, Colt closed the laptop and sat at the other end of the couch, shifting side-to-side as he picked up his pencil.

"What're we gonna do about that month in-between?"

He answered from behind his newspaper. "What we been doin', I figure."

"And what's that, Ev?"

He wanted to believe Colt had little reason to ask, but...it was a fair question.

That first week Colt was out of the hospital, he'd asked himself much the same. He'd all but camped out by his own bedroom door, listening for that shift in Colt's breathing – the one that meant he needed help getting to higher ground. He remembered it from that first time they'd done something like live together. And when it didn't come, Everett would send up a short prayer of thanks and return to the couch, where he'd toss and turn till sleep claimed him as well.

He hadn't expected his own nightmares to show up first.

He was walking through things he'd tried not to see, but had somehow burned into his mind...

Andrea Meyers' fingernails, chipped and crusted with blood –

Chapel altars filled with clothes of bodies whose names they'd never know –

The trigger-light impulse when his eyes fell on Jared...right thing to do, but the way his head burst at the bullet –

"Ev...Everett, c'mon."

But faster than it had happened, he was skipping to the end. In his dream, he was clinging to a blood-soaked Colt, telling lies through a river of red about things like enough –

"No...Col, hold on – "

"Rhett. You're dreamin'."

When he came to, Colt was leaning out of the bedroom doorway, struggling to roll the tops of his borrowed pants. But the man's sleep-rough baritone had cut through the horrors, and Everett was already awake. He'd blinked the terror from his eyes, caught his breath and said, "I'm all right. Get back to sleep."

He snuck a glance over the back of the couch and watched as Colt stood there staring. A long moment later, he sighed. "C'mon, then."

"Colt – "

"Ev, come sleep in your own fuckin' bed."

Everett gave him plenty of time to get situated before picking up his pillow. He walked into the bedroom and placed it on what used to be his side of the mattress. He faced the wall, intentional space between them, much too far from the man he very much wanted to turn to. But that wasn't what this was. Not for a while – if ever, since Everett was trying hard as he could not to assume things anymore.

Then a strong arm tucked around his waist. A warm palm settled over his chest.

Maybe it was the feel of that stitched-up seam at Colt's stomach, pressed tight to his back, or the closeness of the nightmare to what he thought he'd never see again, but Everett had let it out, and he'd cried.

In time, he quieted. But they kept on that way, spoon-fashion, until morning.

* * * *

Colt
Louisiana, 2018

He kept his eyes on his sketchbook when he asked, "What're we gonna do about that month in-between?"

Rhett answered automatically from the other end of the couch. "What we been doin', I figure."

"And what's that, Ev?"

It was because he didn't want to ask that Colt knew he had to. Everett's eyes went distant, then he blinked up from his paper. "How much of this conversation are you wantin' to have?"

Colt sketched and considered his answer.

Since Everett's last night on the couch weeks ago, they'd been sleeping beside each other every night. And in that, a lot was starting to feel like the last time. But some of it weren't the same at all...

Colt's old place had nothing close to creature comforts. In the days before Mira, he didn't have a spare anything, and half the things he needed weren't there at all. One of those was a nightstand. So when Everett started crawling into his bed some kind of regular, his old milk crate – stacked with books to make a flat surface – carried a heavier load.

There were two glasses of water now, two phones charging and two sets of keys among the shrapnel of cans and currency. When Everett asked him to pass his water, it was a normal kind of habit, but what followed was not *Ev's normal response.*

"Thanks, babe."

The word hung in the air like so much smoke.

Everett looked like he weren't so thirsty anymore. And that was good, because Colt couldn't hold a glass steady if he tried. Colt's arm was trapped in limbo, stalled en route to the milkcrate nightstand. He could tell from the tension behind him they were both stuck on that different sort of four-letter word.

Thanks, babe...

"I, uh...I didn't mean to – "

Colt recovered his wits first and passed the damn glass. "It's fine. Never was one for pet names."

"No, it's just...well, you know."

Rachael. Habit. Nothing to worry about.

Yeah, Colt did *know...*

So sitting on the couch now, sketching the view from their window, Colt weighed his options against his dignity and settled for what he could handle in-between.

"Just lookin' for the lay of the land. So I can set my feet."

Everett leaned forward and rubbed his hands. "Okay, then. I uh…" He chewed his lip and started again. "I want you to feel comfortable here. I don't mind bein' the one who's keeping track of you right now. Prolly saving me time, not having to run off and save you from whatever trouble you'd be gettin' into. And you…well, you're getting closer to something resembling upright. Blow right past the grannies on that walker of yours—"

"Fuck off, Ev."

"I'm serious, Colt. I want you here, and I want you all the way on your feet before we're worryin' over long-term plans." Everett waved at the laptop on the coffee table. "That apartment you like's ready in a month, right?"

He shrugged in agreement, but stayed focused on his sketchbook. Everett continued, "Look, we still ain't done up the guest room. Why don't you get some stuff and set it up in there? Make it like your office or whatever. And in a month, if you wanna move it all to your new digs, well…I'll carry some boxes."

"Have you over for a housewarming?" He stilled his pencil and blinked up at Everett. Eyes blue as summer skies lit with promise.

"Or somethin'."

Colt felt his cheeks go hot—and yeah, he knew he was staring, but he also found he didn't want to stop. And it wasn't like he had a damn thing to be shy about with Everett, but he felt the need to mention... "Might still be some time before —"

"Colt. You're alive. If you think I care about more than that right now, the docs need to check you over again."

He felt a subtle warmth in his chest, and the invitation in Ev's smile reminded him of things they both wouldn't admit to missing — circumstances as they were, with nothing they could do about it. Everett broke their staring match before it could get more obvious. He tugged at his collar and stood to clear his mug, swatting Colt's shoulder with the paper as he passed.

"See? Ain't you glad now you followed me home that night? Got laid while you still could?"

Such an asshole...

"Yeah, all right, Rhett."

He turned a page in his sketchbook and pitched his voice so Ev would hear him in the kitchen. "You should call first, when I'm in my new place. Sounds like my landlady might be the hands-on sort."

Everett laughed outright. "Be sure to put that ol' sock on the door."

* * * *

Everett
Louisiana, 2018

Three weeks into Colt's project of finishing the guest room, he learned something new about his one-time partner. After a day too long for cooking, Everett joined him on the couch, a microwaved burrito in tow. Colt sniffed in disgust.

"You ever had real Mexican food?"

He blew over his plate. "Not much of that around here. Y'all had more of that in Texas, right?"

Colt grunted an affirmative. He scratched his arm and kept his eyes on the television, a little too casual when he said, "We should do it up sometime. Get ingredients and all."

"Didn't know you cooked."

Colt waved it off. "Been a while."

That was all they said about it before settling in for another of their now-usual routines, talking smack over cop drama reruns. But in the morning, there was a grocery list on top of his newspaper, ripped from Colt's sketchbook with a short note beneath.

Get this list. I got the rest.

When Everett came home from aisles he didn't usually traverse, he found Colt looking rather comfortable behind the stove. And good goddamn, was Everett glad to be able to blame this on the heat of the kitchen, on the steam rising from the meat in the pan. Because one look at Colt, hip cocked and spatula in hand, with nothing resembling a shirt anywhere near his bare shoulders and chest, standing there steady in *his* pajama pants...

Well. A man might get to having certain thoughts.

Everett put the groceries on the counter and decided the beers should be refrigerated. Immediately. After a blast of cool air had done what it could to ease his suffering, Everett snagged a bottle and popped the top for a healthy swig. He swiped the side of his hand across his mouth and leaned against the wall. Across the kitchen from an unperturbed Colt, he tried not to actually lick his lips.

Because seriously. This just wasn't fair.

Everett looked him up and down, appreciating the view while he could. He pointed with his beer at Colt's chest—and the definition that was working its way back.

"We need to talk about your clothes."

Colt stirred the pan as it sizzled. "What about?"

"Like you *wearin'* some."

Colt laughed once, then turned a kinder eye to where he was sweating in the kitchen. "Not sure what you mean."

Such a liar...

"You do know what you look like, right? Mirrors around the place workin' and all?"

Colt would never admit it, but Everett thought he stood a bit straighter as he chopped the pepper and onion. He slid them cleanly into the pan. "I was napping," he explained as he rinsed his hands. "Don't sleep well with many clothes on."

"I got plenty of respect for your beauty rest. And I got even more for your doctor's orders, though you consider them optional." He eyed the crutches in the living room, and Colt trotted out his now-commonplace complaint.

"I barely need them anymore—"

"My point, exactly," he interrupted, and drained half of what was left of his beer. He crossed arms over his chest. "Let's just say I'm tryin' real hard not to embarrass myself around you, Colt. And I'd appreciate some help negotiating the matter."

"Set some terms of engagement, hmm?"

"Now *there's* a thought."

And Everett could tell, he'd got him good — pulled a gen-u-ine smile from Colt Harkan, professional pessimist. And when he shook his head in that *fuck you* sort of way, Everett thought *yeah*, he could probably jump clear over the house right now. Or anything else Colt might think to ask him.

Everett watched Colt set the spatula aside. He walked easily, under his own power, to where his white cotton tank lay draped over the couch. Colt returned to stand an arm's length away, legs not wobbling at all, and looked him dead in the eye.

"Your house. Your rules."

And like the smug son-of-a-bitch he was, Colt pulled the tank over his head, far easier than he'd done for weeks.

"You ain't got a turtleneck or something?" Everett asked. "That skimpy undershirt ain't exactly helpin' matters."

"Should've been specific. All you said was clothes."

Colt picked up the spatula and returned to the stove.

Everett blew a long sigh from his mouth and finished the last of his beer, setting the empty on the counter. He held fast to his courage, sidled up behind him and wound an arm around Colt's waist — the most he'd reached for since their world was cut apart by an eight-inch blade. Colt's breath hitched at the contact.

Everett traced his fingers under the edge of the ribbed undershirt, and the effect it had on them both was immediate — bordering on visible. He pressed a kiss to the curve of Colt's neck and hummed in thought. "All right. First house rule? The exact *second* the doc gives you anything like a clean bill of health? You tell me."

"Might be somethin' I should mention, then."

That was when he remembered the only thing on Colt's schedule today — *Call doctor for follow-up.*

Oh, Jesus...

Everett's exhalation fell out of him, long and slow and stuttered. He tightened his hold on Colt, rolled his forehead along the line of his shoulder, surprised by how hoarse his own voice already sounded. "Col...don't tease on this."

"I'm not."

He reached his other hand to turn off the burner — because if what Col said was true, everything in the world would just have to fucking wait. He turned Colt in his arms until they faced each other, brought hands to his narrow hips and tried to steady them both. He slid his palms up the sides of Colt's torso, tracing patterns over his barely covered chest.

"Tell me *exactly* what the doctor said."

He moved further up to cup the sides of Colt's face. Noses brushed in the humid space between mouths. The spatula clacked against the counter as Colt followed suit, his thumb sliding soft over Everett's cheek.

Colt swallowed hard. "Ain't like I took anything for a test drive, but we've got the green light. S'long as we start slow on some things."

And damn, if that weren't the best news that Everett had heard in weeks.

"And uh...what about some other things?"

Dark eyes sparked electric as a live wire. "Others..." Colt said, "ain't gotta be so slow."

Everett kissed the corner of his mouth. "How d'you feel about some of that, then?"

Like he had all the right in the world, Colt shoved him flat against the kitchen wall, twisted fingers in Everett's hair and claimed him with a kiss.

And Jesus fuckin' Christ almighty if that wasn't almost enough right there.

All the not-wanting, not-thinking, not-looking of the past several many weeks had built to this, and neither man was keen on anything resembling stopping. Colt's mouth was near-frantic over his in a bruising kiss, tongues sliding fast as Everett pounded his fist against the wall.

Finally...

Quick as he could, Everett was undoing some of Colt's good work and taking that undershirt directly back off again. Colt tugged just as eagerly at his collar. His shirt buttons never stood a chance. Their clattering dance against the kitchen tile had Everett painfully hard, but he held himself to one quick kiss then pulled away to warn, "Careful, Colt, you can't go trippin' on nothin' —"

Colt popped the cuffs open and pushed his shirt to pool on the ground. He nipped at his neck and asked, "Where?"

"Couch. *Now.*"

They sped from the kitchen, and his hands on Colt's hips had little to do with stability.

* * * *

Colt
Louisiana, 2018

Colt barely had time to get his bearings on the couch before Everett was levering over him, straddling his lap. He brought his hands to the small of Ev's back to steady him, and for a moment, they simply sat together and breathed, relishing the beginnings of friction as Rhett rocked his hips into his.

Fuck, but Colt had missed this. He'd known he couldn't trust himself to stop where he'd have needed to during those long weeks of recovery. If there was one thing he'd learned after a decade of Everett Kane? It wasn't ever going to stop at just a kiss.

So now, finally feeling like a person and not an assemblage of broken parts, Colt kissed Everett with all he had, with all the stored-up want of the last few weeks and longer. Colt sucked on his tongue just to hear him moan, willing Everett to read between the lines he couldn't fill in just yet. Ev broke away to mouth a path down his chest with lips and teeth and fuck, but this might be when that rehab paid off after all.

Living might be worth it some if Colt got to have this.

Everett claimed his mouth again, pulling his bottom lip rough between his teeth, licking his way inside like he needed him more than air. Colt kissed him back, accepting all he had to give as two sets of frantic hands pulled at waists of pants. Colt could feel it all fitting into place with Everett settled above him, and he stuttered his last cohesive thoughts against Everett's cheek.

"Ev, if we pick this part of it up…other pieces bound to follow."

It was the last-ditch effort of a desperate man. He half-expected Everett to bolt. The man he'd met years ago would've been gone in a flash.

But this Everett, here and now, only grinned. "They *better*. Kinda countin' on it."

And with a look that said he didn't think Colt was so stupid, Everett slid to his knees, freed his straining erection and took Colt down his throat with a groan.

Oh, shit...

This was always going to be quick — both of them starved for each other the way they'd been — all of it coming to a thundering head as Colt's pulse beat heavy in his ears. His eyes slammed shut as Everett wrapped his hands around his knees, tracing over his thighs as Colt thrust into his throat. He blinked his eyes open as Everett hollowed his cheeks, bobbing in close, leaning forward as Colt tipped into his mouth, circling and sucking just so...

"*Goddamn* it, Ev—"

Colt's legs shook in time with his ragged breathing. His hips bowed up as his hands cradled Ev's neck. He stroked an index finger over the curve of his ear, and the way it all twined with the night sky in the open window, Colt was sure he'd found the taste of starlight, of combustion—

Supernova.

He was blinking at the ceiling when something like coherence stuck. He looked down to where Ev was lookin' up with a smile, way too comfortable on his knees for a man who'd never bent his will for anything. Until maybe him.

"C'mere, Ev."

Everett darted his eyes to the couch, then back to him. "How should...I mean, you need to sit. You ain't have to—"

Colt hauled him up for a kiss, because that was all he could think to do with Everett missing the whole point, and cleared any misconceptions the man might have on the matter.

"None of this is about havin' to. I want to."

I love you.

But Colt wasn't ready to have those words be heard, couldn't get them to fit his mouth any manner of comfortable. He said instead, "Stand up for me."

Everett did so as Colt kicked his legs up under him, kneeling on the cushions as he eased Ev's zipper free, pushing away any fabric that lay between him and what he wanted. Everett's hands fell to his shoulders, then his head, lacing gentle through his dark waves.

Colt looked up as he took Everett in hand, stroking him exactly right by the sound of it. He watched his head fall back, heard him try not to moan and fail spectacularly. Colt kissed down the jut of one hip, then up the other, only stopping when he noticed his legs were shaking. He licked Ev's cock from base to tip before taking him in his mouth — and well, it was a good thing there was no need for pride anymore.

Because when Colt hummed at the crossed-wire taste of him, orange and rosemary bright on his tongue, Everett was already gone.

"Col, I'm —"

Colt had hardly gotten started when Ev's release was on him, and if he hadn't been helping hold the man up, his knees might've given out entirely. Colt eased him through it, didn't want to miss a second of it, and Rhett's chuckling pant sounded like he'd just run a marathon. Colt watched as he sank to the couch, and he couldn't help thinking that Ev looked well and truly fucked, despite the brevity of the thing.

And maybe that was giving Colt too many ideas, at present.

One thing at a time...

Everett pulled him firmly into his chest, kissing light at his temple. "You can make all that tomorrow, right?"

He nodded. "It'll keep."

"Good. Get some sleep. Because in some hours, we're gonna do that again. Properly."

Colt kissed over the pounding in Everett's chest, glad for once they were on the same page. "That right?"

Everett grinned. "Hey, you said it. My house, my rules."

Chapter Twenty-One

Everett
Louisiana, 2018

It wasn't all easy or fun.

They'd been back in the physical swing for no more than a few days when that conversation they never had found its way into mattering again. There were lots of ways it could've broke different, ways that wouldn't have been so bad. But at a certain point, Everett figured he should've known it couldn't last, that their recovery-bright bubble must eventually meet harsh reality.

It was a long day of meeting new clients at coffee shops — a typical occurrence since their names had spent so much time on the news. And maybe, it was because his life looked so different from the last time he'd thought about this. Maybe it was because phone calls with Rach and the kids no longer seemed an imposition or out of place. But when Everett arrived home and saw the blue SUV in the driveway, opened the door to see Rachael in his living room, eyes wide with shock, he figured *yep*. That was about it for that stretch of good luck.

Fuck. Gracie's school shit.

Colt looked no better, blank-faced and barefoot wearing Everett's rolled pajamas — thank God he had a shirt on this time — but the man looked too like a deer in headlights for Everett to be worryin' over details.

For years now, he and Rachael had kept a standing appointment to get Gracie's private school forms in order, and it wouldn't be long before college and the FAFSA game. Rachael made enough money to make things work on her own, but there was still planning to do to keep it fair.

He really should've remembered. She'd even called, but there hadn't been time to check his messages. This was...*oh fuck*. This could be rough.

Because Rachael was holding a bottle of wine.

* * * *

Of the three of them, Everett didn't expect Colt to speak first.

"Rachael."

Not a single thing was conversational about his tone. Colt just...said it. His eyes fixed on that bottle for a millisecond before shooting straight to the wall, to anywhere but Everett.

"Colt, I..." Rachael trailed off. *She never did know what to do when she was the one at fault.* She turned to face the door, blinking fast but recovering. "Everett, I'm sorry. When you didn't answer, I thought we were still on for tonight. Gracie's school stuff...and some college applications." She pulled a laptop from the bag on her shoulder and itched her bare fourth finger.

Colt's jaw ticked as he grabbed his flannel from the couch, pulling it over his faded T-shirt. He shoved feet in shoes that could've been his, but he didn't seem to be looking.

Everett knew he had too much to explain in far too little time. He started with what was easiest. "I'm sorry, Rach. It was a busy day, but I'm still good to talk about the kids."

Colt fished a pack of cigs from his flannel pocket that Everett hadn't known he had. He pulled one free and bounced the filter against the box, eyes black as bullet holes as he propped the smoke on his lip.

Rachael was still apologizing in the background. "I'm sorry. We can do this another time, or you can just email—"

He took a deep breath. Rachael stopped rambling. "No. It's fine."

Everett looked at Colt with all his might, hoping *please just wait* might read in his eyes, and pivoted to face her. "Just sit down. Get your computer set up or...whatever."

Now that she had an occupation, she tried again to talk to Colt—hands busy, eyes away. "You don't have to leave because I'm here. It's boring, but you're welcome to stay or just...be in your room." Rachael nodded at the open door of the guest room, where Colt's desk and futon were just visible. "You moving in finally got Everett to do up the place. It's good."

Colt blinked at her twice, sniffed once then turned to the door, walking straight for it like Everett wasn't standing in his path. Like he would pass right through him instead of checking into his chest.

"Yeah, it turned out real nice," Everett hedged. He held strong against the force of Colt's shoulder and angled his head. "Where you goin'?"

He almost wished he hadn't seen. Colt's eyes were burning red and angry around the rims.

"I'm sure as shit not *sittin' in my room.*"

That was probably the best he was going to get, but he chanced a favor further. "Just...stay close, will you? Got the yard, it's a nice night—"

"Fuck off, Everett. Talk to your wife."

Yep. Me and my good luck.

* * * *

Rachael was quick to the point. "Everett, does he think I don't know?"

And well...that cut a lot of the middle work out. Still, Everett wasn't about to touch that bottle with a ten-foot pole. He strode to the kitchen to get a beer. "Know what?"

"That you're together. Not just living together."

He circled back to grab a beer for Rachael, pointedly not grabbing a wine glass. "And if I were to get some manner of offended at the insinuation here—"

"I'd remind you of photos I only showed you one of. And that the first few days Colt was here, you called me twelve separate times before I let it go to voicemail on principle."

Everett whistled through his teeth, like the way he used to tease her. "Mind like that, you should've been a detective."

"I was married to one. Comes with its own share of tracking down, being a detective's wife."

Rachael always did have to have the last word.

"I s'pose it might."

It was an awkward silence, but not unbearable. They'd certainly had worse. A few more years, something like that might land all-the-way funny. He tried not to notice how they both were nursing their beers.

"He seemed so angry," Rachael said, trying again. "It's something specific. What is it?"

Everett sighed and eyed the wine on the coffee table. He moved it to the center with a weighty clunk. He raised an eyebrow and waved at the bottle. Rachael's cheeks flushed.

"God, no, I didn't — I mean, how does he even know about that? That's not what I meant. Not to *you*, not for *years* — "

"Yes, I know. Thanks for being so clear on it."

Rachael's mouth opened and closed again, quickly. Her eyes lowered as she picked at her nails. "I can't believe you told him. That's...so *personal*."

"Meanin' no disrespect, but Colt and I are two people you ain't got a whole lot of secrets from."

That sent her after a healthy pull of liquid courage. But still, Rachael was right. It was personal, and Everett had shared it with someone. Given it up freely, in fact. Strange how those stories didn't feel as hard to tell when it was Colt listening on the other end.

Divorce meant Rachael didn't have to spend her energy on him or his problems, but Everett knew she still cared about him — and maybe, in her own way, about Colt. Must've done, because she was still sitting there on his couch, taking her lumps better than she ever did when they were married. Maybe one relationship in his life would make it through the day.

The thought choked him up more than anticipated. Everett set down his beer, no longer having a taste for it.

"Look...it's not my place, and you don't have to tell me. But if you wanted to talk, I could listen."

It was a greater kindness than he deserved after all their lives had been, but the worry he'd tamped down was doing a number on his stomach. "It's just...it's still falling together. Haven't really put labels on nothin' yet."

"Everett, he was wearing your favorite pajamas. You didn't let me steal those."

A smile split his face despite it all, because damn, if that weren't true and he'd forgot till just now. He felt a little guilty when he caught Rachael's eye. "Look it's not—they were the smallest I had when he first got here and...well, it wasn't like I'd *planned*—"

He wondered if the beer was hitting a comfortable spot, because Rachael laughed—genuinely laughed—and said, "If there's one thing I've known in all of this, it's that Colt Harkan was never something you planned for." She contemplated her next words carefully. "It's not about...I'm not asking if you're gay, Everett. I don't care and I don't need to know. I'm asking if you realize what's happening here."

The word they'd both been circling for years hit him upside the head. He'd never truly considered that word as something he had to care about—which given his situation, he'd admit was ridiculous, but somehow, it was no less true. That word, what Everett was taught it meant, just didn't feel anything like what was happening now with Colt.

"You've been here all of five minutes, Rach. What could you possibly know about what's goin' on here?"

"I'm asking if you know that Colt's in love with you. Because trust me, Everett. I'd know that look anywhere."

And Lord forgive him if his first thought was selfish, but all he could think was *God, I hope so.* Everett held her gaze as she nodded. The churning in his gut eased.

"I, uh...thanks, Rach."

"For what?"

"I don't know. Just...thanks."

She nodded and closed her laptop, but Everett stayed her hand, brushing the back with his thumb. He stood to get his own laptop and sat on the other end of the couch. "Might as well actually go through this shit. Only takes a few minutes now we know what the fuck we're doin'."

Rachael nodded again, but kept an eye on the door. Everett told her, "He won't be back until you're gone."

"You sound pretty sure."

Everett could tell her all the ways he knew, every bit of anger and betrayal he'd read on Colt's face. But that would be too much to be getting into at present, and he couldn't guarantee a clear frame of mind if he thought about it much longer.

"Just trust me."

* * * *

Rachael left a list of what else she needed, happy not to prolong the visit longer than necessary. Everett walked her out, received a kind pat on the shoulder he didn't deserve then shut the door soundly behind her. He leaned against it and released the breath he'd held since that word he still didn't understand.

"I'm not asking if you're gay, Everett..."

Completely unexpected, advice from a man he'd met twice followed after. *"Don't think gay's your problem, man. Heartbroken is."*

Everett knocked his head against the door, thankful for how it hurt. It was good advice. He should've listened. Two years ago, Carver had called his breakdown play-by-play, leaving him desperate to prove otherwise. He'd never forget the rest of that night as long as he lived.

It should've taken far longer than it did to get back to Mason from Carver's. With a few hours till dawn, he'd decided to split the difference and rolled into the station lot. He'd grab some hours on the couch.

Or that was the lie the whole ride over.

The moment he got to his desk, Everett's fingers had another plan, were searching up a name in files he really shouldn't be pulling for things like this. But the only pull he cared about was the next one from the bottle that'd appeared in his hand, the only thing bitter enough to chase away the taste of another man's mouth.

Wasn't anything wrong with Carver. Just...wasn't right. Wasn't Colt.

Colt, who'd gone and set up some private investigation firm. Colt, hiding in plain sight at the state line – all of thirty minutes from that bar tonight, not that Everett had known. Colt, whose cell was disconnected and he'd only just now confirmed it, muscle memory forcing the call to find that wouldn't be the way to what he wanted.

Maybe the business line had a forward service.

He realized as he was doing it that, being on the office phone, he'd automatically blocked the ID. It rang twice, and despite the clock reading four a.m., a voice scratched over the line.

"Hello?"

Everett's breath froze in his lungs. It was really him. Col...

He was there, listening. Waiting. Maybe even...what? What did Everett think he was going to get from this? The second he said who it was, it was game over. Colt would hang up — or worse, tell him not to call, not to care, not to —

"Ev? Is that — "

The panic acted first. Everett slammed the phone in the cradle.

And if later he was slapping spackle over a hole in the company wall, sporting another set of blood-crusted knuckles, he figured, yeah. That was about what he should've expected...

Still leaning against his own front door, Everett flexed his fist — the same hand he'd plunged bloody into Colt's truck window — and held onto what he'd told himself so often in their years apart. That he should've tried harder to talk to him. Could've listened more, probably. All the same things that pushed Rachael away. Same problems, different day.

But Everett had sworn to himself then if he ever got a chance at having this again, he'd make it a real one. So he waved to Rachael as she backed out of the drive, and watched with hopeful eyes as Colt appeared on the opposite side of the street.

There was no way for her to get to him without crossing traffic. Everett knew he'd done it on purpose. Colt was being obvious. Intending to be seen.

Rachael flashed her lights twice and turned the corner. Colt just watched her go. And Everett wondered what it was she'd tried to say to the shell-shocked man across the street — *I'm sorry. Good luck. I tried.*

* * * *

Everett started talking as soon as Colt was in earshot, and he could give a rat's ass if the neighbors were listening.

"I need to hear you know that nothin' about that bottle of wine mattered. I need to hear you know that, Colt."

He flicked a burning filter to the curb, every line in his body radiating resentment. "Oh, we're gonna *talk* about what you need to hear, Everett. There's a lot you ain't sat through that you ought've."

Back to Everett, then...

And Colt looked madder than he'd ever seen, but he was storming *into* the house. He was talking about talking. He was still there.

Everett decided to take the win, shut the door and try to douse the situation with truth. "It's Gracie's art school. She's there on scholarship. We meet up once the forms go out so we don't get behind or forget. Done it for years now. Completely slipped my mind it was today, or I would've told you. You know I would've."

Colt was already pulling out another cig, hands on autopilot. "She had a key."

"It's my spare. Didn't have anyone else to give it to, and her and I aren't so damaged we can't water a plant now and again. We've got kids together, man. We talk."

Colt's whole body quaked with the strain of holding his silence. Everett watched him pace and for a moment, the mask slipped. Brown eyes flared up panic-wild, that shadow-self from the hospital creeping into his face.

"This is feelin' way too fuckin' familiar."

"Say what you need to say, Col."

His voice was scraped raw, but he managed to ask, "Why'd you go back? That first time? When you knew you weren't plannin' on changing none?"

After all these years, there it finally was. The $100,000 question. The one Everett had asked himself for damn near a decade and never figured out on his own.

Why'd we only get one month that felt like home?

But he'd do anything to have an answer for the man in front of him, even show him all the pieces he'd never managed to make sense of. "You...you deserved someone who could be with you fully. Like Mira. Hell, like Rachael, even. You wouldn't have fucked up somethin' with a good woman like I did. You deserved to have someone who could be with you all the way."

"And that wasn't you?"

Would you have let me? Would the world?

He scrubbed a hand over his face. "The fuck was I gonna do, Col? Stay shacked up with you, us carpooling to the station every day in front of those assholes? Maynard and his crew weren't nothin', there were guys *way* worse than him—"

"Didn't have to go down that way," Colt said quietly. "You didn't have to stay. But you didn't have to leave, either."

Everett barked a laugh but it wasn't a pleasant sound. Even in the middle of the most important conversation of their lives, Colt couldn't help but be on his philosophizing shit. "What kind of circular sense are you tryin' to make now?"

Colt paused before he spoke again. When he did, he sounded more like himself. Like maybe now the fear was out, he could admit what he'd wanted those years ago.

"You...you couldn't have just *stayed*, I know that. Not how things were." Colt swallowed hard. "But you could've got your own place. Let Rachael have her peace. Could've let me know, between us, that we knew what it was."

It wasn't what Everett expected. To make matters worse, Colt was right. The thought of staying gone, getting divorced...back then, the fear was all he knew.

He planted hands firmly on his hips, like that was all that was holding him together. "You were thinkin' that? Then?"

The rest rolled out like Colt didn't know it was happening. He leaned against the couch and picked at stray fibers on the cushions. "Ev, by then I'd been thinkin' that for a long time. Tried to stop the train of thought every time it came up, but..." Colt sighed and almost whispered the rest. "But then...she took you back."

And a memory he hadn't examined in years flooded Everett's mind...

They were in Colt's old kitchen, the night after Rachael first left him. Everett held his breath as the center of all focus, no matter the room, asked a question he didn't want answered.

"What's your play here, Rhett? Just gonna crash on the couch till Rachael caves and takes you back?"

"You think she will?"

And how he ever *thought that blank look of Colt's meant they didn't matter, Everett would never know...*

Shock and something like betrayal fought for Everett's attention. "You thought Rachael was done with me for good. You *lied*."

Colt kept after the thread in the cushion, but didn't deny shit. He closed his lips around his cigarette and pulled hard. "Didn't seem to matter, since she went and proved me right. Always was too smart for my own fuckin' good."

He flicked his filter into an empty coffee mug and Everett decided he was finishing this. Bringing it all out in the open.

"Col...I don't know if you can hear this, or if it even matters but...I *tried* that day. When I left for the house, I tried to say anything I could think. And I knew you weren't happy with me goin' back. But I thought you were fine with it."

It was the wrong thing to say.

Colt's response felt sharper than that blade he'd pulled from his shoulder. "How could I have been *fine with it* if she *never knew*?"

And *that* was a whole new kind of ridiculous, even for them. "Jesus, Colt. Like Mira knew all that? Later on? C'mon."

But he knew how to read that silence by now.

Holy. Shit.

"Colt...when Mira left, you said she wanted a baby."

He flipped his Zippo and didn't look up. The man was chain-smoking now, recovering lung be damned. "She did. But that weren't the straw that did it."

"You really told her. All of it? About...about us?"

Colt laid it out in a huff of smoke. "The way you left from dinner that night? Didn't have to tell her much. Told her it had been happening. That it likely wasn't gonna stop happening. That any life we made together was bound to have you in it." He took a long drag, pulling it deep into his lungs. "Thought if I hadn't managed to shake you yet, it was something she should know."

If he tried to keep standing, Everett was going to need to borrow Colt's retired walker. He sank to the couch instead and dropped his head to his hands. "You told her all that?"

Colt ashed in the mug again, but wasn't about to repeat himself. After a few deep breaths, he asked the final question. "Why?"

Colt pointed the lit end of his Camel right at him. "*That's* your problem, Everett. You keep acting like this...*us*...is different somehow. That you don't know what to do in this situation. Like there's some other rules you need.

"But it's the same. It's *all the same*, Ev. I told Mira because that's what you do when you're in love with someone else. You tell 'em, and let the chips fall where they may."

In love...

"How the hell did Mira take that?"

Everett found he'd like to know. Might be he could take some tips. Because learning Colt *had* loved him? Past tense? Might be the thing that killed him yet.

"Better than you think," Colt said. "Still left though. That and her wantin' family..." He rubbed the line of his brow with his thumb. "She didn't blame you, or me. Which made it worse."

The silence stretched on for far too long. Colt was down to the filter and looked ready to burst when Everett finally found the nerve, wound his way to the word that left him feeling like a well-rung bell and a too-wrung towel all at once.

"Don't, uh...don't remember you taking your own advice all the way, back then."

Colt sniffed, indifferent, and Everett decided something right there. Never again did he want to make Colt look the way he did telling this truth, like what he was saying made all the sense in the world.

Like that shit was obvious.

"'Course I didn't," said Colt. "Back then, surest way to get you to leave was to tell you I loved you. Was never gonna risk somethin' that meant losing you for good. Never managed it...least not till Rachael had her say."

Colt wouldn't look at him as he walked to the guest room. "I'm in here tonight."

"Col—"

"Just...go to bed, Everett."

It was the first night since they'd got it that Colt slept on the futon. In bed, Everett lay awake.

* * * *

Morning found Everett in sheets that smelled too much like the both of them. He wondered when in the night exhaustion had forced his body to sleep. Wasn't anything he'd call restful. But today was another day.

It being a Friday, Everett knew what he'd normally do. Normally, he'd be waking up next to Colt. And he'd watch him sleep some. Or talk to him when he was awake. Most likely make fun of him for something. There'd be coffee and a morning smoke he snatched from his mouth as they bickered about cutting back, his newspaper and Colt's sketchbook and the hum of tuning radio. There'd be a breeze in the trees at the end of the block and cardinals at the backyard feeder.

It had been his life for a while now. Didn't think there'd be a time it wasn't, really. That he'd ever have to re-make a morning routine without Colt.

Everett curled up on his side of the bed, searched his mind for words to describe the ache in his chest and came up blank. But he knew that whatever he found when he opened the door to the guest room, he had to say *something*. Couldn't just let this shit lie. Couldn't go on without knowing a damn thing on where they stood.

"Just...go to bed, Everett."

Well, he'd tried. Now, it was morning.

And this morning, he wanted to have the right thing to say. Because now that he'd spent a night in a bed that used to be theirs...maybe now Everett had something like the proper perspective.

* * * *

Colt
Louisiana, 2018

"Can we talk?"

He lay awake on the futon, facing away from the voice at the door.

"If you got somethin' to say."

"Got plenty to say, Col. Will you listen?"

He breathed in, long and slow, letting it fall out as he sat up and swiveled his legs. From here, he could see the feeder. Good a distraction as any. Might be the only way to get through this, if things went as he expected.

The clock on the desk read seven a.m. and Colt was drinking. He could almost hear Everett hold back from mentioning the hour. More than likely the man wanted to snatch the bottle from his hand, reminders of recovery quick on his tongue.

But Everett made no move to enter the spare room. He stood in the empty doorway and said what he came to say. "I know yesterday was hard, it all coming up again with no warning. But you gotta know…what you were talking about? Not goin' back and getting a place of my own? May sound silly now that's exactly what I've done, but then…it didn't even occur to me. Didn't feel like no kind of option.

"Life without Rachael and the kids…I didn't know how to operate. Home was them, and then…for a while, home was you. And that made *no* kind of sense to me."

Home…

"And somewhere in there I was seein' the kids," Ev continued. "Rachael was askin' for reasons I didn't have and maybe it was easier to just…disappear into that again. But I tell you, Col, a big part of me was hoping she'd just say no. That I'd have no kind of choice. And if that happened…maybe you and I could've…"

Colt had spent too many nights thinking just the same.

"But anyway, that ain't what happened," Everett said, and cleared his throat. "Rachael said okay and…and I didn't know how to be the person she needed. Not without you. Felt terrible to go crawlin' back, kickin' it all up for you again when I knew you were still so mad. But you let me anyway. You gave us those few good years when they were prolly hell for you, tried everything you could to give me what I needed.

"So Colt, I'm gonna do the same," he said, words bright as fresh-polished shoes. "You need your space? Fine. I'm goin' to work like normal and then I'm going to the store. And I'll be home tonight if...if you're wantin' to talk some."

Everett shifted by the door, less certain now his prepared remarks were done. It was more than Colt expected. But Ev was still missing some pretty important pieces.

Colt kept his gaze on the cardinals at the feeder. He drained the bottle in his hand, not caring that it was warm. "Said you're goin' to the store?"

"Yeah. You need anything?"

Colt popped the top on another beer. "Boxes. And some tape."

Chapter Twenty-Two

Everett
Louisiana, 2018

"These should get you started. There's more in the trunk if you need."

He leaned the unfolded cardboard against the open door of the guest room. Colt got started like he'd been handed an eviction notice, taping a box together while Everett surveyed the area.

There were more empty bottles than this morning. Cigarette butts were fucking everywhere. But Everett had run over the absence of other warning signs—no pills, no coke. No more booze than expected. And Everett wasn't really that kind of worried, but still. Checking those facts provided some comfort. It was the only thing he knew for sure right now.

"Need help?" he asked.

"You helpin' 'cause you want me gone?"

He wasn't so blind as to rise to that bait. He'd been turning things over in his mind all day, and he'd come to the conclusion that something more was bothering Colt, something their talk hadn't managed to drag out, and this sunny greeting confirmed it. Colt had more in the tank. There was something else causing this implosion...

As usual, Everett was missing something.

So as he crouched beside Colt on the floor and taped a box of his own, Everett told himself that *boxes don't mean done*. Boxes meant boxes, that Colt was on the mend. He was excited about his new place with the balcony where he could sketch. About that housewarming they were going to have.

Christ...

"I'm helpin' because I said I would," Everett muttered over the plastic screech of tape. "Told you I'd carry some boxes when you were ready to move. Can help pack 'em too."

Colt worked in silence, full attention on whatever he was moving. In time, Everett noticed he was sorting two piles of clothes. He recognized the items in one more than the other, the washed-soft shirts and rolled-up sweats that disappeared from his closet during recovery... that maybe he was okay with never getting back...

Panic unfurled in Everett's gut. "Ain't this a bit early? Your new place won't be ready till next week. And that truck you booked ain't for a week after that."

Colt pulled another shirt from a hanger, folded it rough and tossed it to the pile. "I called the listing. Another unit came open. I'm in tomorrow if I want it." He walked back to the closet. "Might take longer getting my stuff out."

Tomorrow? Well, that...*changed* things.

Because Everett's budding panic was well and truly blooming now, and he wondered if the heat in his cheeks and the sweat on his brow had to do with that rock he'd eaten earlier and must've forgot all about. Suddenly, *boxes* meant *leaving* and Everett was what—helping him *pack?*

"What's, uh...what's goin' on here, Col?"

Another flannel in the pile. "Can't do this again. Can't be the one tellin' Rachael what she should've already known."

"I don't...what are you—"

"*You* pushed her to me." Colt rounded on him, another T-shirt falling from his hands. "You and *your bullshit* pushed Rachael to what she did. And yeah, I made my choices after. But you...you just can't handle your own fuckin' truths. You made it so *I* was the one who had to tell her, confirm what she needed confirmed—"

What is he even talking about?

"What do you mean *you* told her about us?" Everett asked, well and truly confused. "Rachael worked you over 'cause she already knew."

He was met by a look he didn't often get to see—Colton Harkan, surprised. Something more familiar filtered back into his eyes as Everett told him the truth of it. "She had pictures, man. Rachael's known for years. Hell, Rach was tellin' me yesterday to be careful with you. Not to do *you* wrong." He scrubbed a hand over his face. "Jesus, but y'all should start a fuckin' club."

Colt kept still, as if considering those words required his full attention. "So that's why she said...she already knew?"

But it was that first part that caught Everett's attention. "Wait, hold on. What'd she say?"

Colt didn't answer right away, like if he kept quiet, maybe it wouldn't be true. Everett pressed him, wanted to *go* to him, but stayed kneeling on the ground, surrounded by boxes and tape. "Colt, tell me. What'd she say to you that night?"

A removed part of Everett realized he sounded more pissed at Rachael than Colt, which he didn't think would ever happen on this particular topic. But he'd seen time do some unbelievable things and now, he had to know. Because this was the final splinter in Colt's mind changing *home* into *guest room* and *boxes* to *leaving* —

Everett tossed his roll of tape hard against the floor and stood. He marched to where Colt was damn-near trembling, cutting his losses while he could —

"*Goddamn* it, Col, it's me. I was *inside* you yesterday, before this all…just, don't hide from me now. What'd she tell you? What's this all really about?"

Maybe it was how easily those words passed Everett's lips that shocked Colt into talking, but the rest ran out his mouth before he could stop himself. "She said not to go lookin' for something you couldn't give."

"And what's that?"

"Fidelity."

Oh.

Well, shit.

There was a time Everett would've deserved that slap in the face. Would've deserved every bite of that meal, and he'd have eaten it all. But now? After all they'd been through? Everett wondered if anything he did would ever be enough.

How could Colt think that, just because of Rachael coming past unannounced? Did Colt not know what he meant to him by now? How could he —

"I'm asking if you know that Colt's in love with you. Because trust me, Everett. I'd know that look anywhere…"

And it clicked. Of course Colt didn't know. Everett had never told him. Was always too scared, too happy to let it ride, let it all slide as long as whatever they had kept going…

Everett sat on the futon and watched Colt sway at the window, staring out at the lingering hues of sunset. But Everett didn't mind. He knew exactly what he had to do.

"I'm gonna ask a question now. What is it I've done, these months we've been living together, that makes you think I'm still that person? I need you to be specific, here." Everett breathed deep and braced for the worst. "Is it really that you don't trust me? Or do you want a way out and this is the one you're pickin'?"

He dared to catch Colt's eye. "Just tell me, Col. Do you *want* to go?"

Colt's voice was rough and the answer came out hollow. "Ain't about what *I* want."

Hope pounded in his chest. Everett cleared his throat. "Then what…what's this about leaving, huh?" He felt his cheeks getting wet, but couldn't be fuckin' bothered. "Just…just stop. Stop sayin' *leavin'*."

Colt turned fully away from him. He stayed silent, but his shoulders were shaking.

"Col…stay. I *want* you to stay, just…don't you want to stay?"

He held his breath. How'd he let this turn into such a mess?

"If I did," Colt finally said, "it'd be 'cause you knew what it was I was staying for."

Everett knew an earlier version of himself would pretend this sentimental shit didn't matter, but he knew better now. He had to say it. All of it.

And if he had to, he'd tell him every last one of the maddening times he'd realized he was in love with Colt Harkan.

* * * *

Colt
Louisiana, 2018

Ev sat on the worst futon ever made, asking questions that hit too close to home, and Colt wondered how much punishment he had to take in life before he'd finally get to step the fuck off. But like it or not, he could clock Everett's every move in a dark room, blindfolded. He was too attuned to his patterns, the way he rubbed his hands, how it sounded when he shifted foot-to-foot, nervous-like. So Colt knew without looking that Everett was standing behind him, surefooted and unmoving. And when he spoke, it was with a reverent certainty that Colt had never heard.

It was something completely new, and the words burst bright as summer-sunned blackberries.

"I'm gonna be as clear as I can, Colt. What you'd be staying for is the motherfucker who spent two years workin' up the courage to go to some gay bar and confirm what he already knew. That I didn't want anybody — any *man*. Wanted you."

Colt inhaled sharp, felt something ricochet and riot inside his chest, like a bullet trying to escape out his ribcage. Everett stepped behind him, fit hands along the vee of his hips and confessed the rest into his flannel-covered shoulder.

"Did you know that when I stepped out on Rach that second time, I felt worse about cheatin' on you? Never made any sense, but I swear to God it's true. Every time I'd get one of those pictures, I'd be terrified you'd see. Practically left the damn thing out for Rachael to find."

Colt wasn't going to interrupt, couldn't if he tried, but Everett nipped his ear like he had. "You ever remember touching my phone then? Wouldn't so much as leave it in the cupholder, afraid you'd see the ID.

"And after that month we lived together, before I went back to the house?" Everett's voice was rushed now, like if he stopped he'd never start again, or maybe never stop crying –

"Our first time at the store, Rachael reached for her frilly soap and I swear, all it took was seeing the *label* of your rosemary shit to start smellin' you and wantin' *this*. Walkin' 'round the store hidin' a hard-on like a goddamn teenager.

"I'd go out of town for work and get the travel size. Imagine you and that time in the shower." Everett sniffed, laughing at himself. "They stopped making it, d'you know that? Col, I've had that bottle in the shower for years –"

It was too much, *too much* –

"*Ev*...you gotta stop."

"No, you need to *listen*." Everett spun him around, and the world narrowed to a pair of blue-fire eyes that somehow replaced the stars in the sky when he wasn't looking. Everett thumbed under his chin and pulled him close. He leaned their foreheads together.

"Col, I'm far from perfect, but I've lost enough to know...this is as close to right as I've ever been. And you've got a lot to do with that. You're the whole damn reason in the first place.

"So no more of that *leavin'* shit. I fuckin' love you, Colt. And you're *staying*."

And in case there was anything he had to say about that, Ev shut him up with a kiss.

Love with Everett Kane tasted like the fire of cinnamon gum with a scent all honey-warm and brandy, something that filled and kicked and burned in ways Colt had never been able to handle. Everett's kiss was possessive, a perfect replica of the first Colt had laid on him all those years ago. Nothing to prove or disprove. Not something with an ebb or a tide. It was a force of nature, a goddamn hurricane kiss that had Colt swept up and spinning and shit, but he might just need to sit down...

As though Everett could hear him, he anticipated the need, pulling back so Colt could breathe. He let his head fall to Ev's shoulder. Everett brushed his nose through Colt's hair, inhaling every bit of his scent.

"Okay?" he whispered.

I fuckin' love you, Colt...

Well, there wasn't much left to say after that.

"Okay, Ev."

For a moment more perfect than he felt a right to, they stood and breathed together. He cupped Everett's face in his hands, tracing fingers over jawbone, lips, nose and back again, unable to even think for the relief coursing through his veins. Everett's hand slid easy around his waist, thumb riding under the hem of his shirt. Two fingers trailed along the line of his jeans, moved around front to trace the skin below a puckered scar.

Kissing the ridge of his cheekbone, Ev whispered soft as prayer, "Thank *God*."

It was like he'd poured gasoline on a bonfire the way it all bloomed in Colt's chest. Everett's heartfelt confession hung in the air like the good kind of heat, a humid glow that makes the perfect excuse for slow-spinning fans and sweet tea.

I love you, Colt. And you're staying.

Quick as anything, like he was finally seeing clear, actually feeling every place their bodies pressed together, Colt slid his arm 'round the back of Everett's neck, his other hand pressing firm into Ev's side. His breath felt harsh in his lungs and his voice was wet with unshed tears, but deeper than all that was the need to stake a claim —

"You better mean that, Rhett."

"'Course I do."

When Colt realized he was returning Everett's words from a shower long ago, from an apartment he now thought of as *their first place*, he nearly groaned with the want that came with it. He took in every bit of Everett, let him see *exactly* the train of thought Colt was all too prepared to board —

"Need to clear your schedule, Ev. You're gonna finish what you started now."

* * * *

Everett
Louisiana, 2018

Colt shoved firmly against his chest, just enough to stumble and give him a look at his eyes. Slow on the uptake, blood rushing south as it was, he reached again—but Colt hit his hand away. Colt tilted his head and angled over him, feeling into his height as he cowed him out of the guest room, and Everett was reminded of that first time they'd kissed at all, when he'd found himself spun against their car without a clue at how he'd gotten there.

When Colt was like this, he could dare the most dangerous criminal, break the most obstinate mark, read a man's whole life on his face like he was flipping through a newspaper. So when he turned his calculating gaze on Everett—swept him head to toe and back and had the nerve to lick his lips and smile? He almost lost it right there.

"I swear, Col...you do things like that, I can't hardly believe you're real."

A curl of his lips proved that Colt heard him, but he seemed more focused on steering Everett through the living room, behind the couch and down the hall to the bedroom.

Their bedroom.

Colt slid his hands up his own neck as he stalked closer, tying back dark hair in need of a trim. He peeled off his flannel, eyes glued to Everett's all the while.

His mouth was far too dry and his fingers itched with the need to pull Colt close. The mattress hit Everett behind the knees, and his surprised flail backward was probably the least dignified thing he'd ever done. He barely had time to push to forearms and find Colt in the dark, because apparently, Colt had shucked his tee and now, a very shirtless, very determined detective was levering over him, ready to take him completely apart.

Colt tore his dress shirt over his head and arms but left the wrists cuffed, twisting the long sleeves around the buttons to hold him trapped. Colt lowered over him until they fit together, legs sliding and chests brushing, and it was only then that he brought their lips together again, moaning in his mouth as they kissed.

I swear, he does this just to torture me...

Everett couldn't get his hands on him, thanks to Colt's grip on his shirt-bound wrists, but he kissed back for all he was worth. He let his legs fall open to hold hips with his knees, slid his foot along the back of Colt's calf — anything that might feel halfway like an embrace. Colt traced the edges of his mouth with his tongue, pulled Everett's bottom lip between teasing teeth. A hand brushed down his shuddering side, and when Everett thought he just might die if he couldn't touch this man, Colt went and found a way to surprise him again.

"Tell me what else I'm stayin' for. What else you do then I don't know about?"

At that, Everett realized something he should've seen before. For all the man's pessimistic bullshit, Colt Harkan might be the biggest sap of a romantic he'd ever met.

He tried to think as Colt kissed down his jaw, licked over his pulse and rasped the skin with his teeth.

"Uh, it...it took months of being back at the house before I stopped drivin' halfway to your place after work. Had me homesick for some serial killer apartment."

"*God*, Ev..."

"Didn't need you on half the cases I called about. Just wanted a reason to see you, talk to you some. I missed the sound of your stupid voice correcting me." His laugh turned to an outright whimper as Colt sucked over his pulse. He twisted his wrists in vain. "I *know* you know, but that was me callin' your office all those times. Couldn't make myself say a damn word — "

And Everett wasn't sure what was better—the low hum that sounded in Colt's throat at each new confession, or the answering fervor in his attentions. Seemed like every time Everett admitted another thing he should've long ago, Colt's hands were saying *thank you*, his mouth was saying *can't believe you*, his tongue traced patterns that felt like *I love you*, and good goddamn, whenever Col gifted him with those three little words? He planned to spend hours drinking them from his lips.

Colt slipped his belt open and rid him of the rest of his clothes. He kicked it all to the ground and Colt released his hands, tossing his shirt aside too. He kissed down his stomach to where Everett was hard and ready for him, and seeing how well this honesty thing had been going, he bet it all on black and made the ultimate gamble.

"Used to think I hated you. Too pretty for a man by half. Ain't fair. But I was just scared of how much I wanted you...*all* of you, Col."

Colt's intensity remained the same, but the shine in his dark eyes shifted as he looked up. He didn't seem as possessive now as he did intentional, eyes filled with worship, like he couldn't believe what Everett was saying. He kissed over the head of his cock, bobbed his head before pulling back to promise, "I got you, Ev."

Oh, shit...

He was already shaking and they hadn't even started. He forced himself to breathe as Colt settled his legs, circled arms around his thighs and began to work him open with his tongue. And Everett didn't know he could whine like that, but the noise had to be coming from somewhere, and his throat had gone tight like he was yelling something fierce, so yeah, that must be him.

Colt's tongue reached and teased, circled his rim and fuck, but why'd he wait so long to be honest?

"Connection's the real drug..."

And because it was Colt, reaching in the nightstand to press that familiar bottle into another man's hand felt as natural as breathing. Everett knew like he knew the sky was blue that Colt would never — *could* never — hurt him. Not now. And being so connected to someone he loved...well, it was like the man had said. Connection was the only thing that made this rodeo worth it some.

Colt turned him over gently, arranged pillows so he'd be comfortable then flipped the bottle open. Draping his body across Everett's back, Colt stroked him with one hand while slicked fingers reached low, teasing muscles to ease and open.

"S'all right, Rhett. Ain't gotta rush." Colt kissed the dip of his spine. "Relax for me."

Everett couldn't help the nerves. He wanted this, but...

"Might be easier said than done."

Colt slid a hand down his back, and he relished the sensation of gliding fingers over heating skin, the first traces of dewy sweat. "Just breathe," Colt whispered. "And trust me."

"That ain't never been a problem."

Colt teased between his legs as he worked a finger in gentle, and Everett's breathing started to mix with stutters and sighs. Colt kept working until one became two and Everett realized he was starting to rock back. And when Colt reached deep enough to stroke that perfect place, he almost seized to the bed.

"Oh *fuck*..."

He was glad no one other than Colt would ever see him like this — the way he'd started rolling his hips in rhythm, how his hands fisted the sheets clear off the bed, how the flick of the cap pulled an unintended whimper from his throat in anticipation of what he'd always wanted...

"*Col*...can't wait anymore. C'mon now."

Colt shifted on his knees, for once not fighting Everett on something he wanted. "Don't let me hurt you. Ain't gotta do this if you don't — "

He shut that line of thought down fast, desperate for what his body sensed was coming. Everett borrowed his partner's words from the kitchen days ago and said, "Ain't none of this about *have to*, Colt. Now you gonna make me fuckin' beg you or what?"

His answer was an arm wrapping tight around his middle, a solid pressure breaching him where Colt's fingers had been before. And as Colt started to slide in, filling him inch by inch, Everett wasn't sure he remembered his own name.

Jesus fuckin' Christ. This is...

"*God*...c'mon, don't stop."

Colt's voice was strained. "I won't. *Fuck*, Ev..."

They breathed together until Colt was fully seated inside. Everett went limp beneath him — unable to feel all this and hold himself simultaneously, so his body went ahead and picked one.

"*Oh*, you gotta be *kiddin'* me..."

Colt stroked down his arms, cradled his chest and twisted him up to kiss. The voice in his ear was soft, choking through words that sounded like an answered prayer.

"*Ev*, I...I gotta move. You all right?"

He was glad to find his brand of smartass was on autopilot, even in this compromising position. He pushed back against Colt and received a short, surprised shout. "You better shut up 'n' make good on those promises, or I'm gonna think you're some lying sweet-talker after all."

Colt rolled against him, brushed that spot that made him sound closer to a dog in heat than a grown man, and Colt hummed low in his throat. "Can't be havin' that."

The bastard sounded smug, but hell, Col could be anything he wanted if he kept moving like that. On the next thrust forward, Everett was getting his bearings. He found the way to brace on his forearms as the pleasure wound tighter inside. Their fingers locked together on the mattress and Everett relished the words he no longer had to hide.

"*Fuck*, Colt. I—I love you. I love you *so fuckin' much*. You don't even *know*—"

Colt sounded like he'd just won the lotto as he teased, rolling into him until satisfied with his response. "If I'd known all it took to get some honest words was fuckin' you through the headboard..." Colt rocked against him again. "I'd have tried a long time ago."

This arrogant son-of-a-bitch...

"Oh, fuck *you*, Col."

He made a playful correcting sound, tutting his tongue as he slid in hard, angling just so to drive Everett forward. "No..."

Colt's voice went up like a fucked-up impression of a schoolteacher—like he was expecting an answer, or for Everett to try again. And he'd thought his guttural groan should've been enough evidence, but Everett said anyway, "*Fuck me*, Colt. Please just...just fuck me already."

"Yeah, all right." Colt relented, kissing his shoulder. "Hold on, Ev."

That was one thing Colt didn't have to tell him. He was absolutely certain, knew right down to his bones, that he'd never let Colt Harkan go. Ever again.

Colt picked up their tempo, made him see spots with every stroke, and when Everett pressed back in just the right way, Colt couldn't keep his own exclamations any kind of quiet. Every moan he wrung from Col felt like victory. Strong hands held onto his hips hard enough to bruise and *God*, Everett almost hoped he would, wanted to look at the purpling evidence of fingerprints on his skin for days, like Colt's inky birds could transfer through his touch.

But it was the gentleness of Colt's palm sliding around his side, pressing down to feel himself as he rocked and surged inside that pushed Everett past the point of no return, started the tremors in his gut and the twitching in his thighs, because he knew this night had marked him—changed *them*, forever. So when Colt reached around to stroke him, holding his fist tight as Everett rode his thrusts toward completion, he tore down the final barrier in his mind.

"It's the same. It's all the same, Ev…"

*"Colll…*please, baby just—c'mon with me…"

And through a truly inventive string of curses, Colt did as he asked, thrust hard and jerked against him in release as he rode him down into the mattress. Colt stuttered behind him and clamped his teeth down hard on his shoulder and fuck, but that was it. He was done for.

Everett broke apart beneath him, crying out Colt's name loud enough to wake the neighbors. And having lived a moment so perfect, his last coherent thought was that, somewhere among the mistakes of his life, he must've done something close to right.

This here, with Colt? Made one hell of a reward.

After a few shared breaths, Colt tried to roll away, but Everett held him close. "Just...just a second."

Colt eased out gently as he could, then folded into his back and damn the mess. Wasn't like it was nothing they hadn't seen. Colt dropped a kiss to his neck from behind and trailed a hand through sweat-damp hair.

Everett breathed a laugh, still dazed. "Jesus, man. I can't hardly move."

He could hear Colt smirking in the dark.

Such an asshole...

"Don't have to," said Colt. "Stay here. I'll be back."

Colt returned with a warm cloth and took his time cleaning sensitive areas, kissing and caressing a spot on his hip. "Might've left you with something."

He covered Colt's hand with his. "I ain't complaining. C'mon over here."

They faced each other beneath the cotton sheet, still too warm for blankets. Everett twined their hands in the space between bodies and Colt shifted closer, looking calmer than he'd ever seen him. As he wrapped Colt in his arms, it brought a certain kind of warmth to think tomorrow, they'd wake up where they ought to be. Here, together.

Home.

"Didn't mean to go rainin' on your parade with the apartment," Everett told him. "If you still want to look for something, we can find a place we both like. Or hell, keep the place if you want. There's no rule sayin' we have to live together, if you're wantin' your own space."

He felt Colt trace the newest of his scars — the raised line in his shoulder that matched the one in Colt's gut. "Ain't about the building," Colt said. "This here's fine with me."

They traded smiles and Everett breathed easier, eyes blinking with something like slumber as Colt settled against his chest. Sleep was inevitable, but perhaps, so was his teasing.

"So do I have to wait till I can fuck *you* through the headboard to get reciprocation on a certain somethin' here?"

Colt smiled into his neck. "If you're offerin'."

He tightened his arms around Colt's back. "And if I was? In some hours?"

"Then we might see. In some hours."

And while they did sleep eventually, those few hours later...well, Everett couldn't say for sure, since he wasn't the one with all his wires crossed. But if he had to guess, he'd say Colt's cry of "*I love you, Ev*" tasted sweet as apple pie.

Epilogue

Colt
Louisiana, 2018, one month later

"C'mon 'n' pass the clicker, babe."

Rhett sat on the couch just waiting to be corrected, but Colt only handed over the remote. A wry smile broke across his partner's face as he flipped the channel, unable not to make a mention. "That went smoother than last time."

"Mm-hmm."

"Thought you didn't care for pet names."

Colt shifted closer and pulled Everett's arm around his shoulders. He brushed his thumb over the pulse in his wrist. "Times change."

He knew Rhett would hear what he meant — *people* change. And ain't that a wonder Colt thought so.

Ev dropped a kiss to his head. His eyes darted to the framed drawing on the wall, then back to him. "I s'pose they do."

Colt hummed in contentment and thought back on when they'd hung that sketch, the first he'd ever shown his partner. And though Colt hadn't been pleased with how it turned out, Everett declared at first sight it was *"fuckin' perfect."* Went on about how he *"wasn't no art critic,"* but claimed if he was rich as the Maynards, he'd have paid good money for those cardinals at a familiar feeder. Grace had said the same when Ev's family came through last weekend — and since she was the one in art school, she'd told Colt none too gently it was her opinion that mattered, and he could take his humble pie elsewhere. Had the same ring of stubbornness as another blonde in his life.

So fine. He might've let Gracie's praise slide.

He watched Everett scroll the guide for two whole seconds before he couldn't stop himself from saying, "Don't put that NASCAR shit on again."

"Then you pick somethin'."

"You asked for the clicker, I gave you the clicker —"

"Boy, you better shut the fuck up, hatin' on NASCAR in these parts. Show some damn respect."

"It's pointless unless you're driving. No reason to watch it."

"Yeah all right, *sunshine*. That's enough outta you."

With the way Colt leaned against his chest, Everett couldn't see his face. But Colt allowed himself to smile — *really* smile, and filed those words away for a project of his own.

Over the next few days of Everett's experiment with pet names outside the bedroom, Colt added notes to his sketchbook, his part to-do list notepad companion that hadn't ever been tainted by a homicide. Some back pages were getting full with theories for one of Ev's latest clients, but Colt was just helping out. Flexing the muscles from time to time.

He far preferred the notes he took now.

"Sunshine" was sarcastic, tossed over the breakfast table when he was telling Ev some truth he didn't want to hear. *"C'mon, love"* was for shutting off the TV at ten o'clock, because *"we're not some spring chickens"* and these days, they both preferred the routine. *"Babe"* was for when he couldn't find *"a goddamn thing"* in the junk drawer. *"Baby"* didn't slip out unless they were in bed. And every so often, it was *"darlin'."* Just because.

Colt pretty much just called him Ev. But he could tell when he said it — out the side of his mouth with a smile — it was all Everett wanted to hear.

And maybe Ev tracing the back of his fourth finger meant something, especially if considered with that jewelry-store pamphlet he'd found in the garage. God save them all from Everett and his sweeping gestures, but they'd cross that bridge when they came to it. These days, Colt was content just to hold Everett's hand, a bit amazed he was around to be holding a thing at all.

And, maybe, even happier to be home.

Want to see more like this?
Here's a taster for you to enjoy!

At All Costs
Simone Anderson

Excerpt

Riley Hamilton, RJ to his friends, smiled at the pretty brunette behind the bar and slapped his credit card down on the counter. Any other night and he would have tried to sweet talk his way into the cute little bartender's bed. She was his favorite type—petite and slender with a larger-than-average bust size, accentuated by a tight black V-neck T-shirt. He'd never had trouble bedding any woman he wanted. He never lied about his intentions. There was no need. There were more than enough women who would rather have a night of fun over anything long term, especially in New Orleans. The Big Easy was simply crawling with groups of women. Sex hadn't been a problem. Life hadn't been a problem.

"Macallan M, double, straight up. And a beer. Whatever's dark and on tap."

"We don't have that."

Riley scowled. "Well, do you at least have Johnnie Walker Blue? That's drinkable."

The woman nodded and poured him the drink.

Riley paid for his drinks and slammed back the whiskey. He picked up the plastic cup of beer and pushed his way out of the crowded bar and onto Bourbon Street. He mumbled an apology to the group of men he bumped into. This week was supposed to be one last final hurrah with his friends before he started working for his father. He was being groomed to take over the family business. One he had no interest in at all. He hadn't been asked. He'd been told.

Riley blew out a breath and jammed a hand through his hair. He'd managed to stay out of his father's business for nearly five months after graduation under the guise of applying for a job. He had. He just didn't have any experience outside of school. No real marketable experience was what he'd been told more than once. He didn't care. Charles did.

"Hey, handsome, something on your mind?" a pretty blond asked, tracing a long-painted fingernail up and down his arm.

"Ah no," Riley answered, shrugging off the contact. It was a blatant lie. "Not interested, sorry." The phone call from Charles in the early afternoon had effectively killed his mood. Two hours later his day went from bad to worse after an unexpected run-in with a moron who wanted to fit into a world that he didn't belong in. He tossed the empty cup into a nearby trash can then ducked into the nearest bar and made his way to the counter. Unsure why it bothered him still, Riley ordered another shot of whiskey and a beer. Paying for both, he left a generous tip. Riley slammed back the shot and carried the beer with him back outside.

A commotion farther down the street drew his attention before he turned back toward his hotel. Strong arms grabbed him on either side. Beer spilled all over him as the cup tumbled to the pavement. Forced away from the gathering crowd, Riley fought his attackers, struggling to get away. Turning his head from one side to the other, he tried to catch the details.

"You're coming with us, pretty boy," the man on his right said in a thick Southern accent.

Both men had similar builds, slightly taller than himself with muscular bodies and dark hair. The rest of their features were masked by matching New Orleans Saints ball caps.

"Don't think so." Riley's words slurred together even as he pulled and kicked. His stomach rolled and the hair on the back of his neck stood on end. He was overmatched. He knew it without a doubt. Maybe if he threw up on them, they'd let him go. It was a good thought, except he'd been drinking long before he'd been legal and could hold his liquor. There was no way he'd had enough to drink for that.

Riley stumbled and fell to his knees. Shaking his head, he tried to orientate himself. The man who'd been on his right lay several feet away, face down on the street. A man in a black leather jacket kicked the other man, sending him flying backward. Riley pushed himself to his feet. He swayed and stumbled. The newcomer caught him before he fell.

"Let's go." The voice was commanding, the vise-like grip insistent.

"Who are you?" Riley tried to wrench his arm away from the other man. "Like hell! I'm not going anywhere with you. Or them."

People around them started to stop and stare. The newcomer swore and maneuvered him through the crowd and down the next block.

"Come with me if you want to live." The man pulled him down the street.

Riley yanked his arm free. "Okay, seriously, that is the cheesiest pick-up line ever. And completely wasted." Riley shook his head. "I'm not gay."

"First, it's not a pick-up line. Second, gay, straight, in the closet or not, I don't care. You need to come with me if you want to live," the man said, peering over Riley's shoulder.

"The only place I'm going is back to my hotel room to sleep." Riley rolled his shirt sleeves up.

"Riley James Hamilton, we have absolutely no time to stand here and debate this. Your hotel room, your entire life, in fact, has been compromised."

Riley stopped and stared at the man. The buzz he'd been working on disappeared. It was the same man he'd had the run-in at the hotel with earlier in the day. A soldier with the military's Purple Heart patch sewn on his jacket. Riley groaned. He hadn't exchanged names with the other man. There was no way the man should know who he was.

"You're the guy from the hotel. Who are you? How do you know who I am?" he asked, leaning against the wall.

The man pulled him down the block to the next intersection and up the street. "Right now, probably one of the few people who doesn't want you to end up in the morgue. And the only one who can keep you out of it."

"Okay, enough with the cryptic espionage bullshit, James Bond. Not only am I not going anywhere with you, I don't have any idea who you are, and no one wants me dead. If anything, I'm better alive to use as ransom. However, that would mean Charles would have to actually give a shit about me, which he doesn't." Riley stopped outside a small grocery store.

"Shit!" The man grabbed Riley's arm. He pushed and pulled Riley farther down the street.

Riley forced himself to focus on where they were and where he needed to be. They turned onto Bourbon Street. Riley tried to pull away. His hotel was down the street a few blocks. If he could get there, he could shower, change, and sleep off this nightmare.

"In here." They ducked into a bar just as one of the men who had tried to abduct him rushed by them.

Riley's stomach rolled. Several minutes passed before they stepped outside. Still holding his arm, the soldier took a step before he turned and pushed Riley up against the wall. "Play along, or you'll get us both killed," the man whispered harshly. His attacker and another man stopped five feet from them.

Riley resisted the urge to fight the man holding him. Some doors were never allowed to be opened. Not without drastic consequences. He may not like where he was, but the idea of losing everything wasn't worth it. Praying he wasn't making a mistake, he swallowed the forming lump and put his hands on the man's arms before moving them to his waist. He needed to survive long enough to get back to his hotel room.

"That's it." The soldier bent and captured his mouth.

The man shifted positions and Riley's hand bumped something hard. A gun. Riley's head began to spin. The man reportedly trying to save him had a gun. He was beyond screwed. He was a college graduate with a trust fund and a father whose company manufactured and sold perfume and colognes. There was nothing in his life that warranted the current position in which he found himself.

"Hand me your phone!" the soldier demanded.

"My what? No, I'm not giving you my phone." Riley shook his head, trying to push away from the stranger again.

Keeping him pinned to the wall, the man ran his hands over Riley's body. Riley fought the hold, not caring who noticed. The man pulled his phone out of the back pocket of his jeans.

"Enjoying yourself?" Riley bit out.

"Yes, babysitting a trust fund brat in the middle of New Orleans is always how I want to spend my nights," the man retorted. He pulled apart the phone and removed the battery before handing the pieces back to Riley. "Don't put it back together."

"What the —"

"Welcome to the twenty-first-century equivalent of a homing device," the man said. "You can get a cheap burner phone tomorrow."

Riley shook his head, tried to follow the man's train of thought and failed. "A what?"

"A burner phone. You know, a nearly untraceable by-the-minute phone." the man sneered. "You have seriously got to stop drinking."

Riley scoffed. That was not likely to happen. Alcohol made life bearable.

"Look, the French Quarter is packed with people. It's *always* packed with people. Tourists, locals, businesspeople, law enforcement. There are dozens of streets, shops, restaurants, and bars jammed into a relatively small area. There is no way they should have found us that quickly," the man replied, drawing his attention to the swarms of people around them. "Or really at all."

"Great."

"Let's go." The man pulled him back onto the street.

"Who are they? Who are you? What in the hell is going on?" Riley demanded.

"Let's get off the street and we'll talk."

"Do you have a name or will James Bond work?" Riley asked. "I swear this type of shit only happens in freaking Hollywood."

"Yes, but only in Hollywood can the bad guys miss the broad side of a barn from ten feet away with an unlimited supply of ammunition. In the real world, not only is ammunition limited for everybody, both sides have snipers."

"Thanks, *James*, that makes my night so much better. Now, if you don't mind, I'll stop being the heroine in your little melodrama and go back to my hotel. Next time pick a chick to co-star with," Riley bit out, needing to regain control of his life.

"Name's Kaden. Chicks don't do it for me. And you're stuck with me."

Riley groaned. "Great, a gay James Bond. Because that's *so* much better." He blew out a breath and surveyed his surroundings. He recognized some of the bars, but he wasn't completely sure if they were heading back to his hotel or not. The man, Kaden, had checked into the same hotel he was staying at earlier in the day. The streets were filled with people, far from Mardi Gras packed, but enough, Riley admitted to himself, that they shouldn't have been found as quickly as they had. "Who's after me? Why? How many people?" Riley shoved a hand through his hair, Kaden never denied being a spy.

"So you do have a modicum of a survival instinct. Not nearly as dumb as you want people to believe."

Riley repressed the urge to scream and shrugged. "I seriously couldn't care less about what anyone thinks."

"I noticed."

They rounded another corner and their hotel came into view. Relief flooded Riley. He wanted a hot shower and clean clothes. The Royal Sonesta hotel was in the heart of the French Quarter, its elegant and modern interior in turns at odds with and complementing the century-old building and surrounding three hundred years of history. He'd liked it from the beginning and hoped that their return to it meant that either the danger had passed or it was all a big joke meant to humiliate him or blackmail him into doing something he wouldn't normally do.

"I thought you said my hotel room and life were compromised. So, why are we back here?"

"They are. Do you have everything of importance out of your room?"

Riley shook his head. "What does that have to do with anything?"

"Get only what you need. Since I wasn't expecting to have to change hotels so soon, I have to get something from my room."

"I need to change and take a shower."

"You can—"

"I am covered in beer," Riley fumed. "I have what I need in my room."

Kaden sighed and shoved a hand through his hair. "Fine. But, be quick and quiet. You're going to change, then we're going back out to have a night on the town," Kaden ordered.

Riley nodded as the valet opened the door for them. He kept his face carefully neutral. Knowing the hotel would have cameras everywhere was truly only going to help him if they found him dead in the hotel. Kaden bustled him into the lift and punched the number for Riley's floor.

"How do you know—"

"Later."

"My friends are going to know something is wrong. If I don't show up, they'll go to the police."

Kaden nodded. "Probably, but it will take about forty-eight hours. They'll assume you found someone to screw tonight and will wake up late in the day and probably have sex with said partner again. They'll go out, and when you're still not back, they'll think they crossed paths with you. It'll be late afternoon or early evening the day after that before they'll start to get worried and call the police, who will say you're an adult and this *is* New Orleans."

Riley's stomach sank as he digested Kaden's words. "I'm screwed."

"Not yet, but you almost were," Kaden answered.

"I didn't mean that literally."

"You can be screwed in more ways than sex. And I don't do the unwilling." The doors opened and Kaden led the way through the hall to the suite that Riley shared with his friends. Kaden stepped aside to let Riley open the door. Once inside, Riley went to his room, while Kaden searched the suite.

"It doesn't look like anyone has been here," Kaden said, walking in on him. "So much for survival instinct."

"Says the guy with the gun." Riley stripped out of his wet shirt and tossed it into the corner. "Do you mind?"

"Not at all." Kaden smiled.

"Creepy." Riley pulled a pair of clean slacks out of his suitcase.

"Jeans."

"What?" Riley turned to face his unwelcomed visitor. "Can't you wait on the other side of the door?"

"No. For the foreseeable future, I'm not taking my eyes off you."

"Seriously? That's completely unnecessary. This is a hotel. There is no other exit except through that door." Riley pointed behind the other man. "Maybe whatever second-rate rat-infested hotel *you're* used to staying in has multiple exits and adjoining rooms, this is not one of them. I pay too much money to be that close to others."

"Windows. Balconies. Wear jeans."

Riley scowled. "Great. Just great. Now, I'm getting fashion advice from a James Bond wannabe who dresses in holey jeans and a beat-up leather jacket instead of a suit."

"Hollywood. Reality. Two totally different things. Jeans are more durable than dress pants."

Riley shoved the hanger back in the closet and spun around. "Okay, enough. I'm absolutely not going anywhere until you tell me in the hell is going on. No more cute answers. I don't know you. I've never seen you before this morning. But yet, you seem to know everything there is to know about me."

"Afternoon, not morning."

"Morning to me and you're avoiding the question." Riley crossed his arms over his chest.

"I'll tell you what I can. My name is Kaden Tennison and I've been instructed to keep you alive and safe at all costs. As to the men who grabbed you, they're probably nothing more than hired goons. Who hired them and why is the real question. And one I don't have an answer for."

"Alive or dead?"

"Honestly, I don't know." Kaden shook his head. "I suspect alive, at least until you're of no further use."

"Why?"

"Again, I don't know. I was given very little information to go on."

"How is this even possible?" Riley sat down on the edge of the bed. "Why would anybody want me? Seriously? I don't own a business. And kidnapping me isn't going to have an effect on my family. It's not like the family business is guns, medicine, or politics. We make perfume and cologne."

"Which you don't wear."

Riley shrugged. He wasn't going into personal details with a stranger.

"Riley, we need to move. Staying here isn't an option. You post your entire life online."

"And disappearing isn't going to raise suspicions at all," Riley replied sarcastically.

"Phone batteries die all of the time." Kaden smiled. "Get dressed. The sooner we move, the sooner we can figure out who's behind this."

Riley shoved his hands through his hair and stared at the floor. "It still doesn't make any sense. Who hired you? Can you tell me that?"

"An interested party."

"That makes a whole lot of sense. A complete stranger wanting to keep me alive and another complete stranger wanting me dead. How do I know I can trust you?"

"You don't. You just don't have a choice."

"Because you have a gun?" Riley quipped.

"I do, several of them in fact, but in this case it's because right now, I'm the only one who has a chance of keeping of you alive."

"I can take care of myself!" Riley shouted, jumping to his feet.

"I didn't say that. But, have you ever shot a gun before?" Kaden demanded. "Have you evaded capture before? Were you aware that you were being followed since you left the hotel?"

Riley opened his mouth and closed it.

"Now, get dressed. Pack a couple changes of clothes if you want, but we're leaving. Both of us."

"I need to take a shower. I stink and I'm sticky," Riley protested.

"We don't have time. They know where you're staying."

"So what? They know what hotel I'm staying at. It's not a huge secret."

"They know your room number."

"Seriously? You know that how? Nothing in here is missing. Nothing's been missing."

"Nothing's been moved? You and your roommates haven't misplaced anything?"

Riley shrugged and dug out the only pair of jeans he'd brought with him. "We're on vacation, James, and there is maid service." Riley took off his pants, tossing them in the corner with the soiled shirt.

"Silk boxers? A little outdated for you, aren't they?"

"Some of us have taste and style and can afford to wear good clothes." Riley grabbed his jeans and a clean pair of boxers and headed for the bathroom.

"Where are you going?"

"Shower. I cannot stand the way I smell or feel."

"We don't have time."

"Just because you say it's so, doesn't mean it is. I don't know you. I don't trust you. I don't even like you."

"Riley —"

"Man, enough. Joke's over. You've had your fun. You need to leave." Riley tossed his clothes on the edge of the desk.

"I'm not joking."

"Joking. Lying. Same thing."

The room's phone rang, startling him. Riley answered it before the other man crossed the room. "Hello."

He heard only heavy breathing on the other end of the phone.

Riley rolled his eyes. "Dramatic. Very Hollywood of you."

Kaden pulled the receiver away from Riley's ear. "Who is this?"

"That's effective." Riley smirked.

"Your bodyguard isn't going to be able to save you." The voice was robotic.

Riley stilled.

"You should put some clothes on before we get there."

Kaden slammed the phone down. "Now do you fucking believe me? We need to leave."

Riley nodded and stepped into the jeans, pausing for a moment. He hated tight clothes and jeans, even as loose as these were, and it always took him a minute to get used to them. Grabbing a clean shirt, he finished dressing and grabbed his backpack that had doubled as his carry-on. He checked the contents before adding clean underwear, socks, and a couple of changes of clothes. He'd started to throw in his shaving kit and deodorant when Kaden stopped him.

"Leave them."

"But—"

"The toiletries, like your tablet, and power cords need to stay."

"Why?"

"We need the time. If those things are missing your friends will call the police sooner rather than later."

"Isn't that what we want?" Riley asked, tossing the items onto the bed. "Why aren't we going to the police now? Surely, they can handle something like this."

Kaden shook his head, putting the kit and deodorant back from where Riley had grabbed them. "This is out of their—" Kaden paused for a moment. "Jurisdiction."

"Fantastic. So, what, you're a part of a secret group dedicated to saving the world and random people when you're asked to?"

"Something like that."

"Cryptic asshole," Riley said, zipping up the backpack.

"Do you have a jacket?"

"It's New Orleans, there's no need for one." Riley shouldered his bag. "Are all secret agent superheroes assholes or are you just special?"

"Job requirement." Kaden smiled.

Riley scowled as Kaden led them down the hall and around the corner to his room. Kaden entered the room first, pulling Riley in after him. Ordering Riley to wait by the door, Kaden searched the room before grabbing a black duffel bag off the center of the king-size bed.

"So, did you ask for a room on the same floor?"

"Didn't have to."

"You didn't unpack?" Riley asked. "You get to take all your stuff?"

Kaden nodded and checked the contents of his bag. "Unlike you, I don't have roommates, friends, or anyone else who will be looking for me."

"What about surveillance video? I mean, if they start looking for me, they'll see us on the video together. Arriving and leaving together."

"Probably." Kaden slung the bag over his shoulder. "Let's go."

"Where to? Some one-star dump in the warehouse district, I assume," Riley said, adjusting his backpack.

"That's an option."

"Asshole," Riley muttered and followed Kaden out of the room and back outside. Once outside, Kaden handed him a plain ball cap and ordered him to put it on. Despite the crowds of tourists, street performers and musicians filling the streets of the French Quarter, Kaden led them through a dozen bars and restaurants, slipping out of back doors and down alleyways, across Jackson Square, by the St. Louis Cathedral, and through another maze of streets until they ended up at another hotel. Riley raised an eyebrow. The new hotel, the Bourbon Orleans, was four blocks down from their old hotel and two blocks from the gay bar they'd stopped in while evading his attackers.

"Try not to draw attention to us," Kaden bit out, leading them into the hotel.

Riley stayed silent as Kaden led them through the lobby, down a hall to an elevator that took them to the second floor. Their room sat halfway down the hallway. Kaden entered the room first, with a curt order for Riley to stay where he was. Riley heaved a sigh and followed him into the room.

"Well, at least there are two beds." Riley tossed his bag onto the bed closest to the door.

"Do you ever listen?"

"Why? It's a hotel room. It comes standard with beds, bathroom, closet, TV, and a minibar. The good ones have balconies. There is no reason to be cautious." Riley flopped down in a chair.

"There are still plenty of places to hide or booby-trap."

"God, you're paranoid." Riley shook his head. "Your boyfriend must be either super impressed or nuts."

"No time for a boyfriend. Tonight, I'm babysitting," Kaden snapped. "The shower is yours if you want."

"I take it this means we're in for the night?"

"Yes. Go take your shower."

"Seriously? It's not even midnight. I haven't had a curfew in years. And we're in New Orleans, one of America's best playgrounds. I don't think curfews are legal here." Riley pushed himself up out of the chair. To be honest, he'd never paid attention to curfews.

"Maybe you'll get lucky and you'll only have to be inconvenienced for a couple of days, then you can go back to your life of privilege and overindulgence, rich boy."

"You don't like me, do you?" Riley asked, stopping and turning around. There was a bitterness in Kaden's voice that couldn't be missed.

"What I like and don't like isn't important. My job is to keep you alive. Somebody thinks you're worth saving." Kaden turned his back on Riley, set his bag down on the other bed and began digging through it.

Riley picked up his bag and stalked into the bathroom, slamming the door behind him.

About the Author

Gin Vane is your friendly neighborhood bisexual she / they, deconstructing heteronormativity one queer romance at a time.

As a lifelong reader of the genre, Gin refuses to compromise plot for spice and lives by the motto "por que no los dos?" Gin primarily writes MM and MMF, though she enjoys reading and writing lesbian romance as well. Gin lives for the slow-burn that scalds and loves a good character redemption arc. Their novels are always full of heat and often include elements of polyamory and BDSM.

When not at the writing desk, Gin can be found dancing at their pole and circus studio, knitting beside the most perfect cat, watching crime shows and Brit coms with her husband or cooking dinner with friends and partners.

Gin loves to hear from readers. You can find her contact information, website details and author profile page at https://www.pride-publishing.com

Sign up for our newsletter and find out about all our romance book releases, eBook sales and promotions, sneak peeks and FREE romance books!